W9-BFN-620

Titles by Rebecca Hagan Lee

SOMETHING BORROWED
GOSSAMER

Gossamer

REBECCA HAGAN LEE

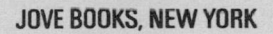

JOVE BOOKS, NEW YORK

GOSSAMER

A Jove Book / published by arrangement with
the author

PRINTING HISTORY
Jove edition / January 1999

The Penguin Putnam Inc. World Wide Web site address is
http://www.penguinputnam.com

ISBN: 0-515-12430-3

A JOVE BOOK®
Jove Books are published by The Berkley Publishing Group,
a member of Penguin Putnam Inc.,
375 Hudson Street, New York, New York 10014.
JOVE and the "J" design
are trademarks belonging to Jove Publications, Inc.

PRINTED IN THE UNITED STATES OF AMERICA

10 9 8 7 6 5 4 3 2 1

DEDICATION

For Karen Marie Dunlap, the original Treasure and the inspiration behind the fictional ones. Thank you for your friendship, support, encouragement, belief in me, and boundless enthusiasm for my stories—and you've read them all—from third grade until now.

I hope I did you justice.

And for the three "guardian angels" who refused to give up on this story and who worked hard to make the dream of publishing it a reality: my friend and mentor, Teresa Medeiros; my agent, Laura Blake Peterson; and my editor, Cindy Hwang.

With love and gratitude.

Prologue

Hong Kong
December 1870

SHE NEEDED ABSOLUTION from him. She couldn't continue without it. But absolution for her sin was the one thing he couldn't yet find in his heart to give. He needed time. Time for the horrible pain to lessen. Time for the terrible wound to heal. Time to forget.

And so, she hid from him. She abandoned the laughter, the gaiety, the joy, the love, and the sunlight that had once made up the parts of her life. She abandoned the beautiful life she had known and existed in the darkness. She covered her face and remained in the shadows, keeping to her room with only her maid for companionship, refusing to look upon the precious countenance of the person she loved most in the world.

She had begged his forgiveness.

But he could not give it.

And her unbearable sin was never spoken of again.

He did not punish her. He didn't speak harshly or starve her or beat her. He didn't do any of the things she thought he should have done to relieve her of a measure of the horrible guilt she carried within her heart. He had done none of the things she expected him to do when he learned of her sin. He had simply stared at her with condemnation and unshed tears in his eyes. Stared at her, unable to speak.

She could not resume her old life, could not pick up the pieces of her life until he absolved her of her guilt, so she stayed to herself and wept. Each day and long into the night.

No one could console her as she wept bitter, heartbreaking tears and prayed for his forgiveness.

And each night as he lay in his solitary bed in the room adjoining hers, he prayed for the strength to look her in the eyes and tell her he understood, that he forgave her for the terrible mistake she had made—for the unspeakable sin she'd committed.

He wanted to forgive her, wanted to love her again, wanted desperately to return to the life they had had together. Before. But now no matter how hard he tried, he couldn't bring himself to say the words she needed to hear. The words of forgiveness he wanted to utter stuck in his throat. He couldn't push them out. And he couldn't lie. She knew him too well, had loved him too long. She would know the difference between truth and lies. She would see it in his eyes, hear it in the sound of his voice, feel it in the touch of his hands. Try as he might, he knew that he couldn't forgive her until he could put aside the horror of the sight burned into his memory. He couldn't forgive until he forgot. And he knew that as long as he lived, he'd never forget what she had done.

And as the days wore on, he continued to lie in bed each night praying as he listened to the sound of her tears. Praying she would find the strength to forgive herself even if he could not. Praying that one day her tears would come to an end.

Until the night they did.

One

THE SOUND OF her heartrending sobs penetrated his sleep.

James Craig immediately identified the sound, opened his eyes, rolled out of bed, and padded barefoot across the dark room to the door connecting his bedroom to hers.

Reaching for the doorknob, he softly called her name. "Mei Ling?"

She didn't answer. And the terrible grief-stricken cries continued as James felt for the doorknob. But there was no doorknob. Or door to attach it to. Only a solid wall, covered in flocked wallpaper.

James leaned his forehead against the wallpaper, remembering. This was San Francisco, not Hong Kong. He was in a hotel thousands of miles away from the bedroom in his dreams and an entire ocean away from his house in Hong Kong. He licked his top lip, tasted the salt of his sweat, and felt another damp trickle of it slide down the curve of his spine. James took a deep breath to steady himself, to gather his bearings as he sorted through the rush of memories triggered by the sound of a woman's grief.

"Are you hurt?" he whispered into the velvet flocking, knowing even as he did so that the woman on the other side of the paper-thin walls couldn't hear him. Knowing, too, that any woman who cried as if her heart was broken had to be gravely wounded—in spirit if not in body.

James heaved a weary sigh. He couldn't begin to count the number of nights he had lain awake listening as Mei Ling cried herself to sleep. He couldn't begin to count the times he had tapped on the connecting door offering comfort, begging admittance, only to be met with more tears. He should go back to bed, bury his head in the feather pillows, pull the covers up over his ears, and pretend he didn't hear. Just close his eyes and will himself to sleep once again. Ignore her pain, her heart-wrenching tears. That's what he should do.

But James Craig had never been one to listen to logic when every fiber of his being told him to listen to his heart.

Pushing himself away from the wall, James groped his way back to the big brass bed. He shoved his long legs into his trousers, then reached for the silk dressing gown lying at the foot of the bed. He located his leather satchel on the floor beside the bed, felt inside until he found a square of clean linen, shoved the handkerchief into the pocket of his robe, then pulled the silk garment over his bare shoulders and knotted the sash at his waist. Closing the bedroom door behind him, James quietly locked it and pocketed the key before making his way down the dimly lit hall to the adjoining room.

He tapped at the door, then put his ear against the cool wood. Hearing her broken sobs and the little hiccuping sound she made as she fought to control her weeping, James knocked at the door again. "Miss?" he inquired softly, his voice, a deep, rough rumble not unlike the rumbling of a big cat. "Is everything all right? Are you hurt? Is there anything I can do to help? Anything I can get for you?" Calling himself three kinds of a fool for standing half-dressed and barefoot outside a stranger's hotel room in

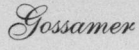

the middle of the night, James heard himself pleading, "Miss? Please, answer me."

He reached down to try the doorknob, thought better of it, and snatched his hand back.

What sensible woman would open her door to a stranger in the middle of the night? It would be as foolhardy for her to open her hotel door to a man in a town like San Francisco as it was for him to stand outside it imploring her to do so.

James leaned his forehead against the molding on the doorframe. What was he thinking? What madness had come over him? He squeezed his eyes closed. Her crying had come over him. The sound of her utter hopelessness. James had no defense against a woman's tears. Tears of grief so overwhelming they made even the strongest of men feel helpless. James tapped on the door again, louder this time. "Miss? I promise I'll go away and leave you alone if you'll just say something to let me know you're fine. Please."

He thought he heard a slight noise on the opposite side of the door. He listened closely and heard the sound of her erratic breathing close by.

"Is there anything I can do for you?" James asked, hearing the phrase as an echo of the many other times he'd asked the same question.

He didn't expect a reply. So he was completely taken aback when the door opened a few inches.

"Please go away," she whispered just loud enough for him to hear. "There's nothing anyone can do."

"I'd like to help if I can." James stared down at her, but she kept her gaze focused on the floor. He couldn't see her face, only the top of her head. He stared at the thick dark strands of chestnut brown hair interspersed here and there with strands of blond and a light brown. Studying the play of light and dark on her head, James was suddenly reminded of a tapestry that hung on the wall of his house in Hong Kong. Her hair was like the threads woven into that tapestry—a mixture of browns, tans, and golds, that made up the colors of the coat of a stylized Chinese lion.

"You said you'd go away," she reminded him. "You promised you'd go away if I answered." Dismissing him, she stepped back and began to close the door.

James stepped closer and pressed his palm against the door. "I promised I'd go away if you could show me that you're all right," he answered.

"Please," she repeated, "you gave your word."

He had given his word. He had told her he would leave her alone if she answered him. And she believed him to be a gentleman of his word. The proper thing to do was to step back and allow her to return to her room and her solitary heartache, but James couldn't bring himself to do so. He was balking at the prospect of leaving her alone, reaching for a way to delay the inevitable. And he knew it.

"My name is James," he said.

Still she didn't look up.

"My name is James," he repeated when she failed to respond, then continued on in a burst of male frustration. "I'm a complete stranger to you and I'm standing outside your hotel room door in the middle of the night like an idiot, barefoot and freezing, because I heard crying." He took a deep breath. "Because crying disturbs—" James broke off abruptly, then impulsively reached out and lifted her chin with the tip of his index finger, tilting her face up so he could look at her. "Because *your* crying disturbs me."

James's heart seemed to thump against his chest. He let go of her chin, took an involuntary step backward, and exhaled all his breath in a rush as he stared down at her face. God in Heaven! A man could lose himself in her eyes. Even red-rimmed and brimming with unshed tears, her deep bluish-green eyes were extraordinary—warm, inviting, and trusting—so clear and revealing, James felt as if he could discern all her secrets and look right into her soul.

Then she blinked and the secrets of her soul were concealed once more. He watched as she fought to control the expressions of fragile vulnerability revealed in her eyes. She almost succeeded. If he hadn't seen the soft, vulnerable

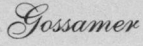

look in her eyes, James would not have believed such a change was possible. But the warmth in her blue-green gaze cooled, even the color changed—hardened—until her eyes resembled a pair of sparkling aquamarine stones. Beautiful, but remote.

In a flash of insight James realized the face he was seeing now was the one she showed to the rest of the world, the one most people saw. He knew, without being told, that only moments ago he had unwittingly caught a rare glimpse of the private young woman the rest of the world never saw. And he had the uncanny feeling that a man might live his entire life without ever again glimpsing the powerful emotions and secret longings hidden deep within her. Looking at her now, he was able to take note of her without the distraction of her extraordinary eyes and find that with her pale ivory skin, her small nose, her squarish jaw and determined chin she presented a capable, no-nonsense appearance. Other than her eyes, there was nothing else about her that gave any hint of the incredible beauty she kept hidden like a light beneath a bushel. Nothing else except her plump, shapely lips.

Her plump, shapely, *kissable* lips.

The idea lodged in his brain and seemed to grow with each draw of his breath until James Craig found himself nearly overwhelmed by the desire to taste those lips. Suddenly he knew he was in danger of being swept away by emotional waters too swift for him to navigate. He took another step backward, trying to distance himself from the powerful and unsettling feelings surging through him.

"I'm terribly sorry." James retreated, running for emotional cover. "I apologize for intruding on your privacy." He gave her a slight bow. "With your permission, I'll say good night and leave you alone."

He whirled around, heading back to the safety of his own room.

"Don't."

James stopped in his tracks, then turned to look at her. "Don't what?"

She bit her lip, clearly startled by her impulsive command. "Don't say good night," she finally whispered.

He hesitated. "I don't understand."

"Don't leave me alone." She opened her hotel room door, then hugging herself tightly, stepped into the breach. "Please, don't leave me alone."

James just stood there, transfixed, staring as her eyes filled with tears, unsure of his next move. Or hers.

A flush stole up her face. Embarrassed, and unable to meet his gaze any longer, she bit her bottom lip again and glanced down at the floor. "Forgive me." Her voice broke and she stepped back into her room. "I never meant to disturb—"

"Wait!" James ordered. "It isn't that I want to leave you alone. It's just that . . ." The awkwardness around women he'd suffered as a twelve-year-old boy returned with a vengeance. "It's just that you shouldn't trust me," he blurted out. "I'm a stranger. You don't know anything about me."

She regained a measure of her composure and shook her head. "I know you. You're good and kind and caring. And your name is James."

"But . . ."

"My name is Elizabeth," she said, in an echo of his earlier declaration, her voice shaky and thick with tears. "And I'm standing in my hotel room in the middle of the night, opening my door to a stranger because he tells me his name is James and his kind eyes and voice offer comfort. Because I arrived in San Francisco this afternoon to join my brother, only to find that my brother has been dead and buried in a potter's field for weeks. Because I lost my teaching position in Providence. Because I have no place else to go and very little money. But mostly because I'm more afraid of being left alone than I am of being accosted by a stranger."

That said, Elizabeth's face crumpled and she could no longer choke back her sobs as she clung to the doorway.

And this time James did what he had not been able to

do for Mei Ling. This time, James did what he felt he should do, what he needed to do. He reached out and scooped Elizabeth up in his arms. Leaning his shoulder against the door, he closed it with a soft final click. Then he carried her over to a chair near the warming stove, where he sat down, and cradled her tenderly against his chest. He held her until her tears were spent, then removed his handkerchief from the pocket of his robe and gently dabbed at the tear stains on her face. "Shh," he soothed. "Close your eyes and sleep. I'll take care of you," he promised. "I'll take care of everything." He cared for her as he would care for a child, comforted her as he would comfort a babe. Relying on instinct and half-remembered bits of old lullabies, James rocked Elizabeth against his chest and sang in a low, rusty baritone until she finally fell into an exhausted sleep.

Two

ELIZABETH SLOWLY OPENED her eyes and recognized the interior of her room at the Russ House. Her eyelids felt weighted down, swollen, and gritty. She tried to stretch but found herself held securely and surrounded by warmth. She luxuriated in the warmth as she breathed in the woodsy, spicy aroma permeating the room and listened to the reassuring thump of a heartbeat beneath her ear and the even, rhythmic breathing of a deeply slumbering man.

Not just any man. *James*. Startled, Elizabeth jerked upright and bumped her head against his chin as the memory of the night before came flooding back. She might have tumbled to the hard floor if not for the strong arms around her and the large hands intimately cupping her bottom, the long lean fingers laced together holding her in place. She wiggled in his embrace and rubbed at the tender spot where her head had come in contact with his chin, waiting for him to awaken. But he simply tightened his grip on her and continued to sleep. Elizabeth sighed. She knew she shouldn't linger. She knew she should get out of his arms right away and feel scandalized by their intimacy, but she didn't. She hadn't had anyone to watch over her or hold her or cuddle her for a very long time.

She waited, barely daring to breath, as he nuzzled her hair with his mouth and murmured unintelligibly in his sleep. She fought against the weakness sapping her resolve, fought against the almost overwhelming urge to burrow deeper against James's chest and cloak herself in his strength. But the night was over and with the dawn came the reality that she wasn't a child any longer. And she couldn't expect to be pampered and petted like a child. She was a woman grown. A woman who didn't waste her breath wishing for things she couldn't have. She had never prayed for miracles or hoped for impossible dreams to come true. She had learned a long time ago that there was no point in wishing for someone to hold her at night, to comfort her and keep the monsters at bay. And she didn't intend to start relying on the kindness of strangers at this late date. Even strangers like James. Especially good, kind strangers like James.

Men like James deserved women with untarnished reputations. They deserved—he deserved—the best. And she wasn't the best. Not anymore. Still, it was nice to think about . . . Elizabeth bit back a wistful sigh and ruthlessly suppressed the hundred unnamed, restless yearnings plaguing her. Don't think about it, she admonished herself, just do what you have to do. She pressed her lips together, flattening them into a firm determined line, and carefully extricated herself from James's protective embrace.

She tiptoed around the room, quietly retrieving her belongings. But Elizabeth couldn't help but glance over from time to time to study him. She'd guessed him to be about thirty years of age when she opened her door to him, but he looked so much younger in repose. His face was relaxed and his lips slightly parted. His piercing blue eyes were closed and shielded from view, and his black eyelashes fanned against his face, drawing her attention. His were the eyelashes of a child—thick and impossibly long—and the way they caressed the curve of his cheekbone made it relatively easy to believe the boyish illusion and to disregard the fine network of lines crinkling the corners of his eyes and the dark shadow of his unshaven jaw that gave proof of his maturity.

Unable to resist the impulse, Elizabeth walked over and gently traced the line of his jaw with her the pad of her thumb, delighting in the sandpapery feel of it. James was an impressive man. The most impressive man she'd ever been close enough to touch. He wasn't as classically handsome as Owen. His looks were too dark, too rugged, but she couldn't deny his appeal. James exuded strength and a masculine vitality, even in sleep, that Elizabeth found impossible to ignore.

But ignore it she must. She had to forget the comfort of his arms, the warmth and feel of his body against hers, and the sense of well-being he offered. She had to dismiss the almost overwhelming desire she felt to lay all her troubles at his feet and let him sort them out. Because she couldn't allow herself to do otherwise. She couldn't allow him to take her cares and concerns onto his shoulders—even if his shoulders were broad enough to carry them. She didn't know why it seemed so important to her, but Elizabeth desperately wanted James to recognize the fact that she wasn't weak or helpless and that she was perfectly capable of handling her own affairs. Especially since he'd seen her at her worst. What must he think of her already? Allowing him into her room in the middle of the night was bad enough, but crying on his shoulder was really mortifying, because she never cried—not when Papa died or Owen left or when Grandmother . . .

Elizabeth bit her bottom lip. *That* didn't bear thinking on. Not when she had so many other worries to tend, not when she was about to do the most cowardly thing she had ever done in her whole life. Not when she was about to sneak out of her hotel room like a thief in the night because she couldn't face James in the morning light and risk succumbing to that age-old female weakness of relying on a man's strength instead of her own. Because she couldn't bear the thought of seeing contempt replace the kindness in his eyes.

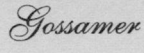

Firming her resolve, Elizabeth gathered her carpetbag, her hatbox, and her room key. She placed her luggage beside the door, then tiptoed over to James still asleep in the wing chair, reached into the pocket of his robe, and carefully eased his hotel key out of his pocket. His handkerchief was entwined with the key. The same handkerchief he had used to wipe away her tears. Elizabeth untangled the key and lifted the silk square to her nose. She breathed in the heady scent of James's cologne. She meant to put it back, to wrap his handkerchief around her hotel key and tuck it back into his pocket, but a sudden yearning gave her pause. Surely, he wouldn't miss one handkerchief? He'd given it to her to use. Would he mind her keeping it? Not when he probably had a dozen or more at home. Not when all she'd ever have were her memories and one tiny memento of the night a very special man had held her in his arms and rocked her to sleep.

Her decision made, Elizabeth clutched James's handkerchief to her breast for a moment before tucking it safely inside the pocket hidden in the seams of her skirt. Afraid to risk another foray into James's pocket, she squeezed her eyes shut, then opened her hand and let her hotel key slide between his muscular outer thigh and the arm of the chair, down between the cushion and the frame. James wouldn't be able to find the key so readily now, and when he did find it, Elizabeth hoped he'd think it slipped from his robe and into the cushion while he slept.

She'd done what she had to do to delay him. She had switched room keys. Elizabeth felt more than a pang of guilt at repaying his kindness with deceit, but she couldn't chance that he would try to follow her. Instinct told her that James was the kind of man who'd be inclined to seek her out—if only to make sure she was all right. He had a room key and could prove he belonged in the unlikely event that the hotel management tried to evict him. She wouldn't have to worry about him not having a place to sleep if he needed one. She wouldn't be depriving him of shelter, only temporary access to his belongings. She didn't want to hurt him. But Elizabeth didn't want him to try to find her, either.

Grabbing her shoes in one hand, Elizabeth opened the door to her room and peeked out. The corridor was empty. She nudged her baggage into the hallway and took one last look around. She meant to check to see if she'd left anything behind, but all she noticed was James. The room that had seemed so big and lonely when she arrived seemed somehow smaller, cozier with him asleep in it. She couldn't help but notice how he dwarfed the chair he sat sprawled on and how he had crooked his head at an uncomfortable angle in order to hold her on his lap. Elizabeth frowned. She couldn't leave him like that. It wouldn't be right.

Quickly, before she had time to think better of it, Elizabeth crossed the room, snatched a pillow from the bed and oh-so-gently worked it beneath James's head and the wing of the chair. He sighed, as if in gratitude, and Elizabeth gave in to a heartfelt impulse and brushed her lips across his hair before she straightened her shoulders and walked quietly out of the room.

An hour later Elizabeth shivered, hugged her double shawl closer to her body, and muttered a sincere, but decidedly unladylike, curse beneath her breath as the fog that shrouded the San Francisco hills seeped through several layers of clothing and into her very bones. She gripped the ends of her shawl in her fists, protecting her hands against the biting cold as she left the cab and started up the steps to the building ahead of her. The thick fog surrounding her diluted the weak sunlight, distorting the sights and sounds of the ordinary urban activity all around her. But the cold and the fog and the fact that she had only been in San Francisco one night and part of a morning could not keep Elizabeth from the task she had set for herself. She'd already endured too much to let anything prevent her from locating her brother's final resting place and that horrible establishment that had caused his untimely death. She was determined to fulfill her duty to Owen, to search the whole city if necessary, and she intended to start at the San Francisco City Police Department.

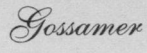

She opened the doors of the station house. The entrance hall was practically deserted at such an early hour, so Elizabeth made her way right up to the front desk. After taking a deep fortifying breath, she announced in a rush, "My name is Elizabeth Sadler. I was here late yesterday afternoon seeking information about my brother, Owen, and this morning I've come to find—"

"Step back, please." A voice, coming from above her head, interrupted her flow of words.

"I beg your pardon?" Standing as close as she was to the front desk, Elizabeth couldn't see the officer seated behind the raised dais, so she wasn't quite certain she'd heard him correctly.

"Step back away from the desk so I can see you, ma'am."

"Why, yes, of course," Elizabeth said, carefully moving back a couple of steps until she could see the officer behind the desk and he could see her.

"Now, ma'am, if you'll give me your name and state your business."

Elizabeth stared up at the policeman. "I've already given you my name and stated my business."

The officer lifted a pen from its holder and opened his log book. "I didn't catch your name or your business," he told her. "So, if you'll kindly repeat it for the record."

"My name is Elizabeth Sadler." She enunciated her name slowly and clearly. "I was here late yesterday—"

"Can you spell that for me?"

"Certainly," she replied. "Y-E-S-T-E-R—"

"Your name, ma'am," he interrupted. "Please spell your name for the record."

Elizabeth blushed. "Yes, of course. E-L-I-Z-A-B-E-T-H-S-A-D-L-E-R." She spelled her name for the policeman, then waited patiently for him to introduce himself.

"What's the matter?"

"You didn't introduce yourself," she said.

The officer gruffly cleared his throat. "Darnell, miss. Sergeant Terrence Darnell."

Elizabeth nodded, then began again. "As I said before, my name is Elizabeth Sadler and I came here late yesterday afternoon."

"What was your reason for yesterday's visit?"

"I was told to come here by the landlady who rented a room to my brother."

"Your brother's name?"

"Owen," Elizabeth replied, standing on tiptoe, trying to peer over the edge of the dais as she repeated, "O-W-E-N-S-A-D-L-E-R."

"Older or younger brother?"

"Why?" Elizabeth asked.

"I need his approximate age for the report, miss."

"Younger," she answered. "Owen is twenty-one." She waited as Sergeant Darnell made a note in his book.

"Got it," he informed her. "Go on."

"My brother, Owen, left home seven months ago bound for San Francisco. He arrived here two weeks after leaving Providence." Elizabeth paused for a moment, waiting to see if the officer would ask her to spell Providence. When he didn't, she continued, "Rhode Island. We grew up there. Anyway, Owen arrived in San Francisco and took a room at Ordley's Boarding House on Montgomery Street. He roomed at Mrs. Ordley's until two months ago—"

"And now you want us to find your brother"—the policeman glanced down at his notes—"Owen Sadler, because he's moved on without contacting you."

"Yes," Elizabeth said. "And no."

The officer stared down at her, impatience written on every line of his weathered face.

Elizabeth hurried to elaborate. "Yes, I do want you to help me locate my brother, but not because he moved away from Mrs. Ordley's, but because . . ." Her voice quivered and she fought to retain control. "He died." She closed her eyes for a moment. "Owen died. And that's why I need your help. You see I only arrived in San Francisco yesterday. I came to live with him, but when I went to Mrs. Ordley's address, she had already rented Owen's room to

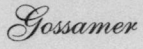

someone else. She suggested I come here. I spoke to Officer Anderson. He told me Owen had died. Nearly two months ago. In an opium den on Washington Street in Chinatown. Officer Anderson said the owner of the establishment identified Owen as a regular customer.''

"I'm sorry, miss." Sergeant Darnell's expression showed genuine compassion.

"Thank you, Sergeant," she replied.

"How can we help you, Miss Sadler?"

"I want to know where my brother is buried. I'll comb this city on foot all by myself if I have to," she told him. "Because I won't be able to rest until I find his grave."

"Did your brother leave any money?"

"No," she answered. "He worked in the Wells Fargo Bank on Montgomery Street. But his account was empty. I arrived during banking hours yesterday. I expected Owen to be at work, so I went directly to the bank. Mr. Knight, the bank manager, told me Owen no longer worked at the bank, that he hadn't worked there for over two months. He said Owen had failed to show up at work, and they had assumed he had left without giving notice. Mr. Knight suggested I try Ordley's Boarding House."

Darnell thought for a moment. "If your brother didn't leave any money for burial, then he's most likely buried in a pauper's grave in one of the city cemeteries."

Elizabeth nodded her understanding. "Sergeant Anderson told me the same thing last evening. But there are several cemeteries with potter's fields in San Francisco, and he didn't know where to begin looking. I came back here this morning hoping for more information."

"You say your brother died in Chinatown?" Sergeant Darnell repeated. "In a den on Washington Street?"

"Yes."

He sighed. "That would be Lo Peng's. And your best bet would be Saint Mary's Church. Go to Saint Mary's and ask for Father Paul. There's a vacant lot down the street from there. I heard that the church had donated the land as a burial ground for the poor victims of Chinatown. Father

Paul sees to the burying of the occidentals who go unclaimed. . . .'' Darnell let his voice drift off.

"How far is it?"

"A few blocks."

"How do I get there?"

"You go down Market, then turn on Kearney toward Portsmouth Square—'' Noting the confusion on Elizabeth's face, the Sergeant brought his directions to an abrupt halt. "I'll draw you a map,'' he told her, before taking his pen and sketching a rough map on one of the blank pages in his log book.

"Oh, thank you, Sergeant.'' Elizabeth's face lit up like a thousand-candle chandelier.

Sergeant Darnell stood and leaned over the high desk to hand the map to Elizabeth. "Take a cab,'' he advised. "The fog's as thick as porridge this morning. And we don't want you wandering around the city getting lost. Saint Mary's is too close to Chinatown. And Chinatown is no place for an unescorted white woman. Even in daylight.''

ELIZABETH LET GO of one end of her shawl, reached inside her skirt pocket, and pulled out the hastily drawn map of the downtown area that Sergeant Darnell had given to her. He'd been right. She should have taken a cab. The fog *was* as thick as porridge—even thicker than it had been when she left her hotel this morning. But she'd already spent a part of her dwindling cash on one cab, and she couldn't afford to spend more money on another one when she only had a few short blocks to go.

Pausing under a street lamp, Elizabeth studied the rough sketch in the eerie glow, then carefully stuffed the map back into her pocket and continued her journey. Only a few more blocks and she'd reach Saint Mary's Church on the fringe of the alien reaches of Chinatown.

Beyond the church, in one of the vacant lots between Saint Mary's Square and Portsmouth Square, was a tiny

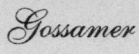

graveyard. A paupers' graveyard. A place where occidental drunks and opium-eaters were buried. Although she and Owen had been brought up in the Methodist faith, Elizabeth felt comforted by the fact that a kindly priest watched over her brother's final resting place.

If only she hadn't stayed behind in Providence. If only she had left her job at the academy months ago when Owen turned twenty-one and told her he was tired of clerking at the bank, when he informed her that he was heading west to seek his fortune in San Francisco. She should have gone with him. She knew he was high-spirited and adventurous and eager to see the world that lay beyond the bank teller's cage. She knew he was a dreamer with a tendency toward laziness, a young man who resented the fact that he had been forced into learning the trade by clerking at the bank their family owned.

Elizabeth bit her bottom lip and fought to keep the tears stinging her eyes from rolling down her cheeks. Owen hadn't been bad, just young and headstrong and, at times, foolish. She was older and more content with her life. Owen had hated the bank, hated answering to others, but she liked Lady Wimbley's Female Academy and had been reasonably happy teaching there. Like Owen, she had needed to escape the two-story stone house on Hemlock Street, where she and Owen had grown up. But unlike Owen, she had been safe and secure at Lady Wimbley's up until two weeks ago, while Owen had been lying in a pauper's grave unmourned and unclaimed for two long months.

Elizabeth hugged herself, then pulled the ends of her shawl tighter around her. She had heard rumors about San Francisco and read accounts of the city's wicked Barbary Coast in the *Providence Journal*, and seen the pen and ink drawings of the interiors of Chinese opium dens in *Harper's Weekly*. She should have foreseen the temptations a city like San Francisco afforded young men like Owen who were far away from home and family for the first time in their lives. She should have been here to watch over him in person, to see that he didn't fall in with the wrong people or fall victim to the temptation of drink and opium. Elizabeth gritted her teeth. Oh, what she would do once she found the horrible place that preyed upon innocent young men like Owen!

She stopped suddenly and peered into the thick fog, trying to get her bearings. Prickles of apprehension ran up and down her spine, lifting the tiny hairs at the nape of her neck. The sounds of the streets had changed. The muffled, distorted cries of street vendors and the snatches of conversations penetrating the thick fog were in a language Elizabeth no longer recognized. The cadence of the foreign language both intrigued and frightened her. It vividly reminded her that she was alone in a strange city, surrounded by cold fog and people she didn't know and whose language and customs she couldn't understand. All at once she longed for the warmth of her room at the Russ House, for the feelings of comfort and security she had found in James's arms. She patted the pocket of her skirt where two brass room keys and a silk handkerchief rested against her thigh. Along with the original key she had a duplicate in her pocket—one she'd talked the hotel desk clerk into giving her so she wouldn't have to bother James, her *cousin*, and traveling companion.

Elizabeth lifted her chin. She wouldn't think of James now. And she wouldn't cry, regardless of how sad or tired or cold or frightened she was. Elizabeth reminded herself that she couldn't give in to weakness, that she despised women who clung and cried and carried on, women who wrung their hands in helpless despair waiting to be rescued, then took to their beds with some imagined illness. She told herself that she'd done the right thing—the only thing—she could do by leaving James behind and that she'd be much happier, much better off on her own.

Her night of grief and weakness was over. And James was in the past. At any rate, she meant to put him out of her mind. She was going to forget all about James of the compelling blue eyes and black hair. And if his handkerchief seemed to be burning a guilty hole in her conscience

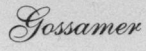

and in her pocket, she was determined to ignore it. She was entitled to one memento. Besides, she needed a handker-chief because she'd suddenly come down with some sort of malady—one that stuffed her nose and made her eyes water and made her jump with fear and nerves when she least expected it.

Why else would she be blinking back tears as she trudged along? Elizabeth glanced to her left and was able to make out the dark gray silhouette of a church. She kept her gaze on the big gray shadow as she made her way off the walkway and onto the church grounds. There was noth-ing to fear. So what if she was near Chinatown and the wicked Barbary Coast and the horrid opium dens? So what if she was surrounded by foreigners she didn't understand? So what if she was a woman all alone? So what if she had made it practically impossible for James to follow her—even if he wanted to? She was intelligent and capable. And about to set foot in a church. What could happen to her here? Elizabeth squared her shoulders, then placed her hand on the big oak door and stepped into Saint Mary's Church in search of the priest.

Three

"BLOODY HELL!" JAMES awoke late in the morning to find himself sprawled in the chair beside the stove, his long body cramping uncomfortably. He had his head pressed against the arm of the chair, and the pillow wedged under his neck didn't prevent his neck from being crooked at a miserable angle. His eyes felt gritty and swollen from long hours spent staring at the orange flames peeking through the stove vents, and even before he opened them, James knew he was alone. Elizabeth no longer slept cradled against his chest.

He pushed himself to his feet, yawned once, then stretched the kinks out of his abused muscles. He glanced around the room looking for some sign of the woman who had rented it, but there was nothing. No sign that anyone else had ever occupied the room. The bed was neatly made. And the single hatbox and traveling bag that had rested on the carpet runner at the foot of the mahogany four-poster bed when James had entered the room were gone.

He might have believed he dreamed the whole encounter with the lovely Elizabeth except for the trace of the deli-cate, violet-scented fragrance that clung tenaciously to the lapels of his silk robe. While James readily admitted a fond-

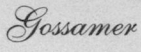

ness for the finer things in life, he had never been known to splash on violet perfume. His tastes ran to the spicier, masculine bay rums and oak mosses. Elizabeth wasn't a figment of his imagination, then, but a flesh-and-blood woman. And as soon as James returned to his own room, bathed, dressed, and grabbed a bite to eat, he intended to find her.

Ten minutes later James decided that, besides being a flesh-and-blood woman, Elizabeth was also a devilishly clever one. She'd left no doubt that she did not want to be found. He'd finally located his room key by fishing it out from under the cushion of the chair where he assumed it had landed after falling from his robe pocket, only to find that the key which should have unlocked the door to his hotel room didn't fit.

He fumbled with the lock again. But the door wouldn't open. There was no mistake. Elizabeth had taken his room key out of the pocket of his robe while he slept and exchanged it for hers. James managed a grim smile. She'd cleverly made certain he had a place to sleep if he needed one, but was denied immediate access to his personal belongings. James glanced down at his bare feet and the wedge of naked chest left exposed by his robe. Personal belongings like socks and boots, shirts and jackets. He wiggled his bare toes. He had to give Elizabeth credit for her resourcefulness. And for limiting his. He wouldn't have any trouble reclaiming his belongings once he got the door to his room open, but he wouldn't be able to gain access to his room without drawing attention to his predicament. As far as he could tell he had three choices: stay in Elizabeth's room until a maid or other hotel employee wandered by, kick in the door to his room, or appear at the front desk downstairs half-clothed and keyless. And no matter which solution he chose, James knew he'd have to do a bit of explaining. A man couldn't be found half-clothed in a room registered in the name of an unaccompanied woman without giving some sort of explanation. Neither could he kick in the door of his room or traipse into the main lobby of one of San Francisco's premier hotels, barefoot and shirt-less, without supplying the management with an apology and an explanation guaranteed to delay his departure. And any delay for James, no matter how brief or how long, provided Elizabeth with more time to disappear into the foggy San Francisco environs.

James clenched his teeth in frustration. Look what he got for trying to be a good Samaritan—for offering comfort and solace to a distraught woman, for spending the night folded into a damned uncomfortable wing chair designed for someone a lot smaller, and at least a foot shorter, than his six-foot-three-inch frame. He was locked out of his room and forced to make explanations to an obsequious hotel staff in order to gain access to his personal belongings.

James was honest enough to admit that being forced to provide explanations for his appearance and his predicament in a hotel jam-packed with his railroad employees galled him more than having Elizabeth sneak out with his room key. After all, Elizabeth didn't owe him anything. He had freely offered his help and words of comfort. Elizabeth hadn't asked him to stick his nose into her personal business. She hadn't asked him to intrude on her private grief. *But she had asked him to stay. She had asked him not to leave her alone. She had allowed him to hold her in his arms.*

He shook his head. It didn't matter if he'd dared to dream a bit while she lay curled in his embrace, or if he'd toyed with the idea of taking a few hours off from his many business obligations to spend the day in the company of a beautiful woman. Elizabeth hadn't been privy to his thoughts. She had no way of knowing he was looking for-ward to escorting her down to breakfast in the hotel dining room, then spending the remainder of his day introducing her to San Francisco.

She hadn't stayed long enough to face him in the morn-ing light. She had sneaked out while he slept, almost as if she were afraid to face him, almost as if she thought he'd think less of her for crying herself to sleep in a stranger's arms. And although James's first inclination was to scour the streets of San Francisco until he found her, Elizabeth had made her feelings perfectly clear. She obviously didn't want him to follow her. She obviously didn't want to be found.

And, James decided, he'd be better off taking care of his own business. He'd be better off if he forgot all about Elizabeth. His railroad and mining interests required all of his attention at the moment. The foremen in the mining and timber camps had reported incidents of labor unrest and he still had a few important details of the rolling stock deal with the Central Pacific to wrap up here in the city before he could return home. And he had several even greater obligations back home in Coryville. The sooner he swallowed his pride and marched down to the front desk, the sooner he'd be able to bathe and dress, take care of his business, and head home to Coryville and to his family.

Because he had no choice, James Craig strolled down the stairs to the front desk of the Russ House barefoot and shirtless to request a spare key to his room. When the desk clerk wanted to know how Mr. Craig became locked out of his room, James had simply stood glaring at the man until Mr. Palmer, the hotel manager, a tall, barrel-chested man with an equally big belly, muttonchop whiskers, and a rapidly receding hairline, arrived and began the search for the spare key to his room. James waited so long for the man to return with the key that he'd almost decided that buying the hotel, emptying it of incompetent staff, and searching for the damned key himself would be easier than subjecting himself to the scrutiny of the hotel employees and guests in the lobby, the public bar, and the dining room. Standing at the front desk, James scanned the restaurant in the halfhearted hope that he would find Elizabeth enjoying a leisurely breakfast. He was disappointed, but not surprised, to discover she wasn't there. She had gone to a great deal of effort to sneak out of the room before he woke up and to keep him from following her. And after going to all the trouble to elude him, James hadn't really expected Elizabeth to linger over breakfast in the hotel dining room waiting for him to appear. But he'd hoped just the same.

Exhaling a long breath, James turned and found himself the object of a half-dozen or so curious glances from his railroad employees who sat sipping coffee and eating breakfast. Acutely aware that he was setting a bloody poor example for the employees at Craig Capital, Ltd., James grimaced, then ran his fingers through his hair in an effort to comb it, straightened his silk robe and tightened the belt at his waist, making himself as presentable as possible. He employed hundreds of men on his railroad lines and in the northern California mines and timber camps, and while James knew the majority of the men were satisfied in their jobs, there were other employees who believed the rumors about him—the rumors that had followed him from Hong Kong. And as a consequence of that, he employed men who didn't trust him, didn't like the way he ran Craig Capital, or the fact that he employed hundreds of Welsh, Cornishmen, and Chinese.

"I apologize for the delay, Mr. Craig," the hotel manager interrupted James's thoughts, "but we've been unable to locate an additional spare key to your room. Perhaps, you should check with your *traveling companion*." He shot James a meaningful glance. "She requested a second key to your room earlier this morning."

"My what?" James's voice rumbled through the lobby causing several hotel guests to turn and stare at him.

"The young lady traveling with you. The young lady staying in the room next to yours."

"Elizabeth?"

The hotel manager nodded, then checked the signature on the guest register. "That's right. Miss Elizabeth Sadler. I believe she said she was your *cousin*," Mr. Palmer informed him.

James digested that information, then scanned the hotel lobby and dining room again before asking, "Did my cousin happen to mention what she was doing up and about so early in the morning?''

"She explained that, although you were her escort, she wanted to do some shopping while you attended to business this morning. The porter hailed a hack for her.''

"What about her room?'' James asked.

"What about it?''

"I'm—we're—leaving San Francisco this afternoon,'' James reminded the manager. "Did my cousin arrange for her bill? Or shall I cover the cost?''

"Oh, no, Mr. Craig,'' Palmer rushed to reassure his guest. "Miss Sadler paid for her room herself in full this morning.''

"What about her baggage?'' he prodded. "Did she have it sent to the Ferry Building in preparation for our departure? Or shall I?''

"She only had the one bag,'' the hotel manager told him. "And a hatbox.'' He glanced at James quizzically. "I assumed she had had the bulk of her baggage sent ahead.''

"Then why did she need a key to my room?''

"She said she'd left a few personal items in your care that she wished to retrieve when she returned from her shopping trip and since she was reluctant to awaken you so early in the morning in order to borrow your key, she asked the clerk on duty for the spare.''

"And he gave it to her?'' James's voice rose.

"Please, Mr. Craig, lower your voice,'' Palmer pleaded. "We have guests.''

"*I'm* a guest,'' James reminded the hotel manager, lowering his voice as he forced his words through his tightly clenched teeth. "And you gave someone else a key to my room without my permission.''

"She said she was traveling with you. She said she was your *cousin*, and we had no way of knowing that the young woman wasn't to be given a key to your room. Or that you would foolishly misplace yours,'' Mr. Palmer added haughtily.

James raised an eyebrow at Mr. Palmer's tone of voice,

then told him, "I didn't misplace my key. Foolishly or otherwise."

"Then what, may I ask, happened to it?" Palmer asked.

James almost told the hotel manager exactly what had happened to his key, but he regained control of his temper in time to stop himself before he could answer that the young woman in question had taken his key from the pocket of his robe while he was sleeping and left hers in exchange. Whatever else Elizabeth was, James would bet his last penny on the fact that she was a lady. A frightened, perhaps even desperate, lady, but a lady nonetheless, and some deep protective instinct inside him refused to allow him to ruin her reputation by relaying the previous night's events. Besides, James had explained more about his situation than he had ever intended. As far as he was concerned, the subject of how his room key came up missing was closed.

He looked the hotel manager right in the eye. "I have no idea. But as I do have business to attend to this morning and my cousin is nowhere to be found, I suggest you call a locksmith."

Mr. Palmer shook his head, then glanced over at James. "This is all highly irregular."

"It will be even more irregular when I kick the door out of its frame."

"You can't do that," Palmer gasped.

"I can and I will."

"But, sir . . . Mr. Craig . . ."

James glanced at the regulator clock hanging on the wall behind the front desk to let Palmer know he felt he'd already dallied too long. "You have ten minutes to find a locksmith," he said. "Starting now."

❧

JAMES SCANNED THE horizon as he waited in the San Francisco Ferry Building at the foot of Market Street for the approaching ferry that would transport him across San

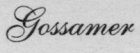

Francisco Bay to the Southern Pacific pier at Oakland, where the Central Pacific Railroad had its terminal. He'd wandered through shopping districts and neighborhoods all over the city looking for Elizabeth. She was somewhere in the teeming metropolis, traveling the streets alone and unprotected. And even though he knew he shouldn't waste any more time worrying about her, James found himself doing just that. She had seemed so fragile and vulnerable. He snorted in disgust. Her looks were deceptive. *Elizabeth had seemed fragile and vulnerable, but she'd proven herself more than capable of outwitting him and spoiling his plans for the day.*

He had stayed in the city as long as he dared, barely making it to the Ferry Building in time to catch the last ferry to Oakland. He'd even briefly toyed with the idea of staying over in San Francisco another couple of days to locate Elizabeth, but James knew he couldn't disappoint his loved ones by staying in the city any longer. He had promised them he'd be home tomorrow, and James intended to keep that promise.

James watched as the ferry pulled alongside the pier, and the crew extended the walkways. He boarded the boat and headed toward his accustomed table in the dining salon. He nodded to several acquaintances before being joined by Will Keegan, his second in command at Craig Capital, Ltd.

Will removed his hat and topcoat, then slipped into a seat opposite James and helped himself to a cup of coffee from the pot on the table. "We missed you at lunch," he said as James turned away from the window.

Lost in thought, James looked at Will blankly, then slapped his forehead with the palm of his hand. "Bloody hell!"

"Not to worry," Keegan assured his boss. "Even without you there to oversee everything, business went on as usual. The papers were signed, sealed, and delivered to the bank for safekeeping." Will reached into his coat pocket and pulled out an envelope. "By the way, this came for you at the office while we were at the meeting." He handed James the envelope.

James accepted the telegram, then wrinkled his brow in annoyance. He couldn't seem to get her out of his mind. Perhaps, it was because he hadn't been able to say good-bye. But even now, as he sat across the table from Will Keegan discussing business, James was reminded of the color of Elizabeth's eyes every time he glanced out at the sparkling waters of the Bay. He'd been so concerned about Elizabeth that he'd forgotten about conducting his business. Instead, he'd spent the day out searching the endless rows of shops, on the off-chance that Elizabeth had meant it when she informed the desk clerk at the Russ House that she had some shopping to do.

"I can't believe I forgot about the meeting with the Central Pacific board."

Will shrugged his shoulders. "Don't worry about it. The deal had already been made. Today's meeting was only a formality, and besides"—he looked over the rim of his coffee cup at James—"I needed the experience and you needed to know the company wouldn't fall apart simply because you missed one meeting." Will set his cup down in its saucer.

"Damn," James said. "I never forget a meeting. That isn't like me at all."

"I figured something important came up." Will's brown eyes twinkled merrily as he gave James a broad knowing wink. "Don't fret about it, Jamie. No one would blame you for spending a day in San Francisco pleasuring a woman in bed. You're entitled. Hell, you're more than entitled, you're due."

"What the devil are you talking about?" James eyed Will suspiciously.

"I heard you created a little . . . um . . . disturbance this morning at the Russ House."

James raised his eyebrow. "You don't normally pay attention to idle gossip, Will."

"I do where you're concerned," Will Keegan answered,

meeting James's unrelenting glare with one of his own. James knew that Will wasn't just talking about this morning's episode at Russ House, but about the other gossip that had followed hot on his heels from Hong Kong. "Don't frown at me, Jamie. You know you'd do the same if our situations were reversed."

James sighed. Will was right. James couldn't blame his friend for paying attention. Will had almost as much at stake in Craig Capital as he did, and any gossip about James that affected CCL affected Will as well. "What did you hear?" James asked abruptly. "How bad was it?"

"I heard you had a helluva morning. I heard you appeared at breakfast at the Russ House in a silk robe and nothing else, that you were arguing with the management because a prostitute named LilyBeth had stolen your clothes and your money and that you kicked your door out of its frame because the hotel management refused to allow you access to your belongings unless you paid your bill in full." Will grinned at James. "In short, I heard that the fabulously wealthy James Craig rolled, and was rolled by, a Barbary Coast whore in one of San Francisco's most exclusive hotels. How close did the gossips come to the truth?"

"I kicked my hotel room door out of its frame."

"Why?" Will couldn't contain his curiosity.

"Because I was locked out of my room and it was taking that incompetent hotel manager too damn long to find a locksmith to get me back inside it."

"No Barbary Coast whore named LilyBeth?"

"Definitely not," James told him, remembering the vulnerable expression in Elizabeth's beautiful blue-green eyes.

"No silk robe?"

James smiled for the first time since Will had joined him at the table. "I *was* wearing a silk robe, all right, but I had a pair of trousers on beneath it."

"Oh, well, I knew it was too good to be true."

"Well?" James demanded.

"Well what?"

"How do you think this latest rumor will affect the company and the men?"

Will began to chuckle. "Oh, I think this rumor will prove beneficial to the company and the men."

"How so?"

"This one will make you seem more human. More fallible. The men will tend to think of you as one of them once they learn you were caught with your trousers down around your ankles just like the rest of us have been at one time or another while in San Francisco."

"But I wasn't," James insisted.

"Doesn't matter," Will told him. "Once the men hear the rumor, that's what they'll believe."

James exhaled a long, slow, deep breath. Why was that? he wondered. Why did everyone always want to believe the worst about someone else? Why would the men in his employ want him to be fallible? Didn't they understand that he couldn't afford to be fallible? Not when he held their livelihoods, and sometimes their very lives, in his hand.

Will Keegan reached over and clapped James on the shoulder. "Cheer up, old man. The men are going to be positively gloating about this one."

"I know," James replied glumly.

"They'll like you better," Will replied.

"I don't care whether they like me or not," James reminded his second-in-command, "but, dammit, I do want them to trust me."

"Trust has to be earned," Will said.

"How well I know it." James focused his gaze on the polished wooden surface of the table.

Will finished his cup of coffee and rose from the table. "Give them time, Jamie. We're still new here in California. Our ways of doing business are new. But I'm certain that once the men who work for us realize that we pay equal wages for equal work to everyone, regardless of background or skin color, they'll relax, learn to work together and to trust our leadership. Once the men figure out that

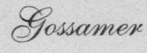

you don't favor one group over the other, everything will be all right."

"I hope you're right," James said fervently.

"I am," Will told him. "You'll see." He clapped James on the shoulder again. "I have to see to the unloading of the supplies we ordered," he said as he prepared to leave the warmth of the salon and return to the deck and the bitter cold. "Don't forget to read your telegram."

"Is it important?" James asked, knowing Will read every telegram that arrived at the San Francisco office of Craig Capital whenever he wasn't there to do it himself.

Will smiled. "It depends on how you look at it," he said. "If I were in your shoes, it would be a tragedy. Your latest governess quit and Mrs. G. is threatening to, unless you find someone else to take care of the Treasures."

James ran his fingers through his thick black hair. "Damn. If I had known about this earlier, I could have hired a new governess while I was in the city. As it stands now, I'll only be able to stay in Coryville a day before I have to turn right back around and return to San Francisco."

"Why not simply spend the night in Oakland and take the morning ferry back to the city and hire a new governess?" Will suggested even though he knew James wouldn't consider it.

"I can't," James told him. "I promised the Treasures I'd be home tomorrow morning. And I can't disappoint them."

"Have you tried to find someone in Coryville?" Will shrugged into his coat, then glanced out the window at the city of Oakland looming on the horizon.

"You know I've hired four governesses in the past month," James admitted. "And they were all from Coryville. Remember? The first one was a former faro dealer, the second one was a former saloon girl. Our third governess was a Chinese laundress from the mining camp, and the last one a widow of one of the miners. Not a one of them met my qualifications. But . . . ."

"But you felt sorry for them and offered them a better-paying job," Will finished for him.

James gave a curt nod. "But only because it was convenient for me at the time."

"I noticed they didn't stay very long, but you never told me what happened to them."

"The faro dealer was in the habit of sleeping all day. She quit because she didn't like the early morning hours. I fired the saloon girl for sampling my Scotch and brandy reserves and because I discovered that when she took the Treasures out for their daily walk, she walked them downtown and left them sitting in their carriages on the boardwalk while she stopped in the saloons for a couple of beers. The Chinese laundress didn't understand why I wanted the Treasures in the first place. She kept encouraging me to sell them and buy myself some sons, so I let her go. And the last one . . ." James reread the telegram. "Who knows?" He pinned his gaze on Will. "We had already had several discussions regarding our differing views of child-rearing. No, this time I think I'll do better to look in San Francisco."

"I think you're right," Will agreed. "Now, I'd better see to the unloading. Don't forget to give my love to Mrs. G. and the Treasures."

"Aren't you stopping by the house?" James asked, hoping Will would be a calming influence on his housekeeper, Mrs. Glenross, and help provide a distraction for the Treasures.

"Nah." Will shook his head. "You decided I should accompany the supplies up to the high timber camps and check on the progress of the track while I'm there. Remember?"

"I changed my mind," James told him. "Send someone else."

"Too late, Jamie," Will shot back, halfway through the door of the salon. "I'm already gone. There's no one else to send. Good luck finding a new governess."

He'd need more than luck, James decided. He'd need a

miracle. Because finding a governess for his three rambunctious girls was next to impossible.

Fortunately, James already had someone in mind and the perfect reason to scour San Francisco searching for her.

Four

"WE'VE GOT ANOTHER one." Helen Glenross, James's Scottish-born housekeeper, met him at the front door with a blanket-wrapped bundle in her arms.

"Already? That's wonderful, Mrs. G." James didn't look up. He stomped the dirt from his shoes on the front steps of his two-story Georgian-style brick home and shook the few flakes of a light spring snow off the brim of his hat and the shoulders of his coat, then stepped over the threshold.

Mrs. G. closed the front door behind him as James dropped his leather satchel, removed his heavy wool topcoat and hat and hung them on the hall tree, and wandered into his study. "Will gave me your telegram on the ferry. I didn't expect to find another one so soon. Tell me, Mrs. G., now that you've hired a new governess, have you decided not to quit?" He picked up the stack of mail on his desk and began to sort through it.

"On the contrary," she replied, finally grabbing James's undivided attention. "Not only have I decided to quit, but the way things are going around here, I may leave tonight."

James whirled around and faced his housekeeper. "I don't understand."

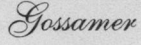

Mrs. Glenross carefully thrust the blanket into his arms. "This should explain it."

James let go of the mail. Envelopes bounced off his trouser legs and fluttered to the hardwood floor unheeded as he accepted the bundle his housekeeper handed to him. James felt the warmth of a tiny body and immediately knew he held an infant in his arms. He shifted the blanket to the crook of his arm, then used his free hand to gently peel back the corners of the soft flannel so he could get his first look at the infant.

As he stared down at the red wrinkled face and body of a female newborn who couldn't have been more than a few hours old, James reached out and stroked the soft black strands of hair covering the baby's head. He marveled at the feel of the baby's tender skin beneath his fingertips, the shape of her nose and mouth, and the length of the dark eyelashes fanned against her cheeks. James ran his knuckles lightly down the delicate skin of the baby's cheek, then touched her tightly balled fist with his index finger. Instinctively the baby grasped James's finger.

James grinned. "She's a strong one, Mrs. G. A real fighter."

Helen Glenross stooped to pick up the mail, then rose to her full height and grinned back at James. Her thin, pinched features were wreathed in a broad smile as she shared the wonder of a new life with her employer. "Aye, that she is."

"Where did you find her?" James asked.

"In the garden behind the greenhouse by the back gate. I had just gone into the greenhouse to pick strawberries for a shortcake. I heard a noise, felt someone brush against the back of my skirt. I glanced around, noticed that a few fruit and vegetable plants were bare, and figured we had another hungry sneak-thief. I went outside to make sure the back gate was secure and found this little moppet lying in a basket in the middle of a row of cabbage—between the regular cabbage and the bok choy. She couldn't have been more than a couple of hours old."

James nodded. "Anything wrong with her?" he asked, an almost hopeful note in his voice as he automatically counted her fingers and toes. "Any deformities? Birthmarks?"

Mrs. G. shook her head. "Not that I can find."

"Damn," James muttered beneath his breath. He didn't want to find that the innocent little girl suffered physical deformities; he only sought a sense of reason, of logic to the ancient Chinese practice of abandoning unwanted baby girls. James could almost understand a frightened superstitious young woman abandoning a deformed child. But this . . . This was beyond his ken. This ritual abandonment tore at his heart, saddened and angered him. Another perfectly healthy, absolutely beautiful baby had been abandoned, left in payment for a few pilfered fruits and vegetables, simply because she'd had the misfortune to be born female in a society that demanded that the firstborn child be male.

"At least they brought this one inside the gate," Mrs. G. said. "You nearly ran over Emerald. Remember?"

How could he forget? The near-accident had frightened him out of ten years of his life. "The word must be finally getting around to every corner of Chinatown," James said. "I've made no secret of the fact that I'll gladly take in any unwanted female children."

Mrs. Glenross placed her hands on her hips and snorted in disdain, her thin lips flattened into a disapproving line. "The leaders of the Tongs most likely think you're going to make slaves or concubines out of these precious little lambs. That's probably why they're allowing the poor mothers to bring 'em here."

"I don't care what the Tongs think."

"But the terrible rumors going 'round about you . . ."

James looked over at his housekeeper. So, Mrs. G. had heard the rumors about him, too. No wonder she was threatening to quit. He couldn't blame the woman for being uncomfortable living in his household, now that she was alone with him, now that the last governess had flown the coop. Hell, he'd be uncomfortable, too. Nobody wanted to live

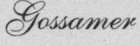

with a murderer—even a rumored murderer.

He'd been lucky to find Mrs. Glenross, and he needed her now more than ever, so James decided to do whatever he could to waylay her fears. "Blast the rumors." James did his best to temper his strong reaction. "I'd rather have the whole nation think of me as a procurer than allow any more of these innocent children to die." He turned his attention back to the baby in his arms, and smiled when she yawned at him. "The rumors about me are just that, Mrs. G.—rumors," James met his housekeeper's hard gaze without flinching. "They don't bother me. And I sincerely hope you don't let them bother you. *We* know the truth. *We* know I'd never do anything to hurt my girls. I want only the best for them—the best life possible. And I'm more than willing to see that they get it."

Mrs. G. gave a sharp understanding nod, before allowing herself, and her employer, another rare smile. "Don't think I pay any heed to gossip," Mrs. G. told him, "nor am I wanting to leave your employ. But"—she hesitated a moment—"with three little ones already, and no governess, and now this little mite, I just don't see how I can manage."

James smiled his most reassuring smile. "Don't worry about a thing, Mrs. G., I already have a governess in mind."

She raised her eyebrows at that.

"I met her at the hotel in San Francisco. She's young, capable, and experienced," James said. It wasn't a lie. He had met her at the hotel in San Francisco. And Elizabeth had told him she'd been a teacher.

Very familiar with the kind of experience James's previous governesses had had, Mrs. G. was more than a bit skeptical. "How experienced?"

"She left a long-standing position as a teacher in a school back East to come west."

"And you think you can talk a teacher with that kind of experience into leaving San Francisco to come to a tiny mining town when she's sure to have plenty of better opportunities in the city?"

"She needs a job," James said simply, praying it was true. "And we need a governess."

Mrs. G. still looked skeptical. "And what if she already has a job before you get back to San Francisco?"

"I'll double her best offer," James said. "Triple it, even. I'll do whatever it takes, pay whatever she wants, to get her here."

Penny-wise Scotswoman that she was, Mrs. Glenross seized the opportunity. "And what about me?"

James bit back a smile. "Well, of course, it goes without saying, that since there will be at least two more mouths to feed and bodies to take care of"—he glanced down at the baby—"I'll be doubling your salary and adding a healthy bonus as a thank-you for staying on. Deal?"

"Deal," Helen Glenross agreed.

"And now that that's settled," James continued, "have you told the Treasures about their newest sister?"

"No, sir, I was waiting for you. I had just gotten them fed and bathed and tucked in for a bit of a rest. And a time I had doing it, too. I finally had to promise I'd wake 'em as soon as you got home."

"We'll go upstairs to see the girls in just a minute, but first we have something very important to take care of." James focused all his attention on his housekeeper. "What shall we name her, Mrs. G.?"

"It's April," Mrs. Glenross replied.

"And what gemstone represents the month of April?" he asked.

Mrs. G. thought for a moment. "A diamond," she replied.

"Then, Diamond, it is." James leaned down and gently nuzzled the infant, inhaling the newborn scent of her. Would he ever tire of seeing a newborn child open her eyes and fix her unfocused gaze on him? Would he ever tire of feeling the warmth of a baby's body in his arms or fail to be enchanted by the simple rise and fall of her tiny chest? Would there ever come a time in his life when he could look at a baby girl and not remember . . . No, James told

himself. Never. He blinked at the sudden stinging in his
eyes as he pressed his lips against the baby's forehead.
"Welcome home, little Diamond. Welcome to the family.
Now, we'll go upstairs and introduce you to your new sisters." James looked over at Mrs. G. "I wonder what our
other Treasures will have to say about this."

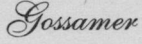

"PAPA!" THE UPSTAIRS nursery vibrated with the high-
pitched squeals of excited little girls. Three-and-a-half-year-
old Ruby scrambled out from beneath the covers of her bed,
climbed over the guardrails, and launched herself at her
father, wrapping her arms around his knees. "What chou
brwing me, Papa?"

James handed the baby over to Mrs. Glenross before
reaching down to lift Ruby into his arms. Two-year-old
Garnet bounced up and down on the mattress before she
followed Ruby's example, lifting her short chubby leg to
pull herself over the bed rail.

Ruby's silky cap of jet black, chin-length hair swung to
and fro as James lifted her above his head before settling
her into his arms. "I brought myself," he whispered into
her ear as he stole little kisses from the ticklish spot on the
side of her neck.

Ruby giggled with glee, then leaned back in the safety
of her father's strong arms, wrinkled her brow, and asked
in all seriousness. "What else chou brwing me?"

"I brought you the sun and the moon and the stars,
happy thoughts, and sweet dreams," he answered.

Ruby wrinkled her brow even harder. "What else?"

James laughed. "Ah, Ruby, my love, you've an avari-
cious nature."

Ruby didn't understand big words. She only understood
that her papa hadn't told her what he'd brought her from
his trip to *Sanfrwansco* and she had been patient long
enough. She began to wiggle, throwing her slight weight

against James's arms. "What chou brwing me, Papa?" she demanded again.

James kissed her again, then set her on her feet. "I brought you a wondrous toy piano all your own," he announced.

Helen Glenross groaned aloud.

Ruby squealed in delight and danced an impromptu jig about the room, bumping into Garnet, who had finally managed to climb out of bed and to toddle over to stand between Mrs. G. and her father. "Where it is, Papa?"

"Where is it," he corrected automatically, reaching down to lift shy little Garnet from behind Mrs. G.'s skirts and into his arms. "It's still packed in my bags." James winked at his housekeeper. "I'm hoping that having a toy piano of her own will keep the little imp from *playing* the one in the parlor."

Ruby crossed her arms over her chest and stared up at her father. "Want it."

"Not tonight," he said firmly.

Ruby stuck out her bottom lip, screwed up her face, and did her best to squeeze out a few tears to sway him before she made up her mind whether or not to wail.

James shook his head at her. "You may have your toy piano tomorrow morning," he told her. "After breakfast." He turned his attention to Garnet, who looped her arms around his neck and pressed her little face against his cheek in a ferocious hug. "Hello, sweet Garnet, Papa missed you, too."

"What chou brwing Garny?" Ruby tried another tack as she marched over to James and tugged on his trousers.

"I brought Garnet the same things I brought you."

"A pinano all her own, too?" Ruby was indignant.

"No," James assured the firstborn and self-appointed ruler of the nursery roost. "I brought Garnet the sun and the moon and the stars, happy thoughts, and sweet dreams. And"—he gave dramatic pause—"a box of story blocks all her own."

Garnet's dark eyes widened in surprise and her tiny face

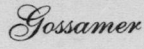

seemed to light up from within at James's announcement. She tightened her arms around his neck and pressed herself even closer to him.

James breathed in Garnet's soap and talcum-powder scent and pondered the differences in his daughters' personalities. Where Ruby was forthright, stubborn, and spoiled, Garnet was reticent, amiable, and generous. Though their looks were similar, there were obvious physical differences. Ruby was small but solidly built, a hardy energetic little girl with a broad, expressive face. Garnet was delicately formed with a smaller oval face and exquisitely formed features. She wasn't a sickly child, only a quiet, retiring one, willing to follow rather than blaze a trail of her own. And where Ruby tended to be imperious and dictatorial toward her younger sisters, Garnet never seemed to take offense. She worshipped Ruby and adored her younger sister, Emerald, delighting in their company and in everything around her. James's heart seemed to turn over in his chest every time she looked at him with love and trust and adoration brimming from her dark soulful eyes.

"Did chou brwing me brwocks, too?" Ruby demanded.

"No," James patiently explained. "I brought you a wondrous toy piano."

"Want brwocks," Ruby insisted, stamping her little foot for emphasis.

"Would you rather have the blocks than the piano?" James asked.

Ruby shook her head. "Want brwocks and pinano."

"I brought the blocks for Garnet," James told his eldest child. "I brought a piano for you." He glanced across the room to where thirteen-month-old Emerald was sitting in her crib. "And a bright red rubber ball for Emerald."

Garnet reached up, placed her small palms on either side of James's face, and turned his head toward Mrs. G. "What 'bout dat?" she asked softly, nodding toward the infant in Mrs. G.'s arms.

James hugged the little girl in his arms even tighter. Trust Garnet to be the first to notice Diamond and to notice that he had omitted the baby from his gift list. "That," James explained, "is your new little sister, Diamond."

Garnet smiled.

Arms akimbo, Ruby stamped her foot. "Wanna see."

James bent at the waist and carefully set Garnet on her feet before taking Diamond from Mrs. G.'s arms. He carried the baby over to the rocking chair beside Emerald's crib and sat down, angling his body so that Emerald could peer through the slats of her crib at the baby and the curious introductions. He made himself comfortable on the rocker, then leaned forward a bit and called Ruby and Garnet forward. "Come on over. Gently now," he cautioned when Ruby made a beeline for his lap. "Come see Diamond."

Ruby and Garnet wiggled closer, pressing their little bodies close against James's legs. Garnet's little face glowed with delight as James peeled back the blanket and held Diamond up so the girls could get a look at her face. She reached out and reverently touched the blanket. "Pwretty." Garnet stood on tiptoe, making smacking sounds with her lips, as she leaned forward to kiss the baby.

James nodded his approval at Garnet and smiled at Emerald, who was reaching through the slats of her crib and babbling excitedly. James brushed his lips against Emerald's hand, then turned to Ruby and asked, "What about you, sweetheart? What do you think of your new sister?"

Ruby frowned at the baby, displeasure written in big bold letters across her face for all the world to see. She backed up a step or two, away from the baby. "Rwuby rwather have her pinano," she said, looking her daddy squarely in the eye. "And brwocks!"

Five

ELIZABETH WATCHED AS Father Paul strolled up and down the narrow path between the rows of graves. She focused her gaze on his feet, watching as the hem of his garment swept back and forth, brushing the tops of his black boots and across the sandy loam covering the newest sites in the ever-increasing potter's field.

"Are you certain this is it?" Elizabeth asked, pointing to the second grave in the row.

Father Paul shrugged his shoulders. "I cannot be certain." He stared down at the row of burial plots. "There are so many new ones."

"Please, Father, try to remember," she pleaded. "Owen had a boyish face, blond hair, and blue eyes. He was only twenty-one."

"So young," the priest remarked, reaching up to reposition his zucchetto on his close-cropped, grizzled hair. "They all seem so young to me." Sighing heavily, he turned his attention back to the row of graves. "Perhaps, it is that one," he told her, pointing to the second grave. "Or perhaps, that one, or the other," he concluded, pointing to the first and third graves. "One of these three, although I cannot say exactly which one."

Elizabeth stood quietly for a moment, absentmindedly chewing on her bottom lip, before making a decision. "That's the one." She pointed to the second grave, then looked over at the elderly priest for confirmation. "Somehow, I just know Owen is buried there. I feel it in my heart."

Father Paul nodded, his faded blue eyes brimming with understanding. "Then that grave is where his mortal body lies."

"Fine, then," Elizabeth agreed. "It's settled." She reached out and grasped the old man's hand. "Thank you, Father." Her next course of action determined, Elizabeth started out of the cemetery. "I'll go order a headstone. A fine one of polished marble." She turned back to the priest.

"See Mr. Dorminey at Dorminey Stone Works near the end of Larkin Street," he instructed. "He's one of my parishioners. Tell him I sent you."

"Oh, thank you, Father. Thank you so much." Elizabeth's gratitude was mirrored in her blue-green eyes.

The elderly priest smiled. "Go with God, my child."

~~⌘~~

TWO HOURS LATER, after having ordered and paid for a white polished marble headstone engraved with Owen's name and dates, Elizabeth concluded her business with the owner of Dorminey Stone Works. Her sense of euphoria at having accomplished the tasks she had set for herself—that of locating Owen's final resting place and purchasing a fine headstone to mark it—faded rapidly once Elizabeth left the stone works and realized she'd spent all but a small portion of her remaining cash on the first payment on the monument and the final payment would be due when the headstone was delivered.

She had planned to secure lodging in another establishment like the Russ House until she decided whether to stay in San Francisco and look for a suitable job or to move on, but staying in a hotel like the Russ House was out of the question now that she had so little money left. And traveling to another town was also out of the question until she replenished her cash. Elizabeth toyed briefly with the foolish notion of telegraphing her grandmother and asking her to send money, but discarded the idea almost as quickly as she'd thought of it. Her grandmother Sadler wouldn't send money for Owen's headstone or for Elizabeth to live on, nor would she acknowledge any plea for help—by letter or by telegram. Elizabeth had created a scandal and Grandmother Sadler had scratched her name out of the Sadler family Bible. She was as dead to their grandmother as Owen was. Grandmother had made that perfectly clear when she disowned her and asked her to leave, not only the Sadler family home on Hemlock Street, but Providence as well.

Elizabeth took a deep breath and willed herself to forget the hurtful things Grandmother had said about her—the names she had called her. What was done was done. She wouldn't crawl back to Providence on her hands and knees to beg Grandmother's forgiveness and she wouldn't send a letter or telegram begging for money, either. She was on her own. And the next order of business was to find an inexpensive place to live and a job.

Her decisions made, Elizabeth took another deep breath and began the long journey back the way she had come—from Larkin Street back toward Saint Mary's Square—in search of inexpensive lodging.

She found exactly what she was looking for on Clay Street, several blocks away from Saint Mary's Church and the cemetery, in a place called Bender's Boardinghouse. The owner of the establishment, Augusta Bender, was a stout, no-nonsense widow in her late fifties, who had sailed around the Horn to San Francisco in forty-nine. Although Mrs. Bender's language was coarse and she wasn't as clean as Elizabeth hoped she would be, she had rooms available and she didn't require references for unchaperoned ladies.

"You can bring gentlemen friends back to your room at

night if that's your leanin'," she said as she explained the house rules to Elizabeth.

"Oh, no, I'd never . . ." Elizabeth began.

But Mrs. Bender held up a hand to forestall Elizabeth's assurances. "That's what they all say. You don't have to worry about explainin' things to me. I know that a girl's gotta make a livin' however she can. But I'll expect an extra two bits a night when your gentlemen friends stay over to cover the cost of the racket and of washing the sheets. And if a cop pinches you for solicitin', I'm telling you now to leave my name and my establishment out of it. The rooms rent for a dollar-fifty a week with no meals. For seventy-five cents a week extra, I'll guarantee you one meal a day. Take it or leave it."

"I'll take it," Elizabeth told her.

Augusta Bender stared at her for a long minute before asking, "You sure you want to live here?"

Elizabeth nodded. "I'm sure." She extended a hand to Mrs. Bender to conclude the agreement, then dug into her purse and counted out the required coins. "Here's my first week's rent in advance. One dollar and fifty cents for the room, plus seventy-five cents for meals for a total of two dollars and twenty-five cents." She beamed at the older woman. "When may I move in?"

"Whenever you want," Mrs. Bender replied. "I'll get you some linens for the bed. And a pitcher of fresh water. The slipper tub's in the room at the end of hall. Full baths are assigned by room number. You're in room four, so your bath time is four in the afternoon. You have the tub room all to yourself for one hour. If you miss your time or need to change your hour, you'll have to negotiate with one of the other residents. And I'm not a lady's maid. I don't fetch hot water or empty the tub, but the kitchen has an indoor pump and I keep the reservoir in the stove full of hot water. You're responsible for emptying the tub when you finish with it. Just tip it over. The water'll run down a pipe and out into the street." She reached into her apron pocket, pulled out a key, and gave it to Elizabeth. "Supper's at six-thirty. Welcome to Bender's."

It took three trips by foot, and the remainder of the afternoon to transfer her baggage from the San Francisco Ferry Building at the end of Market to the boardinghouse on Clay. Elizabeth was exhausted by the time she carried the last of her valises up the stairs to her second-floor room at Bender's. Elizabeth surveyed the sparsely furnished room with its dingy walls, rough planked floors, marble-topped washstand, and cheap furniture, then dropped her bags on the floor beside the narrow wooden bed and walked over to the window. After struggling with the stubborn window, she managed to raise it a couple of inches to allow the fresh air to dispel the musty odor. After removing the stack of clean bed linen and a quilt from its resting place atop the scratched and scarred mahogany bureau, Elizabeth made up the bed.

The aroma of food cooking in the shacks lining the back alleys and in the restaurants fronting the street drifted in with the breeze coming through her window as Elizabeth opened her valise and began to unpack. Her stomach rumbled hungrily. Elizabeth realized she hadn't eaten anything since her arrival in San Francisco the day before. She glanced down at the gold ladies' watch pinned to the bodice of her dress. Her bath hour had long since expired, but the supper hour was rapidly approaching. She had just enough time to finish unpacking and attend to her toilette with a quick stand-up bath before dinner. After laying aside an evening dress and a set of underclothes to change into, Elizabeth pulled open the bureau drawers and placed the rest of her clothes inside them.

When her chore was completed, Elizabeth reached into the pocket of the dress she was wearing and took out two brass hotel keys wrapped in James's handkerchief. She unwrapped the keys and dropped them in the bureau drawer, then stared at the handkerchief and the initials embroidered in deep blue thread on one corner of the square of linen. *J. C. C. James* C. C. After carefully folding the handkerchief, Elizabeth placed it on top of a pile of her frilly undergarments and closed the bureau drawer.

She unbuttoned her dress, stepped out of it, and walked over to the washstand dressed in her camisole and petticoat. She tilted the pitcher of water over the chipped basin, intending to fill it, but halted abruptly when she discovered a cockroach lying on its back in the center of the bowl, its legs pointing toward the ceiling. Shuddering with distaste, Elizabeth set the pitcher down, then picked up the basin, carried it to the window, and emptied the dead roach into the street. She returned the basin to its place on the washstand, started to fill it with water from the pitcher again, then thought better of it. After inspecting the water in the pitcher for signs of more roaches or other vermin, Elizabeth took a clean washcloth from the bar on the side of the washstand, and held it folded in the palm of her left hand, while she used her right hand to pour water from the pitcher onto it.

It was an awkward way to bathe, but Elizabeth managed to do a credible job. She unpinned her hair, brushed it back into a neat chignon and repinned it, then dressed for dinner in a dark blue satin gown edged in matching velvet.

She entered the dining room promptly at six-thirty and discovered she was the only one of the other six female residents of Bender's who had bothered to go to the trouble of bathing and dressing for dinner—or to dress at all. The other women had apparently interrupted their toilette in order to make it to the dinner table on time, for they were all in various stages of dress or undress. Elizabeth glanced around the room. Two young women wore thin dressing gowns and nothing else. One wore a lacy red camisole and matching pantalets. Two more women wore combinations of corsets, camisoles, and petticoats. And the last, a brazen woman of about thirty years of age, came to the supper table wearing a corset and silk stockings held up by frilly garters. Elizabeth blushed at the sight. The woman's corset was laced so tightly her massive bosom threatened to spill over the edge of her corset and onto her plate.

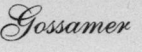

"Wot's this?" The young woman in the red camisole and pantalets turned to glare at Elizabeth as she slipped into a vacant seat at the end of the long dining table. " 'ave we got a bloomin' duchess here at Bender's?"

Augusta Bender placed a huge bowl of mashed potatoes on the table. "What we have here is a lady," she announced to the occupants seated at the table, shooting a warning glance at each of them. "A lady a bit down on her luck. She moved into number four this afternoon." Mrs. Bender abruptly turned and exited into the kitchen. She returned a few moments later carrying a plate of fluffy yeast rolls and a platter of fried chicken. Mrs. Bender set the dishes on the table and began introducing the residents of her boarding house to Elizabeth, nodding her head at each woman as she introduced her. "That's Phyllis seated next to you. She's the Brit. Dove is beside Phyllis. Jennie's the youngest. Trudy's sitting beside Jennie. Eleanor is across from Jennie and Ida's at the end of the table. Girls, this is Elizabeth Sadler. Be nice to her while she's here," Mrs. Bender instructed. "No more talkin'. Dig in to your supper while it's hot. After all, you're paying for it."

There was no further attempt at dinner conversation, and Elizabeth was relieved that she didn't have to try to fill the dinner hour with polite small talk or amusing anecdotes or to remember everybody's names. And she needn't worry about embarrassing lapses in table conversation, for the silence in the dining room was filled by the sounds of eating and the clatter of knives and forks against china. The women at the table ate with gusto, relishing the fried chicken dinner with all the trimmings. And once supper was over, each woman carefully stacked her dishes and carried them into the kitchen for washing. That chore completed, two women hurried upstairs, while the other four withdrew to the front parlor.

After finishing the last of the peach cobbler Mrs. Bender served for dessert, Elizabeth rose from the table. Deciding to follow the example of the four women who had withdrawn to the front parlor, she carried her dishes into the kitchen. She retraced her steps through the dining room and into the front parlor, where one of the women—Trudy, she thought—was playing "Aura Lee" on a slightly out-of-tune piano.

Seating herself on a horsehair loveseat near the doorway, Elizabeth folded her hands in her lap and politely waited to see if the other women would invite her to participate in their after-dinner conversation and entertainment. She wasn't quite sure what to expect in a cosmopolitan city like San Francisco, but back home in Providence it was customary to host after-dinner musical recitals, book and poetry readings or play parlor games like anagrams or charades.

"Some gent taking you out on the town tonight? To the opera or something?" the young woman in racy red camisole and pantalets asked, nodding her head to indicate Elizabeth's evening dress.

"No." Elizabeth shook her head.

"Why you all dressed up?" another asked.

Elizabeth glanced down at her gown. "I've always dressed for dinner."

"I've always dressed for dinner," someone mimicked. "What about the way we dress for dinner? What do you think about that?"

"I didn't think it was polite to comment," Elizabeth addressed the room. "For all I know, your mode of dress may be customary in this part of San Francisco."

A trill of high-pitched laughter drowned out the sound of the piano.

"She didn't think it was polite to comment on our mode of dress!" The young woman in the racy red camisole laughingly exclaimed. "Thought it might be customary in this part of Frisco! Did you hear that, Eleanor?"

Eleanor, dressed in the corset and silk stockings, turned to glare at Elizabeth. "You meeting a gentleman here tonight? Is he coming to the party?"

"I don't know anything about a party," Elizabeth replied. "I just assumed it was customary for the residents to gather in the parlor for after-dinner entertainments.''

"You assumed correctly," Eleanor said bluntly. "And incorrectly. *We*"—she waved her hand to encompass the other women in the room—"do gather in the parlor every night after supper for after-dinner entertainments. But I don't think it's the type of parlor games you're accustomed to."

Eleanor looked over at Augusta Bender. "Did you invite Miss Sadler to our little social gathering this evening?"

Mrs. Bender shook her head.

"Then maybe it would be better if she didn't stick around to witness the gentlemen's arrival." Eleanor leaned so far forward on her chair that Elizabeth could see the rouged tips of her massive bosom peeking out above her corset.

Augusta Bender shrugged her shoulders at Eleanor's suggestion. "Miss Sadler's paid her money," she announced. "In full and in advance. And she's free to stay and receive the gentlemen callers same as all of you if she chooses."

"You're receiving gentlemen callers tonight?" Elizabeth couldn't believe her ears. "Dressed like that?" She blushed when she realized how rude her question was.

"That's right, Sugar," Eleanor drawled as the heavy tread of male feet and the low murmur of masculine voices sounded on the front porch, seconds before the ring of the doorbell. "Any minute now." She arched a black brow at Elizabeth. "Make up your mind. What's it gonna be?"

Elizabeth stood and smoothed her hands over the wrinkles in her skirts. "If you'll excuse me," she said, in a voice full of cool, regal dignity, "I'll retire to my room for the night." She inclined her head slightly at each of the women in the parlor. "Good evening."

"And good evenin' to you, too, Your Ladyship," Phyllis mockingly called out to her as Elizabeth exited the parlor.

Augusta Bender caught up with her before she reached the stairs. Grasping Elizabeth by the elbow, Mrs. Bender turned her around to face her. "Go upstairs and stay in your room until mornin'. I'll let it be known that number four is off-limits. If you stay out of the hallway and keep your door closed, you'll be all right." She let go of Elizabeth's elbow and patted her on the arm. "Now, upstairs with you. Before I let the gentlemen in." She winked at Elizabeth, then smiled before turning to answer the door.

If Mrs. Bender's smile was meant to reassure her, Elizabeth thought as she hurried up the stairs, it had failed miserably. Her hands shook as she closed the door to her room and automatically reached down to turn the key in the lock. There was no key or a lock to hold it, so Elizabeth made do with the only chair in the room—a spindly-legged, rather fragile-looking boudoir chair that sat in front of the dresser. She dragged the chair across the floor, wedged it beneath the porcelain doorknob and piled two of her valises on it. Eyeing her handiwork critically, Elizabeth decided that the chair and valises wouldn't offer much resistance to a determined intruder, but they would make a rather loud noise when they fell to the floor—a noise loud enough to wake her if she happened to fall asleep, which she admitted as she sat, fully dressed, at the foot of her narrow bed, didn't seem very likely.

Shivering, Elizabeth stood up and walked over to the window. Glancing down, she was surprised to discover the streets teeming with life. The yellow glow of lamplight and raucous sound of loud voices and piano and banjo music poured from inside the restaurants, saloons and gambling halls while a steady stream of buggies and carriages deposited passengers on the sidewalks in front of those establishments. And, Elizabeth noticed, the alleys and back entrances leading to those businesses were every bit as crowded and as busy as the main streets and front entrances. Unlike the dark, quiet streets and neighborhoods of Providence, the streets surrounding Bender's Boardinghouse and the adjoining streets of Chinatown were alive with the hustle and bustle of men and women in search of entertainment. And nearly every nighttime form of entertainment in this part of San Francisco appeared to be noisy and boisterous.

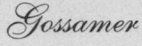

Even the piano music downstairs had grown louder. "Aura Lee" had given way to "Camptown Races," and the quintet of female voices had been joined by several male tenors and one surprisingly good baritone. Elizabeth tried not to listen. The tenors reminded her too much of Owen, and the many happy evenings over the years, when she and he had stood around the piano and sung duets while Grandmother Sadler accompanied them. And the baritone voice . . .

The baritone voice reminded her of the night before, when James had rocked her in his arms and comforted her with lullabies. Elizabeth slowly lowered the window in a vain attempt to shut out the sounds around her. And the memories. Especially the memories. She squeezed her eyes shut and bit her bottom lip to keep from crying at her naïveté and her sheer stupidity. She was surrounded by hundreds of people, maybe even thousands, and yet, she had never felt so alone in her life. Not even when Grandmother had disowned her and asked her to leave the house on Hemlock Street. Although she had found it frightening to be on her own—to lose her job and her grandmother's love, respect, and support—Elizabeth also found the situation oddly liberating. For the first time in her life, she was free from her grandmother's critical eye, impossibly high standards, morals and the social restraints that had weighed on her since birth. For a few short days during the train trip from Providence to Oakland, being a social pariah and the first fallen Sadler woman in generations had been fun. Her grandmother might have disowned her, but she still had Owen. Owen loved her. Owen didn't care that she'd made a mistake. Owen would love her no matter what. But then she had arrived in this horrid city and learned that Owen was lost to her, too.

She was completely alone. Elizabeth rubbed at her eyes with the back of her fist. She knew she was feeling sorry for herself, knew that she shouldn't. But she couldn't seem to help it. So much had happened . . . So much had changed . . . Her plans for a new life in San Francisco had been destroyed. And all because a Chinaman named Lo Peng ran an evil place where young men like her brother, Owen, were introduced to opium and encouraged to spend their hard-earned money indulging. All because Lo Peng had allowed Owen to die from his weakness for opium.

Elizabeth raised her fist and placed it against the cool glass of the windowpane. She wanted to let go of her hard-won control. She wanted to cry and scream and pound at the glass. She wanted to throw a fit, to shout and break things, and to give vent to the frustration and fright building inside her. So much had gone wrong. Right from the beginning. She thought she was so clever when she removed James's key from his pocket and replaced it with her own. She thought she was so clever when she talked the desk clerk into giving her the spare key to James's room to further delay him and keep him from following her. She'd even congratulated herself for her ingenuity when she realized that by sneaking out of the Russ House she could avoid having to face James again. Well, look where her cleverness had landed her! She had run away from a nice, respectable, expensive hotel and a man who had offered her nothing but kindness, and had taken refuge in a shabby, inexpensive boardinghouse inhabited by an assortment of women who could only be described as disreputable. She had run from the Garden of Eden straight into Sodom and Gomorrah—and without a backward glance.

She didn't feel so clever now. She didn't feel anything except stupid. And alone. Completely, utterly alone. What would James think if he could see her now? Would he come to her rescue once again? Elizabeth walked over to the bureau, opened the top drawer, and pulled out his embroidered handkerchief. She held it to her nose, inhaling the faint masculine scent that clung to the fabric. She glanced over at the window. Was he still at the Russ House? Or was he someplace else in the city? Had he left? Had he returned home to a family?

Elizabeth didn't know. But as she climbed onto the center of her narrow bed and sat huddled against the head-

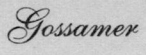

board, she felt comforted by the presence of his handkerchief. By the initials embroidered on it. *J. C. C.*

She sighed. She'd run away from him because she didn't want to face him, but Elizabeth knew that at the moment, she'd give anything to see James's handsome face again.

Six

BY ONE O'CLOCK the following afternoon, Elizabeth had revised her charitable thoughts about James. She'd still give anything to see his handsome face again. But now she wanted to see him so she could have the pleasure of scratching his beautiful blue eyes out!

Two members of the San Francisco police department, including kindly Sergeant Terrence Darnell, had descended upon Bender's Boardinghouse after lunch. San Francisco's finest were engaged in a house to house search of saloons, hotels, boardinghouses, and other less reputable establishments within walking distance of Saint Mary's Church and Chinatown. Augusta Bender had a certain reputation as a successful madam and for offering shelter to petty thieves and "day ladies," ladies who lived in furnished rooms or boarded with respectable families, but who had no visible means of support, fine ladies who offered themselves as companions to gentlemen, who left their photographs and calling cards with the madams of local brothels and prostituted themselves for a living without their families and friends being the wiser.

But the police waiting at Bender's weren't looking for *day ladies*. They were looking for a thief. A thief named

Elizabeth Sadler, who was wanted for burglarizing a very important guest at the Russ House Hotel.

Elizabeth was returning to the boardinghouse after lunch from another morning spent on an increasingly futile quest for a job whose requirements did not include taking off her clothes, painting her face, or dancing a lewd version of the can-can when Jennie, the youngest of Mrs. Bender's girls, intercepted her two blocks away.

"The police are waiting at Bender's," Jennie told her. "They're there to pinch you for stealing some rich gent's handkerchief."

"What?" Elizabeth was appalled.

"The police plan to nab you and take you to the jug."

"For stealing a handkerchief?"

Jennie nodded. "You got to run. Hide. Until they go away."

But Elizabeth suspected there was nowhere to run or to hide. If the police were looking for her, they'd find her. And while jail was a real possibility for the act she had been flirting with all morning, Elizabeth didn't intend to go meekly to jail for the theft of a handkerchief. If she were going to jail, she'd only do so in the name of justice. Owen's justice. Her justice. She looked over at Jennie and asked, "What's the quickest way to the Red Dragon on Washington Street?"

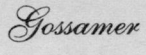

THE POLICE FOUND her there—at the Red Dragon— forty minutes later. They arrived to find Lo Peng and three other Chinamen restraining her. Lo Peng hurried over to the officers. "Arrest her!" he cried. "Arrest the crazy missy. She break up my shop. She wreck the place."

And she had.

Elizabeth smiled with satisfaction. Her hair had come undone from its neat chignon, the pins scattered across the floor. Her bonnet had been ripped loose and crushed in the struggle, and she was missing a button from the bodice of her dress. But the wrecked interior of the opium den was a sight to behold. Elizabeth had oftentimes suspected that she harbored a first-class virago deep inside her, a virago she kept hidden beneath her calm, capable facade, but she hadn't been certain of it until she crossed the threshold of that horrid little opium den and began swinging her parasol. It had taken three men to subdue her as she'd overturned berths and gaming tables, crushed paper lanterns, and shattered pipes, bowls, and lamps. Elizabeth had raged through the den of iniquity that had cost Owen his life and felt an overwhelming sense of satisfaction at seeing it in a shambles.

But the police had eventually shown up at the Washington Street address and Elizabeth had been summarily dragged kicking and screaming out of Lo Peng's establishment and hauled to jail with the sounds of a dozen shouting Chinamen ringing in her ears. She was charged with disorderly conduct, assault, and petty larceny, and escorted to the courthouse by the same policeman who had helped her locate Owen's grave.

She jumped in her seat as Judge Clermont banged his gavel on his desktop and called the next case. "Miss Elizabeth Sadler."

"Here, your honor." Elizabeth raised her hand.

"Rise and approach the bench."

Elizabeth did as she was instructed. After rising from her seat in the third row, she made her way down the aisle to the front of the courtroom. The matron from the city jail went with her and kept a firm grip on Elizabeth's left arm as they stood before the judge.

"Elizabeth Sadler," the judge intoned, "you're charged with misdemeanor crimes of disorderly conduct, assaulting a merchant, and petty larceny. How do you plead?"

Elizabeth bit her bottom lip as she glanced down at the hem of her skirt. Although she was guilty of disorderly conduct and assaulting a merchant, she balked at being accused of petty larceny. She didn't agree that failing to return a handkerchief given to her to use constituted stealing, but honesty compelled her to admit that James hadn't said she could keep his handkerchief, had, in fact, only *loaned* it to her. And, Elizabeth reminded herself, she hadn't kept the handkerchief because she needed it, she had kept it because she wanted a memento, a tangible reminder of James.

"How do you plead, Miss Sadler?"

She looked up at the judge and blushed with shame. "Guilty, your honor."

Judge Clermont stared down at the young woman before him. "The court finds you guilty as charged. That'll be a minimum of fifty dollars or three days in jail and sixty days' probation. And if I see you in my court again, young lady, I'll sentence you to thirty days in jail. Pay the clerk on your way out."

Elizabeth's mouth dropped open as the judge banged his gavel again and called the next case. She had been tried, found guilty, and sentenced, all in a matter of minutes. Her ordeal was over—except for two small details. She had yet to face the man who had accused her of stealing his handkerchief. And she didn't have fifty dollars.

"Come on, Sadler," the matron tugged at Elizabeth's arm. "You're done. Pay the clerk and you're free to go."

"Free to go?" Elizabeth repeated dumbly.

"That's right," the matron assured her. "Once you pay your fifty-dollar fine, you're free to go."

"What if I don't have fifty dollars?" Elizabeth whispered.

The matron studied Elizabeth's stylish walking dress of brown silk edged with taffeta and her expensive leather boots in a matching shade of brown. "You don't have fifty dollars?"

Elizabeth shook her head. "I don't even have five."

"A lady like you? Are you sure?"

Elizabeth nodded. "I only have a dollar and a few cents left. I counted it yesterday long before Sergeant Darnell and Officer Burrows arrested me."

The matron looked at her as if she hadn't heard correctly.

"But your dress cost more than what I make in half a year."

Elizabeth nodded once again. "Too bad I can't sell it for cash. What will I do if I can't come up with the fifty dollars?"

"You heard the judge," the matron said. "If you don't pay the fifty dollars, you'll have to serve three days in jail."

Elizabeth bit her lip to stop its quivering. "Then I guess I'm going back to jail."

The matron let go of Elizabeth's arm long enough to reach for the little leather change purse attached to the belt of her skirt. "How much money do you have? Exactly?"

"One dollar and seventy-eight cents," Elizabeth answered. "But I only have seventy-eight cents with me."

"I have a dollar left from my pay," the matron said. "And I can loan you some of that."

"Oh, no," Elizabeth refused her offer. "I couldn't take your hard-earned money." She drew herself up to her full height, squared her shoulders, lifted her chin a notch higher, then said with a confidence she didn't feel, "It's only three days. I can survive three days in jail."

❧

THREE DAYS. SEVENTY-TWO hours. It might as well have been an eternity. Seated on an edge of the only cot in the cell, Elizabeth pressed herself back against the bars and pulled her skirts close about her to keep them from coming in contact with the clothing of the women pacing the narrow confines of the holding pen. Elizabeth shuddered, wondering how she was going to survive another seventy-one hours in the company of the women sharing her cell. A cell. Elizabeth Sadler was confined to a cell in the San Francisco City Jail along with fifteen other female criminals. Elizabeth knew there were fifteen other women occupying the small space because she'd spent the hour since she'd been incarcerated counting them—counting the number of blondes, redheads, and brunettes, counting the plump

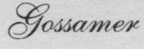

ones, the skinny ones, the ones with visible lice, the ones without, the clean ones, the dirty ones . . . Elizabeth suppressed another shudder and held her breath as long as she could to keep from gagging. The smell of the place was overwhelming. The scent of unwashed bodies, of cheap gin and stale beer, of vomit and urine, and a dozen other odors Elizabeth couldn't identify, nearly took her breath away. Until an hour ago Elizabeth had never realized there were women who regularly spent time in jail, never realized there were women who lived their lives in such a sordid fashion. But the matrons and the officers in the jail knew her cell mates well enough, saw them often enough, to call them by name and ask about their families. Elizabeth had never imagined she would ever experience anything more shocking than the scene she'd participated in in the parlor at Bender's Boardinghouse. The women at Bender's had behaved like harlots. But these women *were* harlots and worse—some of them were criminals. Criminals. And she was one of them. Elizabeth ground her teeth together to keep from screaming. A criminal. Criminal. This situation was criminal. Her temper mounted with each passing moment as she counted down the hours to freedom. She, Elizabeth Sadler, was a criminal convicted of disorderly conduct, assault, and petty larceny. Unable to pay a fifty-dollar fine and in jail because she refused to go to jail without a reason. Because she refused to allow herself to be arrested for stealing a gentleman's fine silk handkerchief.

James's fine silk handkerchief. James. Elizabeth quivered with anger at the thought of him. James, of the gentle voice and kind eyes. James, who had wiped her tears away with that handkerchief, then had pressed it into her hand to use. He must have been furious with her when he discovered she'd taken his room key and replaced it with hers. He had to have been angry and embarrassed to seek revenge for something so trivial when she hadn't denied him access to a hotel room. He could have stayed in her room if he needed a place to sleep. And she hadn't run out and stuck him with her hotel bill, she'd made sure of that. But James would have had her arrested and taken to jail for keeping his handkerchief. Talk about trumped-up charges! She'd never heard of anything so outrageous. No wonder they called it petty larceny. As far as Elizabeth was concerned, her accuser was the pettiest of the petty and he had an awful lot to answer for.

He could start by offering her an apology.

And Elizabeth meant to collect it—just as soon as she got out of jail.

<hr />

"YOU'RE FREE TO go."

Elizabeth recognized Sergeant Darnell's Irish brogue, but she pointedly ignored him by rising from her seat on the cot, lifting her chin a bit higher, and turning to face the wall away from him.

"Did you hear me, Miss Sadler?" Sergeant Darnell asked, his voice full of concern. "I said that you're free to go."

"She heard you."

Recognizing *that* voice as well, Elizabeth whirled around to find James standing beside Sergeant Darnell. There was so much she wanted to say to him, so many angry words she wanted to fling at him, but Elizabeth couldn't give voice to the words. Torn between fury at James for putting her in this situation and tremendous relief at having him come to get her out, she was suddenly shaking with reaction. Her knees threatened to buckle, and because she wasn't sure she could cross the few feet to the cell door without falling, Elizabeth simply stood there staring at him, drinking in the sight of him.

"I came as soon as I could," James told her, taking a step closer to the cell.

She didn't reply.

"I meant to leave my home early this morning, so I could be in the city when the police located you," James

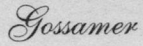

continued. "I should have gotten here in plenty of time to drop the charges, but things got a bit out of hand at home this morning—" James shrugged his shoulders. "My housekeeper couldn't handle things alone and unfortunately I was unavoidably detained." He knew he was rambling, but he couldn't seem to stop the flow of words, nor could he seem to drag his gaze away from her. He was seeing her for the second time and again at her worst, but James realized that Elizabeth Sadler's worst was better than most women's best. She was astonishingly pretty. Much lovelier than he remembered. And those extraordinary blue-green eyes of hers . . . James felt as if he'd been kicked in the gut. He knew it wasn't the time or the place, but he had the incredible urge to kiss her, to feel her against him.

Elizabeth studied James as carefully as she had studied her cell mates. She took note of the whiskers darkening James's unshaven jawline, his rumpled shirtfront, his mussed and hastily tied tie, and what appeared to be a blotch of strawberry jam on the front of his waistcoat. She smiled at the reddish stain on his impeccably tailored garment and found herself wanting to stick out her finger and touch it. Then to lick the tip of her finger to taste it. To see if it was, indeed, strawberry jam. Elizabeth couldn't explain why she felt the way she did. James's slovenly appearance should have put her off, should have helped to fan the flames of her anger, but it didn't. Far from it. For some inexplicable reason, his untidiness made James even more handsome and appealing than before, and Elizabeth had to force herself to remember why she was so angry with him.

"Elizabeth, believe me," James told her, "I never meant for things to go this far."

"You had me arrested!" The accusation, ripe with pain and suppressed anger, seemed to burst forth of its own accord.

"From what I hear, you got yourself arrested for destroying Lo Peng's place on Washington Street."

"But you started it. You meant to have me arrested for stealing a handkerchief you gave me! You had me put in

this place!'' Suddenly regaining her ability to move, Elizabeth waved her hand, gesturing at the interior of the jail,
and narrowly missed backhanding a cell mate whose foul
body odor was enough to make the strongest man gag.
''You would have let them bring me here and lock me up
with these people for no reason. At least I gave them reason!''

James heard the horror in her voice, saw the shimmer of
unshed tears in her beautiful blue-green eyes, and grudgingly admitted understanding Elizabeth's flawed, but honorable, logic. She was right. It was all his fault. He was to
blame for Elizabeth Sadler's situation. She had every right
to be angry with him, to despise him, to refuse to help him.
He had meant for the police to detain her, not throw her
into a cell. But here she was locked in a cell amidst the
dregs of womanhood. Because of him. And now it was up
to him to explain his reasons for doing what he did and, if
possible, to make amends. ''I was desperate.''

''You were desperate . . . ?'' she sputtered. If she only
had her parasol, Elizabeth thought, she'd use it against
James the way she had used it to wreck Lo Peng's place.

''Yes,'' he answered her softly, not offering the word as
an excuse, but as a fact. ''I wanted—'' he stopped. ''I
needed to find you as quickly as possible. Having the police
scour the city streets was the quickest and most efficient
means of locating you, but I couldn't utilize the entire police force unless I had a good reason for wanting to find
you. I had to come up with something. And the theft of my
personal belongings seemed like a fairly innocuous reason.''

''Blast your personal belongings,'' Elizabeth told him.
''You didn't tell them I stole your personal belongings; you
told them I stole your handkerchief!''

James managed a rather sheepish smile. ''I couldn't take
the chance that the police would charge you with a serious
crime.''

''Just a petty one,'' Elizabeth retorted, meaningfully.

''Touché,'' James said with a grimace. ''But I hated the

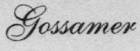

thought of losing that particular handkerchief. It's special."

Elizabeth thought of the carefully embroidered initials, J. C. C., on the corner of the handkerchief. Someone must have given it to him. The woman who'd labored over the beautiful stitches. Elizabeth hadn't counted on James having a special attachment to something as commonplace as a handkerchief. "Apparently."

James raised an eyebrow at her dry retort. "Silk handkerchiefs are expensive. Besides, I used it once, to dry a beautiful woman's tears. I wanted to keep it as a memento."

Unfortunately, so had she. And her desire for a keepsake would have landed her in jail even if her rampage in Lo Peng's had not. Because she couldn't allow herself to be swayed from her righteous anger by his pretty words or his sentiment, Elizabeth fixed her unflinching gaze on him and demanded the truth. "Who are you? The mayor? The chief of police? How is it that you could have me arrested for stealing one of your precious handkerchiefs?"

"My name is James Cameron Craig," he said. "I'm the owner and president of Craig Capital, Ltd., a railroad, mining, and timber corporation. . . ."

Elizabeth gasped as she recognized his name and the name of his corporation. Craig Capital, Ltd., was one of a handful of American corporations owned and managed by men who were members of the Millionaires' Club. James Cameron Craig was one of them. A businessman worth millions of dollars. A businessman who rubbed elbows and made deals with the likes of J. P. Morgan, Jay Gould, Commodore Vanderbilt, Andrew Carnegie, and John D. Rockefeller. "I suppose I should be flattered that one of the richest men in the world decided to have me thrown in jail."

"No." James shook his head. "But you might show a bit of appreciation for the fact that one of the richest men in the world went to a great deal of trouble to get here in time to bail you out."

Elizabeth seared him with a gaze of pure blue-green fire.

"A bail that cost a millionaire all of fifty dollars. I think that's the very least he could do," she replied with a sugary-sweet smile, "since I wouldn't be in here if it wasn't for him."

"Oh, you'd still be in here," James told her. "Lo Peng is sure to press charges."

"But I wouldn't have gone to Lo Peng's if you . . ." Elizabeth clamped her mouth shut.

"If I what?" James prompted, patiently folding his arms across his wide chest, waiting for her to continue.

Elizabeth glared at him.

"Come on," he encouraged, biting back the smile that threatened to overcome him when he recognized the spark of pure fury in Elizabeth Sadler's devastating blue-green eyes. James was surprised to find himself encouraging her, surprised to discover himself attracted, rather than repelled, by her healthy show of anger. He actually liked Elizabeth's spirited, impetuous side—the one so at odds with the more restrained and rational governess-type demeanor. "Spit it out before you choke on it."

"If you hadn't arranged to have me arrested for something so—so—petty. I decided to give the police a real reason to arrest me."

James grinned at that. "Sort of like cutting off your nose to spite your face, isn't it?" Elizabeth stubbornly refused to reply as James motioned to Sergeant Darnell to unlock the holding pen. "I've admitted my guilt and offered my apologies, and you've confessed your sins and repented the crime. Now, come on. Let's get you out of here."

Darnell swung the door of the cell open, then stepped into the breach to prevent the other inmates from slipping through the opening. "You can go now, Miss Sadler," the sergeant told her. "And may I offer my apologies as well. We didn't want anything to do with this. But Mr. Craig being who he is and all . . ." Sergeant Darnell let his voice trail off, then cleared his throat and continued, "I just wanted to let you know that if he"—the sergeant nodded toward James—"hadn't paid your bail and talked to the judge on your behalf, we were going to do it. Lo Peng's out front swearing out a complaint, but we understand about your brother and Lo Peng's and all. And the guys in the precinct are taking up a collection for you even as we speak. We wouldn't have allowed you to spend the night with this riffraff.''

James cleared his throat and impatiently shifted his weight from one foot to the other as he waited for Elizabeth to exit the cell. ''I'm sure Miss Sadler appreciates your kindness and the kindness of your fellow officers,'' James told him, ''but we're late and we really must be going. Come along, Elizabeth.''

James reached for her arm, but Elizabeth recoiled. ''I'm not going anywhere with you.''

''I'm afraid you have no choice,'' James said. ''It's one of the conditions of your release.''

''What?'' Elizabeth glared at him through the bars of the cell.

''I paid your bail.''

''So?''

''Judge Clermont agreed to release you into my custody for the duration of your probation or until you're able to repay the fine.''

''I don't intend to remain in your custody for sixty days,'' Elizabeth protested.

''Fine,'' James replied, most agreeably. ''If you'll just repay the fifty dollars, plus the two percent interest, you owe me, I'll be on my way.''

''I don't have fifty dollars,'' Elizabeth told him. ''And you know it. But I'll repay you just as soon as I can.''

''And what if I'm not willing to wait to recoup my loss?''

''You're worth millions,'' Elizabeth accused. ''Fifty dollars isn't going to break you. It won't hurt you to wait for your money.''

''That depends on how long I'm required to wait,'' James replied.

''I'll repay you, with interest, as soon as possible,'' Elizabeth told him. "But it may take me some time to find a job."

James grinned. "In that case," he said, "I'm prepared to be magnanimous and waive repayment of the fine and the interest."

"In return for what?" Elizabeth hadn't grown up in a banking family without learning something about the business. Any banker or businessman willing to waive repayment of a loan with interest wanted something in return— something worth more than the original loan.

"Your expertise."

Elizabeth stared at him.

"I'm offering you a position in my household," James said.

"As what?" Her face turned bright red as she blurted out the question.

"As governess to my four daughters."

She stood completely still as the nimbus surrounding her half-formed dreams and fantasies about James Cameron Craig splintered into darkness. He was married. He had children. Somehow, she'd never really considered that he might be a family man. Somehow, she'd imagined him as being a dashing *available* loner. Prince Charming to her princess. Now, she realized that if she were released into his custody, she would have to think of him as her prospective employer—as the father of the children consigned to her care. She could never again allow him to be cast as the hero in her girlish fantasies. "You have four daughters?"

James cast a rueful glance down at his wrinkled shirt-front, at the small buttery handprint visible on his tie, and the strawberry jam smeared across his waistcoat. The Treasures had put up quite a fight to keep him at home once they realized their daddy had been recalled to San Francisco after breakfast. "You're a woman of some experience," he said. "Couldn't you tell?"

Elizabeth managed a weak half-smile at his attempt at humor.

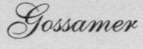

"My girls are three and a half, two, thirteen months, and two days old. I returned home from my trip here two days ago to find that, in addition to three toddlers, I had a newborn daughter and no governess." He turned his most winning smile on Elizabeth. "You mentioned you'd been a teacher at a school." He shrugged. "I needed a governess and I immediately thought of you. But you left the Russ House so abruptly and I had no idea how to contact you, so I . . ." He let his voice drift off.

"You had me arrested because you needed a governess?" She couldn't believe her ears.

"I did what was necessary to find you," he corrected. "I just didn't expect it to go this far. I never expected—"

"A genteel governess wielding a parasol to destroy the notorious Lo Peng's in a fit of temper?" Suddenly seeing the irony in her situation, Elizabeth began to laugh. "I'm afraid you've made a poor bargain, Mr. Craig. You wanted an exemplary teacher for your children and you've gotten an execrable one instead." She stared up at him, her eyes shimmering with mirth. "Are you sure you've made a good bargain with the judge? Are you certain you really want me?"

Her question gave James momentary pause. She'd stirred up a major hornet's nest by wrecking the opium den. Lo Peng and the Tongs would not be pleased, and Lo Peng's displeasure with Elizabeth could ultimately affect James's rescue work, but at the moment none of those things seemed to matter. As he stared down at her, at the shining expression on her beautiful face, her plump pink mouth, and her laughing blue-green eyes, and felt his body's immediate response, James was very much afraid that he would never want anyone more.

"Absolutely," he said. "Cross my heart."

Seven

"YOU GOING OR staying, Miss Sadler?" Sergeant Darnell swung the cell door back and forth in a small arc to
call attention to the fact that Elizabeth stood half in and
half out of the cell.

Having forgotten the policeman was still in the room,
Elizabeth and James both turned to face him.

Elizabeth took a deep breath to steady herself, then
stepped over the threshold of the holding pen and said, "I
suppose I'm going, Sergeant Darnell."

Nodding an affirmative, Darnell closed and locked the
cell door behind her.

She glanced over at James. "Provided the salary and the
terms of my employment are acceptable."

James breathed an audible sigh of relief at the sound of
the key turning in the lock—keeping Elizabeth out instead
of in. "Just name your price."

Elizabeth gave him a mischievous smile. "Shall we start
with fifty dollars a day and go from there?"

James bit the inside of his cheek to keep from laughing
out loud at Elizabeth's audacity. If he agreed to pay her
fifty dollars a day, Elizabeth could repay her fine in one
day—with his money—and be on her way. "Why don't

we start with twenty-five dollars a month, plus room and board, and go from there?'' he countered.

''You did say I could name my price,'' she reminded him.

''I expected you to suggest a *reasonable* price.''

''How very shortsighted of you,'' Elizabeth continued, filled with a sense of recklessness that had nothing to do with her recent adventures and everything to do with the handsome man standing before her. ''Expecting reason from a woman who took on the notorious Lo Peng and his little band of foot soldiers and single-handedly demolished his disreputable establishment.''

James fought to conceal his amusement and retain control of the situation with a businesslike manner. ''Are we agreed on the *reasonable* salary of twenty-five dollars a month during the sixty days of your probation?''

''I don't know.'' Elizabeth hesitated. ''Fifty dollars a day is so much more appealing, especially since it means that one day I could be a lady of independent means.'' She didn't mean to sound mercenary or greedy. But Elizabeth had learned a lesson about money. And the lesson she had learned was that she never wanted to be without it again.

She wasn't being coy, James realized, as he studied the expressions mirrored on her face. Nor was she a true mercenary. The corners of his mouth turned up and into a smile. Elizabeth was a bit naive and perhaps too optimistic, but not greedy. There was nothing wrong with a woman in Elizabeth's position trying to become a woman of independent means. He just hadn't expected her to have the brass to ask him to underwrite her journey to financial independence. ''How much cash do you have?'' he asked, abruptly.

''Enough,'' she answered, attempting to hang on to her last vestige of pride.

''How much?''

Elizabeth turned to him and asked sweetly, ''Didn't your mother ever teach you that it's rude to ask a person how much money she has?''

James laughed. ''My mother's family name is Cameron.

The Camerons made a fortune in banking, mostly by loaning money to Edinburgh merchants. My mother always asks how much money a person has. Banking's in her blood.''

James's laughter surprised her. She hadn't expected a millionaire like James Cameron Craig to have a sense of humor. Elizabeth had to bite her lip to keep from giggling at her own expense. She should have remembered that the Camerons were known for having built considerable banking and shipping fortunes, first in Scotland and later in the British crown colony of Hong Kong. After all, she came from a banking family as well. A much poorer banking family, but a banking family all the same.

''Well,'' Elizabeth replied with an air of snobbery she didn't feel, ''someone should have taught the Camerons, and your mother, in particular, that it's rude to ask a person how much money she has—unless she's sitting inside a bank describing her collateral.''

James looked down at Elizabeth's lovely oval face and recognized the humorous glint in her aquamarine-colored eyes. ''I'll mention that to my mother,'' he said, ''the next time I see her.''

''Come along, folks,'' Sergeant Darnell interrupted, motioning James and Elizabeth away from the cell and toward the door leading back to the precinct headquarters. ''We need to finish Miss Sadler's paperwork and return her belongings.''

James stood beside a long wooden bench set against the plaster wall, a discreet distance away from the desk where one of the jail matrons was returning Elizabeth's crushed bonnet, her battered parasol, and her reticule, taking care to display the contents and count out the money Elizabeth had had in her possession at the time of her arrest. He had done his best not to eavesdrop, but the matron's voice carried and James couldn't help but hear every word she said. ''Seventy-five, seventy-six, seventy-seven, seventy-eight cents. Is that correct, Miss Sadler?''

''Yes,'' Elizabeth confirmed.

''Anything missing from your personal belongings?''

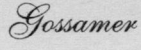

Elizabeth pushed her hair back off her shoulders. "Only my hairpins." She blushed as she glanced down at the bodice of her dress. "And a button. But I suppose they're scattered all over Lo Peng's establishment."

"Probably," the matron agreed, returning the money to Elizabeth's change purse. "Sign here and you're free to go." She produced a form, a pen, and a brass inkwell and handed them to Elizabeth.

Elizabeth signed her name to the form and returned it, along with the pen and ink, to the matron, then reclaimed her bonnet, purse, and parasol.

"Good luck to you, Miss Sadler," the matron said.

"Thank you," Elizabeth replied quietly, frowning in concentration as she attempted to reconnect the broken string on the handle of her misshapen parasol.

The matron smiled. "I heard you did a real good job on Lo Peng's with that dainty little thing." She shook her head. "Who'd have thought it? A lady like you. And with a parasol . . ."

James stepped forward and took Elizabeth by the elbow before she could reply to the matron, then whispered in her ear, "You win. I agree to your salary request of fifty dollars a day. But only if you'll agree to leave it on account until your term of probation is over." He held up his hand to keep her from interrupting until he finished. "I'll provide anything you need until your probation expires. And you may pay me back at the end of sixty days."

"Why?" Fifty dollars a day, fifteen hundred dollars a month, was a princely sum and an entirely unheard of salary for a governess. Any governess. Suddenly suspicious, Elizabeth turned to look at him.

"I have no desire to stand in the way of your becoming a lady of independent means, but I don't plan to underwrite the venture unless you live up to your end of the bargain. I need a governess. And seventy-eight cents isn't going to get you very far."

Elizabeth gasped.

"Don't get any more ideas about using that thing,"

James warned, warily eyeing the way she gripped her parasol in her fist.

"I wouldn't dream of it," she said primly.

"Tell that to Lo Peng," he retorted.

Ignoring James's comment, Elizabeth began a thorough study of the dusty toes of her walking boots. "I have other funds," she continued without meeting his gaze. "I left most of my money at Mrs. Bender's." It was true. She'd left a dollar in reserve against emergencies, tucked beneath her mattress.

"Augusta Bender's?" It was James's turn to gasp in shock.

"Why, yes," Elizabeth answered. "Do you know her?"

James gritted his teeth. Every man in the bay area with more than a couple of hundred dollars to his name knew Augusta Bender. Or knew of her. She ran a house on the corner of Clay and Kearney Streets. Ostensibly a boarding house for young women, Bender's had a well-known reputation for housing and supplying some of the more desirable women in San Francisco and providing a meeting place for the numerous day ladies. And Elizabeth had sheltered there. The very idea horrified him. Good grief, but she was such an innocent. He was amazed she had survived the trip west with her reputation intact, much less two nights in a wicked city like San Francisco.

"I'm acquainted with the madam." He chose his last word with care, curious to see how Elizabeth would react. "How did you come to know her?"

"She runs a boardinghouse and I needed a place to stay."

"Augusta Bender allowed you to stay at her house?"

Elizabeth shook her head. "She didn't *allow* me to stay in her house out of the goodness of her heart. I rented a room and paid for a week, plus a meal a day in advance."

"I hope you locked your door at night," James muttered.

"I couldn't," Elizabeth replied. "The door to my room didn't have a lock."

James groaned aloud. Wasn't she aware of the danger

she'd been in? "Let's hope the money you left at Bender's—if you left money there, which I sincerely doubt," he said, noticing the way Elizabeth's even white teeth worried her full bottom lip and the way she refused to meet his gaze, "is there when we arrive. That part of town is rife with bedchamber thieves, panel thieves, and fences."

Elizabeth blanched at the thought of any of the women she'd met at Mrs. Bender's or any of the constant stream of gentlemen who had made their way up and down the stairs during the night and the early morning hours, rifling through her personal belongings, stealing from her in order to sell her possessions to unscrupulous businessmen who didn't bother to ask if the person doing the selling actually owned the goods.

James took a good look at the expression on Elizabeth's already pale face and could have bitten out his tongue for causing her additional worry. A woman with seventy-eight cents to her name couldn't afford to lose any of her cherished belongings. He eased his grip on her arm and softened his tone of voice. "Let's go see what we find and worry about handling the details once we know what we've got to handle." He urged Elizabeth forward toward the doors leading from the cells and property room of the police station to the main station room where most of the police business was conducted.

The matron stopped him. "Lo Peng is raising a ruckus up front. He's insisting Miss Sadler pay for the damage to his place. It might be better if you take her out the back way." She pointed to a door at the back of the property room.

James hadn't yet asked Elizabeth Sadler why she'd taken her parasol in hand against Lo Peng. He had no idea whether she'd meant to destroy Lo Peng's particular establishment or if her choice had been random. Either way, he didn't look forward to confronting Lo Peng when the man was in a temper, but James didn't care to sneak out of the back of the police station like a thief just to avoid him, either. He expected trouble with Lo Peng sooner or later, and the sooner Lo Peng understood that Elizabeth Sadler was under James's protection, the better off he and Elizabeth would be. The Tongs under Lo Peng's control might attempt to cause trouble later on if James didn't meet Lo Peng's demands for payment for the damages Elizabeth had caused, but facing Lo Peng or not facing Lo Peng wasn't his decision to make. James deferred to Elizabeth. "It's up to you, Miss Sadler. Do we go out the back to avoid Lo Peng?"

Elizabeth pushed her hair back from her face, lifted her chin, and gripped the handle of her parasol tighter. "I'm not afraid of Lo Peng."

"You should be," James told her as he pried the parasol out of Elizabeth's grasp. "He controls over half of San Francisco and most of the high country's Chinese labor force. No one in his right mind would willingly make an enemy of him." He glanced over at Elizabeth and found her glaring at him.

"I'm not sneaking out the back door," she replied stubbornly. "I came in the front door and I intend to leave the same way." Pulling against his grasp, Elizabeth started for the double doors.

"If you're determined to face him," James said, "you'd better be prepared. You'll be at a disadvantage if you allow Lo Peng to see you as you are."

Forgetting the damage done to her hair and clothes during the disturbance at Lo Peng's, Elizabeth demanded, "What's wrong with the way I am?"

James's heart thumped against his chest and his gaze held a curiously tender expression as he gestured toward her. "You look as if you lost the battle."

"I didn't lose," she said, a gleam in her eyes as she recalled the shambles she'd made of the dirty opium den.

"I know that," James answered. "And that's why it's important you don't appear as if you lost. Come here." He led Elizabeth over to the wooden bench that occupied a section of the wall opposite the property room. James

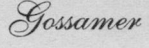

leaned her parasol against the bench, then took a handkerchief—another monogrammed silk one—out of his pocket
and searched the hallway for a water cooler. Locating one,
he drew a cup of water from it and dipped a corner of his
handkerchief into the tin cup.

Elizabeth eyed him warily as he returned to the bench.

"Look up," he instructed.

"Why?" she countered.

James took a deep breath, then let it out in slow calming
ones. The expression on Elizabeth's face reminded him of
Ruby. And just like Ruby, nearly everything he said to her
led to a battle of wills. "You have dirt on your face."

"Oh." She blushed bright red and rubbed at her face
with the back of her hand.

"Allow me," James said as he lifted her chin with the
tip of his finger and used the dampened handkerchief to
clean the dirt from around a nasty-looking scratch that ran
from the corner of her mouth up her right cheek toward her
ear.

"Ouch! That stings," Elizabeth protested as he scrubbed
the beads of dried blood off her face.

"Looks like somebody scratched you."

Elizabeth shrugged her shoulders. "That would be the
big ugly guy. He pulled my bonnet off and hit me in the
face with it. My hatpin must have done it."

James sucked in a breath. A ten-inch hatpin could do a
lot of damage. Elizabeth's had missed her eye by a mere
inch or so. "There," he pronounced, when he had finished
wiping her face with the wet handkerchief. "Now, let's see
what we can do about the rest."

"I haven't a comb," Elizabeth told him. "And I lost my
hairpins."

Smiling, James reached inside his jacket and removed a
tortoiseshell comb from the inner breast pocket. "*Voila!*"
James patted the top of the wooden bench with his hand.

Elizabeth reached for the comb, but James shook his
head. "Sit down."

Realizing his intent, Elizabeth sat at an angle to allow

him complete access to the hair hanging down her back.

James stood behind her and began gently working the comb through the tangles in her thick waist-length hair.

Elizabeth tried to keep her spine ramrod stiff, but the wonderful feel of the comb soon worked its magic. It had been so long since anyone had combed her hair. The feel of it brought a rush of childhood memories of sweet happy days when her mother had brushed and braided her hair each night. Elizabeth closed her eyes and allowed her body to relax against James as he pulled the comb through her hair.

Her hair was thick, but soft and silky. It slipped through the teeth of the comb and curled around his fingers. James loved the feel of it. It had been so long since he'd enjoyed the privilege of combing a woman's hair. He dislodged a couple of stray hairpins caught in the tawny strands of her hair, then watched as the pins slid down her back and settled on top of her bustle. James left the hairpins where they lay, then combed Elizabeth's hair back from her forehead, neatly separated the silky strands into sections and fashioned it into an elegant French braid. "Hold this while I find something to secure it."

Elizabeth stared down in wonder at the end of the neat braid he had fashioned from her mass of thick tangles. "How?"

James winked at her. "I have four daughters. Three of them have hair." Reaching over her shoulder, James removed Elizabeth's crushed bonnet from her lap. He ignored the gold and tiger-eye hatpin stuck through the fabric at the back of the crown and ripped the decorative cording, the wide grosgrain ribbon, and a rosette from around the band and tossed the bonnet onto the bench. James tied the end of her long braid with the cord. Then he looped the length of hair under and secured it at the nape of her neck with the remaining grosgrain ribbon so that the rosette was artfully displayed at the base of the chignon.

When James finished with Elizabeth's hair, he turned his attention to the button missing from the top of her bodice.

Since he couldn't replace the missing button, the best he could hope for was to hide the fact that it was missing. He reached for Elizabeth's ruined bonnet again. This time, the gold and tiger-eye hatpin caught his attention. James removed it from the crumpled hat, then pulled Elizabeth to her feet.

"Pardon me," he said, just before he pushed the hatpin into the fabric of her bodice slightly below the empty buttonhole.

Elizabeth gasped as he worked his fingers beneath the high neckline of her dress. She could feel the rasp of the hair on the back of his hand and the warmth of his skin against the underside of her chin. Elizabeth found it hard to breathe. And she couldn't tell if it was because the neckline of her dress was pulled so tightly against her throat or because James's face was so close to hers and because his long fingers kept brushing against the lace of her chemise. James. She mustn't think of him as James. He was Mr. Craig, her new employer. He had promised to pay her fifty dollars a day to be governess to his children. And she must begin to think of him not as the stranger who had held her in his arms while she cried herself to sleep, but as the man who would soon be paying her salary. She had to remember that his touch wasn't personal. He was simply helping her present a proper, respectable appearance—one befitting a governess. But even as she reprimanded herself, Elizabeth felt the brush of his hand against the hollow of her throat as he bent the shaft of the hatpin and buried the sharp point inside the fabric of her dress away from her tender flesh.

She felt the heat flowing up to her face as he removed his hand from inside her bodice and carefully adjusted the gold and tiger-eye head of the hatpin so that it covered her empty buttonhole.

"There," he pronounced, satisfied with his handiwork. "Now you're ready to face Lo Peng, Augusta Bender, and anything else that comes your way." James smiled at her, then took a moment to straighten his waistcoat and tie, replace his comb, and button his jacket before he offered her his arm. "Shall we?"

Elizabeth nodded and automatically reached for her parasol.

"Leave it here," James told her. "You won't need it."

"But it's the only one I have."

"The sight of you and that battered parasol is only going to fan the flames of Lo Peng's anger."

"That makes it mutual," she muttered. "Seeing him, without my battered parasol, is going to fan the flames of *my* anger."

James laughed. "Be good," he said, tracing the scratch on her cheek with the tip of his finger. "Let me handle it. Remember, I'm paying you fifty dollars a day to be an exemplary governess. Exemplary governesses are seen and not heard."

The need to protest bubbled up from deep within her. Elizabeth opened her mouth to speak, but managed to swallow the words in time.

James noted her struggle, then gave her a nod of approval.

The warm expression of admiration in James's dark blue eyes came as such a surprise to Elizabeth that she forgot all about the need to voice her protest. Suddenly, she had newer, more fundamental needs to worry about—like the need to slow the rapid beat of her heart and the need to remind herself to breathe at an even, steady rate.

Eight

THE MOMENT ELIZABETH saw Lo Peng, surrounded by his three henchmen, standing among the crowd of policemen, witnesses, suspects, and curious bystanders, her knees began to quake. As she watched the little Chinaman gesticulating wildly, his long black queue swinging to and fro across his back as he shouted in a high-pitched mix of English and Chinese, Elizabeth forgot all about her earlier bold brave pronouncement. Her courage seemed to desert her all at once, and if James hadn't kept a firm grip on her arm, Elizabeth would have run right out the back door. She only hoped she looked more confident than she felt.

"You look lovely," James whispered, as if he had read her thoughts. He squeezed her hand in encouragement and continued, "You look serene and confident. Keep that look. No matter what happens, remember not to show Lo Peng any other face. No sign of fear or dismay."

Elizabeth started to reply, but James cut her off before she could say anything.

"Don't speak," he reminded. "Don't utter a sound. Don't look at Lo Peng. Look at the floor." He smiled down at Elizabeth. "I know it's difficult, but try to act submissive. In Lo Peng's world, women only speak when spoken to and never when a man is present to speak for them.'' James nodded toward Lo Peng, then leaned close to Elizabeth. His warm breath brushed her earlobe as he whispered, ''Buck up, Miss Sadler. He's seen you and he's coming this way. Remember to be exemplary. Look down at your feet and leave everything to me.''

Some of her apprehension must have shown in her eyes when she met his gaze, for James leaned close once more before Lo Peng reached them and whispered, ''Trust me.''

There was no time to decide whether or not to trust him, Elizabeth thought as she stared down at the red dragon embroidered on the hem of Lo Peng's trouser legs, the feet in the black cotton shoes, and the white cotton socks mere inches away from her own. All at once, Lo Peng was waving his arms and shouting right at her. He was so close she could feel the spray of his spittle on her hair, could smell the sandalwood and garlic and ginger and the sweet sickly odor of the opium den oozing from his pores, flavoring his breath, and permeating his clothing, could hear the underlying venom and the promise of retribution in the furious rush of foreign words she didn't understand.

Elizabeth felt a wave of nausea wash over her as the combination of odors assaulted her nostrils. She swallowed convulsively, and doggedly kept her attention focused on the feet rocking back and forth on their heels in front of her as Lo Peng's already high-pitched voice took on a highly agitated, screeching quality. Clenching and unclenching her fists within the heavy folds of her skirt, Elizabeth fought the powerful inclination to lose her breakfast all over the little tyrant's cloth-covered feet, then meet his black-eyed stare and dare him to do his worst.

She was so busy concentrating on retaining her breakfast that it took her a moment to absorb the fact that Lo Peng had stopped screeching and was listening intently to what James Cameron Craig had to say. She listened as well, but the rush of foreign words made no more sense coming from James's lips than they had coming from Lo Peng's.

Lo Peng laughed and Elizabeth could stand it no longer. Feeling the massive weight of betrayal weighing on her chest, Elizabeth lifted her face to stare at James Cameron Craig. He was speaking to Lo Peng in the Chinaman's native tongue. And the two men appeared to be on good terms, for they were sharing a hearty conspiratorial laugh at her expense—a laugh reminiscent of the camaraderie shared by the members of the Millionaire's Club—the Chinese version. Elizabeth didn't have to speak Chinese to understand that the rules were the same. In Providence and in San Francisco, American, British, or Chinese, it was still very much a man's world. A man's club. And by virtue of her sex, she was excluded from the membership. She glared at the two men, refusing to return her gaze to the floor. Lo Peng looked over at her, wrinkled his brow, and frowned mightily when he saw that she had abandoned her submissive pose and was staring at him. He spoke sharply to James.

James smiled at Lo Peng, then hissed at her in a firm, steady voice, "Do as you were told, Elizabeth, keep your gaze on the floor. You are a most unworthy woman, not fit to look upon a worthy lord like Lo Peng."

"Unworthy!" Elizabeth turned on James. "How can you—"

"Down!" James's one word rebuke echoed like the crack of a whip.

Elizabeth instantly obeyed.

Lo Peng cackled in delight.

James issued the necessary apologies for Elizabeth's bad manners, waited until Lo Peng had acknowledged his apologies, then resumed his explanation of Elizabeth's behavior, immensely grateful that Elizabeth couldn't understand a word of the banbury tale he was weaving for Lo Peng's benefit. He didn't like lying. He didn't like telling tales at Elizabeth's expense, but if his outrageous explanation amused Lo Peng and kept Elizabeth alive and safe from Lo Peng's wrath, it was worth every lie he told.

James finished speaking, then held his breath, waiting for the old man's reaction.

"Craig's crazy female wreck my shop," Lo Peng replied in an oily voice. "Craig must pay."

"How much?" James asked.

"Four hundred gold dollars."

James raised an eyebrow at the amount. He doubted very much that anything in Lo Peng's shop was worth anything near that price.

Lo Peng watched him carefully, then moved closer to Elizabeth and fingered a strand of tawny hair that had worked loose from her braid. "Five hundred gold dollars."

To her credit, Elizabeth did not flinch when Lo Peng approached her, didn't look up or even breathe as the old warlord touched her hair, but James nodded in understanding. The price had gone up. And it would continue to go up every minute James delayed. Nothing in Lo Peng's shop was worth five hundred dollars in gold, but Elizabeth was. And he and Lo Peng both knew it was Elizabeth's life, Elizabeth's well-being, that was under negotiation. "Agreed."

He reached inside his jacket pocket and took out his wallet. He removed a bundle of blank bank drafts and glanced around for a pen. If the situation hadn't been so serious and if he hadn't feared offending Lo Peng even more, James would have laughed when a pen and a tiny bottle of ink appeared as if by magic from the depths of the sleeves of one of Lo Peng's hatchet men. Bowing in appreciation of Lo Peng's thoughtfulness in providing the writing instruments, James took the pen and ink and carefully filled in the amount on the bank draft, signed his name, and extended the bank draft to Lo Peng. "If you take this to the British American Bank on Montgomery Street, you'll be paid in gold," he said.

Lo Peng let go of Elizabeth's hair and took the bank draft. His hatchet man retrieved the pen and ink bottle. James watched as all the items—bank draft, pen, and ink—disappeared into the depths of two black silk sleeves.

Their business concluded, Lo Peng stepped away from Elizabeth and met James's unwavering gaze and confided, "Craig must be more careful in the future. Craig must teach his unworthy female discipline. He must learn to control her. For if Craig cannot control one unworthy adult female, I must ask myself why he should be allowed to continue to receive our gifts of female children who will also learn how not to obey."

James clenched and unclenched his fists in a reflexive action as he clamped his mouth shut and ground his teeth together in an effort to keep from exploding. The threat, couched in flowery formal Chinese phrases, was very polite and very real. If James didn't cooperate, if he failed in his mission to keep Elizabeth away from Lo Peng and his Washington Street establishment, more innocent girl babies would die because Lo Peng would no longer allow the families under his control to leave their unwanted daughters on James's doorstep. James wanted to yell and curse at the unfairness of it.

"I have respect for Craig and for his powerful family. That is why I must now concern myself with his inside matters. Why I must advise Craig in the way a father advises his son," Lo Peng continued in a smooth tone. "A man must control the women in his household. Especially the ones with tempers." The old man stared up at James, his sharp black-eyed gaze searching James's blue one. "Especially the ones with large feet and hair the color of precious coins. If not—" He broke off, shrugging in a self deprecating way.

James couldn't resist. "If not?" he asked.

"She will die."

With that, Lo Peng clapped his hands. His two hatchet men moved to stand beside the old man, then escorted the Tong leader from the police station and into the sedan chair waiting on the sidewalk beyond the front door.

James looked on in mute, impotent anger. They had been lucky this time. Lo Peng had been willing to be bribed. But Elizabeth's parasol rampage had cost them dearly. Lo Peng would be watching them now. Watching them closely. Looking for weaknesses in James's armor. Waiting for him to make a mistake—or allow Elizabeth to make one. Elizabeth. James let out a sigh of frustration. Elizabeth's act of destruction could bring a halt to James's rescue work, could threaten the futures of his beloved Treasures and other little girls like them, but it could cost Elizabeth even more. If she wasn't careful, her parasol rampage would cost her her life.

Nine

"WHAT DID YOU tell him?" Elizabeth asked in a tight, angry voice once she and James were settled into James's double brougham and on their way down Kearney Street toward Bender's Boardinghouse.

"Whom?" James replied, trying to avoid an impending and unavoidable confrontation.

Elizabeth raised an eyebrow in an imitation of the questioning gesture she'd seen James use on more than one occasion—a gesture that didn't require explanation.

James exhaled. "I told the judge I would vouch for you, that I'd pay your fifty-dollar fine and see that you didn't get into further *mischief*." The corners of his mouth turned up when he recognized the fiery gleam in her eyes. "Mischief." James nodded as if to himself. "I believe that's the term Judge Clermont used."

Elizabeth sucked in a breath and straightened her back against the leather seat until she sat ramrod stiff in a pose that reeked of an old-money, blue-blooded background. "I wasn't talking about Judge Clermont," she enunciated clearly in an effort to control her temper, "and you know it. I was talking about that creature Lo Peng."

James shrugged. "You heard him."

"Unfortunately," Elizabeth continued, "I'm not as talented as you. I'm not on friendly *conversational* terms with Chinese merchants."

She practically spat out the word *conversational* and again the corners of James's mouth curved upward. Elizabeth Sadler was in a fine snit not just because he had raised his voice at her in front of Lo Peng, but because he had attempted to cajole the old man by speaking in Lo Peng's native Cantonese.

"Well, pardon me, but *I* was born and reared in Hong Kong in a house full of Chinese servants," James told her. "I spoke Chinese before I spoke English. Are you going to be unreasonable and hold that against me?"

"I hold your lack of manners against you," Elizabeth replied spiritedly. "It's rude to converse in a foreign language in the presence of someone who doesn't understand it. And you know it."

"How was I to know you didn't understand Cantonese?" James's expression was innocence personified.

The look Elizabeth gave him should have cut James in half. "Unlike you, I didn't grow up in Hong Kong. I grew up in Providence, Rhode Island, where Chinese is rarely, if ever, spoken."

James bowed his head. "Then I humbly apologize for my rudeness."

"That's better." Elizabeth inclined her head regally in acceptance of his apology.

"Of course," James continued, "had I not succeeded in cajoling and amusing the old tyrant with my inventive tale, he might not have been so agreeable."

"He wasn't the least bit agreeable," Elizabeth said. "Not until you bribed him."

"I didn't bribe him," James corrected her. "I paid for the damages you caused to his establishment." He didn't tell her that the money he'd paid for the damages had also insured her a much longer life span. "What did Lo Peng do to make you so angry?"

"I despise Lo Peng," Elizabeth told him. "His very ex-

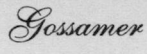

istence makes me angry because he deals in a terrible vice that preys upon the innocent.''

Although he heartily agreed with Elizabeth's assessment of Lo Peng's line of work, James wondered at the depth of her animosity. Had he unknowingly hired a religious zealot or a temperance leader as governess to his daughters? Did she intend to make a habit of wrecking opium dens in her spare time? James shuddered at the thought. ''Did Lo Peng prey upon you?''

''Of course not!''

''Then what made you choose the Red Dragon?''

''The Red Dragon is an opium den,'' she announced.

''That's right,'' he agreed, ''and Lo Peng is within his rights in owning an opium den here in San Francisco. They're perfectly legal. You have no right to wreck it simply because use of the poppy offends your sensibilities.''

''Wreck it? He's lucky I didn't burn the place to the ground,'' Elizabeth muttered beneath her breath as their carriage lurched to a halt in front of Bender's Boarding-house.

''No,'' James said, catching hold of her wrist and encircling it with his fingers, before Elizabeth could open the carriage door. ''*You're* lucky. Lucky he was willing to accept my jumbled explanation of your behavior and an exorbitant amount of gold.'' Watching the way Elizabeth's eyes widened in alarm, James released her wrist, clamped his mouth shut, and quickly unlatched the door. ''Let's go.''

''What did you say to him? What explanation did you give him?''

James stared down at her, wondering if he should lie and spare her and himself the embarrassment of the truth, then decided against it. He wasn't going to begin his association with his children's governess with a lie. As embarrassing as it might be, he was going to tell her the truth. ''I told him you behaved foolishly, because you were jealous. I told him you mistakenly thought I had been spending my nights in the upstairs rooms of his establishment.''

"Why would he think I was jealous?" Elizabeth asked. "Why would a wily little creature like that believe your daughters' new governess would care where you spent your nights?"

"I didn't tell him you were my daughters' governess," James said. "I told him you were my *concubine*."

"What!" Elizabeth's breath left her body in a rush.

"I told Lo Peng you were my concubine. My very jealous concubine who destroyed his opium den in a pique of anger because she thought I was spending time with the prostitutes upstairs instead of lavishing all my attention on her."

Elizabeth's face turned beet red and she stared at him in shock. "Why did you have to make up a fantastic story like that? Why couldn't you have simply told him that I'm the governess you hired for your little girls?"

"I made up that fantastic story," James explained, "because Lo Peng would never believe you're my daughters' governess."

"Why not?" Elizabeth demanded, fully aware that brandishing a parasol and using it to destroy a business was not standard governess-like behavior.

"Because once I explained the function of a governess, Lo Peng would consider me a complete and utterly hopeless idiot."

"For hiring me?" Elizabeth's husky voice rose a notch in tone as she prepared to defend her teaching ability.

James shook his head. "No, for wasting hard-earned cash on a foolish and futile attempt to educate worthless females."

"Is that what you think?" Elizabeth's voice was crisp and sharp, icy with disdain.

The attraction James had felt for her earlier paled in comparison to the kick of desire that coursed through his system at the appalled expression on her face and her frostbitten tone of voice. "We were talking about Lo Peng's notions, not mine," James reminded her.

"What about your notions?" she asked.

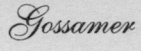

James raised an eyebrow at the question and taking that for her answer, Elizabeth pushed open the door and stepped down from the carriage and onto the sidewalk with all the dignity of Queen Victoria on Coronation Day.

"Where are you going?"

Elizabeth didn't bother to answer. She simply turned and started up the walkway toward Bender's Boardinghouse.

James jumped from the vehicle and followed, catching up with her when she reached the front porch. "I asked you a question, Miss Sadler," he said. "And I'm not accustomed to having my questions go unanswered."

"Neither am I, Mr. Craig. And your question requires no answer because the answer is quite obvious," Elizabeth replied in the same frosty tones she had used before. "I'm going inside Mrs. Bender's. Our arrangement is off. I refuse to work for a man who thinks himself superior and looks down upon females."

"Then I'd say that since most of the men in the known world consider themselves superior and look down upon females, your future employment prospects are severely limited."

Undaunted, Elizabeth lifted her chin. "Then I'll just have to work for a *lady*."

James snorted at the use of that particular word in reference to Augusta Bender.

Elizabeth glanced over her shoulder toward the boardinghouse. "I'm sure I can persuade Mrs. Bender to find a position for me on her staff. And then you'll have your fifty dollars back with interest, in no time."

"Oh, I don't doubt that Augusta Bender would find a dozen positions for you on her staff," James said in amusement. "All of them quite imaginative. Nor do I doubt that you'd earn my—*fifty*"—he emphasized the amount ever-so-slightly—"dollars back in record time if you hadn't made such a powerful enemy out of Lo Peng, but unfortunately for you, I don't think you're going to have an opportunity to ask Augusta to take you on."

"And why not?" Elizabeth had never sparred with a man

in her life, and two days ago she couldn't have imagined
sparring with one of the richest men in the world. But
somehow, she didn't find James Cameron Craig threatening
or frightening and was, quite frankly, exhilarated by their
verbal exchange.

"Because"—James nodded toward a point at a distance
behind her—"if I'm not mistaken, the luggage sitting on
Augusta Bender's porch belongs to you and those two
hatchet men over there in the alley belong to Lo Peng."

"What?" Elizabeth whirled around so quickly she almost lost her balance. Although she didn't see their faces,
she recognized the distinctive red silk dragon she'd come
to associate with Lo Peng embroidered on the back of the
fleeing men's tunics. "They've gone."

"They haven't gone," James told her. "They're still
watching, waiting to report the details to Lo Peng, so let's
make it good."

"Make what look good?" she asked in confusion.

"This." Without giving himself or Elizabeth time to
think about what he was doing, James reached out, caught
her by the hand, and pulled her up against him. Elizabeth
instinctively braced herself, flattening her palms against his
chest to keep from crashing into him as James put his arms
around her, then dipped his head and captured her lips with
his own.

It began almost as an angry kiss, something James
couldn't prevent, but it quickly turned into something more.
Fire erupted throughout James's body as he ravished her
lips and felt her sway against him. He pulled Elizabeth
closer as he deepened his kiss, tangling his hands in the
hair he'd so painstakingly braided back at the jail, before
running them down the curve of her spine. The stiff boning
of her corset frustrated him, but he continued his avid exploration with his hands until they reached the bottom of
her whale-bone cage and slipped beneath her horsehair bustle. James cupped his hands around the curve of her der-
riere, pulling her up against his groin before he groaned in
splendid agony.

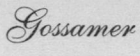

Elizabeth was overwhelmed by her response to his unexpected kiss. She wrapped her arms around his neck and
parted her lips to allow his silken tongue to slip through to
sample the warm recesses of her mouth. Surrounded by his
arms, his mouth, his hard masculine body, and the taste,
touch, and smell of him, Elizabeth melted against him. She
reveled in the hot taste of his kiss, the tangy fragrance of
his shaving soap, the faintest whiff of butter and strawberry
jam as she breathed in his scent and nuzzled closer to its
source. James groaned again. The sound brought Elizabeth
to awareness, and she finally pulled her mouth away from
his. Her senses swam and her knees threatened to give way
at any moment. She tilted her head back as James brushed
his lips against her closed eyelids before trailing down her
neck to place hot, wet kisses behind her ear on the spot
where her pulse hammered to keep pace with her raging
emotions. He darted his tongue into the pink shell of her
ear and Elizabeth gasped in reaction, tightening her grip
around his neck when her legs suddenly refused to support
her weight.

James brushed her lips with his own one last time, then
quickly let her go before his kissing got too far out of hand.
Elizabeth swayed on her feet as he released her.

James reached out a hand to steady her, but Elizabeth
waved him off. She stood in the center of the walkway,
looking shell-shocked and thoroughly kissed, before she
turned and, covering her flushed face with her hands, hurried up the front steps of Bender's Boardinghouse.

"Oh, no." She sank down upon the lid of her largest
trunk, then glanced at the double front doors of the boardinghouse. The outer shutters were closed over the glass-
fronted doors and the window shades were pulled down
against unwanted visitors. Or residents. A note attached to
the brass mailbox on the wall beside the front door requested that Miss Sadler relinquish her front door key upon
her return. And as she stared at the note, the slight movement of one of the window shades settling back into place
caught Elizabeth's attention.

"It looks as if no one is at home," James remarked dryly as he stepped onto the porch.

"Oh, they're home," Elizabeth replied bitterly, remembering the surreptitious fluttering of the expensive lace curtains which hung in the windows of the homes in Providence following her first fall from grace. "But not home to me." She opened her reticule, took out her front door key, then dropped it into the mailbox where it landed with an audible clank. "Now what?" she asked aloud of no one in particular.

"Now we load your luggage," James answered.

"Why?"

"Because you'll probably be needing your clothes," he quipped.

"No," Elizabeth said, "I mean why this? I paid for my room and board a week in advance. Why would she put my things on the porch? Why throw me out into the street?"

"Because you've made a very powerful enemy and even a successful madam like Augusta Bender can't afford to risk her livelihood to shelter you."

"Madam?"

James watched as Elizabeth's blue-green eyes widened in dismay. "Uh-huh," he confirmed. "Madam. And although he has a thriving upstairs business himself, Lo Peng isn't opposed to torching the establishments of independent rivals."

"What about you?"

James smiled. "I've been called ruthless by many people," he told her, being deliberately obtuse. "But I can assure you that I'm not in the arson business, nor am I involved in any upstairs businesses" He held out his hand and pulled Elizabeth to her feet, then bent and hefted her trunk onto his shoulders. The coachman started down from his perch on the brougham to help his employer, but James forestalled him with a quick shake of his head.

"Aren't you afraid an association with me will endanger your family or your livelihood?"

"No. Lo Peng and I have a deal. He won't interfere with my business or my family as long as I see to it that you stay away from him and his businesses." He carried Elizabeth's trunk down the steps and loaded it onto the boot of the brougham. "And I do intend to make sure you stay away from Lo Peng, Elizabeth."

Determined to follow his lead and to appear as unaffected by their devastating kiss as he did, Elizabeth grabbed the handles of two of her valises and followed him down the walkway and around to the back of the carriage. "That might prove harder to do than to say." He turned at the sound of her voice behind him and Elizabeth automatically handed James the bags when he finished stowing her trunk in the boot.

James quirked an eyebrow at her. "I thought our agreement was off."

"It is," she answered. "But since I can't stay here tonight, I thought you might take me to the nearest hotel."

He quirked an eyebrow at that. "I could," he answered, after giving the question some thought, "but I won't."

"And I won't work for a man who thinks his daughters are worthless." Hands on her hips, Elizabeth faced him and issued her challenge. Thoughts of his daughters had reminded her of the existence of his wife, and she felt a burst of indignation that he would kiss her like that—even if merely for the benefit of Lo Peng's men—when he was already married.

"Then, we're in agreement," James told her, before settling the last of Elizabeth's bags into place and closing the flaps of the boot. He walked around to the side of the carriage, opened the door, gently took Elizabeth by the elbow, and ushered her into the vehicle. "Because I happen to think my daughters are wonderfully lovable, highly intelligent human beings and the most precious gifts God has ever entrusted to my care."

"Everyone loves adorable little girls," Elizabeth pronounced, "when they're little. But things tend to change once they grow older, once their family decides they should follow the current vogue and have the young ladies molded into Society's perfect ideals of face, form, and biddability.''

James stared at Elizabeth and the flash of anger in her aquamarine-colored eyes, and couldn't help wondering who in Elizabeth's family had decided to mold her into Society's model of face, form, and biddability and why they had felt it was necessary. Then he thought of his Treasures. His beautiful black-haired, black-eyed Treasures. They would never become American society's models of face and form, and if he had anything to do with it—and he did—they would never become Chinese society's models of biddability. Not his Treasures. They would become the best of both worlds. They would become a spectacular blend of face, form, and independent spirit just like their future governess.

And as Elizabeth stood waiting to see how James would react to her statement, James gave her a mysterious half-smile and cryptically replied, "I don't think you have to worry about ever molding my daughters into perfect models of American society."

Ten

"GOOD EVENING, MR. Craig."

"Good evening, Delia," James replied as he opened the door leading into the luxurious nursery suite in his Coryville mansion some three hours after leaving Bender's Boardinghouse, and found the most responsible of the housemaids sitting beside the fireplace minding the Treasures.

"Daddy!" The trio of little girls looked up from the scatter of blocks and stuffed animals littering the carpet, recognized their father, and began shouting his name at an earsplitting volume, then hurried toward the door of the nursery clamoring for his attention.

James dropped the leather satchel he'd been carrying and bent at the waist to scoop the two oldest little girls up into his arms. "Hello, my lovelies." He turned to Elizabeth. "This is Ruby." He nodded toward the child cradled in his right arm. "And this is Garnet," he said, indicating the child in his left arm. James smothered both girls with kisses, producing more squeals and high-pitched giggles, then set them on their feet. The older girls wrapped their arms around James's legs as he lifted the youngest of the toddlers off the floor in mid-crawl. "And this is Emerald."

He planted a kiss on Emerald's baby-soft cheek, then gave a soft laugh when Emerald reciprocated. "I meant what I said about my daughters, Miss Sadler. I named them after precious gems. And we in the household fondly refer to the girls as the Treasures."

"Good heavens," Elizabeth said aloud before immediately covering her mouth with her hand. "They're . . ."

"A bit overwhelming at first," he said. "But you'll get used to it."

Again, Elizabeth struggled for words. "They're . . ."

Something in her tone of voice alerted him, and James turned his attention away from the Treasures back to the woman he'd hired to be their governess.

Elizabeth suppressed an involuntary shiver. She couldn't stay. She couldn't teach these children. They were too young. Too rambunctious. Too different from what she'd expected. *Too Chinese.* There. She took a deep breath. She'd admitted it. James Cameron Craig's daughters were Chinese. Like Lo Peng. Like the hatchet men who guarded him. Like the minions who obeyed him, like the men who had unceremoniously dumped her brother's body into the street. One of the youngsters—the middle one with the sparkling dark brown eyes and the burgundy hair ribbons sliding through her silky baby-fine locks—loosened her hold on her father's trouser leg and smiled shyly. Elizabeth leaned closer. The burgundy hair ribbon had lost its anchor in the child's soft hair and was in danger of sliding away. She reached out to catch and retie it, but caught herself before she did so. Appalled by her automatic gesture, Elizabeth clenched her fist, then lowered her hand, covering it in the folds of her skirts. The little girl took a step forward. Elizabeth blanched and immediately stepped backward. The child retreated, returning to the safety of her father's long legs, where she hid her face against the lightweight wool of his suit.

James pinned Elizabeth with a sharp gaze as he studied the array of contrasting emotions that flickered across her all-too-expressive face.

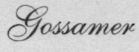

She opened her mouth, stumbled over her words, then cleared her throat and started again. "I apologize, Mr. Craig. I never expected . . . It's just that . . ."

James let out a long frustrated sigh. "They're Chinese. Yes, Miss Sadler, I know." He shook his head. "Although, somehow, this time I didn't think it would matter." He watched Elizabeth closely, noting the way she backed away from the children, the beads of perspiration on her upper lip, and the ashen cast to her complexion.

"I have my reasons," she murmured, embarrassed by the look of supreme disappointment she read in James Craig's face, embarrassed by her instinctive reaction to three innocent little girls, yet not quite able to disguise or to change it. Not yet quite able to come to terms with the fact that the man who had kissed her so passionately just hours ago had a wife. A Chinese wife.

"Most people do."

She had made a promise to Owen. She'd made a promise to herself. And she had to keep it. She wouldn't rest as long as Owen's death went unpunished. As long as people like Lo Peng preyed on innocent young men. People like Lo Peng. Elizabeth stared down at the faces of James Craig's daughters, at their caps of silky jet black hair, their red and burgundy and emerald green hair ribbons, at their dark, deep chocolate, almost black almond-shaped eyes, and the soft golden cast of their skin. She couldn't be responsible for these children because one day, they would grow up to look and think and act exactly like Lo Peng. "You don't understand."

"On the contrary, Miss Sadler," James answered coolly. "I understand this rather mindless prejudice all too well."

Elizabeth sucked in a sharp breath at his words. She had never been accused of prejudice before, quite the opposite, in fact, and the accusation stung. It stung all the more because Elizabeth was forced to admit his accusation was true.

James pretended not to notice the way his words affected her. Shocked her. "Someone told me, not long ago, that everyone loves adorable little girls when they're little." He kissed Emerald again, this time on the forehead. "I foolishly hoped that statement was true even though I knew better. You see, Miss Sadler, everyone loves adorable little babies. Unless, of course, they happen to have a yellowish cast to their skin." He gave a little snort of derision. "Or unless they happen to be female." Holding Emerald in one arm, he bent and gently disengaged his other daughters' arms from around his legs, then turned his back on Elizabeth. He ushered the two older girls into the center of the nursery, set Emerald down on the floor in the middle of the carpet among the wooden blocks and stuffed animals, then turned and escorted Elizabeth to the door. James stopped long enough to tug on the bellpull hanging near the door, then followed Elizabeth into the hallway and closed the door to the nursery behind them. "It's late, Miss Sadler. You've had a difficult day and a long journey. I'll have one of the maids show you to a guest room tonight and see that you get your fifty dollars and that you're on the first train back to San Francisco in the morning."

"I can't go back to San Francisco."

James shrugged his shoulders. "No, I don't guess you can. But you have the rest of the state and the rest of the continent from which to choose a destination."

"I apologize," she said. "Believe me, it isn't your daughters. I have nothing against your daughters personally . . . I just . . ." She shrugged her shoulders and glanced down at the floor, focusing on the way the hem of her skirt skimmed over the top of her slippers, a fraction of an inch above the polished wood.

"Dislike them as a matter of principle."

His crisp, deliberate tone of voice interrupted her perusal of the floor. She looked up at him and saw the flash of emotion he tried to mask. "I didn't mean to hurt you."

James's expression was cool, his reply even more so. "You didn't hurt me, Miss Sadler. You disappointed me."

His face wore a closed, shuttered expression Elizabeth

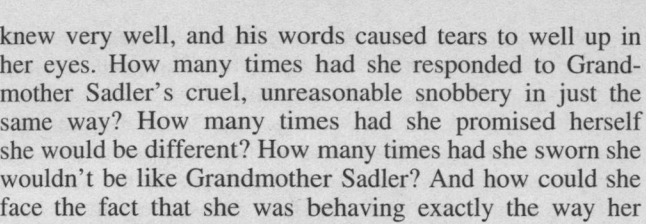

knew very well, and his words caused tears to well up in her eyes. How many times had she responded to Grandmother Sadler's cruel, unreasonable snobbery in just the same way? How many times had she promised herself she would be different? How many times had she sworn she wouldn't be like Grandmother Sadler? And how could she face the fact that she was behaving exactly the way her grandmother behaved, even going so far as to offer her grandmother's feeble excuses for inexcusable behavior?

"I'm sorry," she said, once again.

James quirked his mouth in a brief half-smile. "I suppose it's just as well," he told her, "that you leave before the Treasures have time to form an attachment to you—" He stopped and compressed his lips into a tight, firm line. *Before I have time to form an attachment to you.* James shook the unwanted thought away. "Besides, the Treasures have yet to have the kind of governess they deserve. A governess who sees them for the warm, loving little girls they are and appreciates the unique gifts they have to offer."

Elizabeth opened her mouth to offer a defense, but there was nothing she could say. No defense she could give. No reason she could offer him. No comfort to take away the sting of disappointment. She had already been indicted. She'd indicted herself. She simply stood quietly and waited for James Cameron Craig to dismiss her.

He leaned toward her, and Elizabeth thought he might offer his hand, but James made no move to touch her. "Good-bye, Miss Sadler."

"Good-bye? More like good night, don't you think?"

James and Elizabeth turned as Helen Glenross stepped onto the second-floor landing, walked right up to Elizabeth, and offered her hand in welcome. "I'm Helen Glenross, Mr. Craig's housekeeper. And you must be the new governess. Miss—"

"Sadler," Elizabeth replied. "Elizabeth Sadler." She stared at the housekeeper, taking in Mrs. Glenross's plain, honest face, her graying hair, and her rather gaunt-looking figure.

"Nice to meet you, Miss Sadler." Helen Glenross glanced over at her employer, noted the firm shuttered look on his face, and immediately recognized the tension flowing between Mr. Craig and the new governess. Fearing the desperately needed governess was about to slip away, Mrs. G. plunged ahead, salvaging what she could of the situation. "Miss Sadler, I can't tell you how pleased we are to have a real honest-to-goodness teacher as governess for the Treasures. Mr. Craig and I despaired of ever finding someone suitable. The last four turned out to be disasters."

Elizabeth shook hands with Mrs. Glenross, then glanced over the shorter woman's head, at James. "You've had four governesses?"

"We've had four women who thought they could do the job," Mrs. Glenross quickly replied. "But I would hardly call a faro dealer, a saloon girl, a Chinese laundress, or the ignorant widow of one of Mr. Craig's miners governesses."

"I'm sure you must be busy, Mrs. G.," James interrupted his housekeeper's flow of words. "I didn't realize you'd have to make the trek up the stairs. I expected Annie to answer the bell."

"Annie's having her supper. And I didn't see the sense in having the poor girl jump up in the middle of it. Especially since I was coming up here anyway to put this little mite"—she patted the bottom of the band of silk fabric that was looped over her neck and across one shoulder and rested against her slight bosom—"to bed and help Delia bathe the other ones. Unless, of course, Miss Sadler would like to take over . . ."

Elizabeth reached up and absently fingered a stray lock of her hair as she stared in fascinated silence at the small bulge in the silken sling hanging around Mrs. Glenross's neck. All at once she remembered what James had said to her back at the jail in San Francisco when he'd explained his expert plaiting of her hair by saying, *I have four daughters. Three of them have hair.* Well, she'd been introduced to the three oldest girls—Ruby, Garnet, and Emerald—and while all of them had hair, none had hair long enough to braid. And Elizabeth was willing to bet every penny of her remaining seventy-eight cents that this two-day-old little gem, whatever her name, had no hair at all. The tiny tyke, secured in a makeshift sling around the housekeeper's neck, was the fourth daughter. A two-day-old infant whose mother was no doubt resting in one of the bedrooms lining the second-floor hallway, still recovering from her birth and unable to tend to her needs. *Tend to her needs.* The phrase echoed in Elizabeth's mind. Two days ago that child had been born needing someone to tend to her needs. Two days ago Elizabeth had learned of Owen's death. No one had tended to Owen's needs. But Owen had been a grown man—immature, but grown just the same. While this infant and her solemn-eyed sisters were babies.

James took a deep breath before he broke the bad news to his long-suffering housekeeper, well aware that Helen Glenross's faithful service might come to an abrupt end as soon as she learned the new governess wouldn't be taking the job. "Unfortunately, there's been a mistake, Mrs. G. Miss Sadler feels"—he looked over at Elizabeth, torn between exposing her prejudice to his housekeeper and protecting her feelings—"a bit overwhelmed by the situation here. I'm afraid she isn't going to—"

"Be able to assume my duties until morning." Elizabeth's rush of words surprised everyone. Herself most of all. "I've been in ja—I've been traveling most of the day." Elizabeth let go of the lock of hair and brushed at the scratch on her cheek with the back of her hand. "I need to freshen up. I couldn't possibly touch—" She hastily corrected her wording. "Expose the Treasures, especially the little one, to the grime of the city. So, if it wouldn't be too much to ask . . . If you could manage without me tonight," she glanced back over Mrs. Glenross's head and met James's suspicious gaze, "I'd rather start fresh in the morning."

"We can manage without you," James answered uncharitably. "We've managed this long without you, and

I've no doubt that in the very near future, we'll continue to do so.''

Mrs. Glenross gasped and glared meaningfully at her employer. She knew he expected perfection, but what was wrong with the man? What was he trying to do? Drive the woman off? Feeling overwhelmed by the responsibility of three toddlers upon first meeting them was nothing to be ashamed of—even for a competent governess. Three rambunctious little girls were enough to overwhelm anyone at first glance. And add a newborn into the mix and well . . . She rushed to reassure Miss Sadler before the woman decided she'd had enough of Mr. Craig's surliness and walked out. ''Of course we'll manage. How thoughtless of me even to suggest that you start work before you're even settled in! I suppose I'm feeling my age instead of remembering my manners. Come with me.'' She took Elizabeth by the arm and steered her away from James to the next door down the hall. ''I'll show you to your room.''

Eleven

"NO, I'LL SHOW Miss Sadler to her room." James moved forward and deliberately stepped between the two women, forcing Mrs. Glenross to let go of Elizabeth's arm.

"If you're sure—" The housekeeper hesitated, glancing nervously from her angry employer to the new governess.

"I'm sure," James said. "You're free to go about your other duties, Mrs. G. I'll show our *guest* to her room for the night." He emphasized Elizabeth's temporary status as he released his housekeeper from her hostess role. James motioned toward the doorway that connected the nursery proper to the governess's quarters and gestured for Elizabeth to precede him.

"You got what you wanted," Elizabeth hissed as James took her by the elbow and propelled her through an alcove approximately the size of a butler's pantry, which contained a dumbwaiter, a small sink, a modern icebox, and a tiny range. "There's no reason for you to be so angry."

"Angry? I'm not angry," James uttered through tightly clenched teeth as he glanced over his shoulder toward the open door leading into the nursery. Then, before she had a chance to reply, he threw open another door and ushered Elizabeth over the threshold and into a bedroom before he closed the door behind them with an audible click. "I'm bloody furious! And I demand to know the meaning of this."

"Meaning of what?" she asked.

"The farce you enacted for Mrs. G. Namely, your oh-so-convenient change of heart."

"Just as you said."

James arched one eyebrow in silent question. "Explain yourself."

"There's nothing to explain," Elizabeth answered. "It's just as you said. I had a change of heart. I've decided to stay and become governess to your children."

"Why?"

"Why not?" She took a deep breath, drew herself up to her full height, and straightened her shoulders.

"Why not?" James repeated as if he hadn't quite understood her correctly. "Because you disliked my daughters on sight."

Elizabeth lifted her chin a notch higher and looked him directly in the eye, refusing to flinch under his unwavering scrutiny. "I don't dislike your daughters personally."

"Just on principle," he retorted. "I remember."

"And as I said before, I have my reasons, Mr. Craig."

"And I submit that reason plays no role in that kind of prejudice," he said. "I won't allow my daughters to suffer because the woman I hired to be their governess can't see past the color of their skin. I want an answer from you, Miss Sadler, and I want it now."

"I don't know," Elizabeth answered simply.

"What?"

"I don't know why I changed my mind, Mr. Craig. I was quite prepared to spend one night under your roof, collect the fifty dollars you promised me, pay my debt to you, and leave in the morning on the next train out of Coryville. Then I saw Mrs. Glenross standing on the stairway landing with an infant in a sling about her neck and looking at me with such expectation in her eyes that I couldn't disappoint her."

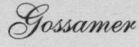

James sighed. "You had no trouble disappointing me."

"Yes, I did."

James's anger dissolved as he studied the earnest expression on Elizabeth's lovely face. He suddenly seemed unable to look away. Her honest statement hung between them, thickening the atmosphere with sharp, palpable awareness that had nothing to do with the fact that he was a man needing a governess and everything to do with the fact that he was a man needing a woman. Her plump, pouty lips seemed to beckon him, and the look in her cool blue-green eyes seemed to challenge him to act on his impulses and taste her again.

Suddenly uncomfortable with the intense, almost hungry, look in James Craig's blue eyes, Elizabeth pulled her gaze away from his and quickly turned her attention to her surroundings. She glanced around the decidedly feminine room with its delicate yellow silk-covered walls and richly carved Queen Anne furnishing and groped for a topic of conversation—something—anything—that would dispel the tense atmosphere hovering between them. "Whose room is this?"

"Yours," James replied. "Unless you have another sudden change of heart."

Elizabeth wrinkled her brow in dismay. "You must be mistaken."

From the looks of it, the bedroom connected to the nursery already had an occupant. Elizabeth walked to the center of the room, then turned and looked askance at the man she had abruptly decided once again would be her employer. Although the half-tester bed was fully made, the coverlet and the feather pillows atop it retained the imprint of the bedroom's former occupant. "Or am I expected to share it?"

James scanned the room and the tips of his ears turned a bright shade of red as he noted the untidy state of the room. Elizabeth's husky voice and her provocative question wrapped themselves around him like a warm blanket. Images of mussed sheets and long, slender feminine limbs entwined with his filled James's mind. He took a deep breath, then cleared his throat. "I didn't realize the room hadn't been tidied."

Elizabeth pointedly fixed her gaze on the heavy woolen topcoat, wrinkled white linen shirt, waistcoat, and suit jacket draped across the foot of the bed.

"I've been catching catnaps in here to be near the children while we've been between governesses." Elizabeth didn't say anything and James raked his fingers through his hair in a visible show of irritation. "I obviously failed to remind Mrs. G. to check this room when I left this morning."

A vivid mental picture of James Craig lying atop the covers without his suit jacket, waistcoat, and white linen shirt added to Elizabeth's nervousness, and she quickly crossed over to the bed and began straightening the covers. "And it obviously never occurred to you to tidy it yourself." Her tone of voice was harsher than she intended, but James's nearness and the unexpected intimacy of occupying a bed James had slept on unnerved her. It reminded Elizabeth of the reason she'd had to come West and all that she'd found and everything that had happened to her since she'd stepped off the ferry in San Francisco two days ago.

"I've been busy," he said.

"And your housekeeper has not?" Elizabeth countered, turning to face him.

"May I remind you that I've been in San Francisco all day?" he replied snidely. "Bailing you out of jail."

"If you hadn't had me arrested needlessly, you wouldn't have had to bail me out," Elizabeth reminded him. "And your housekeeper's been overseeing a mansion and three toddlers and carrying an infant around in a sling all day. You might try being more considerate of the needs of your staff."

"I pay my staff very well," James said, bristling defensively. "That makes me very considerate of their needs."

"And what of your *wife's* needs?"

James froze, barely able to breathe as Elizabeth's im-

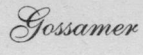

pudent question penetrated his defenses and stabbed directly at his heart.

The rudeness of her question surprised Elizabeth as much as it appalled her. Elizabeth hadn't even realized she was curious about James's wife until she suddenly found herself demanding to know if he fulfilled her needs.

"My wife died," James answered, nearly choking on his guilt. "I can no longer fulfill any of her needs." *And what of your wife's needs?* How many times had he deliberately avoided asking himself that question? How long had it been since he'd been honest enough with himself to admit that he'd never met Mei Ling's needs at all? That he'd never really known what they were?

Elizabeth's knees abruptly refused to support her weight, and she sank down onto the edge of the bed. "I'm sorry." She thought of the two-day-old baby lying cradled in the sling around Mrs. Glenross's neck, thought of the three toddlers next door in the nursery, and of the satchel crammed full of official-looking documents James had attended to over the course of the journey by ferry and train from San Francisco. And the hungry way he had kissed her on the walkway of Bender's Boardinghouse. His wife was dead. His governess had quit without notice, his staff had their hands full with the Treasures, and he had a business to run. Elizabeth hadn't known about his wife back in San Francisco, hadn't understood James Craig's ruthless determination to find a qualified governess at any cost, but now that she understood what prompted him, she was forced to admit his actions made sense. "I didn't realize—"

"It's all right," James cut her off, acknowledging her offer of condolence with a brief nod. "She died a long time ago."

"But the baby . . ."

James shrugged his shoulders. "What difference does it make if Diamond has a different mother? Is she any less mine than her sisters? Would you have me allow the child to go wanting when I can give her a loving family?"

"I owe you an apology," Elizabeth said softly.

"And why is that?" As far as James was concerned, Elizabeth owed him several apologies, but since she hadn't offered to apologize before, he couldn't help wondering what prompted her to do so now.

"I behaved very badly. I was rude and defensive and uncooperative because I thought you were acting out of pity," Elizabeth said. "I thought you felt sorry for me. And that you only offered me a job as governess to your children because you felt guilty for having me arrested." Elizabeth looked up at him, her eyes brimming with sympathy for his loss and for his predicament. "But now I understand that you didn't act out of pity. You really *do* need a governess."

"I never act out of pity," James informed her. But *she* did. He could see it in her eyes, hear it in her voice, and the knowledge that she could salvage her pride by trampling his irritated him more than he wanted to admit. "And I don't need a governess."

"Of course you do," Elizabeth began, "and I'm willing to—"

"My *children* need a governess," James clarified brusquely. "*I* am a grown man."

"Well, yes, of course," Elizabeth stammered, nervously moving away from him, pushing herself back onto the middle of the bed as James stared down at her, his blue eyes dark with emotion.

She sucked in a breath. He looked as if he might touch her. As if he might kiss her.

She stared up at him, waiting for his next move.

Then, without warning, James leaned very close as he scooped his topcoat, suit jacket, waistcoat, and white linen shirt up into his arms and whispered, "My children need a governess. I do not. My needs are very different."

Twelve

JAMES LISTENED TO the sound of water splashing and the happy chatter of little girls as he stopped outside the door of the nursery long enough to retrieve his leather satchel. He paused for a moment, listening to see if Delia needed help bathing the Treasures, before he made his way down the stairs and into the comfort and privacy of his study.

He dropped his armload of clothing onto a leather wing chair just inside the study door, then glanced over at the clock on the mantel. He needed to keep an eye on the time. The Treasures' bedtime was less than an hour away, but he still had a few moments to look over the Central Pacific documents. James set his satchel on top of a massive oak desk, then automatically settled onto the big high-backed chair behind it. He opened the leather case and removed the Central Pacific Railroad rolling stock agreements and turned to the first page.

CRAIG CAPITAL, LIMITED, is hereby granted . . . Craig Capital, Limited, is hereby granted . . . James tossed the contracts aside and looked over at the mantel clock in disgust. He had spent the last quarter-hour reading the same sentence and he couldn't recall any of the information contained in the sentences leading up to it. He pushed his chair away from the desk and stood up, then walked over to the fireplace, leaned against the edge of the mantel, and stared at the logs neatly stacked in the grate. He couldn't concentrate on a railroad contract when his mind was fully occupied with thoughts of the woman upstairs.

Elizabeth Sadler. Lovely Elizabeth Sadler. Mercurial Elizabeth Sadler. Enchanting Elizabeth Sadler. Mysterious Elizabeth Sadler. Bigoted Elizabeth Sadler. James squeezed his eyes shut and pinched the bridge of his nose in a futile attempt to block out the memory of the way Elizabeth had looked as she backed away from the Treasures. He banged the top of the mantel with his right fist. ''Damn it! Is expecting an intelligent woman to look beyond my children's obvious differences too much to ask?'' He lifted his gaze from the fireplace and looked heavenward. He was too old to be an idealist, too jaded. So, when was he going to stop expecting the people he cared about to accept the Treasures, and learn to anticipate their bigoted reactions? When was he going to stop expecting the people he cared about . . . James stopped suddenly, then shook his head as if to clear it. He didn't care about Elizabeth Sadler. He didn't value her opinions or care about her feelings. Or did he?

I have my reasons. Her fervent admission echoed in his mind. She had her reasons. What the hell were they? What reasons could be strong enough to warrant her repulsion at the sight of the Treasures? Had she been so sheltered by her family she hadn't known people came in differing skin tones? And if so, what the hell was she doing traveling out West alone?

James sighed. He'd grown up in Hong Kong. He'd grown up surrounded by people whose beliefs and skin color differed from his own, where he was the minority. And his parents had often commented that growing up in Hong Kong had prepared him for anything. James snorted in derision. Anything except intolerance. Anything except life in America. Anything except how to cope with his massive frustration with, and disappointment in, Elizabeth Sadler. Christ! His mother hadn't reacted as badly as Elizabeth when he'd announced he was marrying Mei Ling. In fact, Julia Cameron Craig had barely batted an eye as her only son announced his plans to marry the girl whose family had given her to him as a concubine. Oh, she'd argued against it later, but his announcement hadn't really caught his mother by surprise. And although Mei Ling wasn't the daughter-in-law Julia Cameron Craig would have chosen for him, she had done her best to secure Mei Ling's position as James's wife within the British community and to make her feel at home. Why couldn't Elizabeth do the same? Why couldn't she welcome four motherless little girls into her heart and make them feel safe and wanted and loved? James sighed. *You must be patient, Jamie. Some things take time.* James heard his mother's voice speaking those words as clearly as if she were standing in his study beside him, as clearly as he had heard them back in Hong Kong when he'd complained to his mother that the wives of the men in the banking community had yet to invite Mei Ling to their afternoon teas or to acknowledge her as his wife.

In fairness to Elizabeth, James was willing to admit that maybe all she needed was time. His mother had spent nearly thirty years in Hong Kong by the time he had brought Mei Ling into the Craig family. Julia Cameron Craig had had plenty of time to become accustomed to the looks and ways of the Chinese people.

And given time, Elizabeth would, too. James squeezed his eyes shut again. He only hoped it wouldn't take her thirty years. He couldn't wait thirty years. He couldn't wait until the Treasures were grown and gone. He needed her now. James shook his head. What was it about Elizabeth? Why hadn't he been able to dismiss her from his mind? Why hadn't he hired a different governess for his daughters? Why hadn't he even tried? Why didn't he walk back upstairs, knock on her bedroom door, and order her to be on the first train leaving Coryville in the morning? James pushed away from the mantel, walked back to his desk, and lowered himself onto his chair. He shoved the railroad contracts out of the way, then bent forward and placed his forehead against the cool oak surface of his desk. Why didn't he escort her to the depot and put her on the train? Because no matter how disappointed or how angry he was with Elizabeth for her honest reaction to her first sight of the Treasures, he wanted her. Not just as governess to the Treasures, but for himself.

A knock on the door startled him. James sat up and pushed his chair away from his desk. "Come in."

His housekeeper opened the door, and James quickly got to his feet. Mrs. G. had removed the sling she'd used to carry Diamond in from around her neck and replaced it with a starched white bibbed apron.

"Pardon the interruption, Mr. Craig, but Delia has finished bathing the girls. They're ready for you to come tuck them in."

"I'll be right up."

"Fine, sir. I'll let Delia know you're on your way," she replied as she stepped inside the study and began gathering up the clothes James had dropped on the chair. "Shall I take these to your bedroom, sir?"

James started to give his approval, then remembering Elizabeth's earlier comments, thought better of it. "No, thank you, Mrs. G. If you will, just leave them on the chair. I'll take them when I go upstairs."

Helen Glenross gave her employer a curious look. "If you're sure."

James smiled. "I'm sure."

Mrs. G. draped the garments over the arm of the leather wing chair. "One more thing, Mr. Craig . . ."

"Yes, Mrs. G.?"

"Shall I serve dinner in the dining room?"

James met his housekeeper's gaze. "Will I be dining there alone, Mrs. G.?"

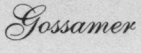

Helen Glenross hesitated. "Miss Sadler asked to have a tray sent up to her room."

James took a deep breath, then slowly exhaled it. "I suppose the staff's already eaten."

His housekeeper nodded.

"Have you?"

Mrs. G. didn't quite meet his gaze as she answered, "Yes, sir."

James knew better. Helen Glenross was nothing if not conscientious. She would never dream of having her dinner until she was certain he had eaten. But he also knew that after a life spent in household service, Helen Glenross wasn't about to break with tradition and sit down to supper with her employer.

"Then I'd prefer to have a tray sent here," James said. "If it won't be too much bother."

"No bother at all."

"Are you certain, Mrs. G.?" He hesitated, nearly stumbling over his words in an effort to show her the consideration she deserved for three years of devoted service to him. "That is . . . I mean to say, that I realize you've had extra work thrust upon you since the governess left. I know you've been putting in longer than usual days to take care of all your household duties and little Diamond."

Mrs. G. grinned, her plain face glowing with pleasure. "I'll have your dinner ready in three-quarters of an hour. Will that give you enough time to tuck the girls into bed?"

"Plenty," James answered. "And, Mrs. G., thank you. For everything."

⌒⌒⌒

"WEAD THE STOWY, Daddy," Ruby demanded imperiously, pulling a thick leather-bound volume from beneath the covers and shoving it into James's hands.

James took the book, lowered the bedrail, then climbed onto the bed and settled back against the headboard. Ruby climbed across his lap and burrowed into the crook of his right arm, while Garnet and Emerald leaned against his left. Diamond, the baby, lay fast asleep in the crib. He opened the book and turned to the page marked with a sky-blue ribbon. "Where were we?"

"Sir Knight," Ruby replied, "and Sancho Panza."

" 'To wight wongs and come to the aid of the wet-ched,' " Garnet quoted.

"How right you are, little one," James said as he leaned forward and planted a kiss on Garnet's shiny cap of black hair. "Don Quixote is on his quest to right wrongs and come to the aid of the wretched. All right, here we go," He cleared his throat and began reading, "Chapter Twenty-two."

⸻❦⸻

IN THE BEDROOM next door Elizabeth pushed her dinner tray to the side, untouched. Although the food smelled delicious, she couldn't bring herself to eat it. She was too tired to eat, too tired to think about her stupidly impulsive decision to remain as governess to James Craig's daughters. No good could come of it. She was too green, too inexperienced, too frightened. Her years at Lady Wimbley's Female Academy had been spent first as a day student and then as a teacher to girls old enough to be sent away to boarding school. Even the youngest of the academy students had been six years of age.

She had no practical experience with children as young as the Craig Treasures. She didn't know how to handle them, how to talk to them or teach them, how to entertain them, or bathe and clothe them—especially the baby, Diamond. And heaven help her if they started babbling in that heathen Chinese language, because she'd be lost. Elizabeth paced the bedroom as she unbuttoned the bottom buttons on the bodice of her brown silk walking dress and removed the hatpin James had used to fasten the top of it. She took off her bodice, shook it out, and hung it on a hanger inside the massive Queen Anne armoire. She dropped the hatpin

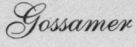

into a porcelain dish sitting atop the dressing table as she walked by, then unhooked her corset and the fasteners on her skirt, sucked in a deep breath, and let both garments fall to the floor. She'd be lost? She was already lost and completely out of her depths. What had possessed her to open her big mouth? James Craig had been about to dismiss her, to release her from her obligation to him.

Elizabeth paced to the tall bedroom window and realized it was a door that led to the balcony overlooking the back garden. She opened the door a crack to let in the night air, then turned and retraced her steps, bending to pick up her discarded clothing along the way. What made her disregard her sense of fear of and unease about the Treasures? Elizabeth hung her skirt beside the bodice in the armoire and stuffed her corset and corset cover into a drawer. Her trunks had arrived from the depot shortly before her dinner tray, and, stripped down to her chemise and stockings, Elizabeth leaned down and began rifling through the smaller one, searching for a nightgown and robe. Finding what she needed, she pulled on a white lawn nightgown, draped a satin wrapper within easy reach on the footboard, then kicked off her shoes, and climbed onto the bed. She rolled onto the center of the bed and wrapped her arms around a pillow. The answer to her questions was all around her. The faint scent of his cologne clung to the pillowslip and the sound of his voice penetrated the silk-covered walls.

Elizabeth lay quietly listening as James Craig read to his daughters. Not some frivolous little children's story or rhyming song, but Cervantes. She smiled at the image. He was reading *Don Quixote de la Mancha* to toddlers, relating the story of a dreamer who tilted at windmills and did his utmost to right incorrigible wrongs. A man, Elizabeth suspected, not as far removed from James Cameron Craig as James would have everyone believe.

Elizabeth doused her lamps and lay in bed staring up at the half-tester canopy and listened to the accounts of Don Quixote's adventures until James's voice trailed off into nothingness and the soft sighs and gentle snoring told her that the story was done for the night and that the Treasures were fast asleep.

She listened to the sound of James moving quietly around the room and was amazed that a big man could move about so silently. She imagined him going through the bedtime routine—straightening and tucking in the covers, leaning down to kiss each child good night, and blowing out the lamps. She heard the quiet click of the door as he closed it behind him and exited the nursery. And for a brief moment Elizabeth listened to the sound of his quiet tread as he paused outside her door.

She smiled up at the darkness.

Thirteen

"GOOD MORNING, MRS. G.," James said as he walked out of the master bedroom just after dawn the following morning and met the housekeeper exiting the governess's room with a heavy silver tray in her arms. James drew his brows together in a show of irritation. Having her dinner sent up after a long eventful day was one thing, but asking Mrs. G. to bring her breakfast was quite another. Elizabeth Sadler was not the lady of the manor. She was an employee—a temporary one, perhaps—but for the time being, she had a job to do and responsibilities that did not include breakfast in bed. From now on he expected her to have the Treasures up and dressed and sitting at the dining room table to share breakfast with him. "Is this our new governess's breakfast tray?"

Mrs. G. shook her head. "No, sir. This is her dinner tray from last night, and she barely touched it."

"What?" James reached over and lifted one of the silver covers from the tray. It was identical to the one Mrs. G. had left on his study desk last night. He stared down at the cold, untouched half of perfectly roasted Cornish hen on a bed of wild rice, then replaced the cover and lifted another one, and another. Even the slice of cherry pie was untouched. "I didn't see her eat a thing all day yesterday. She had to have been starving, but she didn't eat anything."

"I know," Mrs. G agreed. "The tray and everything on it was still sitting where I left it last night."

A streak of alarm shot through James as he remembered staring at the open balcony door outside Elizabeth's room last night while he sat smoking a cigar on his own balcony several doors down from hers. "Is she still with us? Or has she flown the coop?"

Mrs. G. raised her eyebrows at that and frowned.

"I had a cigar on my balcony last night and noticed her door was open," James explained. "I thought that after the day she had yesterday, she might have changed her mind again about staying and climbed out the window while we were all asleep in our beds."

Mrs. G. shook her head. "She may have felt a bit overwhelmed by the long trip yesterday and the fact that the Treasures weren't what she expected, but she's got more grit than you think. She won't be climbing out windows in the middle of the night or stealing the silver. If she decides to leave, she'll tell you straight out."

It was James's turn to frown. "So you knew how she reacted. I wondered."

"I heard most of it while I was coming up the stairs," Mrs. Glenross admitted. "And Delia told me the rest."

"What do you think?" James asked. "Should we keep her because we desperately need a governess? Or shall I give Miss Sadler a train ticket out of Coryville and keep searching for a governess?"

"We should keep her," Mrs. G. answered firmly. "For her sake if not our own."

James nodded in agreement. "I think you're right. As far as I can tell, she has no family out West. She said something the first time I met her about having a brother who lived in San Francisco, but he died before she arrived." He wrinkled his brows in concentration. *There was something else about the brother. Something that nagged at his memory, taunting him.* James shook his head. "And

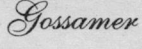

she's right about not being able to return to San Francisco. Her confrontation with Lo Peng has made it impossible for her to even consider it for a while.''

Helen Glenross shuddered at the idea. "She's had a confrontation with Lo Peng?''

James couldn't keep from grinning. "After only two days in San Francisco our Miss Sadler has managed to become one of Lo Peng's most bitter enemies.''

"How on earth did she manage that?''

"By single-handedly wrecking his Washington Street opium den with a brown silk parasol.''

Mrs. G. pursed her lips in thought, then turned her attention to her employer. "Well,'' she said, "that explains what she did to earn Lo Peng's enmity. The question is: What did *he* do to earn hers?''

"Of course.'' James stared at his housekeeper with an incredible sense of awe, the same sense of awe he would have felt if she had just created the heavens and the earth and presented it to him on the silver platter she held in her arms. It was so simple. "A proper schoolteacher like Elizabeth Sadler would never take her brown silk parasol to an opium den without reason. And religious zeal isn't the reason. We know what Miss Sadler did to Lo Peng. What did *he* do to her?'' And then it came back to him—that niggling memory that had plagued him since Elizabeth Sadler had quietly and defiantly informed him that she had her reasons for disliking the Treasures. James heard the answer clearly in Sergeant Terrence Darnell's Irish brogue: *"Lo Peng's out front swearing out a complaint, but we understand about your brother and Lo Peng's and all. And the guys in the precinct are taking up a collection for you.''* We understand about your brother and Lo Peng's and all. There was something between Elizabeth's brother and Lo Peng. Something so terrible Elizabeth had taken her parasol and wreaked havoc on Lo Peng's primary place of business. It wouldn't be hard to check the facts. A telegram to Sergeant Darnell or the desk sergeant in charge of the San Francisco City Police Precinct should net results. If he scheduled the inquiry into Elizabeth Sadler's brother's fate as first order of business when he reached his office this morning, he could probably have the facts in hand by late afternoon, and then he'd know what caused Elizabeth Sadler to go on her rampage at Lo Peng's. But for the moment, he needed to know why his newly hired governess hadn't started her work day.

James smiled down at Mrs. G. "Then, we agree, Mrs. G. As far as we know Miss Sadler has no one to rely on and nowhere else to go. For the moment she needs us as much as we need her. As long as she does no harm to the Treasures, we'll allow her to stay."

Mrs. Glenross tried hard not to smile at his high-handedness. "I don't think you have to worry about Miss Sadler damaging the Treasures. She isn't that sort of person."

"What do you mean?" James asked. "You heard how she reacted upon seeing them."

"Yes, I did," Mrs. G. agreed. "And it was no worse than anyone else would react upon seeing three little Chinese girls when they were expecting blond-haired, blue-eyed beauties who looked like their father."

"I don't have blond hair," James pointed out. "And you didn't react badly at your first sight of Ruby."

"I'll wager you had blond hair as a child," Mrs. G. retorted. "And like you, I'm accustomed to the looks and ways of the Chinese. My late husband was a construction engineer who supervised gangs of Chinese laborers during the building of the Central Pacific Railroad back in the late sixties. I traveled right alongside my husband and became quite accustomed to being around Chinamen and seeing the half-Chinese offspring of the soiled doves who set up camp behind the railroad construction crews. I've got nothing against the Chinese. They helped build this country, are still building it, but you introduce me to one of those Apache warriors I read about terrorizing the settlers, and I just might react the same way Miss Sadler did."

"We're not talking about Miss Sadler's behavior toward

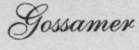

an Apache warrior, Mrs. G. We're talking about innocent children and the damage she might do to them emotionally if her initial reaction continues."

But Helen Glenross just smiled mysteriously and said, "I don't think you have anything to worry about."

"You've said that before, Mrs. G.," James replied. "Now, tell me what you mean by it."

Mrs. G. nodded toward the door to the nursery, then turned and started down the hall toward the stairs and the kitchen. "See for yourself."

Knowing he was being baited, yet unable to resist the bait, James walked to the door of the nursery, turned the doorknob, and entered. He walked through the play area to the Treasures' bedroom, and his heart seemed to stop beating when he realized that the bed Ruby and Garnet shared—the bed he'd securely tucked the girls into last night—was empty. And one glance at Emerald's crib told the same story. Ruby, Garnet, and Emerald were gone. Only Diamond lay sleeping peacefully. James calmly checked the closets and under the beds, then tossed the covers on the bed and the crib. He took deep breaths and fought the overwhelming sense of panic by reminding himself that Mrs. G. hadn't seemed concerned. But Mrs. G. hadn't shared his past. She had never returned from a business trip and discovered an empty crib. James opened his mouth to shout for the housekeeper and demand an explanation when he noticed the door leading from the Treasures' bedroom through the kitchen, to the governess's private quarters was open.

The balcony! James rushed through the kitchen alcove like a shot, intent on reaching the open balcony door before the Treasures stumbled upon it. The balcony! Bloody hell! How could he have forgotten to tell Elizabeth to keep the balcony door closed and latched? The wrought-iron railing surrounding the balcony was secure and the rails were close together—too close for small bodies to slip through—but James had a horror of discovering the Treasures had somehow breached the four-and-a-half-foot-high railing and fallen onto the flagstones in the garden below. James rued the day he'd given the architect his approval to build it. He'd worried about the balcony ever since he'd brought Ruby home to live there.

James clenched his fists as he focused solely on the balcony, not bothering to glance around the room or at the half-tester bed as he crossed the room to the French doors in a few quick strides. He swallowed hard, and flicked his tongue at the tiny beads of perspiration on his upper lip, then squeezed his eyes shut and forced himself to wipe away the grisly images of the three shattered little bodies he was afraid he'd find. I can do this, he told himself as he breathed deeply through his nostrils and opened his eyes again. *I can survive this.* He knew the sight would be terrible. But he also knew he'd seen worse. Survived worse. Still, James thought he would scream as the sheer drapes blew in on the morning breeze coming from the balcony and wrapped themselves around the legs of his trousers. He batted them away, then grabbed a handful of sheer fabric in a fit of frustration and started to rip the drapes from the rods.

"Hi, Daddy. Whatcha doing?"

The soft voice startled him.

James let go of the curtains and his breath at the same time. He glanced down to find Ruby curled up on the chaise longue near the balcony door. As he watched, she sat up straighter, rubbed at her eyes with the back of her hands, and yawned widely as if it were perfectly natural for him to find her on the chaise longue in her governess's room every morning instead of in her own bed.

Suddenly James's knees refused to support him. He sank down onto the end of the chaise.

"Hi, Daddy," Ruby repeated, her tone of voice demanding an answer to her greeting.

James leaned over and hugged her tightly, pressing her warm little body against his chest, breathing in the baby-soft scent of her until she squirmed in his embrace. "Hi, Button."

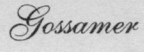

Ruby pushed at his chest until James realized he was holding her too tightly and reluctantly let go. "Whatcha doing, Daddy?"

"I came looking for you and your sisters," James answered. "I went to your room to wake you up and you were gone. What are you doing here sitting all alone in the dark in Miss Sadler's room?"

"Waiting," Ruby replied matter-of-factly.

"Waiting for what, Button?"

"For Garny and Emmy to get up."

"Where are your sisters?" James gently prodded.

"Over there," Ruby pointed toward the big half-tester bed, where Garnet and Emerald lay sleeping, snuggled close to Elizabeth. "I waked up in the dark and Emmy and Garny were gone. I was sleeping all by myself. So I came to get you. Onlys you weren't here. *Her* was."

James automatically lowered his voice to a whisper to keep from waking Elizabeth and the other two girls. "Have you been here a long time?"

The Grandfather clock in the hall downstairs chimed six times. Ruby turned toward the balcony, saw the pinkish streaks of sunlight lightening the sky and realized it was morning. "I been here since it was weal dark. When the clock didn't make so many noises."

"Are you hungry?" James asked.

Ruby shook her head.

"Thirsty?"

Ruby nodded.

James smiled. It was too early for Ruby to want to eat, but she had been awake long enough to want something to drink. "Why don't we go down to the kitchen and see if we can scrounge some warm chocolate for you and a cup of coffee for me?"

"Okay." Ruby scrambled off the chaise and made a bee-line for the bed.

"Shh!" James put a finger to his lips to remind Ruby to try to be quiet, then whispered, "Where are you going?"

"Don't we want to get Garny and Emmy to go to the kitchen wid us?"

Staring at Elizabeth's lovely slumbering form and watching as the lace trim on her virginal nightgown rose and fell with each breath she took, James realized the impropriety of his actions—the impropriety of entering the bedroom of an unmarried woman in his employ regardless of the reason. James weighed his decision. Should he risk waking Elizabeth to get his daughters and have her discover he'd disregarded her right to privacy and barged into her bedroom while she slept? Or should he allow her to awaken on her own and risk her reaction at finding two of his Chinese daughters in bed with her? Should he take matters into his own hands or trust Elizabeth to do the right thing?

James shook his head. After witnessing her first reaction to the Treasures yesterday, it wasn't easy to walk away. But he'd decided to entrust his daughters to her care, and he had to start somewhere. He had to believe, as Mrs. G. believed, that Elizabeth wasn't the sort of person who would intentionally cause the Treasures emotional pain. He had to trust her. And to trust her, he had to take Ruby and walk away and hope for the best. "It's early yet," he said to Ruby. "Let's let them sleep a while. You and I can have our morning coffee all by ourselves."

"Just us, Daddy?" Ruby asked, her little face alight with joy. "Me and you?"

"Just us," he reaffirmed, reaching out to lift her into his arms. "You and I."

"Good, Daddy," she continued to beam at him. "But first . . ." Ruby leaned close and whispered in his ear.

James hugged her closer to him, planted a reassuring kiss on her cheek, bypassed the bath and water closet opposite the tiny kitchen which connected the governess' quarters and the nursery, and carried Ruby down the hall to his bedroom and the water closet in his private bath.

Fourteen

ELIZABETH OPENED HER eyes and found herself face to face with a small child—one with dark black hair and deep brown, almond-shaped eyes. Startled by her near proximity to an Oriental child, Elizabeth tried to move away, but as she watched warily, the delicate-featured child gently patted her on the face. Garnet, she remembered. The second daughter was Garnet. The third was Emerald and the infant was named Diamond. Precious and semiprecious gemstones. Treasures.

"Wake up, lady," Garnet said.

Elizabeth levered herself up from the mattress and leaned back against the feather pillows propped against the headboard. She blinked in confusion. Another, smaller little girl with one arm twisted at an awkward angle slept with her feet pointed at the pillows and her head pointed toward the footboard. And each time the feather mattresses shifted beneath Elizabeth's weight, the smaller child rolled up against her.

"I'm awake," she whispered. She glanced over at Garnet, then gingerly reached over and repositioned Emerald's arm, turning her so that her head rested closer to the pillows and her feet pointed toward the foot of the bed. "What's

wrong? What's happened?" In her concern for ⌐
Elizabeth forgot all about her aversion to the col⌐
skin. "Are you all right?"

Garnet nodded. "Emmy broked her rails down. Sh⌐
out of her bed in the dark and waked me up, so we c⌐
to sleep with Daddy." Garnet lifted the edge of the be⌐
spread and peered under the covers. "But I can't find him.
Where's mine daddy?"

"I don't know," Elizabeth said.

"Mine daddy here." Garnet patted the bed, then looked
over at Elizabeth, tears sparkling on the base of her eyelashes as her bottom lip began quiver. "Daddy gone to
work? Mine Daddy gone Sanfrwansco?" She asked, in broken little gasps. "Daddy leave? Daddy go back Sanfrwansco?"

"No," Elizabeth told her. "I'm sure your daddy
wouldn't leave you without saying good-bye. I'm sure he's
here somewhere."

"I want mine daddy," Garnet said.

Eager to allay Garnet's fears, Elizabeth shoved the
covers aside, swung her legs over the side of the bed,
grabbed her satin wrapper draped over the bedpost, and got
to her feet. "Then, we'll go find him." She lifted Garnet
and set her down beside the bed where she stood shifting
her weight from foot to foot. Barefooted herself, Elizabeth
realized the wooden floor was cold—too cold for a small
child. "Do you have slippers?"

Garnet nodded.

"Where are they?"

"At mine bed."

"Let's go get them, shall we?" Elizabeth reached for
Garnet's hand, but Garnet refused to budge.

"What's wrong?" Elizabeth asked. "Aren't your feet
cold? Don't you want your slippers?"

Garnet nodded again. "Emmy." She pointed to her sister, who still lay sleeping in the center of Elizabeth's bed.

Elizabeth made a rueful face. "Of course! We can't leave

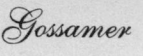

here all alone.'' She looked to Garnet. ''What
with her?''

hers back in hers bed,'' Garnet sagely replied.
pull the rails up taller.''

izabeth leaned down and rolled Emerald from the mid-
e of the bed toward the edge. The muscles in her back
ached from the awkward angle, but Elizabeth managed to
roll Emerald into her arms without waking her. She
straightened and cuddled the sleeping child closer, suddenly
aware of how small and vulnerable she was and how de-
pendent she was on the tender care of the adults around
her. Elizabeth looked to Garnet for further instruction.
''Okay, we've got your sister. Now what do we do?''

Garnet grinned. ''We get mine slippers and find mine
daddy.''

Elizabeth grinned back. It sounded like a good plan to
her and the fact that she was seeking guidance and instruction from a precocious two-year-old didn't escape her notice. But what else could she do? She had a wealth of
experience handling school-aged girls, but she was at a
complete loss with toddlers. Even Garnet knew more about
caring for her younger siblings than Elizabeth did. She
shifted Emerald in her arms, then took Garnet by the hand
and allowed the little girl to lead the way into the nursery.

As they entered the nursery bedroom, Elizabeth discovered she and Garnet had other problems to attend to. The
baby, Diamond, was awake and fussing in her crib, and
Emerald had wet her undergarments.

''Di hungry,'' Garnet said, stepping into her slippers before pushing a child-sized step stool from the foot of her
bed and using it to peer through the slats of the crib at the
crying and squirming baby.

''And Emerald's wet.'' Elizabeth felt the warm wet liquid on her arms and on the front of her nightgown as she
lowered the protective rails and placed Emerald on her bed.
She tugged the end of Emerald's nightie up over her hips
and legs and stared down at the soggy diaper. ''Where are
the diapers?'' she asked.

"Over there." Garnet shifted her weight ⌐
foot and pointed to two neatly folded stacks of cⱱ
and infant dresses sitting atop thin, flat cotton padⱱ
tecting the surface of a rather squat and unadorned ⱱ
"Mine bring you," she answered, hopping off the
stool and pushing it over toward the bureau, eager to hⱱ

Elizabeth watched as Garnet stopped several times on heⱱ
journey across the nursery floor, pausing for breath and
wiggling back and forth from one foot to the other. Understanding dawned and Elizabeth feared Garnet had the
same urgent need as her younger sister.

"Emerald's already wet," Elizabeth said, pulling the
rails on Emerald's bed firmly into place as she addressed
Garnet. "She can wait a moment longer for her diaper. Do
you need to use the pot?"

Garnet looked blank.

Elizabeth searched for an expression Garnet would understand. "Do you need to use the potty? The privy? The
convenience?" She thought for a moment. James Craig was
British. What did the British call it? "Do you need to use
the water closet?" Still, Garnet didn't reply. "The w.c.?"

"Wacee." Garnet beamed, then nodded her head.

Elizabeth heaved a sigh of relief. She didn't remember
seeing a child's nursery chair anywhere about, so she assumed they used the same water closet Mrs. G. had pointed
out to her. She knew Delia had bathed the Treasures there
the night before because the floor was still slightly damp
when she used it. And since she didn't see another water
closet in the nursery, she turned to Garnet for guidance.
"Go on. Go on to the wacee."

Garnet frowned. "Mine not go by self."

Elizabeth spared a glance at Emerald, who still slept
soundly, despite the wet diaper, then at Diamond who was
making her presence known by crying louder. Elizabeth
walked over to the crib and carefully lifted Diamond, cradling her against her shoulder and feeling, once again, the
unmistakable dampness of a wet diaper staining her night-

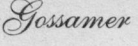

l right, Precious," she cooed to the baby, jig-
a bit on her shoulder, "I know you're hungry and
ut we must take care of Garnet's needs first, then
take care of you and Emmy." Elizabeth smiled down
Garnet. "Lead the way to the wacee, sweetheart. Dia-
nond and I are right behind you."

Garnet did as she was instructed, leading Elizabeth
through the bedroom to the tiny kitchen, where she turned
and opened the door to the bath and water closet. Elizabeth
took note of the second porcelain doorknob on the door of
the water closet—one set inches lower than the regular
doorknob. One she had failed to notice the night before.
Elizabeth followed Garnet into the necessary, and leaned
against the vanity, watching as the little girl walked around
the toilet and pushed aside the privacy screen at the foot of
the large bathtub to reveal a step stool identical to the one
in the nursery bedroom and a child-sized invalid's chair
complete with porcelain pot.

When Garnet finished with the invalid's chair, Elizabeth
helped her set her nightgown to rights and maneuver the
step stool into place beside the tub so she could wash her
hands at the bathtub faucet. Elizabeth was feeling quite
proud of herself as she led Garnet back into the nursery
bedroom. She thought maybe even Mrs. Glenross would be
proud of her for correctly interpreting Garnet's needs and
learning to assist her, while she soothed the fretful baby—
and all at one time.

Diamond had discovered her thumb while Elizabeth was
helping Garnet in the bathroom and her crying had subsided
to little satisfied sucking sounds as she dozed. Elizabeth
softly patted the baby on her back, then placed Diamond
in her crib. All that remained was the task of diapering the
two wet bottoms and Elizabeth decided to start with Emerald and work her way down to Diamond. She grabbed
two of the neatly folded cotton cloths from the top of the
bureau and two infant sacques and walked over to Emerald's bed.

Lowering the rails, Elizabeth leaned over the bed. She

studied Emerald's diaper carefully, noting the ⌐
of the three corners and the way it was fastened,
pinned it and rolled Emerald from one hip to the ◄
order to remove it. Elizabeth lifted the sodden diaper
from Emerald and from herself, holding it gingerly by
corner as she looked around for a place to deposit it.

"Here," Garnet said, lifting the lid from a large pail.

Elizabeth dropped the diaper into the pail. Garnet shoved
the lid into place, then hurried out of the room. Elizabeth
heard the splash of water running in the necessary next
door. Alarmed, Elizabeth called out to her, "Garnet? Garnet, what are you doing?"

Garnet returned to the nursery carrying a dripping facecloth that she shoved at Elizabeth.

Realizing that Garnet knew more about the running of
the nursery and the changing of diapers than she did, Elizabeth made use of her little fount of helpful information.
"Show me."

Garnet lifted her nightgown and pretended to wash.

Balancing on one foot, Elizabeth toed off the lid of the
pail, held the facecloth over it and wrung out the excess
water before she used it to wash Emerald. Emerald awoke
at the first touch of the cold cloth. She smiled sleepily up
at Elizabeth, then lay quietly, playing with her fingers, her
dark, almost liquid, black eyes taking note of her new governess's every movement.

Finished with the bathing, Elizabeth dropped the soiled
facecloth into the pail with the wet diaper and positioned a
fresh diaper beneath Emerald. She pulled the triangular
pieces of linen together until the ends met in the middle of
Emerald's chubby little belly and loosely pinned them together with a large safety pin, taking great pains not to pull
the fabric too tightly or to bind Emerald in any way. She
was about to celebrate her accomplishment when Garnet
bumped her elbow with a decorated metal can of Fine Nursery Talcum Powder.

Elizabeth looked down and found that Garnet had already sprinkled some of the fine powder onto her hands

usy rubbing it across her abdomen and down her
couldn't help but smile at the sight, for the clever
was rubbing the talc into the fabric of her bunched
ghtie. "I know you think I'm hopeless in the nurs-
," Elizabeth said, making a funny face to emphasize her
oint to Garnet. "But, believe it or not, I know what to do
with talcum powder. I just didn't realize you used it on
babies." Elizabeth unpinned Emerald's diaper, held out her
hand and motioned for Garnet to fill it with talc, then sprinkled the powder on Emerald. As she rubbed the superfine
powder into Emerald's tender skin, Elizabeth marveled at
the contrast between the very white, very soft powder, and
Emerald's much darker, much softer body.

Emerald giggled as Elizabeth touched a ticklish spot as
she carefully repinned the diaper, and Elizabeth found herself cooing to the little girl, "Does that feel good to you?
Is that ticklish?"

"Mine." Garnet said, bumping Elizabeth's elbow again
with the box of powder and lifting the hem of her gown to
allow Elizabeth access to her stomach. Elizabeth poured
more powder into the palm of her hand and coated Garnet's
midriff with it.

In a matter of minutes both little girls were giggling with
delight at the new game. Elizabeth took advantage of their
amusement to whisk Emerald's soiled nightgown over her
head and grab the fresh one meant to go on in its place
from the bed rail. Emerald laughed uproariously as Elizabeth played peekaboo with her, pulling the old gown off
over her head, momentarily covering Emerald's face and
tousling her dark, black hair.

"What's going on in here?"

At the sound of the deep baritone voice, Elizabeth automatically let go of Emerald's nightgown. It slipped out
of her grasp and fluttered to the floor, forgotten, while Elizabeth, twisting her hands in the folds of her nightgown like
a child caught with her hand in the cookie jar, turned toward the door.

James Craig stood on the threshold watching.

Fifteen

"DADDY!" GARNET AND Emerald squealed with glee and reached out to him.

"Hello, my little beauties." James entered the bedroom, then knelt down and opened his arms to welcome Garnet. "What's been keeping you? Your sister is already downstairs with Mrs. G. awaiting her breakfast." He hugged Garnet close, lifting her into his arms as he got to his feet and walked over to Emerald's bed. "Hello, Miss Sadler," he said, his voice low and husky as he noticed that she was barefoot, and that the smoke-colored satin wrapper she wore had come untied allowing tantalizing glimpses of her delicate white lawn nightdress to show. James decided he liked the way she looked in the morning when her exceptional blue-green eyes were heavy-lidded and languid and her face still bore the marks from her pillowcase and the braid confining her thick tawny mane of hair was rumpled from sleep. And although his visits to the nursery before breakfast were a part of his everyday routine, the chance to glimpse Elizabeth Sadler looking as she looked right now gave him added incentive to continue to rise early to check on his children.

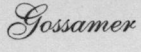

"Mr. Craig." Elizabeth nodded to her employer in what she hoped was a professional manner.

James quirked his lips into a half-smile, then turned his attention to Garnet and Emerald. He planted a kiss on Garnet's forehead, then listened intently as she babbled happily. When Garnet finished speaking, James nodded gravely as if he had understood every word of her nonsensical chatter, then replied, "You two look like you raided the flour bin again. What's going on up here? What mischief have you gotten into while Miss Sadler's back was turned?" James pretended to ask Garnet and Emerald, but he looked over their heads and directed his gaze—and his questions—at Elizabeth.

"N-n-no mischief, Mr. Craig." Elizabeth barely managed to get the words out. There was something in his look, something in his tone of voice that made her breath catch in her throat. Her heart began to pound. Her mouth went dry. And she seemed to be having trouble regulating her breathing. She stared at James Craig—at his expensive suit and the fine white powder smeared across the front of his waistcoat and tie. Elizabeth cringed, remembering the many times she had run to her mother, eager to show her love and affection by offering a hug, and received a scolding for mussing her dress instead. She gritted her teeth, straightened her shoulders, and steeled herself for James's stinging rebuke, knowing it would come once he realized that the child he held in his arms had marred his immaculate appearance.

But James Craig surprised her. He noticed the talc on Garnet, then glanced down at the powder dusting the front of his suit, shrugged his shoulders as if to say, "oh, well," then looked up at the ceiling and laughed.

And in that moment Elizabeth knew she was in danger of giving her heart away. She remembered the buttery handprints and the blotch of jam that had stained the suit he'd worn to the jail. She remembered catching an intriguing whiff of what smelled like strawberries and wanting to reach out a finger and touch the stain, then taste it to see if her sense of smell had deceived her. She wanted a taste this time, too. Not of the talcum powder on the front of his suit, but of him. James Craig. She knew how talc felt against her skin, and she knew how his lips tasted; now she wanted another longer taste. She wanted to press her lips against his, to feel the texture of his lips and share his breath. She wanted to kiss him. And she wanted him to hold her in his arms the way he had held her the first time they met and kiss her the way he had kissed her at Bender's. Until she was breathless. Until she needed his breath to sustain her. Until she recognized every nuance, every flavor of his mouth and breath and touch.

"Miss Sadler?" James repeated for the second time. "Have my busy little Treasures been giving you problems?"

"N-no problems, Mr. Craig," she stuttered, her cheeks reddening with embarrassment as she struggled to put aside her outlandish daydreams and concentrate on her job. She was a governess now. She must remember that—must remember that honorable men like James Craig did not kiss their children's governess—except in times of emergency— like yesterday when they'd needed to put on a show for Lo Peng's hatchet men She wondered, suddenly, if any of the men in the black silk tunics emblazoned with red silk dragons had followed them from San Francisco to Coryville— and if they were watching now. She shivered at the thought of another emergency kissing.

"Miss Sadler? Elizabeth?"

"Yes?"

Staring at her bemused expression, James said, "If they haven't been into mischief, how did they"—he glanced down at his suit and over at Elizabeth's satin dressing gown—"*we* all become covered in talc?"

"Garnet was helping me change Emerald's diaper. See?" Elizabeth smiled broadly, then turned to Emerald and proudly lifted her out of the baby bed to show off her handiwork.

And she watched in horror, as in the instant that Emerald

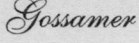

hung suspended by her arms, the diaper slid over Emerald's narrow hips, down her legs, and onto her feet.

James bit his bottom lip to strangle his laughter as Emerald kicked free of her diaper.

"Oh!" Elizabeth's incredible blue-green eyes widened in utter disbelief. "Oh! I'm so sorry!" She hugged Emerald close to her body, then looked at James. "I don't understand what went wrong. I've never—" She stopped abruptly. "I've never had this happen to me before."

"Not to worry," James said as he set Garnet on her feet, then crossed over to where Elizabeth stood and held out his arms for Emerald. The bare-bottomed tot released her hold around Elizabeth's neck and slipped into James's welcoming embrace. "It happens to me all the time."

"Really?"

"Yes, indeed." He bent and retrieved the lost diaper and the nightgown Elizabeth had dropped on the floor. He draped the garments over his shoulder, then carried Emerald over to the low bureau that doubled as a changing table. Shifting Emerald to one side so that she rode on his left hip, James opened the top right drawer of the bureau and quickly shoved the freshly laundered stacks of clothing inside. That done, he pushed the drawer closed and lay Emerald on top of the thin pad.

Elizabeth was stunned by James's proficiency in the nursery. She watched, open-mouthed, as he pulled the diaper from his shoulder and carefully unpinned it. He stuck the safety pin into the fabric of the breast pocket of his jacket, well out of Emerald's curious reach, then grasped the little girl by the ankles, lifted her hips, and positioned the diaper beneath her.

"It's been my experience," he confided as he pulled the three sections of the cloth together and pinned them snugly into place, "that children are a lot like Shetland ponies. They tend to puff out their stomachs and if you don't pull the cinch tight enough, the saddle slides down around their bellies."

He glanced over his shoulder at her, and Elizabeth saw

that his brilliant blue eyes were sparkling with mirth. "I never had a pony," she said.

"Well, of course! That explains it," he pronounced as he pulled Emerald into a sitting position, took her nightgown from its resting place on his shoulder, and dropped it over her head and tied the satin bow at her neck with a flourish.

"Explains what?" she asked, unable to resist the teasing note in his voice.

"Why you didn't know to tighten the cinch." James smoothed Emerald's gown into place and carried her back to her baby bed. "I knew a teacher with your experience and *vast* knowledge of children would know her way around a nursery."

Elizabeth frowned. "I never claimed to have a vast knowledge of children. You took it for granted . . ."

James stiffened. Elizabeth watched as the sparkle in his blue eyes disappeared, replaced by something harder and colder.

"I never take anything for granted," he told her. "I knew yesterday afternoon how much, or should I say, how little practical experience you had with small children."

"How did you know?" she asked.

"I knew from the bewildered and dismayed expression you had on your face when I first told you about the Treasures."

Elizabeth could have informed her new employer that her bewildered and dismayed expression had come from the fact that she had thought of him as single and available and had never once considered that he might be a married man with four little girls. And while she was on the subject, she could have pointed out the fact that James hadn't told her anything about the Treasures except their ages, and that he hadn't dared breathe a word about the fact that his daughters were Chinese. But Elizabeth tactfully managed to refrain from making those points. She concentrated, instead, on pulling together the pieces of her already battered sense of pride. "Is that why you came up here?" she asked, more

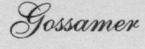

sharply than she intended when she realized her satin wrapper had come untied and hung open, revealing her nightgown and adding to her nervous, unsettled feeling. "To supervise an *incompetent* governess?"

He glanced over at Elizabeth as she snatched up the ends of the sash of her robe, pulled them tight, and tied them in a bow at her waist. *She certainly is defensive and prickly this morning.* "There's a big difference between incompetent and inexperienced," James told her as he lifted Emerald from her bed and held her in his arms. "And no, I didn't come to stand over your shoulder and pass judgment. I came to the nursery because I thought Diamond would be awake and fussy and ready for a fresh diaper and breakfast. Not necessarily in that order. She usually—"

James broke off abruptly and watched as Elizabeth slapped her palm against her forehead.

"Diamond!" she said as she rushed to the cradle. "Oh, my goodness, Garnet, we forgot about Diamond!"

"What about Diamond?" James was standing at Elizabeth's side in an instant. "Is she all right?"

"She's fine," Elizabeth answered, staring down at the baby who lay quietly gazing up at the ceiling and contentedly sucking on her fingers.

"Are you certain?" James wrinkled his nose in distaste as he leaned over the cradle and caught a whiff of Diamond's soiled undergarment.

"I'm certain," Elizabeth replied, turning her attention away from the baby in the cradle long enough to study James's profile. "Absolutely certain that you were right about Diamond. She's hungry and she needs changing. And not necessarily in that order."

James gave her a boyish grin. "Be my guest," he invited, reaching out to hand her another fresh diaper.

Elizabeth blanched. Practicing on Emerald was one thing, but Diamond . . . Diamond was so small.

Seeing the look on Elizabeth's face, James relented. "Here, you take Emmy." He handed Emerald over to Elizabeth. "And I'll change Diamond." He carried the baby over to the changing table and held out his hand for the clean diaper, which Elizabeth gladly relinquished. "Now, watch closely and pay attention," he instructed. "This is your last lesson in diaper changing. I'm not always going to be around."

"You're not going away again?"

James recognized the hint of alarm in her tone of voice for what it was—not panic, but genuine disappointment. "Not out of town," he told her. "But to the office. I do work for a living, you know." He unpinned and removed the baby's dirty diaper, then held out his hand like a surgeon demanding a scalpel. "Warm damp cloth."

Elizabeth rushed to the bathroom to get one, then returned and placed it in his hand.

"This is the tricky part," James explained, lifting Diamond's hips and gently, thoroughly washing her. "Be sure you get her clean. Babies have very sensitive skin." He shoved the dirty diaper and face cloth to the far end of the bureau, positioned the fresh linen into place. "Powder," he demanded, and Garnet bumped his leg with the can. James reached down and took the powder from her. He nodded toward the powder on Garnet, then winked at Elizabeth and Emerald. "I think you've got the powdering part down pat." He sprinkled talc on the baby, gently rubbed it in. "As for the cinching and the pinning, same procedure as before," he told Elizabeth. "But on a smaller scale. Any questions?"

Elizabeth bit her bottom lip and shook her head at the same time, then blurted out, "What about that? What do you do about that?"

"What?"

Elizabeth pointed to the baby's raw belly button. "What do you do for it? Emerald's doesn't look like that."

"Neither does Garnet's or mine," James replied. "Or yours." Suddenly intrigued by the idea of intimately exploring Elizabeth's belly button, he gave her a smoldering

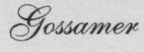

look. "But that's because ours have healed. Diamond's hasn't had time."

"Healed from what?" Elizabeth hated to sound ignorant, but her curiosity got the best of her.

James chuckled. "From birth, Miss Sadler. You're looking at what's left of Diamond's umbilical cord—the cord that attached her to her mother while she was inside the womb."

"Oh," she replied, her cheeks turning a most becoming shade of pink.

"Yes, oh," James agreed. "How refreshing to have a novice governess!" he teased.

"I'll learn," Elizabeth promised.

"You already have," James said, flashing her a truly devastating smile. "Any more questions?"

"No."

"Then, we'll pin Diamond together," he announced, doing just that by fastening the safety pin in the center of the three sections of her diaper, "and begin lesson number two."

"Lesson number two?" Elizabeth parroted.

"Breakfast," he announced.

"Yours? Mine?"

James shook his head, then nodded toward Garnet, Emerald, and Diamond. "Theirs. And we'll start with Diamond." He lifted the baby from the changing table, cradled her against his chest, then reached down and took Garnet by the hand. "Let's go eat, shall we?"

"I can't go down to breakfast dressed like this," Elizabeth protested, suddenly remembering she was still barefoot and wearing nothing but a satin wrapper and nightgown.

"Of course you can," James told her, shrugging his shoulders. "Everyone else is in their nightclothes." He nodded to indicate the little girls.

"You're not," Elizabeth said.

James glanced down at his suit and noted the blotches of white talcum powder across the front of it. "Only because I have an early meeting with my associate, Will Kee-

gan, at the office this morning. Otherwise, I'd have
breakfast in my dressing gown every morning. Come on,''
he urged. ''Or our breakfast will be cold.''

Still, Elizabeth hesitated. ''This isn't proper.''

''Sure it is,'' James told her. ''House rule number one:
Everyone eats breakfast dressed in their nightclothes.''

Elizabeth smiled. ''I don't believe you have any such
rule.''

''It's true,'' he fibbed. ''It's a Craig family custom. One
my mother adopted from the Chinese servants. And believe
me,'' he continued, embellishing the story, ''it's quite a
practical custom when you have small children. Look at all
the powder on my suit. Dressing gowns are easier to
clean.''

''The powder will brush right off and you know it.''

''Maybe so,'' James agreed, ''but what about spilled
juice and milk and porridge? And buttery handprints and
splotches of jam?''

''Surely, you're exaggerating.''

''You saw me yesterday,'' James reminded her. ''Did I
look as if I were exaggerating?''

''That was one day out of many,'' Elizabeth told him.
''And you said yourself that you'd had a little difficulty
getting away on time because you were without a governess. But you're a successful businessman, and I'm willing
to bet your morning routine usually goes as smooth as
clockwork.'' She recalled her experience as a child sitting
fully dressed beside her brother and father at the breakfast
table every morning while her mother and grandmother
dined on trays in their bedrooms. In a businessman's world
everything ran according to schedule. Owen's tutor escorted
them downstairs and stayed to report her younger brother's
progress in mathematics and economics while her father
read the morning financial pages and drank exactly one and
one-half cups of coffee. At precisely eight o'clock her father rose from the table, checked the time on his watch
against the time of the casement clock in the hall, instructed
Elizabeth to say good-bye to Owen and Mr. Frederick, then

her out the front door and down the street to
bley's Female Academy two blocks away from
. He never asked about her progress at school,
asked anything at all, and Elizabeth was expected
r to volunteer information or start a conversation on
own. She was a girl and girls were pretty decorations
meant to be seen, never heard.

"My schedule ran as smooth as clockwork before I had
the Treasures," James told her. "Now I've learned to make
allowances. Every morning brings a new adventure."

"At breakfast?" Elizabeth laughed at the idea.

James raised an eyebrow at her charming, blissful naïveté. "My dear novice governess," he said in a wise, pa-
tronizing tone. "You shouldn't worry about whether your
mode of dress is proper or improper, but if it will make
you feel any better, I'll have someone bring my dressing
gown to the dining room so I can wear it over my suit at
breakfast. In the meantime, I suggest you simply prepare
yourself. Lesson number two, the Treasures' breakfast adventure is about to begin."

Sixteen

BREAKFAST WAS A bigger adventure than Elizabeth could ever have imagined. It bore absolutely no resemblance to the staid, proper mealtimes she had endured growing up. Breakfast at the Craig mansion was homey, cheerful, and at times, chaotic. Elizabeth soon learned that feeding a hungry newborn and three equally hungry, energetic, and demanding toddlers required the instigation of a battle plan that would impress a British army field marshal.

Upon sitting down at the table to a dish of warm oatmeal, sweetened with applesauce and cream, that Mrs. G. had assured Elizabeth was Ruby's favorite breakfast food, Ruby had decided she hated, not the meal, but the bowl it was served in and refused to eat until her porridge was transferred into another bowl. At last count, they had gone through three bowls with James finally dishing the current serving of oatmeal into a crystal sherbet glass that Elizabeth was certain would be sacrificed in a show of temper before the meal ended. Although James appeared to be surprised by Ruby's oatmeal rebellion, Elizabeth was amazed at his seemingly unending patience. James seemed more than willing to allow Ruby to express her feelings as long as

ner feelings didn't include sweeping her bowls
ge off the table and onto the floor. James had in-
Ruby's whim, changing bowls three times, and still,
dn't once raised his voice in anger or lifted a hand to
ak her or to send her away from the dining table. *Her*
ther hadn't been as patient. He had insisted on excruci-
atingly correct table manners, and every little spill or clank
of silver against china brought an instant rebuke.

And while she admired his handling of the situation,
Elizabeth couldn't help wondering how much longer James
would continue to be patient, how much longer he would
accept Ruby's behavior before he lost his temper. Especially since the normally easygoing Garnet and Emerald
had decided to follow Ruby's lead and had also joined the
oatmeal revolt, insisting on crystal sherbet glasses as well,
which upset Ruby even more because she apparently
wanted to be the only one eating porridge off crystal.

Happily feeding Diamond her bottle, Elizabeth watched
as the battle of bowls continued into a second round.

James Craig didn't believe in the maxim that children
should be seen and not heard. Nor did he believe in confining the children to the nursery for every meal. He liked
sharing breakfast with his daughters. He enjoyed seeing
their precious faces first thing in the morning—even if
those faces were smeared with porridge and fruit compote.
He supposed the aristocratic society in which he belonged
considered his ideas low-class and foolish, maybe even rad-
ical, but he preferred to spend as much time with his children as possible, not shunt them off to the upper reaches
of the nursery until they were considered old enough and
civilized enough to be allowed to share mealtimes with
adults. James didn't mind the chaos of mealtimes with toddlers. He enjoyed them, especially breakfast because it gave
him one last opportunity to be with his little family before
he went out into the often hostile world of business.

This morning was fairly typical of the way his mornings
had gone for the past few days—with one exception. This
morning Elizabeth Sadler, dressed in a nightgown and robe,

sat at the dining room table sharing with him
reverently referred to as the breakfast advent.
couldn't begin to describe the feeling of conten
felt when he gazed over the three older Treasures
and watched Elizabeth feeding Diamond with a nu.
bottle filled with goat's milk. It was as if the huge hole N
Ling had left in his heart had finally begun to heal.

James tried to recall the last time he'd shared the breakfast table with anyone except the children, Mrs. G., or Will
Keegan. Oh, he'd instituted the policy of sharing breakfast
with the Treasures and three of the last four governesses,
but unfortunately, he hadn't been able to successfully en-
force it. The former faro dealer and the former saloon girl
he had first hired to act as governess to the Treasures had
been in the habit of sleeping late—much too late to breakfast with him—and at the time, he'd needed them too badly
to insist that they bring the girls downstairs for breakfast.
And the Chinese laundress James had hired after the departure of the first two governesses had flatly refused to go
against a lifetime of training and sit down at the same table
with her male employer. And although the last governess
had complied with his wishes, she had done so grudgingly,
protesting all the while that children as young as Ruby,
Garnet, and Emerald shouldn't be allowed to eat with adults
or express their likes or dislikes when it came to eating.
She insisted that allowing them to do so was upsetting for
the children and impossible for the adults.

Now that she was gone, James was determined to prove
her wrong. And he was going to use Elizabeth Sadler to
help him. Starting today. And today was proving to be
every bit as challenging as the day he had taken over as
director of Craig Capital, Ltd. James wasn't sure, but he
thought that after privately sharing morning "coffee" together, Ruby was upset because he had allowed Elizabeth,
Garnet, Emerald, and Diamond to intrude on their father-
daughter early morning tea party by joining them at the
dining table for breakfast.

"No, Ruby," he said softly but firmly as Ruby decided

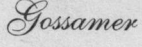

out her earlier threat and sweep her sherbet dish
oatmeal off the table and onto the floor. James put
the spoonful of oatmeal he was feeding Emerald and
Ruby's sherbet dish up and out of her reach. "That's
ough."

"Don't like!" Ruby announced.

"Fine," James said, "you don't have to eat any more
oatmeal." He set her dish of porridge beside his cup and
saucer. "Would you like to share my breakfast?" He
glanced down at his plate of scrambled eggs and kippers.
He scooped up a forkful of fluffy yellow eggs and held it
out to her.

"No!" Ruby pushed his fork away. "Taste bad! Want
oapmeal!"

"Oatmeal," James corrected, automatically emphasizing
the *t* in oat. "All right." He ate the forkful of scrambled
eggs she pushed away, then picked up Ruby's dish of oatmeal and set it before her.

"No, that bowl!" she insisted.

James fed Emerald another spoonful of oatmeal, took
another quick bite of the excellent eggs and kippers on his
plate, then pushed back his chair and got to his feet. "If
you will excuse me for a moment," he said to Elizabeth.

"Certainly," she answered, then held her breath, watching and waiting for the explosion of temper she knew was
sure to come.

James walked over to the breakfast buffet and surveyed
it for a moment, then left the dining room. He returned a
few minutes later carrying a sterling silver sugar basin
shaped like a sea shell and lined with a pink cut glass dish,
a green china egg cup, and a ruby red crackled glass candy
dish in the shape of a grape leaf. James placed the ruby-
red bowl in front of Ruby, then picked up the sherbet dish
containing her oatmeal and scraped the contents into the
candy dish. "Here you go, Ruby," he said, making a big
production of presenting her breakfast to her. "A ruby-red
bowl fit for a queen."

Ruby squealed with glee.

Anticipating disappointment on the part of ⊂
Emerald, he set the sterling silver sugar basin with
glass liner in front of Garnet and raked the oatme
her sherbet glass into the sugar basin. Then, he rep
the process with Emerald, using the green china egg
as her porridge bowl. "There," he announced when he
finished, "you each have a beautiful and unique bowl from
which to eat the delicious porridge Mrs. G. made for you."

"Not eat kips yeggs. Eat oapmeal, Daddy." Garnet announced, testing the waters a bit. She dipped her curved
child's spoon into her oatmeal, then thrust it up in James's
direction.

"Maybe that's the problem," Elizabeth ventured.

James raised a questioning eyebrow at her.

"Maybe their rebellion isn't about their bowls, but
what's in them. Maybe they've wondered why you eat kippers and eggs when oatmeal's supposed to be so delicious."

"You mean they expect me to eat porridge, too?"

Elizabeth bit her bottom lip to keep from giggling at the
horrified expression on James's face as he stood gazing
across the table at her. "It looks that way to me."

"But I haven't eaten oatmeal since I was in short pants.
Surely they don't . . ."

The giggles Elizabeth had been trying to suppress did
escape her lips at the image of a grown-up James Cameron
Craig eating oatmeal in short pants. "Why not? You expect
them to eat it every morning. If it's good enough for
them . . ."

James thought about it for a moment. Elizabeth was
right. It *was* a bit hypocritical of him to expect the Treasures to eat the same breakfast of oatmeal every morning
when he had a buffet of foods from which to choose. "All
right," he capitulated. "I can't argue with all of you. You
win. I'll have oatmeal." Before reseating himself at the
table, James picked up his breakfast plate, carried it to the
small table beside the buffet reserved for dirty dishes, and
left it. Then he picked up a clean porridge bowl and . . .

"Uh-hem," Elizabeth loudly cleared her throat.

...es glanced back over his shoulder at her and seeing ...knowing expression, replaced the bowl and picked up ...up and saucer in its place. He lifted the top from the ...afing dish containing the oatmeal, set it aside, then filled .he teacup with oatmeal. That done, he spooned a generous helping onto the matching saucer. "Just for that," he said to Elizabeth, "we all eat oatmeal."

He walked back to the dining table and set the cup of oatmeal down on the table in front of his chair, then carried the saucer over to Elizabeth and placed it before her. "I was going to be gracious," he added. "And allow you to select from the buffet, but as you so helpfully pointed out, if it isn't fair for me to eat kippers and scrambled eggs in front of the Treasures when they eat oatmeal, it isn't fair for their governess to eat kippers and eggs or sausage or ham or steak in front of them either."

"You're *too* kind," Elizabeth replied sweetly. Too sweetly.

"Yes, I am," James acknowledged, picking up a spoon and digging into his cupful of oatmeal. "Mmm," he announced to the Treasures. "Delicious."

Elizabeth looked down at the baby she held. "Diamond's finished her bottle. What should I do now?"

James set his spoon aside. "Hand her to me and I'll take care of her," he suggested, reaching for the baby. "While you eat your porridge like a good little governess."

"Oh, no, you don't." Elizabeth eyed him warily. "You're not going to get out of eating your porridge that easily. Just tell me what to do next and I'll do it. After all," she added, "you can't keep giving me these free lessons."

Outmaneuvered, James handed Elizabeth a white linen napkin. James's fingers brushed hers. Elizabeth started at the jolt of awareness she felt at the merest touch of his fingers against hers. She looked up and met James's gaze. She could tell by the expression on his face that he'd felt the same jolt. He let go of the napkin. She caught it. "Now what?" she asked, nervously moistening her lips with her tongue.

"Drape this across your shoulder." James issued in-structions in a brusque, husky tone of voice. "Then Diamond facedown against it and lightly pat her on back until she burps."

"How do you know she'll burp?"

"Trust me," James said, "she'll burp."

And after a few minutes of patting, Diamond did.

Amazed, Elizabeth looked down at the baby, then over at James. "She did it."

"Of course she did," he answered. "And now that you know how, be sure to burp her just like that after every meal. Once she's been fed and burped, she usually sleeps for a while."

"She's already sleeping," Elizabeth told him. "In fact, that's about all she's done since I've been here."

James shrugged. "Babies are like that." He reached over and picked up the little silver bell beside his coffee cup and rang it.

Delia appeared at his side almost immediately. "Delia, would you please take Diamond up to her bed and sit with her until Miss Sadler and I have finished our breakfast and discussed the nursery schedule?"

"Of course, sir." Delia lifted Diamond from Elizabeth's arms and carried her out of the dining room and up the stairs to the nursery.

Elizabeth looked bereft.

"Don't worry, Miss Sadler," James said, nodding to-ward the Treasures. "I'm sure you'll have plenty to keep you busy with these three moppets."

"What's that about my moppets?" Will Keegan boomed from the doorway.

Ruby squealed at the sight of him and hurriedly scram-bled down from her chair to fling herself at his legs. Garnet followed right behind her, both little girls demanding that Will pick them up and hold them.

Will obliged by lifting Garnet into his arms first, then hoisting Ruby into place as he strolled over to the buffet and sniffed at the dishes covering the array of eggs, pota-

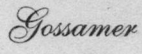

toes, ham, kippers, bacon, kidneys, steak, porridge, and pastries on the sideboard.

"Good morning, Will," James said, when Will walked over to the dining table and deposited the Treasures in their usual seats. James then turned to Elizabeth and said, "Elizabeth, this is my closest friend and associate, Will Keegan, senior vice president of Craig Capital, Limited. Will, may I present Miss Elizabeth Sadler, our new governess?"

Will Keegan studied Elizabeth for several minutes, taking in each nuance of her appearance, before he reached out and grasped her hand in a firm handshake. "Pleased to meet you, Miss Sadler."

"Likewise, Mr. Keegan," Elizabeth politely replied.

"Call me Will," he suggested. "All my friends do. And, Beth, I'm willing to bet you and I are going to be friends."

"Thank you, *Will*," Elizabeth murmured, a bit taken back by the bold, teasing expression in his golden-brown eyes. Suddenly conscious of how she must look dressed in her wrapper and nightgown and with her hair straggling free of its braid, Elizabeth shifted in her seat, straightened the lapels of her satin wrapper, and tightened the sash. "You have my permission to call me Elizabeth."

James watched the interaction between Will and Elizabeth, and for the first time in many years, he felt the swift bite of competitive rivalry nipping at his heels. A few months older than he, Will was the eldest son of the minister of the First Presbyterian Church in Hong Kong. Refusing to follow in his father's footsteps after finishing University, Will had gone to work as a clerk at Craig Capital. He had begun work five months before James graduated and had been the clerk assigned to James when he entered the family business. But Will hadn't stayed James's clerk. Once he realized he'd been unfairly promoted over Will, James had prevailed upon his father to promote Will and had begun his work at Craig Capital as Will's clerk instead. The two young men had become very close over the years, rising through the ranks of the shipping and banking firm Randall Craig had founded in Hong Kong to be-

come director and vice president of an international
organization. They had grown up together and become as
close as brothers. And although he knew it was quite natural to feel a sense of rivalry at times, James didn't like
the feeling. He loved Will like a brother. He trusted Will
with his money, his corporation, and his life, trusted him
as he had never trusted anyone in his life. But he didn't
like the way Will seemed to look through Elizabeth's mod-
est satin wrapper or the cozy way he tried to flirt with her.
He wasn't convinced it was harmless. Because all at once,
James wasn't so sure Will could be trusted not to poach in
his domain. "Pull up a chair, Will, and sit down," James
said abruptly. "Your leering is making *Miss Sadler* uncomfortable."

Will threw James a sharp look. "I wasn't aware I was
leering. My apologies, Elizabeth."

"Apologies accepted," she answered. "Please, won't
you join us for breakfast?"

She issued the invitation so naturally that Will decided
to pay closer attention to the familiar surroundings. What
at first glance had seemed like a normal breakfast in the
bachelor household of James Craig was something else entirely. Will looked over the dining table crowded with sherbet glasses and china and crockery, at the two oldest girls
happily plunging their spoons into the sugar basin and a
red grape-leaf candy dish and dipping out porridge, at Emerald jabbering to her father and pointing to a green egg
cup as he fed her a spoonful of oatmeal. And Elizabeth and
James sitting cozily together at the dining room table
dressed in their nightclothes exchanging intimate looks and
making reference to things in a language that included the
Treasures, but seemed to exclude everyone else. Will
fought to keep his jaw from dropping in amazement as
James wordlessly refilled Elizabeth's teacup without asking
and as she bent to retrieve the napkin he dropped and
handed it to him so that he could wipe oatmeal from Emerald's ear. A miracle was taking place right before his
eyes. James and the new governess were laying the foun-

...ons for a new family. Although he wasn't all that hun-
y, Will decided this morning's meal was too good to pass
p.

"Smells delicious," he said. "What's for breakfast?"

"Oatmeal." James and Elizabeth answered in unison.

"In the most unusual container of your choice," Elizabeth added.

Will raised an eyebrow at that. "Oatmeal? What about all that food going to waste on the buffet?"

"We're experimenting with a new breakfast policy," James told him. "As of today, we eat what the Treasures eat. And they're eating oatmeal."

"All right," Will agreed with a frown. "As long as it stops there."

"What do you mean as long as it stops there?" James asked.

"Well, I assume this new breakfast policy is part of Elizabeth's new regimen for the Treasures," Will elaborated.

"That's right," Elizabeth answered.

"Well, just how far do you plan to go with your changes?" Will teased. "If I continue to join you for breakfast on a daily basis, may I make suggestions as to the menu occasionally or will it be written in stone? And shall I continue to wear a suit and tie or has a dressing gown and slippers become de rigueur?"

Seventeen

"OF COURSE NOT!" Elizabeth looked over at Will Keegan and burst out laughing at his outrageous teasing. She knew she should be mortified at the mere suggestion that she or James Craig had behaved improperly after the scandal she caused back home in Providence. But Providence was an entire continent away and Grandmother Sadler's harsh actions seemed to have lost a good bit of their sting—especially after the scandal she had caused yesterday at Lo Peng's. Not that she intended to scandalize the citizenry of Coryville by vandalizing businesses or terrorizing the Chinese merchants. Nothing of the sort. As far as Elizabeth was concerned, her brief days of impulsive, reckless behavior were over. She had learned her lesson. From now on, Elizabeth meant to be the very model of decorum. But even proper models of decorum needed, she had learned, a sense of humor—especially now that she was working with three demanding Treasures and a newborn baby. Will Keegan hadn't meant any harm. He was James's friend and there was nothing malicious about his teasing.

"As long as we understand each other," Will replied. "I'm not one to turn down offers of breakfast. . . ."

James snorted.

"...'ll even eat whatever mush you serve up to the ...es," Will continued. "As long as you allow a little ...y now and then. But I draw the line at sitting down ...t breakfast in my birthday suit."

"I should think you'd be accustomed to it by now," ...lizabeth retorted, blushing prettily at Will's brashness.

"How so?" Will asked.

"After hearing you speak, I assumed you were originally from Hong Kong and that you had known Mr. Craig for a good many years," she told him.

Will poured himself a cup of coffee from the silver coffee urn and sat down across the table from James. "That's true," he said. "I guess we've known each other about twelve or thirteen years now." He looked over at James for confirmation.

James nodded at Will, then shrugged his shoulders in a gesture meant to convey the idea that he hadn't the slightest idea where Elizabeth's questions were leading.

"And your habit of sharing breakfast is a long-standing one?" she asked.

"I suppose so," Will admitted warily.

"Then I should think you'd be accustomed to sitting down to breakfast in your nightclothes"—she paused for effect—"seeing as how it's a long-standing tradition Mr. Craig's mother adopted from the Chinese."

Will pretended to be aghast. "Where did you hear such rubbish?"

Elizabeth cast a pointed look in James's direction.

James set his coffee cup into its saucer and quickly covered his mouth with his hand to disguise his laugh.

"Hah!" Will exclaimed. "Nobody would dare sit down at Julia Cameron Craig's table—at breakfast or any other time of the day—unless they were properly turned out, and the entire British population of Hong Kong knew it."

"Uh-hem." James cleared his throat, trying to interrupt before Will exposed him any further.

"Jamie, what were you thinking of to spin Elizabeth a yarn like that?"

"I suspect it was to put me at ease about my attire and my untidy appearance," Elizabeth admitt. consciously pushing back a lock of hair that had es the confines of her braid and fallen across her foref. "You see, I didn't want to come downstairs for breaki until I'd had time to dress properly."

"Well, if that's what's worrying you," Will tried to make amends for putting Elizabeth on the spot, "don't fret about it. Jamie's not dressed yet, either."

"Oh, but he is." Elizabeth told him. "He's wearing his dressing gown over his suit."

Will lifted the tablecloth and peered under the table. Sure enough, beneath his silk dressing gown, Jamie wore a pair of woolen suit trousers and socks and dress shoes polished to a high sheen.

"What are you doing here, Will?" James asked when Will straightened up in his chair and opened his mouth to speak.

"We have a meeting this morning, remember?" Will answered, taking James's cue and wisely deciding to refrain from pursuing the topic of nightclothes and dressing gowns any further.

James set down the spoon he was using to feed Emerald and reached over and wiped the little girl's face with his napkin. He glanced over at the clock on the dining room wall. "Our meeting is scheduled for nine sharp. What brings you by so early?"

"I came for breakfast," Will told him. "And because I thought you might like the opportunity to go over the details we didn't get to discuss yesterday...." He threw James a sharp look.

"I had to leave for San Francisco early yesterday morning," James explained. "There wasn't enough time to let you know that I wouldn't be in the office. Didn't you get my message? I asked Mrs. G. to send word."

"I got your message when I returned from the mining camps late yesterday morning, but the train had already left for the city," Will said. "Otherwise, I might have joined

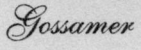

..., We could have gone over the fine points of these rail-
...ad contracts en route. How were things at the Montgom-
ry Street office?''

"I didn't go to the office," James replied. "I had other
more important business to attend to." James picked up his
coffee cup and downed the contents, then took his napkin
off his lap and placed it on the table. The Treasures had
finished eating. It was time to help Elizabeth get them upstairs to the nursery and get them cleaned up. And he
needed to talk to her about her daily schedule and what he
expected of her.

"More important than our negotiations with the Central
Pacific?" Will raised his voice in exasperation. "What's
more important than that?"

James pushed back his chair back from the table and
stood up. "The Treasures, Will. Three, no, four, innocent,
defenseless little girls who rely on me for food and shelter
and love and support.''

Will held up his hand. "That goes without saying, Jamie.''

"Maybe so, but I'm saying it. The needs of four little
girls are more important to me than the Central Pacific Railroad rolling stock negotiations. And acquiring a governess
to help me take care of those four little girls is more important to me than the Central Pacific negotiations." James
bent down and lifted Emerald from her high chair. "And
if I ever allow myself to forget that my family comes before
Craig Capital, I'll sell it." He stared across the table at
Will. "So help me, God, I'll sell it, Will. Lock, stock, and
barrel, right down to the last brass paper clip. I'm not going
to make the same mistake twice." Balancing Emerald on
one hip, he eased Ruby's chair away from the table, helped
her down, and took her hand. "Now, if Miss Sadler has
finished her meal . . ."

Elizabeth nodded quickly, blotted her lips with her napkin, and rose to her feet.

Will politely stood as Elizabeth helped Garnet out of a
high chair identical to Emerald's and into her arms.

"If you'll excuse us, we'll take the girls upstairs," Jar continued.

Will nodded.

"And I'll need a few moments to go over Miss Sadler's schedule and her responsibilities as governess before I can join you to discuss the Central Pacific deal," James added. He glanced back up at the clock on the wall. "Twenty minutes at best."

"Fine," Will replied, rather coolly. "That will give me time to finish my breakfast."

"I'm sorry," Elizabeth said as she and James started up the stairs leading to the second floor nursery.

"For what?" James asked.

"I'm sorry you missed that important meeting with Will yesterday."

"As you so pointedly reminded me last night, that trip to San Francisco was of my making," James told her as they reached the door of the nursery. "There's no reason for you to apologize. If I hadn't asked the police to track you down and pick you up for questioning, you would never have been arrested."

"Maybe," Elizabeth agreed with a shrug of her shoulders. "Or maybe not. I was so hurt and so angry about Owen's—about my brother's death,"—she paused for a moment and fought for control—"I think I may have been secretly spoiling for a fight." She looked up at James. "Not that I regret what I did to Lo Peng's establishment. Because I don't." She looked up at James, and lifted her chin a notch higher, until he could see the challenge glinting from the depths of her aquamarine-colored eyes. "But I've learned my lesson."

The determined glint in her blue-green eyes and the thrust of her chin dared James to contradict her. That she thought it necessary to convince him that she was a lady worthy of the position of governess to his children made James want to tease her just a little. "Then you *are* ashamed of yourself for destroying Lo Peng's establishment."

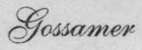

"Ashamed?" She bristled like a wet cat. "Of course I'm not ashamed of my actions. Why, if I was still in San Francisco, and the circumstances were the same, I'd do the same thing today!"

James smiled down at her. "Please, not again today. One skirmish a day is all I can handle, and we've already been through the Oatmeal Wars."

"You don't have to worry." She stiffened and became all prim and proper once again. "I don't intend to cause any more scandals."

Lord, but he wanted to kiss her! The thought popped into his brain and James realized that nothing he had ever thought was truer. She made her promise to him with so much fire and conviction in her voice and on her face that James had to stop himself from pulling her into his arms and following through with his inclination. Hadn't she learned that oftentimes scandals weren't controllable? That some scandals were caused by the overactive imaginations of bored gossips and like beauty, were found in the eyes of the beholders? "Don't make promises you can't keep, Elizabeth." His voice was deep and thick with emotion.

"But I do intend to keep it, Mr. Craig. I assure you I won't be participating in any more scandals. Not in Coryville. Not while I'm in your employ and responsible for the lives and reputations of the Treasures."

James cocked his head in Elizabeth's direction and stared at her with a puzzled look on his face. "There's plenty of time for that. It's a bit early for you to concern yourself with their reputations, don't you think?"

"Oh, no," Elizabeth replied earnestly. "It's never too early. A girl's reputation is her most precious endowment."

"Oh, come now," James scoffed. "Surely a woman's intellect and her accomplishments are much more important than her reputation."

It was Elizabeth's turn to scoff. "Men don't marry women for their intellect."

James smiled. "Men don't necessarily marry women for their spotless reputations, either."

"Maybe not," Elizabeth agreed. "But a girl with a spotless reputation is much more likely to marry well than a girl with a ruined one. It's the duty of girls from the best families to marry well."

"I'd say it depends upon the girls," James told her. "And the men doing the marrying."

"It should be that way." Elizabeth smiled a sad, far-off little smile that spoke of heartbreak and personal experience. "But all too often people don't look beyond the surface of things. That's why girls from good families must be beyond reproach. They must aspire to higher standards than girls from lesser families, and in your daughters' cases, it will be so much harder for society to believe that it's possible for the Treasures to attain them because they're . . ."

"Chinese?" James queried, wondering if Elizabeth was going to balk at that again.

"Well, that, too." She had the grace to blush. "But I was going to say 'without their mother.' "

"I don't understand," James said. "It looks to me that if having Chinese blood flowing through their veins and imprinted upon their features is the problem, then being without their Chinese parent would be beneficial in society's eyes."

"Yes, but everyone knows girls of a certain breeding need their mothers' guiding hands, and that no matter how loyal and dedicated the household employees, no matter how good the teacher or governess, hired help cannot teach girls the refinement and breeding society requires. That level of refinement can only come from the teachings of the mother."

"Hogwash!" James exploded. "Who taught you that rubbish? Your mother?"

Elizabeth looked startled. "My grandmother."

"And you believed her?"

"Of course I did," Elizabeth said. "I had no reason not to. She was teaching me the lessons of life."

"*Her* lessons of life, not yours. And what she taught you

was that you weren't quite up to her impossible standards,''
James muttered beneath his breath, angry at the injustice
society heaped on innocent women and young girls, angry
that women like Elizabeth's grandmother not only believed
in such garbage, but preached it. ''And where was your
mother while your grandmother was spouting that worthless
tripe?''

''Upstairs hiding in her bedroom.'' Elizabeth nearly bit
her tongue, unable to believe that after all these years she'd
admitted a truth to a virtual stranger that she hadn't even
admitted to herself. Her mother had avoided her responsibilities and her duties to her children and had kept herself
hidden away in her bedroom for years to avoid Grandmother Sadler's vicious tongue.

''Why didn't your mother teach you about duty and refinement and the inferiority of household servants?''

''Because she didn't know those things.''

''Why not? Wasn't she a member of a best family? She
must have been to have married into your father's family.''

''Of course she was,'' Elizabeth said. ''But her mother
died when she was small, and she couldn't benefit from her
mother's guidance. My mother didn't have the proper background for entree into society.''

''It figures,'' James muttered.

''What?''

''Your grandmother felt that your father married beneath
his station,'' James said.

''Yes,'' Elizabeth admitted. That was part of it. But there
was something more, another deep family secret Elizabeth
had only heard mentioned twice in her lifetime—the day
her father died suddenly of apoplexy at the age of thirty-
seven and the day her grandmother had disowned her. It
had tainted the family atmosphere for years and hung un-
spoken and unacknowledged, like a pall in the air until the
whole house reeked of it. Elizabeth couldn't bring herself
to acknowledge it aloud, but she was to blame for her
mother's unhappiness and her father's distance. She was to

blame because she was the reason her father had been forced to marry her mother.

"And I'll bet your Grandmother never let you or your mother or your father forget it."

"No."

James let go of Ruby's hand and bent low to ask, "Ruby Button, will you please open the door for Miss Sadler and Daddy?"

Ruby looked up at her daddy, then at the new governess. "No," she answered defiantly.

"I'll get it," Elizabeth volunteered, reaching for the doorknob.

"No!" Ruby exclaimed, running ahead of Elizabeth to grasp the doorknob. "I open door for Daddy!"

James shook his head. "It figures. One rebellion a day is never enough." He stepped back to allow Elizabeth to enter the nursery, then set Emerald on her feet. She crawled over to watch as Ruby ran over to the shelf lining the play-room wall and began pulling down a pile of building blocks.

Eager to join her sisters, Garnet squirmed in Elizabeth's arms. Elizabeth put her on the floor, then watched as Ruby built a tower of blocks and ruthlessly knocked it down, sending wooden blocks flying across the floor.

"Ruby, please," Elizabeth said, firmly but gently. "Not so hard. You'll hit your sisters."

"No!" Ruby looked to James for approval.

But James shook his head. "Ruby, you must listen to Miss Sadler now. She's in charge of the nursery. You must mind her."

He turned to Elizabeth. "You're the governess and it's important that the Treasures understand that when they are with you, you're in charge."

Elizabeth nearly panicked. She couldn't be in charge of the nursery, because she had no idea what to do. "What about you?" she asked James.

"I'm going to work."

"What do I do?" She lowered her voice to a whisper,

not wanting the girls or Delia to hear. "You know I don't know what to do. I've never done this before."

James reached under his dressing gown, searching his jacket pockets until he found what he was looking for. He took out a folded piece of Craig Capital stationery and handed it to her. "It's the Treasures' daily schedule. I wrote it down for you."

Elizabeth unfolded the sheet of paper and read it aloud. "Six A.M.—up and dressed for seven o'clock breakfast with father. Eight-thirty A.M.—supervised play time in the nursery. Ten A.M.—lessons." She glanced over at James. "Lessons? What kind of lessons?"

He shrugged. "Start with the basics. The alphabet, counting to ten, colors. Read them a story. Be creative."

Elizabeth nodded in agreement, then read the remainder of the schedule. "Eleven A.M.—lunch in the nursery. Twelve P.M.—nap. Two P.M.—daily walk in park for everyone including Diamond."

"Mrs. G. will show you where the carriages are kept, and Delia will accompany you."

"All right," Elizabeth said.

"Four P.M.—return home. Four-thirty P.M.—dinner in nursery. Six P.M.—baths. Seven P.M.—story. Seven-thirty or eight P.M.—bedtime." Again, she looked over at James for an explanation.

"Sometimes they fall asleep before the end of the story," he said. "And sometimes the story is interrupted because, even though we're weaning her, Emerald often cries for a bottle at bedtime."

"That's a long day," Elizabeth told him. "And a very full schedule."

"Yes, it is," James agreed. "And I'm afraid your day is even longer. You see, although we try to keep Diamond on the same basic schedule as the others, she requires an early morning feeding or two." He winced as he said the words.

"How early?" Elizabeth asked.

"I feed her before I retire for the night," James said.

"Then she usually requires another bottle around two or three in the morning."

Elizabeth gasped. No wonder the man had been desperate to find a governess. No wonder he was willing to have her arrested, bail her out of jail, and agree to pay her the princely sum of fifty dollars a day to come to Coryville. No wonder he looked so tired. No wonder his wife had died. A schedule like this could kill an ox.

Recognizing the note of alarm in her voice and the expression on her face, James tried to reassure her. "Mrs. G. and Delia will help you during the day. And I'll do my share at night. I'm usually home in time to help with baths, get them ready for bed, and read them a story."

"I'm relieved to hear it," she replied.

Realizing her sarcasm masked her apprehension, James gave her a knowing look. "And not only that," he said, "but you'll be relieved to see me as well."

"Is there anything else?" she asked, glancing back down at his bold handwriting on the schedule he'd written out for her to follow, suddenly uncomfortable with the warm, understanding expression on his face and in his eyes.

"You did well this morning." He walked over and lifted her chin so he could look into her eyes. This time James didn't attempt to rein in his impulses. Taking full advantage of her speechlessness, he gently caressed her full bottom lip with the pad of his thumb. "You did *very* well this morning. I'm quite proud of you, Elizabeth." His voice took on a rough husky quality. "Don't worry. You'll do fine. Forget everything your grandmother ever taught you or said to you, and follow your own instincts and you'll do just fine." He winked at her. "Any more questions?"

"Are you sure you have to go to work this morning?"

She looked so appealing, standing there in her nightgown and bare feet, imploring him not to go to work, that James forced himself to fight the urge to give in and stay home and show her everything he knew about babies, including how to make them. Instead of kissing the worried look off her face the way he longed to do, he managed to laugh. "I most certainly do,'' he said. ''Especially if you expect me to pay you the outrageous sum of fifty dollars a day.'' Unable to resist, he leaned closer until he was within an inch of exchanging breath with her. ''It's time to go to work, now. Time for you to earn your money.''

''It's time for you to earn money,'' Elizabeth rebounded. ''As much as you can. Because when I'm done with today's schedule, I may decide fifty dollars isn't enough!''

James laughed again. ''There is one more thing, Elizabeth.''

''What now?'' she asked, rather ungraciously, wondering what other surprises he had up his sleeve.

''Dinner for grown-ups is served at eight,'' he said. ''And I would consider it a very great honor if you'd join me.''

Eighteen

"DO YOU WANT to talk about it?" Will asked when James reentered the dining room.

"What?" James gave Will a blank look and tried to avoid the question by pretending not to understand.

But Will ignored James's pretended ignorance and pressed on. "Don't try to fool me, Jamie. You're no good at it. I've known you too long. If you don't want to talk to me about what's bothering you, all you have to say is, 'Will, I don't want to talk about it.'"

"Will, I don't want to talk about it," James replied.

"Well, you need to," Will decided. "I haven't seen you so snarling and territorial in years."

James clenched his teeth and pinched the bridge of his nose, then heaved a resigned sigh and shrugged out of his dressing gown. He draped the silk garment over the back of a chair, then, realizing he was still covered in talcum powder, began brushing at the front of his suit. "Have you finished your breakfast?" he asked Will.

"Yes." Will pushed back his chair and stood up.

James glanced up at the ceiling. "Then let's go. We can talk in private while we walk to the office. I'll let Mrs. G. know we're leaving." He left the dining room and walked

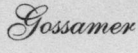

...ne kitchen, where Helen Glenross sat drinking a cup
...ea at the large oak worktable.

"Breakfast was delicious as usual, Mrs. G."

"Thank you, sir."

"Ruby settled down a bit once I gave her the red dish.
Thanks for the help."

"You're welcome, sir." Normally Helen Glenross didn't
interfere in her employer's business, but Mr. Craig had
been having such a hard time of it since that last poor
excuse for a governess left, and she wanted to reassure him
that this time he'd made a wise choice. "How did our Miss
Sadler do?"

James grinned. "She did fine, Mrs. G. You were right
about her. She's not as experienced with small children as
I had hoped, but she handled herself and the Treasures very
well."

"I'm glad to hear it, sir."

"Mr. Keegan and I are leaving for the office. I said good-
bye to the girls," James told her. "And I made it clear to
them that Miss Sadler is in charge of the nursery, and I
wrote out a schedule for her to follow. She's to come to
you for help if she needs anything. It may take her a while
to settle in and become accustomed to the Treasures and
the way in which we do things, but her presence should
help relieve some of your responsibilities. I would appreciate it, however, if you can continue to help with Diamond.
Miss Sadler is a bit apprehensive around her."

Mrs. G. nodded. "That's perfectly understandable. A society lass like our Miss Sadler probably hasn't been around
many newborns."

"No," James agreed. "But she'll learn soon enough."

"That's for certain," Mrs. G. said. "And it will be a
right good training for her. She'll be an old hand at caring
for babies by the time her own little ones come along."

James paused and looked at Mrs. G. as if the idea that
Elizabeth might one day choose to leave his house to marry
and have children of her own had never occurred to him.
"I suppose you're right."

Helen Glenross raised an eyebrow at him. "Well, s
you weren't thinking our Miss Sadler will stay in ser
forever." She shook her head. "Oh, no, that one will fi.
a husband before too long and raise children of her own
She'll not run out on you like the last governess did or
cause herself to be dismissed like the others, but you can
wager that she won't be staying on permanently."

James knew better than to ask, but he couldn't seem to
help himself. "Why not?"

"Because one day you may decide to bring home a
bride," Mrs. G. answered. "New brides always make
changes in the household staff. And our Miss Sadler won't
want to stay where she isn't needed." *Or wanted.* Helen
Glenross had eyes. She understood, even if James Craig did
not, why Miss Sadler had decided to stay. And if Mr. Craig
got tired of being a widower and brought home a new bride,
Miss Sadler would be on her way. Not that Miss Sadler
was after his money. Nothing of the sort. From what she'd
seen of her, Elizabeth Sadler looked very much like a
young lady on the verge of falling in love. It wouldn't hurt
to give Mr. Craig a tiny warning not to take his new governess for granted.

James cleared his throat as he headed for the dining room
door. "I don't think you have to worry about that any time
soon, Mrs. G. What innocent young girl would be willing
to take on a man of my reputation? Especially when I come
equipped with four Chinese daughters?"

"Maybe an innocent young Chinese girl," Mrs. G. replied, teasing.

But James Craig didn't hear the teasing note in her voice.
He only heard the suggestion. He glanced down at the
sheen on his highly polished shoes. "Not again, Mrs. G.
Never again. I don't think I could survive it."

⸻⸱⸱⸱⸱⸺

"I THOUGHT WE were going to talk." Will Keegan
lengthened his stride to keep pace with James. James hadn't

d a word since leaving the house. In fact, he hadn't said word since he'd left the kitchen. And James had left the kitchen in a hurry. He'd paused long enough in the study to retrieve his leather satchel, then headed straight out the front door at such a pace, Will immediately suspected the kitchen might be ablaze.

"Will, I don't want to talk about it."

"Well, that's just too bloody damn bad," Will told him. "Because something's got your tail tied into knots, and I'm not going to let you keep it all bottled up inside. It makes you too bloody hard to live with! Now, what is it about Beth that's got you all lathered up?"

"What makes you think that what's bothering me has anything to do with Elizabeth?" James snapped.

Will burst out laughing. "How can it not? Two days ago you were the same Jamie Craig I've come to know and love, and today you're a virtual stranger. So what's changed in the one full day since I last saw you except that you've gone and hired yourself a right beauty of a governess named Beth?"

"Her name is Elizabeth, Will," James said. "As in LilyBeth. Does that name ring a bell?"

"San Francisco Lilybeth? Russ House Lilybeth? The one the men were gossiping about?" Will stopped dead in his tracks in the middle of the brick-paved path that led from James's house around the park to the Main Street office of Craig Capital, Ltd., beside the First National Bank of Coryville.

"The same," James said.

"Thunderation, Jamie! What were you thinking to bring her to Coryville and into your home?"

"I hired her as governess for my children," James reminded him.

"After you spent the night with her in San Francisco," Will added. "Are you sure that's wise? How many nights have you spent in her company? What do you know about Elizabeth Sadler?"

"I've only spent one night in her company." James

paused, frowning. "Two, if you count last night."

"Exactly my point," Will said. "I know you're desper ate for a governess, but you don't know enough about this woman to take her into your home and into your bed."

James sighed. "I didn't take her to bed, Will. I spent the night in her room at the Russ House, but not in her bed."

Will glanced over at James, a skeptical look on his handsome face. "She looked awfully cozy in her nightclothes, Jamie, with her hair still in its braid and her feet bare. She looked completely at home and natural—as if she was accustomed to sharing an intimate breakfast with you."

James laughed. "You call the presence of four children, a housekeeper, two maids, and yourself intimate?"

Will quirked an eyebrow at James. "She invited me to join you as if she had the right—as if you'd given her the right. What was I supposed to think? The other governesses you hired didn't come to breakfast in their nightclothes."

"That was my fault," James said. "I rushed her. I didn't give her a chance to bathe and dress because I—"

"What?" Will asked, although he had a very good idea that James's next words were only going to confirm his suspicions.

"I wanted to be sure she ate something," James said.

"Why?"

"Because she didn't touch her supper tray last night. Because I thought that—" He stopped and raked one hand through his hair. "Oh, hell, what does it matter what I thought?"

"Don't read anything into her skipping supper, Jamie," Will warned. "You know how women can be. Maybe she's watching her waistline. Maybe she just wasn't hungry. Maybe she had a big lunch."

James shook his head. "She didn't have any lunch, Will. They don't serve lunch at the San Francisco City Jail."

"What?" Will was genuinely surprised.

"I couldn't wait for you to get back, Will. I left for San Francisco without you yesterday because I needed to get there before the city police arrested her. I had asked for a ouple of favors and set a few wheels in motion . . ." James felt, rather than saw, Will's censure and held up a hand to forestall the outburst he knew was coming. "I regretted it immediately, Will, and I was doing my damnedest to get into town before the police hauled her into jail for stealing a handkerchief from me."

"So, that's why you commandeered the express train," Will interrupted.

"Yes. But I was too late. The Treasures were being difficult yesterday morning and Mrs. G. had her hands full so I had to stay and help out as long as I could, and by the time I arrived, Elizabeth had already been arrested, charged with theft and destruction of private property, and jailed because she didn't have enough money to pay the fifty-dollar fine Judge Clermont levied against her," James told him.

"Whoa." Will held up his hand. "Whose property did she destroy?" He shook his head. "Wait, don't tell me yet. Just start at the beginning."

James took a deep breath and began. He told Will everything. And by the time they left the brick path and entered the elegant American headquarters of Craig Capital, Ltd., and the private suite of offices James and Will occupied on the second floor, Will Keegan knew as much about Elizabeth Sadler as James did.

"So you see," James concluded, dropping his leather satchel on his desk. "I need you to do a little digging for me. Lo Peng will have members of the Tong watching me too closely. I need you to use your contacts outside Craig Capital to discover what happened to Elizabeth's brother and why she risked so much by alienating a powerful warlord like Lo Peng." He sat on the edge of his desk.

"Does she have any idea how powerful Lo Peng is or how much she's risked?" Will asked, pulling James's desk chair around to the side of the big mahogany desk where he sat down on it, propped his feet up on the desk and crossed his ankles.

"No," James said. "I warned her to stay away from him

and his business, but I think that as far as she's concerned, Lo Peng is just the angry owner of the Washington Street opium den she vandalized. And I don't want her to know any differently unless it's necessary.''

''It may not be wise to keep her in the dark about the danger she could be in,'' Will replied.

''It may not be wise, Will, but it's necessary,'' James said. ''Elizabeth already has the typical American distrust and dislike of the Chinese. So, even if she doesn't quite understand how powerful an enemy she's made in Lo Peng, she knows enough to be wary of him, perhaps even afraid of him. As long as Lo Peng keeps his word and Elizabeth keeps her distance, she's safe. I don't want to alarm her by telling her the truth about Lo Peng. I don't want to fan the flames of her prejudice. I won't risk having her dislike of the Chinese, in general, or her fear of Lo Peng, in particular, adversely affect the Treasures.''

Recalling the scenes he'd witnessed at breakfast, Will said, ''I don't think you need worry about Elizabeth's fears adversely affecting those little gems.''

''I hope you're right,'' James said. ''But you didn't see the way Elizabeth reacted to the sight of them when we arrived at the house yesterday. She actually recoiled in horror and refused to get close to them, much less touch them.''

''She seems to have gotten over her fear,'' Will commented with a shrug of his shoulders. It wasn't that he dismissed James's parental concern or Elizabeth's disappointing first reaction to the Treasures lightly, but from what Will had seen this morning, she seemed to have come to terms with her feelings. ''Thunderation, Jamie! Neither one of us wanted to touch little . . .'' He let his voice trail off for a moment, then continued, ''If the truth be known, I didn't want to touch Ruby the first time I saw her, either. Not because she was Chinese, but because she was so blamed little. I was scared I'd damage something. Did you ever think that maybe Elizabeth's reaction had more to do

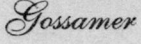

with the Treasures' ages and sizes than with the color of their skin?''

No, he hadn't. The fact that she might have been afraid of his little girls because they were so small compared to the girls she must have taught at the girls' school she'd worked in had never occurred to him.

"Give the woman a fair chance, James," Will told him. "After all, not every one is brought up with a working knowledge of infants."

Will was right. Not every one was brought up with a working knowledge of infants. This morning Elizabeth hadn't known how to diaper a baby or how to feed and burp one, but then, three and a half years ago, neither had he. James steepled his fingers, propped his chin on his index fingers, and nodded. "I'd forgotten," he admitted to Will. "Ruby has been a part of my life for so long now, it's hard for me to remember what my life was like before diapers and bottles and governesses."

"Is it really so hard to remember, Jamie?"

"No," James answered truthfully. "Sometimes it seems like yesterday. I wake up in a cold sweat and I remember . . ." His voice broke for a second before he regained his composure. "I remember what life was like before Ruby. And then I find myself standing in the doorway of the nursery in the middle of the night just watching her sleep. I'll never forget. I can't forget."

"I know, Jamie." Will straightened, took his feet off the desk, then reached out in a show of emotion and clapped James on the shoulder. "I know."

They sat quietly for a moment, each lost in his own thoughts until Will broke the silence. "Will tomorrow morning be soon enough? Or would you like me to leave after the meeting this afternoon?"

"You just got back from the mining camp," James reminded him.

"So? You just returned from San Francisco," Will retorted. "Besides, if I'm going to be digging for information that's weeks or even months old, I'd best get started before the trail gets much colder.''

"Do you still have that friend at the *Chronicle*?" James asked.

"Yes," Will answered. "And he likes to entertain the ladies, but he doesn't usually have two copper pennies to rub together. I figure this will cost me a few theater tickets, a few bottles of good brandy, and some champagne.''

James threw open his arms. "My wine cellar is yours. And I'll be more than happy to reimburse you for theater tickets, hotel rooms, whatever . . .''

Will winked at him. "I'll remember that.''

James shook his head, then grinned at Will. "I owe you an apology, Will, for my behavior this morning. I don't know what came over me.''

Will laughed. "I do. It reminds me of old times, except that this time, she's about five feet, eight inches tall, with streaky golden brown hair, extraordinary blue-green eyes, and an independent spirit.''

"Not my usual type." James's smile was sadder this time. "I don't understand it.''

"You've suffered enough, Jamie, and more than paid for any imagined sins," Will said. "Perhaps it's time for a change.''

Nineteen

IT WAS TIME for a change. Elizabeth took a clean diaper from the stack on the bureau and positioned it in the center of the thin cotton pillow atop it. She opened the lid on the tin of talcum powder in preparation and placed it, along with a damp facecloth, within easy reach, then approached the newborn lying in her crib with equal measures of determination and trepidation.

"Need any help, miss?" Delia called from the playroom where she was wiping down the small round table and setting out the bowls and spoons in preparation for the luncheon of chicken and rice Mrs. G. was sending up to the nursery for the Treasures.

Help? She didn't need help. She needed rescuing. But she wasn't about to let Delia know that. Instead of handing over the diaper, the facecloth, and the talcum powder as any normal obviously out-of-her depths woman would do, Elizabeth called back, "No, thank you, Delia. You finish the lunch preparations. I'll take care of Diamond." She leaned over the crib and lifted Diamond out of her little bed, carefully supporting the baby's head as she had watched James do, and carried her over to the bureau. "We can do this, can't we, Diamond?" Elizabeth flattened her lips into a thin, determined line and prepared for battle. "We can do this."

To Elizabeth's immense surprise and satisfaction, Diamond seemed to agree. She demonstrated her cooperation by quietly submitting to the procedure, enduring Elizabeth's awkwardness and inexperience with grace and patience.

When Diamond's fresh undergarment was pinned firmly into place, Elizabeth, feeling the first flush of renewed confidence, gently eased the baby's arms out of the sleeves of her nightgown, then pulled the damp garment over Diamond's head and replaced it with another white cotton gown. She lifted Diamond from the cotton padding and held her cradled securely in the crook of her left arm, while she deftly gathered the dirty garments and facecloth and deposited them into the laundry pail. Wanting to share her victory with someone, Elizabeth hummed beneath her breath and rocked Diamond to and fro in her arm as she reentered the playroom.

"That was fast, miss," Delia commented when she looked up and saw Elizabeth standing near the doorway with Diamond in her arms.

"Yes, it was." Elizabeth's voice fairly crackled with triumph. "I changed her diaper and she slept right through it."

"You're lucky, miss," Delia said. "Some babies ain't so accommodating. My mam always says she ain't going to risk bothering a peaceful baby just to change a nappy." She circled the table, setting a small wooden bowl and spoon in front of three chairs. "Besides it's a waste to change 'em every few minutes when they're just going to need another changing soon as they suckle or wake up from a nap. Lots of times my mam doesn't even bother with a nappy on the little ones."

"They go without clothing?" Elizabeth was shocked. "Inside the house?"

"Of course, inside the house," Delia told her. "The little ones are too small to be outside yet. Letting 'em go without saves on laundry." She shrugged her shoulders once again as if having naked children running around a cottage soiling themselves was an accepted part of life. And indeed it was, for children less fortunate than James Cameron Craig's precious Treasures.

"What about their beds? Doesn't letting them go with a diaper ruin the bedding?" Not to mention the unsanitary conditions in the house and the smell and the mess.

Delia shook her head. "Nah. The little ones don't sleep in beds like these. My mam spreads layers of newspaper on the floor in the corner of our house and the little ones sleep there."

"How many little ones are there?" Elizabeth asked.

"Well," Delia paused. "There's Mam and eight of us. One older than me and six younger. And my cousin, Rose, and her little one lives with us."

Elizabeth gasped. She couldn't imagine eight children, nine if you counted Cousin Rose's child, in one family. Nor could she imagine the responsibilities Delia, who couldn't be a day over fourteen, as the second oldest had had to bear. "What about your father?"

"He died two winters ago, miss. He took the sniffles and died." Delia shivered at the memory. "Imagine a big strong man like that dying of the sniffles after traversing the prairie building the railroad out from Missouri. I tell you my mam still ain't got over it. Him up and dying and leaving us alone in Coryville. If he was gonna die of the sniffles, he could've done that back in Ireland. Not come all the way to the promised land to do it." She turned away from the table to look at Elizabeth "I already rang the bell for lunch. Annie should be up here with it any minute now."

"Will Annie be bringing up Diamond's bottle as well?" Elizabeth asked.

"Not yet, miss," Delia told her. "She brings it after lunch when the Treasures go down for their naps. Little Di there usually sleeps right through her sisters' lunch and wakes in time for a bottle while the others are napping. But you know how babies are.'' She shrugged her shoulders. ''If she wakes up fussy, you can take her down to the big kitchen and Mrs. G. will fix her up with a bottle quick as a flash. Is she waking early?''

''Oh, no,'' Elizabeth assured the housemaid. ''She's sleeping like an angel.''

Delia smiled. ''She's a good one, Di is. Cheery and quiet most of the time. Not like the Queen Bee over there.'' Delia nodded toward Ruby, who was arguing loudly with Garnet over a set of wooden building blocks, then walked over to the small sink in the kitchen alcove, turned on the tap, and ran her dishcloth under the water. She turned the tap on and off several times, staring in fascination at the flow of running water.

''How long have you worked here?'' Elizabeth asked.

''A couple of weeks,'' Delia told her. ''Mr. Craig hired me to help the last governess.''

''Mr. Craig hired you?''

''Yes,'' Delia said. ''He didn't want to. He said I was too young to go to work, but my mam convinced him that we needed the money.''

''Why didn't Mr. Craig hire your mother as governess? Why doesn't she work?'' Elizabeth asked.

''My mam does work,'' Delia said. ''She does the washing and ironing for us here at Craig House and several other fine families in Coryville. She and Rose wash and iron and take care of all the little ones. And if Mam was governess here who would take care of her little ones? Okay, girls,'' Delia called to Treasures. ''Time to wash up and eat.''

Not yet ready to part with Diamond, yet knowing she would have to help Delia with the Treasures' lunch, Elizabeth took Diamond into the bedroom, placed her down gently in the small wooden cradle, then carried the cradle back into the playroom and set it on the floor far enough from the table to be safely out of range of dropped food and spilled juice, yet close enough for Elizabeth to reach if necessary.

''You'll be lucky if she sleeps through this,'' Delia commented as she took Ruby by the hand and prepared to wash her face with the dishcloth.

"Wait!" Elizabeth hurried over to the sink.

"What is it, miss?"

Elizabeth took a clean dishcloth out of a drawer, wet it under the taps, and handed it to Delia. "Use this one."

"What for?"

"You used the other one to scrub the table," Elizabeth explained.

"So?"

"The cloth you used to scrub the table is dirty."

"Well," Delia protested, "Miss Ruby's face is dirty."

Elizabeth laughed. "I know. But I think it would be best if you used one cloth for wiping food and spills from tables and chairs and floors and another separate *clean* cloth for the Treasures' faces and hands." She held out her hand for the dirty dishcloth and Delia reluctantly handed it over.

"Seems like a waste to me," Delia grumbled, wiping Ruby's face and hands. "Dirty is dirty. And your way will mean a lot more laundry for Mam and Rose to wash."

Elizabeth pulled another cloth from the drawer, wet it, and called Garnet and Emerald over to the sink. "From now on, we'll use separate dishcloths and facecloths and," Elizabeth added, thinking about how uncomfortable she had been this morning in her soiled nightgown and how eager she had been to bathe and change into her favorite blue-striped morning gown, "we'll change dirty clothes and wet and soiled diapers as soon as we realize they need changing. I won't have the Treasures walking or crawling or lying around in filth. As my grandmother is so fond of saying, 'cleanliness is next to godliness.' "

"Well, begging your pardon, miss," Delia replied uncharitably, eyeing the fine fabric of Elizabeth's morning dress and her soft white hands. "But your grandmother probably had hot and cold running water. And she probably hired somebody like my mam to do her washing."

Elizabeth paused for a moment. "Then, look at it this way, Delia, the more laundry we dirty, the more money your mother and Rose will make washing it.''

Delia frowned. "It don't work that way, miss. Mam and Rose get paid the same every week no matter how much laundry they wash.''

Elizabeth snapped her fingers in the air and grinned. "Then I'll just have to talk to Mr. Craig about paying your mother and Rose an additional nursery bonus.''

"Really, miss?'' Delia's brown eyes widened in something akin to awe as she stared at Elizabeth.

"Of course,'' Elizabeth assured her, bending down and following Delia's lead by washing Garnet and Emerald's faces and hands. "Children dirty more clothes than anyone else, so it makes perfect sense that laundresses should be paid a nursery bonus for the additional wash.''

"Oh, miss,'' Delia breathed, "if you can do that for me and Mam, I'll be glad to change more diapers and dirty more dishcloths.''

"Fair enough,'' Elizabeth said. "I'll hold up my end of the bargain, and I will expect you to do the same.'' And if James Cameron Craig didn't agree to supplement Delia's mother's and her cousin's income, Elizabeth would request an advance against her salary for expenses and pay the supplement herself.

~~∞~~

ELIZABETH SIGHED. SHE pulled the empty baby bottle out of Diamond's mouth and set it on the table near the rocking chair. She eased the sleeping infant out of the crook of her arm and carefully patted Diamond on the back until she heard her burp, then Elizabeth stood and carried the baby to her crib and carefully placed her on her side in the bed. Elizabeth stood for a moment and watched Diamond sleeping, then pulled herself up to her full height, lifting her arms high above her head to stretch the tired muscles in her lower back.

All the Treasures were fast asleep at last.

Elizabeth gave a satisfied smile. The hours since breakfast seemed to have flown by. So far, Elizabeth had accomplished everything on James's list: six A.M.—breakfast; eight-thirty A.M.—supervised play; ten A.M.—lessons—lessons that had consisted of singing the alphabet song and several remembered counting and color songs. She smiled when she remembered the exuberance with which Garnet and Emerald and even at times, Ruby, had filled the nursery with song. Ruby. Elizabeth reached into the crib and pulled the light cotton sheet up over Diamond's back and shoulders and gently tucked it into place. Ruby. It hadn't escaped her notice that Ruby was reluctant to join in the singing games or to do anything Elizabeth wanted to do. Ruby was standoffish. She kept her distance from Elizabeth. Ruby didn't want to follow, she wanted to lead. Elizabeth wrinkled her brow and frowned. Ruby didn't like her. And unless Ruby learned to like and trust her, the nursery would be torn between its two rulers and Garnet and Emerald would follow Ruby just as often as they would follow her.

Elizabeth gave Diamond one last pat on the back and brushed the soft curls on the back of her head. She tiptoed back to the rocking chair and picked up the infant feeding bottle. She carried the bottle with her as she tiptoed across the nursery bedroom, through the open connecting door, and into the kitchen alcove. She placed the feeding bottle in the tiny sink, then eased open the door that connected the alcove to her bedroom. She listened, for a moment, to the satisfying sounds of the children snoring before she pulled the bedroom door almost closed, leaving it slightly ajar so that she could hear the Treasures should any one of them call out for her. She had done it. She had survived her first morning on the job. All of the Treasures were fast asleep. And Elizabeth had earned a much needed two-hour break.

Quietly leaving the nursery, Elizabeth entered her bedroom and resumed the task of unpacking she had begun the night before. She folded the remaining stack of lingerie and placed it in the top drawer of the armoire, then leaned into the deep trunk and removed her last precious belonging from the bottom. Portia. How could she have forgotten Portia? Elizabeth held her breath as she unwrapped several layers of cotton batting and unrolled the protective length of cotton fabric until a delicately painted bisque face and startling blue-green eyes stared back at her. Elizabeth tossed the cotton fabric aside and cradled Portia in her arm. She anxiously scanned Portia's face and ran her fingertips over the painted features, feeling for cracks and chips in the porcelain. Finding none, Elizabeth hugged Portia to her chest, feeling the same rush of warmth and love for the doll she had felt the morning her father had presented Portia to her as a boon to help soothe her ruffled feathers at finding herself presented with a baby brother. And although she'd never really been allowed to play with her because she was such an expensive doll, Elizabeth had loved Portia instantly. Elizabeth thought they were twins. They had the same color hair, the same mouth and chin, and the same color eyes—even if Portia's were painted—and Elizabeth knew instinctively that her father had chosen the doll because Portia looked like her. Portia had been her closest friend and dearest confidante, even though she'd never left the bedroom shelf until the day Elizabeth's grandmother had disowned her and Elizabeth had moved out of the house on Hemlock Street. Elizabeth lovingly smoothed back the locks of tawny brownish-blond hair that had escaped from Portia's elaborate coiffeur. She'd spent the most important hours of her childhood talking to Portia, confiding her deepest desires and secrets to her, and as she fingered the creases in the doll's blue velvet gown, and checked to make sure both of her matching blue velvet slippers were still on her feet, Elizabeth realized that, other than her clothes, Portia was the only personal item she'd taken with her when she left her grandmother Sadler's house.

Elizabeth breathed a heartfelt sigh. Portia had endured the journey across country and arrived in California without so much as a new nick or scratch. She hugged the doll to her chest again, then carefully settled Portia against the

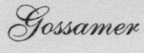

headboard and on the pillows in the center of her bed. Elizabeth looked down at the gold watch pinned on her own bodice. If she were lucky, she'd have time to take a brief nap herself before her charges woke up.

"Miss?"

The knock on her bedroom door and the sound of Delia's voice startled her. Elizabeth walked over and opened the door. "Yes?"

"I finished my meal and Mrs. G. sent me up to mind the nursery while you go down to the kitchen and have your lunch."

"The Treasures are napping," Elizabeth answered, swallowing a yawn.

"Yes, miss, I know. But Mr. Craig doesn't like the Treasures to be left alone. I'll just sit in the nursery and work on this basket of mending until the little girls wake up. You go eat. Mrs. G. is expecting you."

Elizabeth shook her head. "Thank you, Delia, but I'm not very hungry." She eyed the bed longingly. "I think I'll just skip lunch and take a short nap."

Delia looked shocked. "Oh, no, miss. That won't do."

"I'm not allowed to take a nap?"

"Of course you are, miss," Delia said. "But Mr. Craig insists that everyone in the household eat three square meals a day."

"Even if I'm not hungry?"

Delia nodded. "Even so."

"But why?" Elizabeth asked.

The young maid shrugged her shoulders. "I don't know. But everyone eats three meals a day at Craig House. That's one of the three cardinal house rules."

She wasn't accustomed to eating three meals a day. Lady Wimbley's Female Academy offered only breakfast and dinner. Lady Wimbley had done away with luncheon for the staff and students in order to economize and keep the school operating within its budget. No one ate luncheon except Lady Wimbley herself, and her luncheons for parents and society patrons were the stuff of legends. "What are the other cardinal rules?"

Delia shifted her feet from side to side and glanced over at the sheer draperies billowing in the wind from the breeze coming in through open French doors leading onto the balcony. "We must watch the Treasures at all times and the French doors in the governess's room must be kept closed and locked whenever the Treasures are in the nursery," she muttered uncomfortably.

"Oh." Elizabeth walked over and closed and latched the doors.

"Mr. Craig must have forgotten to tell you about the rules."

And as a consequence Elizabeth had already broken one rule and nearly broken the other two. She looked over at Delia's tense expression and shrugged her shoulders good-naturedly. "I suppose breaking one cardinal rule a day is enough." She smiled at the young housemaid. "Thank you for agreeing to sit with the Treasures, Delia, while I go downstairs for lunch."

"Thank you, miss," Delia breathed. " 'Cause I'd sure hate to have to get used to another governess's ways of doing things or lose the bonus money you're going to get Mr. Craig to pay Mam and Rose."

That gave Elizabeth pause. "If Mr. Craig feels that strongly about the rules, we won't worry him by telling him how close I came to breaking them."

"Right, miss," Delia agreed. " 'cause Mr. Craig ain't going to allow anything bad to happen to his Treasures and he ain't going to let anybody in Craig House go hungry for any reason. Nobody in Craig House is ever going to starve to death. Go on, miss, before your luncheon gets cold. I'll watch over the Treasures."

Twenty

THE BELL IN the tower of the First Protestant Episcopal Church pealed three times, announcing the end of school. Elizabeth watched as the double doors of the church opened and a dozen or so school-age children hurried down the front steps and ran for the park.

Elizabeth, Delia, and the Treasures followed the crowd of children toward the park. It was Elizabeth's first look at the town in daylight, and it hadn't taken her long to learn that Coryville was laid out on a square grid. Main Street was routed around a large expanse of park land dotted by tall pines at one end and enclosed by a black wrought-iron fence. A brick-paved pathway led the way from Craig House, through the stone and wrought-iron entry gate, into the park, then continued around the perimeter of the park. Wrought-iron benches and lampposts lined the path at quarter-mile intervals. Having already made one revolution around the town square, stopping off to mail a letter with her forwarding address and a request to Mr. Dorminey at the stone works for a final accounting once Owen's headstone was in place, Elizabeth wheeled the carriage through the stone gate and entered the park. She maneuvered Diamond's wicker carriage off the path to a nearby bench and

parked it before she allowed Delia to let go of Ruby's hand
or Emerald and Garnet to get out of their twin perambulator
for a romp in the park.

Elizabeth sat on the nearest bench and gave a nod of
approval for Delia to lead the girls to the play area. She
wheeled Diamond's pram back and forth to keep the baby
entertained while her older sisters played tag and hide-and-
seek with each other and with Delia.

Elizabeth sighed. Coryville was a beautiful, model
town—full of green areas, trees, brick pathways, lamps and
wrought-iron fences—so different from many of the other
towns Elizabeth had passed through on her way out West.
She shivered at a blast of cool late April air and stared out
past the town to the snowcapped mountains far off in the
distance. Situated as it was in a protected valley, Coryville
could very easily have been one of those quaint little Alpine
villages she had heard so much about. Elizabeth pulled her
wool cape closer around her, then checked to make sure
Diamond hadn't kicked off her blankets. Ruby and Garnet
were warm enough playing tag with Delia. And Emerald
was sitting, securely bundled against the chilly breeze, a
few feet away in the center of a large sandbox happily
pouring sand from one metal pan to another smaller one.

Hearing the little girls' delighted squeals and high-
pitched laughter made Elizabeth want to join in the fun.
She called to Delia and asked if she would mind watching
Diamond and Emerald while she joined Ruby and Garnet
in a game of ring-around-the-rosy. Delia quickly ran over
to the bench and sat down to rest while Elizabeth took her
place.

Gathering the two little girls to form a circle, Elizabeth
reached down to take Ruby by the hand.

Ruby backed up a step, refusing to grab hold of Elizabeth's hand.

"What's the matter, Ruby?" Elizabeth asked as she knelt
on the grass to look Ruby in the eyes. "Don't you want to
play anymore?"

"No!"

Tears welled in Garnet's dark brown eyes and her little bow-shaped mouth began to tremble.

"Don't you want to play ring-around-the-rosy anymore?" Elizabeth asked, trying again.

"I don't want to play wif you," Ruby told her. "I want Delia."

Elizabeth recoiled at the vitriolic tone in Ruby's voice. The little girl's words stabbed at Elizabeth's heart, cutting deep. She took a deep, steadying breath to keep from crying and managed a very calm, "I see." She slowly rose from her knees and walked over to the bench, where Delia sat watching the two younger girls.

"I think it might be best if I sat and watched Diamond and Emerald while you play with the older girls, Delia."

"Why, miss?" Delia asked. "I thought you wanted to romp around a bit."

"I did," Elizabeth replied, "but Ruby doesn't want me. She wants to play with you, and it's more important for her to get her exercise than it is for me."

Delia left the bench and walked over to Ruby. "What's the matter with you? Stop being so mean and let Miss Elizabeth play, too."

"No." Ruby shook her head. "Don't like Miss Libeth," she announced. "I like you."

"Ruby! You shouldn't say such things."

"It's all right, Delia," Elizabeth said as the burn of unshed tears stung her eyelids. "Ruby is entitled to her own opinions. If she doesn't like me and doesn't want to play with me, I understand. And I agree that she ought to have playmates she likes. So, I'll keep an eye on Emerald and Diamond while you entertain Ruby and Garnet. Agreed?"

"Okay, miss," Delia replied glumly.

Elizabeth blinked back the tears and smiled over at Delia. "Good. And now that that's settled, why don't you run along and play ring-around-the-rosy with Ruby and Garnet?"

‐‐‐‐‐‐◦✦◦‐‐‐‐‐‐

"DAMN." JAMES STOOD staring out of his office window overlooking the park in the center of the town square where, two stories below, his darling domineering Ruby was engaged in a war of wills with her governess.

"What is it?" Will asked.

"Ruby," James answered. "Come see for yourself."

Will got up from his chair, walked around James's desk, and moved to stand beside him at the window. Far below, James's four daughters, their new governess, and Delia, the housemaid, were playing games in the park.

At least, Ruby, Garnet, and Delia were playing tag on the grass. Emerald was playing in the huge sandbox, and Elizabeth was sitting on a park bench pushing Diamond's pram back and forth with her foot.

"What happened?" Will asked.

"Ruby's refused to participate in any of the games if Elizabeth plays." James's voice held a resigned note. "I was afraid of this," he admitted. "I was afraid Ruby wouldn't accept Diamond and a new governess."

"Still jealous, is she?" Will chuckled, understanding that Ruby enjoyed being the queen bee of the nursery, enjoyed twisting him and James around her little fingers, and lording it over her younger sisters.

"Very much so." James plowed his fingers through his hair and shook his head, before turning his attention back to the scene in the park. As he watched, Elizabeth straightened her shoulders and surreptitiously brushed the back of her hand beneath her eyes. Although he couldn't see it from this far up, he felt in his heart that Ruby's hostility had wounded Elizabeth deep enough to make her cry. James turned away from the window and started toward the door.

"Where are you going?" Will asked.

"To see about Elizabeth and to have a little talk with Ruby," James replied, torn between his love for his daughter and his desire to comfort Elizabeth.

"She won't appreciate you interfering."

Will's words stopped James in his tracks. "No, she won't," he agreed. "But Ruby needs to understand that she has to mind Elizabeth."

"Elizabeth needs to teach Ruby that lesson. Otherwise, her authority in the nursery will be undermined."

"I know," James said. "I know. But—"

"Leave it alone, Jamie." Will slapped James on the back. "Come on, the sooner we get these contracts in order, the sooner I can leave for the city and find out what happened to Elizabeth's brother."

James didn't say anything else. He simply walked back to his desk and resumed his review of the Central Pacific contracts.

~~~

ELIZABETH GLANCED AT the gold watch pinned to the bodice of her dress, then pulled the schedule James had copied down for her out of her pocket and read it once again. According to the schedule, the Treasures had another hour of fresh air and exercise in the park before it would be time to return to Craig House and get the girls bathed for dinner.

She shoved the schedule back into her pocket and lifted a fussy Diamond out of her perambulator. She draped Diamond's soft wool blanket over the infant's head, then hugged Diamond close, gently bouncing her up and down against her shoulder to soothe her. A young blond woman with two small children approached the bench, and Elizabeth scooted to the edge of the seat in order to make room on the bench for the woman.

"Hello." Elizabeth shifted Diamond to her left shoulder, smiled at the other woman, then offered her hand in introduction. "I'm Elizabeth Sadler."

The other woman whispered instructions to her children—a small boy of about Garnet's age and a girl who appeared to be two or three years older—and sent them off to play in the sandbox.

She looked Elizabeth up and down. "I don't remember seeing you before. You must be new in town."

"Why, yes, I am," Elizabeth said. "And you must be . . ."

"Lois Marlin," the blond-haired woman replied. "Mrs. Joseph Marlin, Esquire. That's Deborah," she said, pointing to her little girl. "And Joseph Junior." She pointed to the little boy sitting beside Emerald in the sandbox. "Joseph Junior," she called out to her son. "Move over. I thought I told you to stay away from the little Celestial."

Elizabeth sucked in a breath, stiffened in her seat, and hugged Diamond a bit closer.

Lois Marlin didn't seem to notice. Done giving instructions, she turned her attention back to Elizabeth. "We've been in Coryville since the beginning. My husband is . . ."

"The local attorney," Elizabeth said. "I passed his office as I was strolling with the baby."

Lois Marlin leaned closer. "May I see your baby?"

"Yes, of course," Elizabeth moved Diamond from her shoulder and settled her into the crook of her left arm.

"Boy or girl?"

"A girl," Elizabeth answered proudly, pulling the edges of the blanket back away from Diamond's little face so that Mrs. Marlin could see her.

"My stars!" She gasped. "She's a Celestial heathen, too."

"A what?" Never having heard the term, Elizabeth didn't know what it meant, only that it was in some way derogatory and that Lois Marlin used it on a regular basis.

"A Chinese. Good heavens, don't tell me she's yours!" Lois Marlin dropped the corner of Diamond's blanket and moved away, farther down along the bench. "You didn't actually . . . marry . . . one of those. Did you?" Lois wore an expression of rabid curiosity.

"Diamond is the youngest of Mr. Craig's four daughters," Elizabeth answered coolly. "I'm their governess."

Really? When did he hire you?'' Lois asked.

''He didn't hire me,'' Elizabeth replied, not liking Lois's rude question or her superior tone of voice. ''I'm an old friend of the family. Mr. Craig arranged for me to come to Coryville shortly after his wife died.'' She crossed her fingers beneath the folds of Diamond's blanket and said a few silent prayers to excuse the little white lies she was telling. Elizabeth wasn't about to let a woman like Lois Marlin think she knew all of James Craig's business. ''Surely you had heard.''

''What took you so long to get here?'' Elizabeth didn't think it was possible for Lois Marlin to look more shocked or surprised or rabidly curious, but it was.

''What do you mean?''

''James Cameron Craig's wife died over three years ago.''

Elizabeth was stunned. Over three years? Ruby was three and a half. Ruby's mother had died? But what about Garnet and Emerald? Where was their mother? And where was three-day-old Diamond's mother? What had happened to them?

''Were you marooned or shipwrecked or something?'' Lois asked eagerly.

Elizabeth had to think fast. That was the trouble with little white lies. They got you into trouble so fast that soon you were forced to weave a whole fabric of bigger, darker lies. ''Oh, no, nothing so dramatic. You see, my family and Mr. Craig's family are both in banking and finance.'' That part was true enough. ''And well, they've been business associates for as long as I can remember.'' Elizabeth began warming up to her story and telling it in the light, gossipy tones of a society debutante. ''You see, I had just begun my course of studies at the academy when Mr. Craig spoke to my grandmother about my coming to Coryville after graduation and after my year of finishing school in Europe. At the time, his wife was very much alive. But then, I decided to extend my educational tour of Europe to include a—a—course of Italian and Greek art history—at the Vat-

ican City and in Athens, of course. And by the time I
turned to the States to accept his invitation to come
California, James—I mean Mr. Craig—was a widower.''

"Wasn't your family afraid for you to come here? Aren't
you afraid?''

"Of what?''

"Of Mr. Craig,'' Lois breathed. "Of James Cameron
Craig, of course.''

"Why should I be afraid of Mr. Craig?'' Elizabeth asked.
"He's an old family friend, a well-respected businessman,
and a perfect gentleman.''

"He *appears* to be a well-respected businessman and a
perfect gentleman,'' Lois corrected. "But appearances are
deceiving. He's a criminal, you know.''

"Don't be absurd!'' Elizabeth snapped. "Mr. Craig isn't
a criminal.''

"Yes, he is,'' Lois said. "Oh, everything is very hush-
hush now. You were away in Europe and your family probably didn't think anything of it because, after all, she was
a Celestial. But James Craig didn't come to California because he wanted to. He came because he was forced to
leave Hong Kong to escape punishment.''

"Punishment for what?'' Elizabeth didn't believe a word
of Lois Marlin's gossip, but her curiosity got the best of
her.

"He killed his wife,'' Lois whispered. "He killed her
with his bare hands.''

"I don't believe you,'' Elizabeth said flatly. James Cameron Craig was no more a killer than she was. He was too
patient, too understanding. Too loving. He would never kill
the mother of his child. The idea was unthinkable. James
Craig could not have murdered the mother of his child. He
loved Ruby too much. And his love for her was the pure
love of a father for his child. There wasn't a hint of guilt
attached to it. And James wouldn't be able to look Ruby
in the eye if he had committed the horrible crime of which
Lois Marlin accused him. "Mr. Craig is one of the few

men I've ever known who genuinely likes women and children. In fact, he adores them.''

"So what?" Lois didn't appreciate Elizabeth's superior tone of voice. "Everyone knows he prefers Celestial women. His wife was one and he must have at least one or two mistresses over in Chinatown." She nodded toward the row of buildings beyond Main Street to the right of the square. "How else could he keep spawning these heathens?''

"How dare you suggest . . ." Elizabeth began in a voice shivering with cold fury.

"I'm not suggesting," Lois told her. "I'm telling you the truth. Everybody in town knows it. If you don't believe me, ask him. Ask him what happened to his wife. Ask him how she died.''

"I would never presume to ask Mr. Craig such a personal and hurtful question." Elizabeth's voice cooled even more.

"Oh, you'll ask him," Lois Marlin asserted smugly. "You'll ask him. You won't be able not to ask him now that your curiosity has been aroused. But, take my advice, Miss Sadler, and leave while you still have the chance. The other governesses didn't stay because they were afraid to. Why do you think he's still eligible? Surely you don't believe a handsome, rich bachelor like him could remain unmarried in a town full of eligible women, if there wasn't something horribly wrong with him?''

Elizabeth got to her feet, then bent and gently placed Diamond in her perambulator before she signaled to Delia to bring the other Treasures. "I suspect you have it backward, Mrs. Marlin," she said in an oh-so-sweet tone of voice, "I don't think Mr. Craig has remained a widower because the women in Coryville are afraid he murdered his wife. I doubt they care if he murdered his wife. After all, she was only a *Celestial heathen*." Elizabeth sneered the term. "I suspect the reason James Cameron Craig has remained a widower, in a town of plenty, is that he's afraid the town is full of women with narrow-minded attitudes like yours.''

"Why, I never!" Lois Marlin got to her feet, red-faced and sputtering.

"And you never will, Mrs. Marlin. You never will." Elizabeth grabbed hold of the handle of Diamond's carriage, pulled it behind her as she left the brick walkway, and stalked over to the sandbox to rescue a squirming Emerald from Joseph Junior, who had her in a bear hug and was plastering her face with wet sloppy kisses. "If I were you"—Elizabeth turned to give Lois Marlin one last parting shot—"I'd work on broadening my view with an eye toward the future. Joseph Junior doesn't seem to mind sharing the sandbox with *Celestials*. In fact, he seems to rather enjoy it." Elizabeth lifted Emerald out of the sandbox, hefted her onto her hip, then grabbed hold of the handle of Diamond's pram and pulled it behind her. "Good afternoon."

Twenty-one

"CELESTIAL HEATHEN! THE nerve of that woman to call a precious little gem like Diamond a Celestial heathen!" Elizabeth was still fuming as she watched carefully while Mrs. G. showed her how to bathe the baby in the sink in the kitchen alcove of the nursery while Delia fed Emerald and supervised Ruby and Garnet at supper.

Mrs. G. shrugged as she cupped her hand and gently scooped warm water over Diamond's little body. "Now you know what you're up against." She had lived a long time. She was wise enough to listen to Elizabeth's ranting, yet clever enough to keep her counsel until she knew where Elizabeth's loyalties lay. She glanced slyly over at Elizabeth and added, "Now you know what you *and* Mr. Craig are up against."

"He built this town," Elizabeth continued furiously. "He built this beautiful little town, and yet the people who live here shun and insult his children and repeat horrible mean-spirited rumors about him."

"That's about the size of it," Mrs. G. agreed.

"I don't believe the things Lois Marlin said about Jame— I mean Mr. Craig—are true. I don't believe he killed his wife, and I don't believe he keeps a stable of mistresses in Chinatown.''

Mrs. Glenross raised an eyebrow at that. "So, that's how the townspeople account for the Treasures? How do you account for them?"

"I don't," Elizabeth said. "I accept them for what they are—James Cameron Craig's daughters." Elizabeth leaned against a kitchen cupboard and paused. "It doesn't matter who their mothers are or if they have mothers. He loves those girls, Mrs. Glenross. I've only been here a day and I already know that if I live to be a hundred, I shall never see a man who loves his children more than James does."

Mrs. G. lifted Diamond out of her bathwater, carefully wrapped her in the large towel Elizabeth had waiting, and handed her to Elizabeth. "You've learned a lot in one day, Miss Sadler," she said with a knowing grin. "More than most people learn in a lifetime."

Elizabeth carried Diamond into the bedroom and placed her on the bureau that doubled as a changing table, finished drying her, then picked up the tin of powder and sprinkled her with talc before pinning on a fresh diaper.

Mrs. G. followed Elizabeth into the bedroom and stood in the doorway watching as she quickly pulled an infant sacque over Diamond's head. "Now you know how the townspeople feel about James Craig—especially the women," Mrs. G. said. "Although the local businessmen appreciate his talent for making money, their wives refuse to accept him or forgive him for having been married to a Chinese or for keeping and raising the Treasures as his own. And the women in town will never willingly accept the Treasures into Coryville society."

Elizabeth wrinkled her brow in thought, then straightened her lips in determination. "Then, we'll just have to change their minds."

"How do you intend to do that?" Mrs. G asked.

"We invite them to tea," Elizabeth replied, suddenly remembering her grandmother's solution to recalcitrant society women. "We host a couple of splendid spare-no-expense

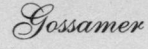

invitation-only teas. We start with a very exclusive guest list, then expand. Before we know it, every woman in town will want to come.''

''We?'' Mrs. Glenross demanded.

''Yes, we,'' Elizabeth answered firmly. ''After all, this was partly your idea.''

Mrs. G. smiled, a bit sheepishly at having been so transparent. ''I guess it was, at that.''

Elizabeth wasn't fooled by Helen Glenross's casual offer to help bathe Diamond. She knew the housekeeper had come up to the nursery to oversee her progress with the Treasures on James's instructions, and Elizabeth had taken full advantage of Mrs. G.'s willing ear to relate her conversation in the park with Lois Marlin. Mrs. G. knew more about James and the Treasures than she was letting on, and Elizabeth meant to enlist the housekeeper as an able ally in her fight to prove how wrong the people of Coryville were in their assumptions about James and the Treasures.

Elizabeth suspected Mrs. G. missed having little Diamond all to herself and was willing to supervise the nursery and its new governess, not only because James expected her to, but because Mrs. G. had overheard her conversation with James in the hallway the night before and was worried about Elizabeth's handling of the Treasures. But she also knew that unless she did something wrong, Mrs. G. would respect her dominion over the children and the upstairs nursery wing because James had hired her as governess and put her in charge, just as Elizabeth respected Mrs. G.'s dominion over Delia and Annie and the rest of the upstairs and everything downstairs because Mrs. G. was the housekeeper.

Elizabeth gave the housekeeper a quick decisive nod. ''That's settled. Now, would you like to feed Diamond her bottle or shall I?''

A wide, joyful grin transformed Helen Glenross's plain features into something akin to beauty. ''Let me go downstairs and get the bottle I've got warming for her,'' she said to Elizabeth. "I'll be back in a flash to feed and rock our precious little angel."

JAMES ARRIVED HOME from the office around half-past five. Eager to see his daughters and to find out how Elizabeth had fared on her first day on the job, James made his way upstairs to the nursery after briefly stopping in his study to drop off his leather satchel. He was late.

He entered the nursery after the Treasures had had their supper and during the scheduled bathtime. James recognized the sound of voices and of water splashing coming from the water closet as he walked into the playroom. He didn't see Elizabeth, nor did he see Garnet or Ruby. A freshly bathed Emerald stood patiently, near the warming stove in the playroom, as Delia knelt on the floor in front of her and made a game out of drying Emerald off with a fluffy terry-cloth towel. James decided Elizabeth must be busy bathing the older two girls.

"Good evening, Mr. Craig," Delia greeted him as she looked up from the game of peekaboo.

"Good evening, Delia."

Emerald shoved the towel away from her face, grinned broadly, and reached out for her daddy.

James bent and lifted her into his arms. "How's my little sweet pea?"

"Da," Emerald gurgled happily. "Da."

"That's right," James said, hugging her naked little body close to his. "Your daddy's home."

Emerald hugged him one last time, then squirmed, struggling to get down and return to Delia and the peekaboo game. Realizing Emerald had tolerated all the loving she could stand for the moment, James reluctantly set her down on the floor. He glanced over at Delia. "Where's Miss Sadler?"

"Washing Ruby and Garnet," Delia replied, confirming James's earlier supposition and one of his biggest fears.

"By herself?" he asked, somewhat alarmed by Delia's casual disregard of what was likely to turn into chaos. Ruby could be notoriously stubborn during the best of times, and bathtime was not one of her best times. She hated the very mention of the word *bath*, despised the bathtub, and did her absolute best to avoid the water and the whole process. He had forgotten to warn Elizabeth, and had no idea how she would manage.

"I warned her about Miss Ruby," Delia replied.

"And?" James was on pins and needles.

"She said she'd manage." Delia reached beneath the edge of her skirt and produced a white cotton nightgown, then grabbed hold of Emmy as she made a dash for the freedom of continued nudity and quickly dropped the garment over her head. Delia got to her feet, lifted Emerald from the floor in mid-yelp, and carried her into the bedroom to diaper her.

James marveled at the fourteen-year-old housemaid's adeptness. "How long has Miss Sadler been in there with them?"

"A while," she answered.

Unable to contain his curiosity, he called to Delia, "I think I'll go see how Miss Sadler is faring with Ruby."

"She managed just fine with Miss Emerald."

"Ruby's an altogether different kettle of fish," he replied. "I think it might be a good idea if I go see how she's doing for myself."

"Suit yourself," Delia called from the bedroom.

Fully intent on doing just that, James left the main room of the nursery and walked through the kitchen alcove to the bathroom. He paused before knocking on the bathroom door, listening to the exchange of conversation from within the room.

"I can't reach you over there, Ruby," Elizabeth said in a cajoling tone. "Please come over here and sit by Garnet."

He didn't hear Ruby respond to Elizabeth's request, and James imagined his eldest daughter standing at the far end of the large bathtub defiantly shaking her head.

"All right, Ruby, you leave me no choice."

James recognized the note of resignation in Elizabeth
voice, heard the whisper of rustling fabric, and the sound
of water sloshing against the deep claw-footed cast-iron
bathtub, and experienced a brief moment of perverse satisfaction. He knew it was wrong to feel a sense of fulfill-
ment in knowing his latest governess had failed, but he
couldn't help the swell of love and pride he felt at being
the only person Ruby found worthy of her complete faith
and trust. Having grown accustomed to Ruby's adamant
refusal to allow anyone but him to bathe her, James expected the bathroom door to open any moment and yield a
victorious Ruby and the latest in a long line of defeated
governesses. What he didn't expect, when he knocked once
on the door before opening it, was Elizabeth Sadler's solution to the problem.

"Please slide over a little, Garnet, and make room so I
can reach your sister." James overheard and comprehended
the meaning of Elizabeth's instructions in the same moment
he stepped over the threshold into the heavy, moisture-
laden air of the small steamy bathroom and discovered Elizabeth kneeling in the center of the tub.

Instantly aware of the intimate nature of the situation,
James took a hasty step backward, bumped into the open
door, and accidentally pushed it shut.

Elizabeth was too busy trying to hold on to Ruby long
enough to finish bathing her and to corral the bar of French-
milled lavender soap that had slipped from her grasp to turn
at the sound of the door slamming. Expecting Delia, she
said, "Garnet's ready to get out if you're finished with
Emerald." She paused, then chuckled. "And you were
right about Ruby. She positively hates a bath. We've had
quite a battle of wills. And while I know this method is a
bit unorthodox, it seemed the best and most efficient way
of accomplishing our task, didn't it, Ruby?"

Ruby didn't bother to answer. Her attention was focused
on the shadowy figure trying his best to escape from the

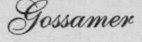

room without notice. "Daddy!" she squealed with
ght.

Elizabeth turned and half-rose from the warm soapy wa-
er as James stepped into view. Her lips parted, but all she
could manage to say was "Oh."

"Oh, yes." He gave Elizabeth a rather sheepish smile.
"And although your solution to Ruby's problem *is* rather
unorthodox, it appears to be working."

Before Elizabeth had time to formulate a reply, Ruby
lunged for the side of the bathtub and her father, drenching
Garnet with bathwater in the process. "Daddy!"

"Ruby!" Elizabeth reached out to catch her as Ruby
dashed for the side of the tub.

Garnet began to cry as Ruby sloshed more water on her,
and Elizabeth, who, up till now, had managed to keep her
batiste camisole fairly dry, quickly pulled Garnet against
her, then gently moved back a little bit so she could brush
Garnet's wet hair off her forehead to keep the droplets of
soapy water from running onto the little girl's face.

James caught Ruby against his thigh as she scrambled to
get out of the bathtub and hoisted her into his arms. Holding Ruby securely against his chest, James looked down at
Elizabeth.

She looked up at him.

Their gazes met and locked while the humid atmosphere
around them seemed to grow thicker and heavier.

Transfixed by the sight of the water droplets shimmering
on Elizabeth's flushed face and the soaked and transparent
undergarments tenaciously clinging to her stunning cleav-
age, James sucked in a breath and shifted his weight from
one leg to the other to accommodate the sudden swelling
in his groin. He stared at the water around her and the
rapidly dissipating lavender-scented bubbles. He hadn't
counted on this incredible assault on his senses. He hadn't
counted on the warm water, the humid air, the scent of
lavender permeating the room, or his gut reaction to it. He
simply hadn't counted on finding Elizabeth in the bathtub,
hadn't counted on the powerful surge of desire that shot

through him. He knew he should do the gentlemanly t
and leave. Simply back out the door the same way h
come in, but once again, gentlemanly behavior was beyo.
him. He wanted too much. He wanted to look at her, t
drink in the sight of a beautiful woman once again. He
wanted. James bit back a groan. He wanted. After three
long years of loneliness and pain and guilt and denial, he
wanted Elizabeth so badly he could feel her, could taste
her. Even though he knew he shouldn't—couldn't—touch
her. Not while she was under his protection. Not while she
was in his employ. Not while she lived beneath his roof.

Recognizing the sudden intense interest in his gaze and
realizing she was the focus of it, Elizabeth decided discre-
tion was the better part of valor and stood up to make a
hasty exit from the bathroom to the relative safety of her
bedroom.

"Stop!" The word erupted from James's lips and rever-
berated through the small room.

Elizabeth's eyes widened in surprise. And Garnet began
to cry.

"Sit down," James managed in a softer tone of voice,
holding out his hand as if to ward her off. "Wait right
there." He leaned over and gave the water taps a vicious
twist, then picked up a bottle of lavender-scented bubble
bath from the bathroom shelf and shoved it into Elizabeth's
hands. "Here. Add some more bubbles."

Elizabeth clutched the bottle of bubble bath to her chest
in self-defense, turned the water off, and quickly sank back
down into the soapy water. She reached up, with her other
arm, for the face towel hanging on the bar above the tub
and snatched it down to wipe Garnet's face. "See what
you've done!" she snapped, chafing under his tone of
voice. "I was managing quite nicely until you walked in.
And I could have continued on quite nicely without your
interference."

"I—I . . ." James was momentarily taken aback by the
flash of fury in Elizabeth's blue-green eyes. Didn't she realize he'd reacted on instinct to prevent her from further

xposing herself to his view? Didn't she realize the bath-water made her undergarments transparent? He shook his head. Of course she didn't. The explanation for his bizarre behavior hadn't yet occurred to her. She was too angry or too innocent to understand the effect her near-nudity had on him. James automatically lowered his gaze to the floor in a noble effort to keep it, and his wayward thoughts, from reveling in the entrancing sight of his daughters' lovely governess flushed with anger, semi-nude, and soaked. As he worked to curb his uncomfortably vivid and suddenly overactive imagination, James discovered, to his dismay, a rather untidy pile of feminine garments strewn across the marble tile. At the bottom of the pile was the striped morning gown he'd seen Elizabeth wearing in the park. And on the top of the pile of clothing was a veritable sea of white cambric petticoats and under-petticoats, a chemise, an embroidered corset cover, and a small horsehair bustle. But it was the pair of almost-sheer navy blue silk stockings lying draped across Elizabeth's leather half-boots that played havoc with his control. James squeezed his eyes shut and clamped his teeth together in a determined effort to will away the image of Elizabeth's long slim legs, encased in navy blue silk, and locked around his waist, but the erotic image continued to tease his senses.

"Daddy's quash me!"

James hadn't realized he was holding Ruby too tightly until she began to wiggle in an effort to relieve the pressure of his embrace. A sheepish expression crossed his face as he immediately loosened his grasp to allow Ruby more freedom of movement. "Oh, Button, Daddy's so sorry."

"Humph," Ruby snorted, still disgruntled about her bath and because her father wasn't paying attention to her.

James glanced down at his daughter and recognizing the pouting expression on her face, shifted her to one arm, then tilted her chin up to look at him with the tip of his index finger. "Daddy didn't realize he was squashing you, Ruby-button. He's very sorry." He let go of her chin and planted a tender kiss against Ruby's forehead.

"He should be sorry for barging in uninvited," Elizabeth retorted, embarrassed and the tiniest bit envious of Ruby as she watched the way James tenderly cuddled his daughter close and kissed her forehead. "He owes us all an apology."

James gave a nod in Elizabeth's direction as he walked over to the closet and reached inside for a couple of thick terry-cloth towels. He wrapped one towel around Ruby, then set the child on her feet beside the bathtub. "I *did* knock," he pointed out ungraciously, focusing his gaze on Elizabeth. "Although I don't suppose you heard me. In any case, I owe you an apology for barging in on your toilette without awaiting permission to enter. All I can offer in my defense is the fact that I was worried because I forgot to warn you about Ruby's unfortunate bathtime phobia and the fact that I was expecting to find you bathing two toddlers, not bathing *with* them."

His blue-eyed gaze saw too much. Elizabeth felt her face redden beneath James's intense scrutiny. And in spite of her best efforts to prevent it, her breath quickened and her breasts rose and fell in cadence to her rapid breathing. "Ruby was frightened," she replied, somewhat defensively. "And climbing into the bathtub myself was the only way to reach her."

Thunderation, but she was killing him. The strain of struggling to behave normally was killing him. James ground his teeth together again and a muscle in his jaw began to tick from the pressure. He had to get out of there. Elizabeth couldn't possibly understand how her innocent explanation for climbing into the bathtub evoked images he was valiantly trying to control. Reaching out, he unfolded the second towel and held it out in front of him almost as a shield, then ground out, "For Garnet. She's turning into a prune."

"I know," Elizabeth agreed, bracing her hands on the sides of the tub to lever herself up and out of the water. "We're behind schedule. I should have finished their baths

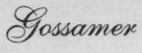

half an hour ago. You go ahead with Ruby. Garnet and I will be right behind you.''

"No!" James replied in a rather strained voice. "You stay right there. Just hand me Garnet and I'll leave you to fill up the tub and finish your bath in peace."

"I'm not bathing." Elizabeth said as she helped Garnet get to her feet, then kept a hand on her until James leaned forward, wrapped the child in the towel, and lifted Garnet out of the tub.

"You might as well," James said, staring down at her. "You've had a long, busy day. Relax and enjoy a hot bath. Delia and I can look after the Treasures for a while."

"I appreciate your thoughtfulness," Elizabeth began to protest, although the idea of filling the bathtub full of hot water and bubbles and soaking her tired body appealed to her more than she liked to admit, "but it really isn't necessary."

"Oh, but it is," James insisted. "You're joining me for dinner at eight, remember? And if you don't take advantage of your opportunity to bathe now, you may not get another chance before dinner. Besides"—he bent low to turn the hot water tap back on and whispered—"the question of whether or not you're bathing has already become a moot point. In case you haven't noticed, it's transparent . . . uh . . ." James could have bitten out his wayward tongue. "*Apparent* that you're soaked to the skin."

Elizabeth looked down at the wet fabric clinging to her chest, revealing more than it concealed, and gasped. "I didn't realize . . ."

Unable to stop himself, James grinned an impish grin, then whispered his confession. "I did."

The glint of blue-green fire in her eyes warned him before her furious squeal did. He opened the bathroom door and shepherded Ruby and Garnet through it just seconds before Elizabeth's wet, soapy camisole landed against it with loud, watery *thwack*.

"Missed me," he commented as he opened the door seconds later and stuck his head inside. "You throw like a girl," he taunted, adding insult to injury.

Maybe so, but the facecloth that followed her camisole came closer to its mark and left a trail of soapy water splashed across James's handsome face before it slipped down the door and landed on the marble floor.

Much to her disgust, Elizabeth couldn't prevent a silent chuckle from escaping her lips when she heard James's roar of laughter on the other side of the door.

Twenty-two

ELIZABETH FINGERED THE edges of her smoke-colored satin wrapper before she loosened it and untied the matching sash. She sat on the edge of her half-tester bed and carefully moved Portia off the pillows to the far side of the bed before she flung herself backward, so that she lay in an unselfconscious sprawl in the center of the bed. She had been about twenty minutes into her long soak in the bathtub when James knocked on the bathroom door to inform her that the wrapper she'd worn at breakfast was hanging on the doorknob whenever she was ready for it. Elizabeth had childishly stuck her tongue out at the door and muttered a few uncomplimentary names about him beneath her breath before reluctantly admitting that she was rather glad he'd thought to leave it for her. Her undergarments were wet and a good many of her outer garments were, too, since the water from the camisole and the facecloth she'd thrown at James had pooled and run across the marble floor to the pile of clothing she'd left lying there.

How could she go downstairs and have dinner with the man after what had happened in the bath? But how could she think of not going? Elizabeth glanced over at the armoire. She was going. And she was going to wear her fa-

vorite dress. The elegant and sophisticated green silk gown
showed off her figure in just the right places. She knew she
should probably wear a dress more sedate—more gover-
nessy—but there was something about the way James Craig
looked at her that sent ripples of excitement shivering
through her. When he looked at her, Elizabeth experienced
a sense of expectation and an acute awareness that triggered
goose bumps on her flesh and an intense yearning deep
inside her. She wanted very much to explore those feelings.

What was it about James Craig that brought out that restless, unbridled, untamed, unladylike side of her? Elizabeth
frowned, suddenly confused and thrilled and dismayed by
this new and unexpected aspect of her personality—all at
the same time. Less than an hour ago she had knelt in a
tub full of water while her employer looked on. That she
hadn't known the undergarments she'd left on, for modesty's sake, were transparent when wet did not excuse her
behavior. She shouldn't have been in the tub in the first
place, and he certainly shouldn't have barged in and seen
her.

But he had seen her, and though embarrassed by her lack
of modesty, Elizabeth was also secretly thrilled at the way
her body quickened and her heart pounded in response to
the look in James's eyes. Two days ago she had vandalized
a business in broad daylight in downtown San Francisco
and been carted to jail for her efforts. She should have been
ashamed of herself, but she wasn't. There was a part of her
that rejoiced at her having had the courage to strike a blow
for Owen and all of the other unfortunate young men who
had succumbed to the lure of opium. Less than a week ago
she had allowed a strange man to enter her hotel room in
the middle of the night and not only offer words of comfort,
but to hold her in his arms while she slept. And she'd allowed that same man to kiss her senseless on the front
walkway of a boardinghouse run by an infamous madam.
That the stranger had been James still did not excuse her
behavior. And yet it did, because Elizabeth knew in her
heart that she would never have allowed any other man past

her door in the middle of the night or allowed him to kiss her so thoroughly. But how could she explain feeling like a butterfly emerging from its chrysalis when she didn't even know when or why or how the metamorphosis had begun? She only knew that James had somehow recognized and responded to it.

And what a metamorphosis she had had so far! Elizabeth grabbed a pillow and hugged it to her chest. Today had been an adventure in itself, thanks, in large part, to Ruby. Ruby. Who would have dreamed a three-and-a-half-year-old child could be so demanding and strong-willed? Or so terrified of water? Or so overwhelmingly possessive of her father?

Her father. Still pleasantly warm and damp from her hot bubble bath, Elizabeth stared up at the half-tester and covered a yawn as she listened to the sound of James's deep melodic voice coming from the room next door. Elizabeth had purposely left her bedroom door slightly ajar so that she could hear the story as James resumed his reading of the adventures of Don Quixote to the Treasures. She liked the way he read aloud, the way he dramatized the story, the way he patiently endured endless interruptions to answer the Treasures' questions or to explain the nuances of the story so toddlers might understand it. Tonight they were finishing chapter twenty-two. Pasamonte and his gang were about to stone Don Quixote and Sancho and steal their clothes, and James was skimming over the passages the Treasures might find disturbing and making a great to-do over the knight's heroism. Elizabeth smiled at the notion of James Cameron Craig shielding his daughters from the more disturbing events in the life of the fictitious hero, Don Quixote, just as he shielded them, every day, from the more disturbing events that might touch their real lives. Elizabeth closed her eyes and let James's voice fill her imagination with images of courtly knights and their lady loves. Chivalry hadn't died at all. It still flourished in the heart of one extraordinary man.

꧁ꕥ꧂

JAMES STOPPED HIS nervous pacing and focused his attention on the rapidly melting beeswax candles in the silver candelabrum on the table. He glanced over at the clock on the dining room wall to check the time again. Twenty-six minutes past eight. Three minutes later than the last time he'd checked. He raked his fingers through his hair. Elizabeth was late. Or worse yet, she had decided not to come downstairs and join him for dinner.

He walked around the table to his customary seat, lifted a small silver bell from beside his plate and rang it. Annie appeared in the doorway almost instantly, almost as if she'd been waiting just outside it listening for the sound of the bell.

"Shall I begin serving now, sir?" she asked as she lifted the skirt of her white apron a fraction and bobbed a respectful curtsey.

James shook his head. "No. Not yet." He walked to the opposite end of the table and gazed down at the place setting laid out for Elizabeth. He hesitated for a moment, then lifted the plate and silverware and carried it to the chair sitting to the right of his own and relaid the place setting on the table in front of it.

"Shall I do that for you, sir?" Annie asked.

"No, thank you, Annie. I can manage. There's no need to bother you with this." He walked back down to the opposite end of the table and removed the bread and dessert plates and the glassware.

"I'll be glad to do it, sir," Annie insisted. "It's no bother."

"Actually, I would rather do it myself," he told her. "I think I've gotten quite good at this during the last half hour. I've already removed and reset Miss Sadler's place three times." James flashed the timid little kitchen maid a crooked half-smile. The tips of his ears warmed in embarrassment at his uncharacteristic admission of nerves. Suddenly he turned his full attention on Annie. "What are you

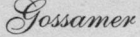

doing here? It's late. You should have had your supper and left for home an hour ago.''

"I asked Mrs. G. if I could stay a bit later tonight. I thought there might be something I could do to help out.'' Annie shrugged her shoulders self-consciously and looked down at a scuff mark on her polished, but well-worn, boots.

"Why would a pretty young girl like you want to work later than necessary?'' James asked.

"Ah, I'm not pretty, Mr. Craig. I'm plain,'' she informed him. "I'm way too skinny, too. All elbows and knees with no boo—no figure to speak of. And I've got this flaming red hair and no eyebrows or eyelashes and spots on my face. It's common knowledge that I'm never going to be passable, much less pretty. Everyone says so.'' She hunched her shoulders and seemed to withdraw from him.

James studied Annie's downtrodden expression, the flush of bright red color that stained her cheeks, the way she tried desperately not to meet his gaze and the way she attempted to hide her under-developed body by hunching her shoulders and looking down at the floor. She did have flaming red hair, but it was thick and curly and he'd bet his last cent that in five or six years, her hair would darken into a rich, burnished copper color. In a few years Annie's facial blemishes would fade, and women throughout the town would envy her pale ivory complexion and big blue eyes. "Who told you that nonsense?"

"My brothers and the boys in town. And''—she lowered her voice to a tortured whisper—"my dad.''

"How old are you? Fourteen? Fifteen?"

"Sixteen.'' She cringed as she answered.

"And how old are your brothers?'' he asked.

"Eleven, fourteen, and eighteen.''

"Well,'' James pronounced in a voice full of confidence and authority, "that explains it.''

"Explains what?'' Annie's blue eyes widened with curiosity.

"It explains what's wrong with your brothers and the

boys in town," James told her. "Everyone knows that boys
that age are louts. Especially to their sisters. As for the boys
in town, well, they've not yet matured enough to be able
to recognize beauty when they see it. You mark my words.
In five or six years those same callow fellows who make
fun of you now will be begging for a scrap of your attention. You see, Annie, your red hair and coloring have been
passed down for generations from the beautiful women of
Scotland, Ireland, England, Brittany, and Wales. You're an
unmistakable Celtic beauty. But the boys you know are too
ignorant to notice."

"Really?" she asked hopefully. "You think they'll notice in a few years?"

"I'll stake my fortune on it." He smiled at her.

"What about my dad?" Annie whispered.

James frowned. "There's no excuse for your dad," he
replied harshly. "Some men never appreciate the unique
and wondrous beauty around them. But that doesn't excuse
them. Certainly there's no excuse for a father who doesn't
think his daughter is the loveliest creature the good Lord
ever put on earth." James paused to let his words sink in,
then waited until he thought he recognized a glimmer of
trust in Annie's blue eyes. "Now, why don't you tell me
the real reason you wanted to work late tonight?"

"Because it's Friday night," she replied as if that explained everything.

"I'm sorry, Annie," James apologized for his ignorance
on the subject of Friday nights in Coryville. "But I don't
understand what Friday night has to do with your wanting
to work late. I would think it would be just the opposite—
that you would want to get off early."

"My dad drinks," Annie confided. "And my oldest
brother, Calvin, drinks. And on Friday nights they invite
all their friends home to drink at our house. And, well"—
tears sparkled in her bright blue eyes and her voice caught
in her throat—"sometimes it gets ugly with them all paw-
ing at me and saying that they might have to put a bag over
my head, but they'll be more than willing to suffer in order

...o me a favor and teach me all the things a girl needs ...know in order to please a man.''

"Has anyone ever touched you?" James clenched his ...sts to contain his rage. His immediate concern was Annie's safety, but his rage extended to her brothers and to her father, who had failed to see her inner beauty as well as her potential outer beauty and had demeaned and belittled her during the most awkward and confusing time of her life. James was furious with her brothers and her father for failing to care for and appreciate Annie as she deserved to be cared for, and appreciated and loved, just as she was—just for being herself.

"No, sir, not yet, but it's hard to avoid 'em when they get mean and drunk every Friday," she admitted.

"I believe there's an extra bedroom beside Mrs. G.'s suite. If you like it and want it, Annie, it's yours," James said.

"For Fridays?"

"For any day you want, for as long as you want," he told her.

"Oh, Mr. Craig, thank you." Forgetting herself, Annie rushed forward and flung her arms around his neck and hugged him. She then quickly stepped back and blushed. "Beg pardon, sir."

"That's quite all right, Annie," James said, "I needed a hug to reassure me, for I seem to have lost my dinner companion tonight." He glanced back at the clock on the wall as his stomach rumbled, then turned his attention to the two empty place settings on the table. Eight thirty-three. "Have you eaten?"

"Yes, sir. Ages ago." She shifted her weight from one leg to the other. "May I go tell Mrs. G. about the room now, sir?"

James managed a rueful smile and gazed longingly at the table before he turned his attention back to Annie. "Sure, run along. I don't think I'll be needing you to help serve dinner for a while."

Annie was halfway through the dining room door before

she remembered what she wanted to say to him. She tu.
and smiled at James. "I don't believe a word of what th
say about you, Mr. Craig."

James's heart seemed to skip a beat. Could Annie have
possibly heard the rumors about him killing his wife? He
swallowed hard. "Really?"

Annie nodded her head. "I don't believe a word they say
about you being daft in the head where those little girls of
yours—the Treasures—are concerned."

"Is that what the townspeople say?"

"Yes, sir. They say you're real queer about them and
that you're teaching them to be uppity instead of knowing
their place in the world like all the other Celestials. Everybody says you're teaching the Treasures to think they're as
good as white folks *because* they're Celestials, not in spite
of it."

James sucked in a breath. He had known the townspeople
didn't share or appreciate his love for his daughters. But
he hadn't known how much the townspeople resented his
educating them. "What do you think, Annie?"

"I think you treat the Treasures the way you do because
you love them," she said simply. "Because you're a man
who sees and appreciates the unique and wondrous beauty
around him and because you really and truly like *girls*.
Even girls like me."

"Every girl is a Treasure, Annie. Every girl is a rare and
precious gem. God thought so or he would have bestowed
the greatest gift of all on men by giving them the ability
to carry and bear children." James winked at her. "You're
descended from a long line of wonderful women. Prin-
cesses, every one of them. And don't you ever forget it. Or
let any mere man tell you differently."

"I won't, Mr. Craig. I promise." Annie left the dining
room and headed toward the kitchen, and as she did so,
James noticed that she held her head higher and her back
straighter and carried with her a newfound sense of dignity
and self-esteem.

Moments later James's housekeeper, Helen Glenross, ap-

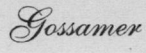

peared in the doorway of the dining room. "What did you say to Annie?" she asked.

"I told her how much we valued her," James answered.

"Well, whatever you said sure made a world of difference in her. I've never seen her stand so tall and proud. She's practically bubbling over with excitement at having a room to herself whenever she wants it. Heaven only knows how she's managed so far as the only girl in a house full of boys, headed by a drunken and neglectful father. Her mother ran off, you know."

"No," James admitted, "I didn't know." It seemed there were quite a few things going on in his storybook town that he didn't know about. But he intended to remedy that situation as soon as possible.

"I came to add my thanks to Annie's, Mr. Craig. She's a good girl and a hard worker, and she ought to be rewarded for it. Besides, a girl her age needs a room of her own. And I hope you don't mind, but I sort of promised her that she could paint it any color she wanted."

"That's fine," James said. "And take her to pick out wallpaper and all the trimmings if she wants it."

Mrs. G. wiped her hands on the skirt of her apron. "I've got to get back to the kitchen and make sure I don't scorch your dinner. I don't know how much longer I can keep it hot without ruining it. When I heard the bell, I thought for sure that you'd finished your sherry and were ready for the first course. What's the holdup?"

"Miss Sadler's the holdup," James replied. "She hasn't come downstairs for dinner yet."

"What?" Mrs. G. glanced around the dining room and seemed to notice, for the first time, that Elizabeth wasn't there.

"I thought, perhaps, she had changed her mind about joining me for dinner," James admitted. "And I thought that you might have sent a supper tray to her room instead."

"Miss Sadler didn't request a supper tray," Mrs. G. denied. "And I know I didn't prepare one for her."

"I know I embarrassed her," he muttered beneath his breath. "But . . ." James turned to Mrs. G., a look akin to fear on his face. "You don't suppose she decided not to eat again?"

Mrs. G. shrugged her shoulders. "It's possible," she replied cautiously. "Why don't I go upstairs and find out?"

"No." James shook his head. "You stay down here and take care of dinner. I'll go upstairs and find out what's keeping Miss Sadler. I embarrassed her earlier this evening. If she's decided she doesn't want to join me for dinner, that's fine. We'll work out a dining schedule. But she's going to have to tell me she doesn't want to share a table with me face to face. I'm not going to allow her to miss meals by hiding away in her bedroom." He paused for a moment, then lowered his voice and said to himself, "I can't allow it. Not again."

Helen Glenross watched as her employer stalked out of the dining room. You never could tell about people. To look at him, no one would ever think that such a fine, fit figure of a man, without an ounce of spare flesh on him, would have such a predilection for eating three full meals a day. But she had learned early in her employment that James Craig was fanatical about mealtimes. Nobody missed meals in Craig House without his knowing why.

Elizabeth Sadler had already missed one dinner served to her at Craig House. She'd better have a darned good reason for missing another one.

Twenty-three

ELIZABETH HAD A very good reason for missing dinner, James discovered as he walked through the quiet nursery, past the bedroom where the Treasures were sleeping, through the kitchen alcove to Elizabeth's room. He raised his fist to announce his presence by knocking, then found it wasn't necessary. Her bedroom door was ajar and through the crack James could see that Elizabeth lay sprawled in the center of the half-tester bed, fast asleep.

He started to obey his first impulse and walk away, but James gave into an almost overwhelming need to push the door open a little farther and quietly step over the threshold into her room. He pushed the door open with his elbow, thinking as he did so that, in the short time he'd known Elizabeth Sadler, he had conveniently managed to disregard a lifetime of gentlemanly manners and ethics. James frowned. So far he managed to barge in on her at least three times without an invitation—four times, if he counted the night at the Russ House in San Francisco, and James was honest enough to count the night at the Russ House, because although Elizabeth had invited him to enter her room, he had known he was preying on her sorrow and had been the one to force the issue. And not only had he suddenly

developed the habit of barging in to wherever Elizabeth was
just to see her, James was forced to admit that he had also
been willing to have her arrested on trumped-up charges of
theft and even jailed if necessary, so that he could act the
part of the magnanimous rescuer and bail her out of trouble.
He snorted in self-disgust. Even that part of his despicable
scheme had been a lie. Elizabeth hadn't needed rescuing.
The members of the police department had recognized the
trumped-up charge and Elizabeth's character for what they
were, and had already taken up a donation to bail her out
of jail. There had never been a real reason for him to step
in and practically browbeat her into accepting the job as
governess to the Treasures except that he had wanted her
and had been unwilling to settle for anyone else.

James shook his head. My, how the mighty had fallen!
And at what price? Elizabeth lay in the center of the half-
tester bed in what could only be described as an exhausted
slumber. A small lamp glowed with a steady flame on the
dresser in preparation for her toilette and the door of the
armoire was open, but Elizabeth had apparently made no
further progress in her efforts to dress for dinner. She still
wore the smoke-colored satin wrapper she had worn at
breakfast—the one he had fetched from this room and hung
on the bathroom doorknob while she was bathing. The
wrapper had come loose and twisted around her in her
sleep, leaving a tantalizing inch or so of naked torso and
her long slim legs exposed to his view. James forced himself to ignore the fantasies that popped into his head at the
glimpses of tender flesh she revealed. He concentrated, instead, on the way her long tawny-colored hair fanned out
across the bed and the way baby-fine wisps of it curled
around her face. She slept as soundly as a child, clutching
a pillow to her chest. An apparently much-loved doll rested
on the pillow beside her.

The sound of her heavy breathing reminded him of his
daughters' in the bedroom next door, as did the way she
slept with her lips slightly parted. A strand of hair was
caught in the corner of her mouth, and James reached down

and gently pulled it away, brushing his knuckles against the satiny soft curve of her cheek as he did so. The flawless ivory skin of her face was every bit as soft as the Treasures'. James marveled at the feel of it. But it was the network of fine blue lines crisscrossing her eyelids and the dark purplish bruises beneath her eyes that caused the first swift kick of guilt to hit him in the gut when he realized how tired Elizabeth must have been to have fallen asleep so quickly and so soundly. She couldn't have had much sleep in the past few days, not after journeying from the East Coast to California by train. He remembered thinking how exhausted and fragile she had seemed as she slept in his arms that night at Russ House. How could he have forgotten how tumultuous her arrival in California had been? James shook his head at his lack of consideration.

His life had become equally tumultuous since he arrived in California. His life had changed so much since Ruby had joined the family, that he sometimes didn't recognize it as belonging to James Cameron Craig. He could barely remember a time when he hadn't slept with one eye and one ear open, afraid to sleep too deeply for fear that he wouldn't wake up if Ruby or one of the other girls needed him during the night. It seemed he'd spent the past three years existing on catnaps while he managed to maintain a full work schedule at Craig Capital. He wasn't complaining. He would gladly sacrifice any amount of sleep in order to be there if the Treasures needed him, but James had existed on so little sleep for so long that he had forgotten Elizabeth wasn't accustomed to keeping up with three toddlers and a newborn infant. Or the long hours and the full schedule he'd devised for her as the Treasures' governess.

He leaned forward and carefully eased himself down on the edge of the bed, careful not to jostle the bed and awaken her. His conscience nagged at him. Elizabeth had fooled him. She had a core of strength that made her seem strong and invincible when she stood up to him at every turn, but she also had a vulnerable, fragile streak. He'd recognized both her strength and her fragility the first night he'd met her. He should have remembered how small she was, how delicate and light she'd felt as he held her in his arms. James stared down at her. She was tall and slim, and from what he'd seen in the bath, there wasn't a spare ounce of flesh on her anywhere. She couldn't afford to miss anymore meals. And now, because of him, she'd missed two. James let out a breath. And he had thought requesting her company for dinner was a foolproof means of killing two birds with one stone—of seeing that she took care of herself—and of getting to know her better. James shook his head. Well, he'd certainly botched the job by working her too hard. Besides, it was time to be honest with himself. His reasons for inviting her to dinner hadn't been nearly as noble as he wanted to believe. Certainly he wanted to get to know Elizabeth better and to see that she took better care of herself, but his sole purpose for inviting her to join him for dinner had been to charm her.

He was attracted to her and he fully intended to do everything in his power to charm her, to woo her, and to eventually win her over. He had tried to tell himself that the attraction he felt for Elizabeth could be contained within the boundaries of the governess–employer relationship. And maybe he had believed it when he first decided to hire her. Maybe it had been possible then. But breakfast this morning had shattered that illusion. James had looked at Elizabeth sitting across the table holding his infant daughter to her breast, and he had wanted that reality more than anything else on earth.

Right there and then he had finally understood why he'd tossed aside the ethics of a lifetime to locate her. Why he'd called in markers and political favors in order to have Elizabeth detained on the flimsiest of charges. It wasn't enough that Elizabeth act as mother for his children—he wanted her to *be* their mother. As he sat at the breakfast table watching while she fed Diamond her morning bottle, James had been struck by a desire so pure and so powerful that had he been standing, it would have brought him to his knees.

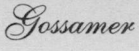

He wanted to see Elizabeth at breakfast every morning. He wanted to watch her care for his children every day and most of all, he wanted to love her, to give her more children to love—including a few of their own. And then he wanted to share the privilege of bringing those children into the world and watching while they nursed at their mother's breast. It was as basic and as incredibly complex as that.

James sighed. He was so tired. So bone-numbing tired of being alone. Of course he had Ruby and Garnet and Emerald and Diamond and he loved them more than he had ever dreamed possible, but it wasn't enough. He was a man who had taken a portion of his family inheritance and made himself a millionaire in his own right. He was greedy. He didn't want to settle for less when there was every wondrous possibility that he could settle for more. Suddenly James realized that the best part of himself had been missing for over three years. Mei Ling had taken it to the grave with her but Elizabeth had somehow found and resurrected it.

Elizabeth shivered and James leaned forward and closed the folds of her dressing gown around her, then carefully reached over her and pulled the coverlet of the bed up and tucked it in around her legs. This was what was he had been missing. This incredible feeling of tenderness for a woman, the sense of rightness in being with her and touching her.

Mei Ling been dead for over three years, and in all that time, he hadn't wanted any woman for more than an hour or so. There hadn't been anyone of any duration since he'd arrived in California. No one he wanted to hold during the night, no one he trusted enough to put in charge of the Treasures or to hold him while he slept. Until Elizabeth. James watched her as she slept and wondered what it was that had prompted his attraction to her beyond an appreciation for her beauty, her spirit, her willingness to tackle any challenge, and her resourcefulness. Was it because he had met her at a time when Mei Ling lay heavily on his mind? Or perhaps, in spite of it? Was it because he had awakened in the middle of the night, heard her crying, and thought it was his wife? Or was it because at first, when he had thought she was Mei Ling, hope had sprung to life deep inside him and James had somehow known that if he could only get past the barred door to her room, he would be granted a miraculous second chance to put back all the pieces of his life and to make things right? Or because the hope had stayed even after he knew she wasn't Mei Ling? Was it because Elizabeth reminded him of Mei Ling in some way? Or because Elizabeth was nothing like her? James didn't know. He only knew that when he looked at Elizabeth he felt hopeful again, felt alive in a way that he had not felt since Mei Ling had torn their world apart.

James frowned. Elizabeth and Mei Ling were as different as night and day. As far apart as any two women could possibly be in all the ways that mattered except one—he had wanted both of them the first time he saw them.

James ran his hand through his hair. Even their entrances into his life were as different as night and day. He'd had to pursue Elizabeth to bring her into his home, while Mei Ling had been delivered to him—as a gift. His sixteenth birthday gift.

James smiled at the memory. His father had been amused and his mother appalled at the fact that one of Randall Craig's oldest and most trusted Chinese advisers had purchased Mei Ling at auction and offered her to Randall as a birthday gift for his son. And there had been no way for Randall Craig to graciously refuse the gift. Not when he knew that to do so would cause his old friend Cho to lose face, and not when he had known that refusal to accept Mei Ling into the household meant she would most likely be turned out on the street to starve. Times were hard in the Canton province, and Mei Ling's family had sold her to a flesh broker who had smuggled her off the mainland and taken her to Hong Kong to be sold as a serving girl or prostitute or concubine. Randall Craig's employee, Cho Xing, had seen her at the auction and presented her at the house of his noble employer, Randall Craig, because he

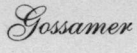

knew Craig had a young son who would welcome such a gift.

And on James's sixteenth birthday, fourteen-year-old Mei Ling had become a member of the Craig household. Cho had presented her to James with great ceremony and fanfare, and the willowy beauty known as Mei Ling had become his. James knew his mother and father would never allow him to keep Mei Ling as a concubine, but he also understood the importance of saving face. He had played along as Cho extolled Mei Ling's virtues and listened to his assurances that she was skilled in the art of lovemaking and had been taught all the secrets of pleasing a man. And from the moment he saw her, James made up his mind that when the time came for him to learn the art of lovemaking, he wanted Mei Ling to teach him.

In the end they had taught each other. Mei Ling was welcomed into Craig House, not as concubine or servant, but as Randall Craig's ward. She was sent to the Presbyterian Mission School run by Will's father, the Reverend Francis W. Keegan, and educated there. James knew his mother and father hoped that welcoming Mei Ling into the family and treating her as a daughter would foster a brother–sister relationship between them, and he tried to oblige them by doing his best to ignore Mei Ling during the two years he lived at home, before he left for England and the university. But knowing Mei Ling was his carried a certain aphrodisiacal cachet all its own. They had both known from the beginning that she'd been given to him as a concubine. And although James tried to please his parents and treat Mei Ling as a sister, he couldn't. He didn't want a foster sister, he wanted a lover and he wanted Mei Ling. His feelings for her weren't brotherly or platonic. He was in love for the first time in his life.

James frowned, amazed in retrospect at how well soft-spoken, timid Mei Ling had known him. She never set out to win his love, she simply took it for granted that she had it. She had been given to him, but he belonged to her as well. Fate had placed her in Cho Xing's path on the day of James's sixteenth birthday, and from that day forward she felt that her destiny and his were intertwined. They belonged to each other. Mei Ling never set out to seduce him, she simply assumed that one day they would fulfill their destiny by becoming the lovers they were meant to be. And while she was quiet and reserved and demure in public, Mei Ling was anything but weak. She was young and beautiful and she believed in the strength of her beauty as only the young and the very beautiful can. She was spoiled and petted and pampered by the Craig household from the day she joined them, and in her own way, Mei Ling became a stubborn force to be reckoned with. Her role as foster daughter to Randall and Julia Cameron Craig failed to satisfy her need to be loved. She wanted to assume the role for which she had been chosen. She didn't want to settle for being James's foster sister when she could be his wife. His first wife, not his concubine.

They became lovers shortly after James returned home from England and the university. He was twenty-one. Mei Ling was nineteen. He had learned a great deal about the art of pleasing women while away at school in England. Beautiful, virginal Mei Ling had known nothing about pleasing men, and yet, he'd been pleased because she was his—at last.

When his parents learned of the affair, they decided it would be best to let it run its course. Once the passion between James and Mei Ling burned itself out, they could be married to other, more suitable, spouses. For James, that meant marrying a European heiress to one of the many commercial banking and shipping firms in Hong Kong. For Mei Ling, it meant marrying a young Chinese man from a good family and with good prospects for the future. But James and Mei Ling had other ideas, and three months after they became lovers, James told his parents that he and Mei Ling were going to be married.

"You can't be serious!" Randall Craig had blustered, knowing full well from the expression on his son's face that James was completely serious.

"Think, Jamie," his mother, Julia, had pleaded, "I know you love Mei Ling. We love her as well, but you're British and she's Chinese. She'll never be accepted by society here."

"She's already accepted, Mother," he had argued. "She's lived with us for years. You've treated her as your daughter for years. Mei Ling and I simply want to make it official."

His mother's face had hardened. "Mei Ling is accepted in society because she's our *ward*, Jamie. But that's the only reason she's accepted. Don't you understand? She's accepted now because one of the wealthiest men in Hong Kong chose to do his Christian duty and offer a poor Chinese girl food, shelter, clothing, and a place to live. She's treated like a member of the family now because everyone knows she isn't."

"What does it matter?" Flush with the passion and idealism of youth, James hadn't understood. "Once we're married, she'll be my wife. She'll be part of the family."

"It may not seem like much to you now, Jamie, because you've always taken acceptance for granted. You've always had a place in society and understood where you belong and you couldn't care less what society thinks of you. You're a man. You have that luxury. But Mei Ling is different. She adores attention. She adores the parties and fetes and society gatherings. And she can have those things as long as she's our ward. She may even be able to have them once your *affaire d'amour* has run its course and she's safely married to some enlightened Chinese gentleman."

"Mei Ling isn't some whore I picked up in a dockside brothel," James said. "You know her. You know who she is and what she is. She's lived in your house and been treated like your daughter for years. She's a lady, for God's sake. And she was a virgin until *I* took her maidenhead."

"Jamie!" His mother had gasped at the crudity.

"Are you planning to marry her out of some sense of guilt or of responsibility because you took her maidenhead?" Randall asked.

James shook his head. "I'm marrying Mei Ling, with or without your blessing, because I love her and she loves me. And I want you to understand that ours is not an *affaire d'amour*, but an *affaire de coeur* that isn't going to run its course, Mother, simply because you feel it should. We're in love. We have been for years. And we want to get married and have a family and we want your blessing."

"But, Jamie," Julia had protested, "if you go through with this romantic and foolish marriage, Mei Ling will be snubbed by the same people who profess to adore her company now, and what's worse is that she'll be shunned by the Chinese as well. You both will. You'll be excluded from polite circles and ostracized from society because you will have overstepped the boundaries of what is and is not acceptable. You may not care about that. You may think that those things don't matter because you're a man and able to do as you please. But Mei Ling will be trapped, Jamie. She'll be caught between our two cultures as surely as a fish is caught in a net. She'll be miserable and she'll make you miserable because even though I've no doubt that she loves you with all her heart, she also wants to be somebody. She's ambitious, Jamie. She wants to rise above her humble beginnings and be Mrs. James Cameron Craig."

"And she will be," James asserted.

But Julia sadly shook her head. "No, Jamie. She won't be. Not here. Not in our lifetime. No matter how many times or how many ways you marry her, to the people here in Hong Kong, she will always be the little *Celestial heathen,* the little concubine that Randall Craig took in because she was given to his son as a birthday gift. And the fact that you love each other won't matter at all to the people you've always thought of as friends, because they're going to be horrified at the fact that James Cameron Craig *married* a girl he could have accommodated anytime he wanted without resorting to a ring and a license."

"Is that what you think?" James demanded.

"No," Julia replied honestly. "But it's what all your friends will think. It's what they'll say."

"I don't care what they say," James announced. "I love Mei Ling and she loves me and that's all that matters."

"I pray you're right, son," Julia said. "I pray with all my heart that you're right."

He had naively thought that nothing mattered except the love he shared with Mei Ling, but he'd been wrong. Very wrong. His parents had known the lay of the land much better than he had. Although Julia did her best to open the doors of Hong Kong society to her new daughter-in-law, Mei Ling never received the acceptance she craved.

Julia tried to assuage Mei Ling's bitter disappointment and sense of isolation from the community that had once embraced her, by hosting all manner of parties and events at their Victoria home that most of the premier British and American families in Hong Kong felt obliged to attend. But it was to no avail. James and Mei Ling had broken the unwritten laws of the British Crown Colony and of its Colonists, and they had to be punished for doing so.

James watched as the beautiful, witty, and vivacious young woman he married retreated further and further into the customs and the teachings of her childhood. It was as if Mei Ling had decided to reject everything British as the British had, ultimately, rejected her. She gave up Western dress and Western customs and transformed herself into a model of Chinese womanhood. When Julia refused to allow Mei Ling to extend her redecorating of the wing she and James occupied to the rest of the house, James had bought a house for himself and Mei Ling on the edge of the British community, in an area reserved almost exclusively for Chinese merchants. James allowed Mei Ling to decorate it as she pleased and to hire a completely Chinese staff.

James was happy and content. And Mei Ling seemed equally happy and content with the life they'd built for themselves. They accepted invitations to events held at his parents' home and invited the Craigs and Will Keegan and one or two other bachelor friends of James's over for dinner on a regular basis. But none of James's married associates or any of Mei Ling's former friends or acquaintances ever accepted invitations to their house for dinner or for any reason. He and Mei Ling lived in relatively blissful isolation from the rest of the British community. James ignored the fact that his home reflected nothing of his Scots heritage, or contained any remnants of his Western culture except the clothes he wore to work. He ignored the fact that Mei Ling had retreated into the comforts of a thousand years of traditions. She was his wife and he loved her. He wanted her to be happy, and if shunning the Western world made her happy, he would gladly shun it and become as Chinese as he could possibly be. To please her, James adopted her customs and accepted her way—the Chinese way of life. And for nearly seven years, it worked, but then Mei Ling became pregnant and the world they had carefully constructed seemed to unravel like a paper lantern in the rain.

Unable to sit still any longer, James carefully eased himself off Elizabeth's bed and stood up. He slipped his feet out of his shoes so his footsteps wouldn't wake her, then walked over to the French doors and quietly slipped the bolt back from the lock. James opened the doors and stepped out onto the balcony, where he reached into his jacket pocket and pulled out a slim cigar case. He walked to the wrought-iron railing of the balcony that overlooked the garden, removed a cigar from the case and lit it. He took a drag on his cigar and exhaled. His eyes stung and watered, but whether from the painful memories or from the first puff of cigar smoke, he couldn't tell. The tip of his cigar burned red-orange in the night as James turned his back on the view of the garden and leaned against the railing, stretching his long legs out in front of him. Mei Ling was gone and he desperately wanted to be able to look back at their life together and remember the good times, but all he really remembered was the horror of their last months together and the overwhelming anger and loss.

James stared at the soft glow of the lamp coming from Elizabeth's bedroom. Elizabeth Sadler was the second chance he'd been waiting for. The chance he needed to

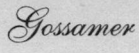

redeem himself from the nether world of lost and lonely souls he'd called home for so many years. Perhaps Will was right. Perhaps it was time to learn to change. To learn to let go of the past. To finally forgive Mei Ling for her tragic mistake and for leaving him alone without saying good-bye.

James took another puff on his cigar. He'd given his heart freely once. And he nearly hadn't survived the breaking of it. And there was even more than his own heart at stake this time. He had the Treasures to think of. He might be ready to risk his heart again, but he couldn't risk theirs.

For now it was enough to know that he wasn't entirely alone anymore. Elizabeth was waiting nearby.

Twenty-four

THE INSISTENT, ANGRY cries seemed to reach her from across a vast distance. Elizabeth opened her eyes. The faint aroma of an expensive cigar drifted in on the breeze from the balcony and the dim glow of the lamp on the dresser dispelled some of the darkness of the room. She stared up at the underside of the half-tester and waited for the sound that had awakened her. It came again. Stronger. More insistent; more urgent. Diamond. Elizabeth jackknifed into sitting position, swung her legs off the side of the bed and got to her feet. Something was wrong with Diamond. Bleary-eyed and half-asleep, she tripped over a pair of shoes lying by the side of her bed and stumbled out of her bedroom, heading down the short hall toward the nursery, guided by the sound of Diamond's cries and the small gas night light that burned in the hallway at the entrance to the nursery.

"Shh, shh."

The sound of the low voice stopped Elizabeth in her tracks.

"Shh," James repeated, bottle in hand, as he carried Diamond from her bedroom and into the main room of the nursery. He set the bottle on the Treasures' little table, then

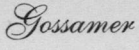

disappeared into the nursery bedroom for a moment. He reappeared with Diamond cradled in his left arm, the big wooden rocking chair beneath the other arm. He carried the chair into the main room and positioned it between the warming stove and the little round table. A fire burned low in the grate, casting flickering shadows against the wall.

James bent down and picked up the infant bottle. "I know you're hungry, but we mustn't cry so loud. We'll wake up Elizabeth and we don't want to do that. She's had a long hard day and she needs her sleep. Please, sweetheart, try to be patient for a few more seconds." Settling down onto the rocker, James hooked one stockinged foot under the rung of one of the small chairs that matched the round table and pulled it forward to use as a footstool. He rocked back and forth as he brought the rubber nipple of the feeding bottle to Diamond's mouth. "There. There it is. That's my girl," he soothed as Diamond latched on to the bottle and began to suck.

He leaned his head back against the chair and closed his eyes as he rocked.

Elizabeth paused in the doorway, watching. Her breath seemed to catch in her throat. Still dressed in evening clothes, James sat on the rocking chair holding Diamond in his arms. Sometime during the evening, he'd yanked the tail of his starched white dress shirt free of his trousers and unbuttoned it. His shirt hung open all the way down the front, the black onyx studs still precariously balanced in the buttonholes. His black satin tie was untied and the ends of it dangled from beneath his collar points. Elizabeth stared in fascination at the pattern of dark curly hair visible though the opening in his shirt. Her pulse quickened and her heart seemed to swell in her chest at the sight of James cradling his infant daughter against his starched shirt front while he fed her a bottle. Watching him, Elizabeth felt the full force of desire. All at once she was bombarded by feelings she'd read about, but never experienced. Suddenly she understood the passion that had driven Tristan and Iseult, Heloise and

Abelard, Romeo and Juliet. Suddenly she understood how it felt to look at a man and want him as a lover.

Diamond squirmed in James's embrace and he opened his eyes and looked down at her. "Are you uncomfortable, sweetheart? I don't blame you," he told her, "I don't like the feel of it, either." James shifted her slight weight higher in his arm and balanced the bottle against his stomach for a moment as he nudged his shirt out of the way. His stomach muscles rippled in reaction as the smooth glass bottle came in contact with his skin while he repositioned Diamond in his arm so that her tiny face rested against his warm flesh instead of the stiff and scratchy fabric of his shirt.

Elizabeth felt as if her heart was bumping against her rib cage. Her mouth went dry and she seemed to have trouble regulating her breathing. Her flesh began to tingle in anticipation and her body grew warm and moist and uncomfortable in the most intimate of places. She didn't think she'd made a sound, but she must have, because James suddenly looked up and saw her. "Good evening," he said softly. "Or good morning." He stared at Elizabeth for what seemed like an eternity before he asked, "Did she wake you?"

There seemed no point in politely pretending she hadn't. Elizabeth nodded.

"I heard her crying."

James frowned. "I was afraid of that."

"What was wrong with her?"

"She was hungry." He shrugged his shoulders. "That's the way it is with babies," he said. "There's no warning. One minute they're sleeping soundly and the next minute they're crying loud enough to wake the neighborhood. By the time I got from the balcony to the nursery and got her bottle warmed, she was really frustrated and upset."

"What were you doing on the balcony?"

Watching over you, James almost said as he mentally cursed his slip of the tongue. "I sit on the balcony to smoke," he said.

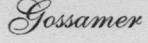

"This late at night?" Elizabeth pushed her hair out of her eyes. "When do you sleep?" Then before he could answer, she asked, "What time is it anyway?"

"I couldn't sleep." James smiled at her and Elizabeth noticed the network of fine lines at the corners of his blue eyes. "That's why I was still out on the balcony. And it's a little after three. I heard the clock downstairs chime a little while ago."

"I didn't hear anything." Elizabeth admitted. "I was dead to the world until Diamond started crying."

"Uh-oh." James clucked his tongue against his teeth and shook his head as if to he meant to commiserate with her. "That's a bad sign. It means you've got it."

"Got what?" She thought he was teasing her, but she couldn't be sure.

"Maternal instinct," he answered in a solemn tone of voice.

"That's bad?" Now she knew he was teasing. No one would ever think having a governess with maternal instinct was bad.

"It depends on how you look at it," James explained. "It's good for me because as your employer, I'm delighted to know I won't have to worry any longer about your not hearing the baby cry or the other girls call out should they need you at night. But it may not be so good for you." He shook his head as if he fully understood her new dilemma. "Because once you have children and discover you have maternal instinct, you never quite sleep as soundly again. You never quite feel you can relax your guard until the children are grown and able to take care of themselves."

Elizabeth shivered at the daunting prospect of never having another moment's peace where your children were concerned. "Is that how you feel?"

He nodded. "Every day of my life."

She smiled at him. The responsibility she'd accepted as governess was an awesome one, but somehow the idea of caring for the Treasures didn't seem quite as daunting knowing that James was equally committed to sharing the responsibility with her. Parenting didn't seem quite so over-whelming when two people were committed to the task. "You know," she said softly, "I should be doing that."

"Doing what?" He looked up at her, genuinely sur-prised.

"Feeding the baby."

Her quiet words evoked an image in his mind that rocked James to the core. Elizabeth feeding the baby—their baby. Elizabeth lying propped upon a mound of pillows in the center of his bed with him beside her watching as she opened her nightgown to share a plump breast with a beau-tiful dark-haired infant. He envisioned her lovely pear-shaped breast so engorged with milk that the aureole surrounding her pink nipple was twice its normal size. As he listened to the sucking sounds Diamond made as she pulled on the nipple of her bottle, James imagined her tiny bow-shaped mouth greedily suckling Elizabeth's lovely full breasts instead. And he vividly imagined himself sucking them long after the baby was satisfied. "Yes, you probably should be," he agreed at last. "But I don't mind."

"I really should be doing it," Elizabeth insisted. "It's what you're paying me for."

James grinned. "I haven't paid you yet. Besides," he said, pulling the empty bottle from the baby's mouth and setting it on the floor beside the rocking chair. "She's al-ready finished her bottle and I'm too comfortable to move." He gently turned Diamond onto her stomach, across his knees, and began to pat her back. He wasn't too comfortable to move. He was too *uncomfortable* to move. He was rock hard behind the front of his trousers and not about to stand up in front of Elizabeth and reveal the results of his erotic imagination. "You look tired. Why don't you go back to bed?"

"I *was* tired," Elizabeth told him. "So tired that the last thing I remember is Pasamonte throwing stones at the don and Sancho Panza."

James raised a questioning eyebrow in her direction.

"I was listening to you read *Don Quixote* to the Treasures while I was dressing for dinner.'' She stopped abruptly and widened her eyes in horror as she remembered. ''Dinner.'' Elizabeth stared at James, willing him to understand. ''I'm terribly sorry. I don't know what else to say. I forgot about our dinner.'' She moved farther into the room. ''How was it?''

''Lonely.''

The atmosphere seemed to thicken around them. Finding it hard to breathe normally or to think rationally when she was standing in front of the half-dressed man of her dreams wearing only a satin dressing gown, Elizabeth glanced down at her waist, then picked at a loose thread on the sash that encircled it. She pulled at the thread until it came away in her hands, unraveling the hem at the end of her dressing gown sash. Realizing what she'd done, Elizabeth tried to cover her attack of nervous energy and repair the damage done to her clothing by twisting the end of the sash into a tight little roll. ''I meant the food,'' she whispered.

''I don't know,'' he answered. ''I didn't eat.''

''Then you've broken one of your own cardinal rules.''

She moved with such grace. James couldn't stop looking at her, watching her. He couldn't help but feast on the way her satin dressing gown molded itself to her breasts and hips and thighs, the way the flicker of light from the stove seemed to reflect on the satin covering the slightly convex mound below her waist. ''Which are?'' He sounded as if he'd never heard of them.

''They're your rules,'' she replied. ''You should know what they are.''

''Refresh my memory,'' James answered in his deep, husky voice.

Elizabeth frowned at him.

''Humor me.''

''All right,'' she recited. ''Rule number one: Never leave the Treasures alone. Rule number two: Never leave the balcony door open. And rule number three: Never, ever, miss breakfast, lunch, or dinner.''

James closed his eyes. Those were rules he insisted his

staff abide by. He supposed they could be called cardinal
rules. And if breaking them meant punishment, he was already destined for purgatory. Because he hadn't just broken
one cardinal rule. Tonight, he'd broken all three. And he
was in serious danger of breaking cardinal rule number
four: never seduce your daughters' governess—or allow
your daughters' governess to seduce you. James's breath
caught in his throat as Elizabeth moved closer, then glanced
around the room, searching for some place to sit. He lifted
his feet from the seat of the chair he was using as a footstool and pushed it toward her. Elizabeth lowered herself
onto the tiny chair as James reached out with his foot,
hooked another one by its bottom rung and pulled it to him.

"You're quite adept at that," Elizabeth commented.

"I've usually got my hands full," he told her. "I've been
forced to learn to make good use of my other body parts."

"I'll bet," Elizabeth blurted out, staring not at James's
stockinged feet, but at the ripple of his muscles below the
thick wedge of hair on his chest. She didn't realize she'd
spoken the comment aloud until she heard the deep rumble
of his laughter.

Elizabeth blushed red from her neck to the roots of her
hair.

"Making comments like that can get you into trouble,"
he warned.

She lifted her chin a notch higher and defiantly flipped
a section of her long hair back over her shoulder. Elizabeth
felt as if she were walking on the edge of a precipice. One
wrong move and she could go tumbling over the rim, and
yet, she couldn't back off the path. She was compelled to
disregard the danger, to dance along the rim of the precipice, and to continue the thrilling journey into uncharted
territory. "Can it?"

"Aye." All traces of the crisp, proper British businessman vanished. James's one word answer was pure Scots
seduction.

Elizabeth wet her suddenly dry lips with the tip of her
tongue.

Her unconscious signal made James tense even more. And he was already wound as tightly as a clock. His body ached, practically screaming with the need for physical relief despite the fact that he'd been running all day long on less than four hours of sleep and was currently sitting in a rocking chair burping his three-day-old daughter after her early-morning bottle. "Doing that can get you into even bigger trouble."

Elizabeth looked up at him from her seat on the chair beside his feet. "I think it's too late for the warning. I think I'm in big trouble already," she whispered softly, fervently. "What should I do?"

James stared down into her extraordinary blue-green eyes and read the hot desire and the confusion mirrored in them. "Run," he whispered. "Save yourself while you can."

Elizabeth pushed herself to her feet. "Is that what you want?"

James's jaw tightened and he looked at her, willing her to understand. No, it wasn't what he wanted. Or what he needed. But it was the best thing for her. Elizabeth needed to understand that, needed to understand the noble sacrifice he was trying to make on her behalf. He patted Diamond one last time and listened as she let out a satisfied burp, then James lifted the baby from her place on his lap and held her out to Elizabeth. "What I want," he said bluntly, "is for you to do what you're paid to do. Take Diamond and put her to bed and—"

Elizabeth had the baby in her arms before he finished speaking.

James breathed a sigh of relief as she disappeared into the Treasures' bedroom. He stood quietly for a few moments, contemplating his next move. They were safe. At least for the moment. It was time for him to disappear. He turned and started toward the door, then came up short when Elizabeth blocked his path.

"And?" she asked softly, provocatively, deliberately moistening her lips with the tip of his tongue.

James stared blankly at her.

"You said you wanted me to put Diamond to bed and . . ."

James's whole body vibrated with the effort he was making to restrain himself. Every nerve he possessed hummed with tension, and he clamped down on his natural inclination to sweep Elizabeth off her feet and carry her to his bed. He gritted his teeth. "Oh, hell."

Elizabeth's face fell. Tears welled up in her eyes and threatened to spill over her bottom lashes.

James stared at the glimmer of tears and the stricken expression on her face and all of his good intentions evaporated. "And," he whispered as he reached for her and pulled her up against him. "Kiss me good night."

Twenty-five

THE FIRST BRUSH of his lips against hers set Elizabeth's heart racing and her nerve endings jangling. She leaned into him, wrapped her arms around his neck, and tilted her head back to better accommodate him. James cupped one of her firm plump breasts in his hand as he teased the seam of her lips with his tongue, tasting, probing until she parted her lips and allowed his tongue to slip through.

Elizabeth shivered as James used his tongue to woo her. He deepened his kiss. Elizabeth tasted him, feeling the roughness of his tongue as he raked the warm recesses of her mouth and taught her tongue how to answer his demands. She lost herself in his kiss—lost herself in the warmth of him, the scent of him, the feel of his hard body pressed to hers. If kissing was an art, James was the master of it and she, his most avid and ardent student, willingly learning everything he wanted to teach her.

Elizabeth burrowed her fingers into the thick hair at the nape of his neck and held on—wanting more of him, needing more of him.

Suddenly James broke the kiss. His breathing was heavy and irregular and his heart seemed to beat at a much faster rate than normal as he backed up a few steps to put some distance between them. James stared down at Elizabeth. Christ, but she was beautiful! Her lips were red and swollen from his kisses, the expression in her blue-green eyes slightly dazed, dreamy-eyed, and sensual. She looked as thoroughly kissed and as well loved as a new bride—even the creamy skin of her cheeks was suffused with color and slightly abraded by his unshaven jaw.

"Damn me," he muttered as he reached out with his index finger and gently traced a line along her cheekbone. He opened his mouth as if to say something more, then closed it and quietly walked away, leaving Elizabeth alone and quivering with emotion in the playroom of the nursery, and wondering how she had managed, in the space of four days and two kisses, to fall head over heels in love with him.

SHE HAD NO idea how she was going to face him. What could she say to the man who had kissed her as if he never wanted to let her go, then had walked away and left her standing alone? Should she try to forget the most wonderful thing that had ever happened to her? Or should she remind James that he seemed to have enjoyed kissing her as much as she enjoyed being kissed? And if she needed to remind him, how should she go about it? How did you show a man you had fallen in love with him if he wouldn't let you? Especially when he wouldn't let you? Elizabeth took a deep breath as she pushed the last hairpin into the thick chignon at the nape of her neck. She smoothed her hands over the form-fitting bodice of her dark green morning dress and brushed away invisible wrinkles, then bent to make up her bed. It was six in the morning. Time to wake the Treasures and get them downstairs for breakfast. Actually, it was a few minutes after six, past time for her to wake the girls, but Elizabeth had taken far more care with her toilette than usual. Somehow, it seemed vitally important that she look her best when James saw her this morning. More than her pride had been affected when James had left her standing alone in the playroom. He'd pricked her vanity as well, and Elizabeth wanted him to see exactly what he'd walked away from.

Elizabeth removed Portia from her resting place on the pillow beside hers, then placed the doll on the little chair in front of the vanity. Then she straightened the sheets on her bed, plumped the pillows, and pulled the quilted coverlet up over the pillows and tucked it into place.

"Who's tat?"

Elizabeth whirled around at the sound of the voice behind her and stumbled over a pair of shoes. Big shoes. Men's shoes. James's shoes. Lying halfway under her bed. Elizabeth stared at the shiny leather shoes. Not only had he sat on the balcony outside her room, but he'd apparently spent enough time inside it to take off his shoes and make himself comfortable.

A vivid image of James as he'd looked earlier in the morning in the nursery came to mind. James with his dress shirt unfastened and untucked pushing a chair toward her with his stockinged foot. Elizabeth retrieved his shoes and placed them on top of the dressing table.

"Daddy." Garnet grinned up at her.

"Yes, Daddy's," Elizabeth confirmed as she bent and lifted Garnet high over her head, then lowered her and held her anchored on her hip. "What are you doing up? And what do you suppose your daddy's shoes were doing beneath my bed?"

Garnet smiled shyly, again, then looked over Elizabeth's shoulder and repeated her earlier question, "Who's tat?"

Elizabeth followed Garnet's gaze in the mirror over the dressing table. "That's Portia," Elizabeth told her. "My oldest and dearest friend. My father gave Portia to me to take the sting out of having a baby brother when I was a little girl not much older than you."

Garnet opened and closed her small hand in gesture that indicated she wanted to hold the doll.

"Would you like to hold Portia while we get you dressed and ready for breakfast?" Elizabeth asked.

Garnet gave her an enthusiastic nod and Elizabeth reached for Portia and handed her to Garnet.

Garnet hugged the doll to her chest. Elizabeth couldn't help but wince at the abuse Portia's elaborate coiffure and velvet suit were taking. But when Garnet impulsively reached out a hand to include Elizabeth in the embrace, Elizabeth decided that it was time Portia had a little girl hug her and muss her clothes. It seemed a fitting reward for all the years she had sat untouched on the shelf of Elizabeth's bedroom.

"All right, little gem," Elizabeth said, her heart swelling with love every time she looked at Garnet, "let's take you and Portia to the bathroom, then get you dressed for breakfast."

CHANGING EMERALD'S DIAPER and Garnet's drawers and dressing and combing their hair and fastening ribbons that matched their frocks into their baby-fine hair went faster than Elizabeth expected. And bathing and changing Diamond was easy compared to Ruby.

Ruby resisted Elizabeth at every turn. She fought when Elizabeth took off her nightgown. She squirmed and cried when Elizabeth dressed her in a red dress and white pinafore. Ruby twisted and turned and pulled away as Elizabeth combed her hair. She yanked the matching red ribbon from her hair and threw it to the floor in a fit of temper. Elizabeth discovered that dressing Ruby was as much a war of wills as bathing her had been, but for different reasons. Ruby had fought the bath because she was afraid of water. She fought Elizabeth's attempt to dress her simply because she had decided she didn't want Elizabeth to speak to her, much less touch her. Delia arrived to help in the nursery during the fray, but Elizabeth gave her the easier task of taking care of Diamond instead of the older girls and continued

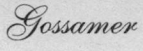

dressing Ruby herself. Elizabeth claimed a moral victory in the battle because she had managed to dress all four girls by herself. That she was ten minutes late for breakfast was of no consequence compared to her incredible accomplishment. But when all was said and done, Elizabeth wasn't sure who had emerged the victor. Ruby was wearing the dress Elizabeth had selected for her, but she had managed to foil Elizabeth's best attempts at putting on her stockings and shoes. Elizabeth had finally conceded the stockings and shoes after Ruby had pulled them off and thrown them at her—not once, but twice. Ruby's victory in the stocking skirmish meant that she was on her way to breakfast barelegged, barefoot, and furious.

All because Elizabeth had allowed Garnet to carry Portia into the nursery and Ruby had decided to lay claim to her.

"Good morning." James glanced pointedly at the clock on the wall, then rose from his place at the table where he'd passed the time waiting for Elizabeth and the girls to come down to breakfast by perusing the latest bundle of newspapers from San Francisco that Will had brought with him on the morning express mail train. "You're ten minutes late."

Elizabeth, who had Ruby by one hand and Emerald on her hip, shot him a dirty look. "So dock me."

James raised an eyebrow at her just as Ruby pulled out of Elizabeth's grasp and ran to him, hugging him around the knees.

"What's wrong with Ruby?" he asked.

"She's angry," Elizabeth replied, thrusting Ruby's stockings and shoes into his arms along with Emerald. "Here, you try. And take Emmy. I've got to go back upstairs to get Garnet and Diamond."

Will picked up his coffee cup and took a sip of the hot liquid while he focused his attention on James and Elizabeth and the thick tension hanging all around them.

James kissed Emerald's forehead, then shifted her into one arm, while he reached down with the other and untangled Ruby from around his legs. Ruby began to cry. "What upset her?'' James asked as he placed Emerald in her high-chair before he lifted Ruby into his arms to comfort her.

"You'll see," Elizabeth answered as she headed back up the stairs to the nursery.

"I'll see?" James called back to her. "What does that mean?"

"It means," Elizabeth replied cryptically, "that you should take those fancy dolls off those high nursery shelves and let your daughters play with them. They should have dolls to hold, to dress and undress, and to love. Dolls of their own."

"What's she talking about?" Will asked in puzzlement.

James shrugged his shoulders. "I've no idea. The Treasures have plenty of toys to play with."

But when Elizabeth returned moments later, leading Garnet by the hand, her comments became clearer. Garnet had the tawny-haired doll James had seen lying on Elizabeth's bed in a death-grip hug. She moved at a snail's pace, apparently afraid to move too fast for fear of dropping the doll.

James had Ruby on his lap and was patiently buckling her shoes when Garnet toddled up and all hell broke loose. When Ruby saw what Garnet held in her arms, she kicked off the shoe James hadn't yet buckled and began screaming for the doll. But Garnet gripped the doll tighter and stubbornly refused to relinquish her prize. The louder Ruby screamed and the harder Ruby cried, the more uncharacteristically stubborn Garnet became.

"*That's* why we're late," Elizabeth announced with a smug expression on her face.

"Rwuby want baby!" Ruby shouted.

"No!" Garnet shouted back.

Ruby looked stunned by Garnet's reaction, then furiously more determined than ever. She reached for the doll and tried to snatch her out of Garnet's grasp. Garnet backed away, cradling Portia protectively. Ruby tried again, before James intervened.

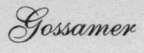

"Enough!" he commanded in a voice only a fraction louder than usual.

But it was enough. Having never heard their father raise his voice, both girls quieted instantly. Ruby's tears miraculously disappeared as he lifted her off his lap and set her on her chair at the table. Then James stood up and walked over to where Garnet stood sucking her thumb and holding the doll. He squatted down beside her. "Who's this?" he asked.

"Libeth," she answered softly.

He glanced over at Elizabeth for an explanation.

"No, sweetie, her name is Portia. Remember?" she replied.

"Libeth," Garnet insisted stubbornly.

"You know," Will said thoughtfully, "I believe Garnet's right. She looks exactly like Elizabeth—only in doll form."

James studied the doll, then turned to Garnet. "Where did you get her?"

"She's mine," Elizabeth answered. "I gave her to Garnet to hold when she came into my room early this morning. And since she seemed so taken with her, I allowed Garnet to carry Portia into the nursery to keep her company while I got her dressed." Elizabeth looked over at Ruby. "Once we reached the nursery, Garnet refused to part with her. And I never dreamed Portia's presence would start the Craig House War of 1873," she replied sardonically.

James couldn't help but smile at her apt description as he tried again to reason with Garnet. "Will you let Ruby hold Portia—Libeth—for a while?"

Garnet removed her thumb from her mouth. "No."

"Will you let Daddy hold Libeth until breakfast is over?"

"Her name is Portia," Elizabeth interjected.

"Not to Garnet," James said. "May Daddy have her?"

Garnet shook her head.

"For a little while?"

"No." Garnet shook her head even harder.

Unaccustomed to negotiating with Garnet, who was always so generous and good-natured, James tried a different tack. "Would you like Portia to have breakfast with us?"

Garnet nodded.

James smiled in triumph. "Would you like Portia to sit with Daddy?"

"No," she said, smiling shyly back at her father. "Libeth." Garnet ran to Elizabeth, handed Portia to her, then flung her arms around Elizabeth's skirts.

Elizabeth felt her breath catch in her throat and tears sting her eyes. James may have rejected her after kissing her last night, but Garnet clearly approved of her. It was a start.

"I've been thinking," James announced to Elizabeth after she had regained possession of Portia and they'd all sat down to eat their breakfast of oatmeal from an amazing assortment of unusual containers, "that perhaps I've been unfair to you."

Will groaned.

"In what way?" Elizabeth asked in a sharp tone of voice.

"I prepared the Treasures' schedule with myself in mind."

Will groaned again as Elizabeth stiffened in her chair and James appeared too busy formulating his ill-advised thoughts to notice that he was about to put his big fat foot in his mouth.

"So, I've decided that it might be best if . . ." he continued.

"If I were to leave your employ," Elizabeth finished for him, straightening her back in a defensive gesture.

James looked stunned.

"Isn't that what you were going to say?" she demanded. "After what happened in the nursery this morning?"

"What happened in the nursery this morning?" Will couldn't contain his curiosity any longer.

"Stay out of this," James and Elizabeth directed at Will in unison before James asked Elizabeth a question of his

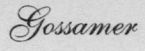

own, an echo of the question she'd put to him last night. "Is that what you want?"

"Of course it isn't what I want." Elizabeth put her napkin aside. "I want to stay here with y—the Treasures. I want to do the job you hired me to do."

"That's what I want, too," James said softly, staring at Elizabeth's lovely face, remembering how it felt to hold her in his arms, completely forgetting that they had an audience. "I want you to stay."

"Then why were you about to dismiss me again?" she asked.

"I wasn't going to dismiss you," James contradicted. "I just wanted to make your job a little easier by modifying your schedule. I thought that you and the Treasures could sleep later if you didn't join me for breakfast."

It was Elizabeth's turn to look shocked. "But you enjoy having breakfast with the Treasures."

"Who told you that?" James wanted to know, thinking that someone in the household had told her that his sharing breakfast with the Treasures was another cardinal rule that couldn't be broken.

"Nobody had to tell me," she said. "I can see for myself that you enjoy—no—you thrive on this morning chaos." She nodded toward the table, to the spills that dotted the tablecloth and the spoonfuls of oatmeal that didn't quite make it from bowls to mouths. "I'm not willing to deprive you of this."

"You were so tired you missed dinner," James reminded her. "*Again*," he added for emphasis. "That's two nights in a row. You fell asleep while you were dressing."

Elizabeth suddenly beamed at him, understanding at last, that James wasn't questioning her ability to do her job, just suggesting that she be allowed to work up to the current schedule until she became accustomed to keeping track of three small children and a newborn baby on a daily basis. He wasn't criticizing her, just showing his concern. And that changed everything. "You worry too much," she replied indulgently, lovingly.

"I wasn't worried," James denied quickly.

"Really?" Elizabeth cast a saucy glance at him. "You were sitting on the balcony outside my room last night."

"I've already explained that I sat out on the balcony to smoke a cigar," James answered, beginning to feel a bit uneasy, wondering what Elizabeth would say next.

"Was that the only reason? Just to smoke a cigar?"

"Of course," James lied. "What other reason could there be?"

"I don't know." Elizabeth shrugged her shoulders in an elegantly nonchalant gesture. "But I thought there must be some other reason because"—her eyes sparkled with mischief—"you forgot your shoes."

James's mouth fell open.

"I found them under my bed this morning."

Twenty-six

"WHAT DID YOU find out?" James asked as he and Will walked down the brick path from Craig House to the office after breakfast. "Did your friend at the *Chronicle* know anything about Elizabeth's brother?"

"Old Cromartie was a veritable fount of information about Elizabeth Sadler's brother, Owen." Will grinned at James, showing off a bit because he'd been able to get the information James wanted in less than twenty-four hours. Of course, James could have gotten the same information in less time if he hadn't been in such a hurry to get Elizabeth away from San Francisco and safe in Coryville. "Owen Sadler died a little over two months ago in Lo Peng's Red Dragon on Washington Street in San Francisco."

"How?"

"He succumbed to the lure of the poppy," Will explained, pulling out a little notebook and glancing at it. "According to Cromartie, who interviewed everyone he could find who knew Owen Sadler, young Sadler came out from Providence, Rhode Island, on a grand California adventure. Unfortunately, a young friend of his introduced Owen to the pleasures offered at the Red Dragon. Sadler's friend apparently frequented the upstairs business, but Owen preferred the opium. He ran out of money, and instead of writing home and asking for more, his friend told Cromartie that Owen began clerking in the Wells Fargo Bank on Montgomery Street. His friend remembered that bit of information because he'd found it strange that Owen would rather work in the bank than wire home and ask his grandmother, who owns a bank in Providence, for money. Did you know Elizabeth's family owned a bank.''

James nodded. ''She mentioned it. Go on.''

''Apparently, Owen wrote home to Elizabeth because when she arrived in San Francisco, four days ago, she knew Owen lived at Ordley's Boardinghouse on Montgomery Street and she knew he worked at the Wells Fargo Bank. What she didn't know was what happened to him. When she got to the boardinghouse, Mrs. Ordley sent her to the police station, and the sergeant on duty informed her that Owen had died more than two months ago—presumably in the Red Dragon, since his body was found in the place where Lo Peng's men always dump dead occidentals.''

James closed his eyes and pinched the bridge of his nose, imagining Elizabeth traveling three thousand miles to join her brother, and then finding out he was dead. James knew first-hand how the news had devastated her. ''Anything else?''

''She spent the night at the Russ House Hotel, left early in the morning in a hired hack, and went back to the police station. She spoke to Sergeant . . .'' Will consulted his notebook. ''Darnell, who told her about the paupers' cemetery near Saint Mary's Church. Elizabeth left the police station on foot—''

''She *walked* from the police station to Saint Mary's?'' James interrupted. ''Through Chinatown? Alone?''

''I'm afraid so.''

''What happened when she got to Saint Mary's?'' James asked.

''Father Paul, one of the priests there, took her to the

paupers' graves. He didn't remember Owen exactly, but he remembered that there had been three young men, over the past few months, whose bodies had been found dumped nearby. Elizabeth chose one of the three fresh graves, proclaimed it Owen's, and set off for Dorminey's Stone Works on Larkin Street, where she ordered a polished marble headstone. She paid for half of it on order and promised the rest when it was delivered." Will paused. "Do you want me to pay it off?"

"Not yet," James said. "But contact him and have him notify me when he's ready to set it up and have him send the final bill to me. Anything else?"

"Elizabeth also made a rather generous donation to Father Paul for the upkeep of the cemetery. She left the stone works and found lodging at Augusta Bender's and spent one night there. She went on her rampage at the Red Dragon the following afternoon *after* she was warned by one of Augusta's girls that the police planned to 'pinch her for stealing a rich gent's handkerchief.' The police arrested her at the Red Dragon some time later, on charges of theft and vandalism. She went before Judge Clermont and was fined fifty dollars or three days in jail. Apparently, she didn't have fifty dollars, because she elected to serve time in jail."

James held up his hand. "All right, all right. I know the rest." He looked over at Will. "I'm impressed. Tell me, how did Cromartie get this information?"

"I told him what you told me of her background and her whereabouts and he followed her trail right up to the jail, where you're spoken of in less than complimentary terms at the moment." Will grinned at James. "By the way, you owe me three bottles of Napoleon brandy and a case of champagne, oh, and a pair of season tickets to the opera."

James whistled through his teeth. "Cromartie's information didn't come cheaply."

"He was risking a lot in telling me," Will reminded him.

"I'm not complaining about the price, Will," James said.

"The fact that the information cost so much tells me exactly how much Cromartie was risking."

Will nodded. "Cromartie didn't have any trouble getting the information. The risk was in giving it to me." He looked over at James. "Our reputation has preceded us, my friend. Lo Peng not only knows just about everything there is to know about you, he knows what there is to know about me as well. And Cromartie will have to walk a very fine line for a while in order to show Lo Peng and the Tong that he isn't siding with us," Will said as he and James reached their offices in the Craig Capital building.

"I'm sorry." James sighed. "I shouldn't have embroiled you or your friend in this."

"What are friends and partners for?" Will asked with a shrug. "Besides, I'm already embroiled in it. There's more to this than Elizabeth and Owen Sadler, Jamie."

James raised an eyebrow at that.

"There's trouble in our high timber and mining camps," Will told him. "Labor unrest. The Welsh and the Cornishmen aren't happy sharing a camp with Chinese."

James swore viciously.

"It gets worse, Jamie. I heard this morning that the Tong has put out the word against you. Permission has been revoked. You won't be getting any more baby girls."

"Lo Peng and I have an understanding," James said. "He knows that I'm as powerful in my own way as he is. And my reach into Hong Kong and China is almost as long as his."

"You *had* an understanding that kept him from openly warring with you and with me," Will corrected. "But this thing with Elizabeth changed all that. Lo Peng blames you for the destruction on the Red Dragon as well as what happened back in Hong Kong."

"Why should the old hypocrite care about what happened in Hong Kong?" James demanded. "He's the one who sold her to that Cantonese flesh peddler in the first place."

"Mei Ling was his niece and he holds you responsible for her death."

James sucked in a breath. He hadn't heard Mei Ling's name spoken aloud by anyone but himself since she'd died. "I *am* responsible for her death," James said heavily.

"Jamie," Will said softly, "Mei Ling was responsible for her death, not you."

James turned to his friend, his face a mask of pain and torment. "Tell that to my heart! All she asked was that I forgive her. And I couldn't! I couldn't forgive her."

"She wanted your forgiveness to make things right, Jamie. I can't count the number of times during your marriage that Mei Ling did things she knew you wouldn't like, then begged your forgiveness for her actions. She thought forgiveness equaled approval. If you forgave her, it meant that you approved of what she'd done."

"I know that," James said, tears sparkling in his eyes. "I wanted to forgive her. But I couldn't. And she died because of it."

"Mei Ling died because she couldn't forgive herself. She couldn't live with what she'd done. If you had forgiven her, she'd have convinced herself that she did what she did because you wanted it done—even if you couldn't bring yourself to do it. She'd have convinced herself that she was right to do it. For you. For her husband."

James turned to Will, pinning him with his gaze. "You could have forgiven her."

Will blinked twice and stared at James without saying anything.

"You loved her as much as I did, Will."

"Jamie, I . . ."

James held up his hand to forestall any argument. "It didn't matter, Will. I loved her. You loved her. We both loved her. I've known that from the start." James shook his head. "You couldn't help it any more than I could. And I never held it against you. How could I? You're the brother I never had. We're as alike as two men can be. Why wouldn't we fall in love with the same woman?"

"I never wanted you to know," Will said. "I never wanted Mei Ling to know."

"Did she?"

Will shook his head. "She wasn't interested in me. She had you."

James nodded in understanding. Neither one of them was willing to say aloud what they both knew to be true. Mei Ling had chosen the heir to Craig Capital. And if the situation had been reversed, if Will had been the heir to Craig Capital, Mei Ling would have probably chosen him.

"You wouldn't have let her die, Will," James said. "Your heart is bigger than mine, your well of forgiveness is deeper." He squeezed his eyes shut, squeezing back the pain, blocking the tears. "If she'd married you, Mei Ling would still be alive. Because you could have found it in your heart to forgive her."

"No, Jamie," Will said. "You're wrong. I didn't see what you saw. I didn't suffer all you suffered, and yet, I have nightmares just like you do. I couldn't forgive her while she was alive, and I haven't forgiven her now that she's dead. There are some things only God can forgive. Mei Ling's crime was one of them."

James nodded. He had spent the past three years wondering how Will felt and now he was satisfied. He didn't know if the knowledge that Will didn't hold Mei Ling's death against him would help him sleep better at night, but the sleep didn't matter. The knowing was enough. He held out his hand to Will, then reached over and clapped him on the shoulder. "Thank you, my friend."

"All you had to do was ask, Jamie. Like you said before, I'm the brother you never had." Will walked over to the cabinets behind James's desk, opened the top one, and took out a bottle of aged Scots whisky and two glasses. He poured a shot for James and one for himself. Will handed James a glass, then lifted his in salute. "Here's to old friends and better times."

"Amen." James clinked his glass to Will's, then took a sip of the mellow whisky.

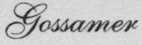

ELIZABETH, DELIA, AND the Treasures returned from
their daily walk in the park at four in the afternoon as
scheduled. Ruby was still out of sorts and refusing to have
anything at all to do with Elizabeth. At ten minutes past
four Delia began preparations for the Treasures' supper and
sometime between four-thirty and six P.M., Portia disappeared from her customary place on the extra pillow on
Elizabeth's bed.

Ruby quickly became the prime suspect in the abduction.
It didn't take a genius to figure out why Portia had disappeared, but it took every bit of Elizabeth's self-control not
to lash out in anger. Her most precious possession—the
only personal thing she'd brought with her from the house
on Hemlock Street other than her clothes—had disappeared
because both Ruby and Garnet wanted her and there wasn't
enough of poor Portia to go around.

By the time the Treasures' supper was over, the rest of
the household had been made aware of the crisis and the
search for Portia had begun. Mrs. G. and Annie searched
the downstairs, and Delia searched the nursery while Elizabeth bathed Diamond, Emerald, and Garnet and dressed
them for bed. The housekeeper and the two maids turned
Craig House upside down, searching all of Ruby's favorite hiding places—all the nooks and crannies that a three-
year-old child might find intriguing. But Portia remained
lost.

Elizabeth tried to talk to Ruby, but reluctantly gave up
when Ruby failed to respond. There was nothing she
could do except wait and hope that Ruby would get over
her anger and that Portia would eventually reappear. Garnet, however, did not understand Elizabeth's patient approach. She wanted Portia and she couldn't understand
why nobody could find her. And when Garnet began to
cry and beg for the doll, it was all Elizabeth could do not
to do the same.

Not trusting herself enough to do battle with Ruby in the

bathtub, afraid of losing her patience and her temper, Elizabeth wisely decided Delia could give Ruby a stand-up bath and put her to bed.

By the time James arrived home from work to continue the adventures of Don Quixote, Elizabeth had retired to her room.

THE KNOCK ON his bedroom door late that night startled James. The Treasures were all asleep. Even Diamond had had her bedtime bottle. James got up to answer the door and found Mrs. G. standing on the other side.

"Mrs. G., is there anything wrong?" James asked.

She frowned. "I hate to bother you in your room like this, Mr. Craig, but I thought you would want to know that Miss Sadler didn't come downstairs for dinner again tonight. And she refused the tray I sent up."

"What?" James had missed dinner himself, but Mrs. G. had brought a tray of roast beef sandwiches to his bedroom study soon after he finished reading the Treasures their bedtime story.

"She's been upset all afternoon," Mrs. G. volunteered. "Ever since her doll went missing."

James was clearly surprised. "What happened?"

"Well," Mrs. G. explained, "after Miss Sadler returned from her outing with the Treasures in the park this afternoon, she discovered her doll—you know the one that Miss Garnet sets such a store by—had disappeared from her room."

"Oh, no," James muttered, anticipating the worst. "Ruby."

Mrs. G. nodded. "We think so," she admitted. "But we turned the house upside down, and we didn't find a trace of Portia. If Miss Ruby's hid her, she did a real good job of it."

"What can I do?" James asked.

"Well, you might try talking to Miss Ruby in the morning,'' Mrs. G. told him. "And I think you ought to talk to Miss Sadler tonight. She's very upset."

"What do I say?" James wanted to know.

"Just tell her you want to talk to her about the Treasures, about the nursery, anything. But please talk to her, Mr. Craig, because I've become very fond of her. And I'm worried."

"All right, Mrs. G.," James said. "I'll see what I can do."

"Thank you, Mr. Craig." Helen Glenross breathed a grateful sigh. "Thank you so much."

James waited until Mrs. G. left, then wrapped a leftover sandwich in a linen napkin and stuck it in the pocket of his robe before he walked down the hall from his bedroom to the nursery. He paused for a moment in the Treasures' bedroom and stood looking down at the little girls all curled on their beds. They were still sleeping peacefully. James smiled at the angelic expression on Ruby's face. Looking at her like this, no one would guess the chaos she'd caused today. He shook his head. And over a doll! He looked up at the shelves high on the wall, far above the Treasures' heads. Three beautiful dolls stared down at him. All the dolls were different. One had curly red hair and big green eyes. Another had brown hair and blue eyes, and the last had white-blond hair and blue eyes. He had bought them in San Francisco for Ruby when she was much too young to play with them. So he and Mrs. G. had placed them on the high shelf in the nursery bedroom, and to his knowledge, none of the Treasures had ever paid any attention to them or ever asked to play with them. But today Ruby and Garnet had had a battle royal over Elizabeth's doll. He glanced down at the bed where Garnet slept, her thumb in her mouth and a frown on her face. James walked to the side of Garnet's bed, bent down, and gently rubbed the pad of his thumb across Garnet's wrinkled brow, smoothing out the lines, as if to erase them and the worry that put them there. James stood and blew a kiss to all the Treasures before he walked silently out of the bedroom.

He knocked on the door twice. "Elizabeth?"

She didn't answer but James knew she was in there. He could hear the muffled sounds she made as she wept into her pillow. He reached out and turned the doorknob. The door was locked.

James knocked again. "Please answer the door, Elizabeth."

Still she didn't answer.

"You didn't eat dinner. Are you all right?

Elizabeth let go of her pillow at the sound of James's voice and sat up in bed.

"I'm very sorry about your doll, Elizabeth," he said softly. "I'm sorry about Portia." James let go of the doorknob and walked away—back to his room.

Elizabeth rolled off the bed and went to the vanity. Her eyes were puffy and her nose was red from crying. She didn't want James to see her when she'd been crying over something so foolish as a doll. But she didn't want to miss seeing him, either. She walked to the door and turned the key in the lock. She opened the door and stepped out into the hall, but it was too late. James was gone. He'd already walked away. Again.

Elizabeth closed the door, then crossed the bedroom and unlocked the French doors that opened onto the balcony. She dragged the chaise longue from her bedroom to the balcony, then sat down and waited.

"My father gave her to me the day my younger brother was born," Elizabeth said soon afterward, when she heard the scrape and smelled the acrid sulfur odor of a match, seconds before she saw the flare of a blue-orange flame as James lit a cigarillo. "Other than at Christmas and my birthdays, Portia was the only gift my father ever gave me."

"Then I'm doubly sorry she's missing," James answered, crossing from his end of the balcony to stand just a few feet away from where she sat on the chaise. He was

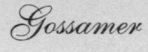

shirtless and barefoot, as he'd been the first night she met him, wearing only his favorite silk robe and a pair of trousers. And he didn't appear to be the least bit surprised to see her. James took a handkerchief from the pocket of his robe and handed it to her.

Elizabeth stared at it, searching in the dim light for the initials she knew were embroidered on the corner. J. C. C. "Am I going to jail again if I accept this?"

James shook his head. "No, but if you don't take this"— he stuck his hand in his other pocket and removed a bundle wrapped in a linen napkin and gave it to her—"I may consider it."

Elizabeth unwrapped the bundle and found what smelled like a slab of roast beef sandwiched between two thick slices of bread.

"Dry your eyes and eat your sandwich," James instructed.

"I'm acting like a baby," Elizabeth sniffled. "Crying over the loss of a doll like this." She took a bite of the meat and bread and then another.

"I'd say you're entitled," James replied. "First Owen, and now, this."

Elizabeth looked surprised by his mention of Owen's name.

"I know about Owen, Elizabeth. I did some checking around," he admitted. "I know where and how Owen died. And why you used your parasol to destroy the interior of the Red Dragon."

Elizabeth let out a breath. "That's a relief," she told him. "I was afraid you might think I intended to crusade against other dens of iniquity and make a habit of destroying other people's property."

"Opium dens are legal," James reminded her. "They may be dens of iniquity, but by law, they're allowed to operate. Your brother was over twenty-one. He made his choices."

"I know. That's the sad part. People like Lo Peng operate businesses that thrive on other people's weaknesses.

Owen was *barely* twenty-one. He was young and he was weak-willed, but I loved him anyway and he didn't deserve to die or to have his body dumped on the side of the street like so much trash.''

"So you struck out against the Red Dragon." James shook his head. "Why didn't you tell me this before?" He glanced around for a place to sit.

Elizabeth shrugged. "What was there to tell? Owen's dead. His body was dumped in the street. I can't change those facts." She curled her legs beneath her to make room for James to sit on the end of the chaise.

James sighed. "I know it won't lessen your grief or the pain of knowing what was done to Owen, but dumping your brother's body in the street wasn't personal, Elizabeth. I'm not saying that it isn't horrible, and I'm certainly not defending the practice. I'm just saying that Lo Peng considered it a necessity. You see the Chinese in this country don't have many legal rights. They're forced to cross the street if a white man walks down the same sidewalk. They can own and operate businesses, but they're always in danger of being harassed by local police and the citizenry. The owners of opium dens and gambling houses are at greater risk because men can and do get killed in fights, or die from overindulgence in the poppy." He took a puff on his cigar. "When a Chinese dies, nothing much is said or done about it, but when an occidental dies, for whatever reason, a great deal is said and done about it. Chinese merchants have been accused of murder and of poisoning customers, and lynched for having a white man's body on their premises." James sat on the end of the chaise longue and blew out a puff of cigar smoke.

Elizabeth shuddered. "It's still a despicable thing to do."

"Yes," James agreed, "it is."

They sat without speaking for a while, until James broke the companionable silence by asking, "Did you know Owen was addicted to opium? Is that what brought you out here from Providence?"

"A train brought me out here from Providence." She

managed a slight smile at her weak attempt at humor. "But my own faulty judgment precipitated the journey. I didn't know anything about Owen's frequenting of the Red Dragon until I arrived and learned of his death."

"What happened?" he asked, getting up from the chaise and moving to lean against the balcony railing.

Elizabeth gave a little unladylike snort. "My grand-mother Sadler disowned me. She scratched my name out of the family Bible and asked me to leave the house I'd grown up in—and to leave Providence. I didn't have any place else to go, so I decided to come stay with Owen."

James didn't believe Elizabeth could have done anything bad enough to warrant her grandmother's harsh punishment. "Why did she disown you?"

"I allowed myself to be compromised."

"I don't believe it," James said flatly.

"It's true," Elizabeth told him. "At least, that's the way my grandmother saw it."

"How do you see it?" He'd already heard enough about her grandmother to know that the lady made moral judgments and set impossibly high standards for the people around her to follow.

"I saw it as taking care of an old family friend who was ill when he arrived in town for his Christmas visit."

"He?"

Elizabeth nodded. "His name is Samuel Wright. He and my father were schoolmates."

"Go on," James urged.

"I've known Samuel all my life. So when he arrived for his visit earlier than planned, I didn't think anything of accompanying him to his hotel room. You see my mother and my grandmother were out of town. I was staying at Lady Wimbley's with some of the girls who didn't go home after term, so our house was closed and the servants were still on holiday. Samuel was feverish and very ill. So I accompanied him to his hotel room and sent for the doc-tor." Elizabeth looked down at her tightly clenched fists. "I couldn't leave him. There was no one else to take care

of him. He was alone and sick and burning up with fever.
The doctor suggested I stay until Samuel was better or until . . .'' She let her voice drift off. ''And I agreed. I didn't
think about propriety or my reputation or the fact that Samuel was a widower. I didn't care about any of that. All I
cared about was Samuel and the fact that without my help,
he might die.''

''But your grandmother did care about propriety,'' James
guessed.

''Yes,'' Elizabeth answered. ''My grandmother cared
about propriety more than she cared about me or Samuel's
well-being. She cared about propriety to the exclusion of
all else. And because I'd spent three days and two nights
in the unchaperoned company of an unmarried man, I was
compromised.''

''And then what happened?'' James asked softly.

''As soon as he recovered his health and realized what
had happened, Samuel went to see Grandmother Sadler and
asked her for my hand in marriage.''

''She turned him down?'' James couldn't believe it.

''Of course not,'' Elizabeth said. ''Grandmother was delighted. I turned him down.''

''Why?''

Elizabeth gave another unladylike snort. ''He was old
enough to be my father. And what's more, Samuel didn't
love me. Not the way a man should love his wife. Samuel
loved me like a daughter. And I loved him like a father. I
couldn't marry him. It wasn't right. It would have felt too—
too—incestuous.'' She glanced at James, willing him to
understand.

''I take it your grandmother didn't agree.''

Elizabeth shook her head. ''She thought I was crazy.
She said I was a fool to turn him down, then she ordered
me to rethink my position and to say yes when Samuel
asked again. Grandmother knew Samuel would ask again
because he felt responsible for destroying my reputation
and the only way to repair the damage was to marry me.
She knew he would keep asking until I agreed. So when

I refused Samuel's second most generous proposal, I was ostracized by my friends, relieved of my teaching duties at Lady Wimbley's, disowned by my grandmother, and asked to leave not only her home, but the town of Providence as well.''

James winced. In the time he'd known her he'd compromised Elizabeth far worse than Samuel Wright had done. But Samuel had felt honor-bound to offer Elizabeth marriage. Not once, but twice. ''Because you were compromised, or because you refused Wright's gentlemanly offer?''

Elizabeth shrugged. ''Either way, the price was too high.'' She studied James's profile in the faint light moonlight. ''What about you? What made you leave Hong Kong?''

''I had my reasons,'' he answered in an echo of the words she'd given him the first time she met the Treasures.

Elizabeth frowned at him.

''All right,'' he said. ''Finish your sandwich and I'll tell you.''

Elizabeth did as he told her, polishing off the rest of the food in three bites.

James smiled. ''That wasn't so bad, was it?''

She blotted her lips with the napkin, then shook her head. ''Now, tell me what brought you to California.''

''A ship,'' James teased, walking back to sit on the end of Elizabeth's chaise longue.

''Why?'' she asked. ''Why did you leave your home and family to come here?''

''Too many memories,'' he admitted at last. ''There were too many ghosts back in Hong Kong. Too many reasons not to sleep at night.''

''You still don't sleep enough at night,'' Elizabeth pointed out, reminding him that they were both sitting out on the balcony long after they should have been in bed asleep.

''And you don't eat enough.''

Elizabeth agreed. ''We're a fine pair.''

James looked at her, then reached out and cupped her chin in his hand. "If you think that, Elizabeth, then you can't have heard the rumors about me."

"I heard."

He quirked an eyebrow at her.

"Lois Marlin told me," she explained. "In the park yesterday. But I don't believe a word of them."

He was tempted to kiss her, so James dropped his hand from her face and stared up at the stars. "I didn't kill her," James said starkly. "I couldn't forgive her for what she did, but I didn't kill her."

"I never doubted that for a moment," Elizabeth answered, her eyes sparkling with fierce emotion and loyalty.

"I did," James said. "Oh, logically, I understood that she killed herself. But until today, I never understood that I wasn't responsible. I kept telling myself that if I'd just been able to forgive her for what she'd done, she'd still be alive. But I couldn't forgive her. And when she died I felt I was responsible. I thought I killed her." He looked at Elizabeth. "Be glad you got here after Owen died. It's horrible to sit helplessly by while someone you love dies slowly, little bit by little bit, until they simply waste away. That's why I worry so. I try not to, but I can't seem to help it. Every time someone misses a meal, I think it's happening all over again."

Elizabeth sucked in a breath as understanding dawned and the horror of what James had endured sank in. "Oh, my God, what did she do?"

"I have money," he said. "Lots of it. Millions of pounds of it. And I could have bought her anything on earth she wanted to eat. I tried. But she wouldn't let me see her. Wouldn't let me near her. And by the time I realized what was wrong, I couldn't stop it. I couldn't force her to eat."

Tears sparkled in Elizabeth's eyes and ran unchecked down her face. "Oh, James, I'm so sorry." Impulsively offering comfort, Elizabeth leaned forward, wrapped her arms around his waist and pressed her cheek against his shoulder.

"So am I," he said softly. "But every day I live with the knowledge that even in a house of plenty, there was nothing I could do to prevent my wife from deliberately starving herself to death."

Twenty-seven

THE MOMENT JAMES turned in her arms, nothing on earth could have prevented Elizabeth from offering him the solace he needed. Desire arced between them like lightning. She leaned forward and closed her eyes as James sought her mouth with his own.

She deserved gentleness, James reminded himself in an effort to go slow. She deserved tenderness. So he devoted himself to giving Elizabeth everything she deserved. He nibbled at her lips, then traced the texture of them with a light brush of his own. James touched the seam between her lips with the tip of his tongue, showering Elizabeth with pleasure as he tasted the softness of her lips and absorbed the feel of her mouth, poring over every detail, every nuance of her lips and mouth and teeth and tongue, with the same single-minded attention to detail he used to orchestrate million-dollar deals. He leaned into her, pressing the lower part of his body against the cradle of hers and Elizabeth opened her mouth and parted her legs to grant him access. Acknowledging her generous offering, James reached up, tangled one hand in her hair, and sent her hairpins scattering in all directions as he pulled her closer to deepen his kiss. He used his tongue to delve deep into the lush sweetness of her mouth. Her tongue mated with his, mirrored his as he plundered the depths, then retreated before plundering again.

Elizabeth sank against him, shivering in delicious response as James left her lips and kissed a path over her eyelids, her cheeks, her nose, brushing his lips lightly over hers once again before he continued on his path to the pulse that beat at the base of her throat. Elizabeth had always prided herself on her independent spirit and her education, but she found she was sadly, shamelessly, lacking in both those attributes as she lay in James's arms. She was a little bewildered to discover she was more than willing to relinquish her independence and become a willing slave to her desires.

James rubbed his nose into the hollow below her ear, inhaling the fresh lavender scent of her, as he laved the spot where her pulse throbbed with his tongue. He nibbled and teased and coaxed his way from her mouth to her throat, to the dainty pink shell of her ear and back again with a finesse he'd almost forgotten he possessed. A fierce longing flowed through him, making him shudder with the need to touch all of her, to taste all of her. He remembered the way her breasts had looked through the wet transparent fabric of her chemise, the way their pink tips puckered like ripe lips awaiting a lover's kiss. His kiss. And, ever the gentleman, James vowed not to disappoint them.

She melted back on the chaise and gazed up at the twinkling stars as James cupped her breast with his hand, pushing it up and out of the confines of her corset so that only the fabric of her chemise and bodice separated her breasts from him. Elizabeth started as he rubbed the pad of his thumb over the tip of her breast until it hardened against the fabric, then kissed his way down the front of her bodice, past the row of tiny buttons that kept her fastened inside her dress, and pressed his lips around the hard little nub in the center of her breast.

Fire, like the fire of a glass of brandy on an empty stomach, shot through her, only this fire was a thousand times better than anything alcohol induced. Elizabeth gasped as the warmth of his breath against her breast made her nipple swell and harden even more until she ached in the dark secret recesses of her body—all the places proper ladies didn't admit to having. Elizabeth arched her back, filling the night air with little incoherent sounds she made in her throat. She wiggled in his arms, moving steadily closer until she finally reached up, clamped her fingers into his thick black hair and held him pressed against her. She whimpered hoarsely as James dampened the satin of her bodice with his tongue, then forced his warm breath through the fabric, igniting spontaneous little brush fires of desire that flared throughout her body.

James chuckled deep in his throat, thrilled with Elizabeth's impatience and heady with the powerful sensations swirling around them and with the incredible realization that she enjoyed his touch as much as he enjoyed touching her. He turned his head so that he might breathe once again, then slowly worked his way over the satin fabric, past the little jet buttons to her other breast. He wanted to bite off the buttons and tear the linen covering her breasts away with his teeth, but he fought to control that urge, freeing her breast from her corset, instead, by cupping his hand beneath it and pushing it up and over the top of the whalebone in the same way he'd freed her other one. Once his mission was accomplished, James lavished her nipple with a rush of hot, moist air. God, but he wanted to touch her. All of her. He wanted to suckle at her breast and taste the sweet hot essence of her. He wanted to bury his length inside her warmth and to feel the heat of her surrounding him as he throbbed and pulsed within, and he wanted to capture her lips and swallow her cries as they careened toward the heavens and where desire and passion were forged like iron and carbon melded into steel, forming an exquisite blend of love and faith and trust.

James worked his way from her breasts back to her lips. His tongue, warm and rough, plundered her mouth as he slipped a hand under her skirts and worked his way through the sea of petticoats until he felt the lace of her drawers just above her knees. He reached beneath the lace ruffle at her knee and ran his hand up her silken clad thigh as far as the give in the fabric allowed. Frustrated by his lack of progress, he withdrew his hand from the leg of her drawers and began again. His second foray yielded better results as he ran his hand over the top of her thigh and down into the valley between her legs. He located the opening in the fabric and gently eased his fingers inside it, through the nest of silken curls, to the damp swollen flesh hidden beneath them.

"James, please," Elizabeth moaned and begged as she thrust her hips against his incredibly talented fingers while James traced the contours of her sleek flesh and teased the tight little bud hidden within the petal-like folds of her most secret place. There were no words to describe the shock of the myriad delicious and forbidden sensations she felt as James slid his skilled fingers into her soft folds. She felt the impact of those sensations deep inside her womb as her body clenched uncontrollably, yearning to fill the desperate emptiness that James had created with his touch. Elizabeth knew she should be scandalized by James's familiarity with the forbidden places on her body, knew she should be alarmed at the way he played her like an instrument, coaxing sweet music from her. But he stroked and probed her with such infinite tenderness and such agonizing care that she couldn't be outraged. How could she be shocked and angry when all he gave was unimaginable pleasure?

"Please," she murmured again with such anguish that James couldn't tell if she was inviting him to continue or begging him to stop. He deliberately deepened his caress and circled his fingers. Elizabeth immediately pressed her legs together in reaction, before opening them again to give him access. And James had his answer.

Elizabeth squirmed as pleasure—hot and thick and dangerous—surged through her body, filling her with urgent longings she never knew she possessed. She thrust her hips upward as she moaned her delight and gasped out his name in short frantic little breaths.

James continued to kiss her, gently at first, then harder, consciously matching the action of his fingers to that of his tongue as he feverishly worked his magic on her. He knew she was desperately close to finding wondrous satisfaction, even if she didn't quite know what was happening to her. His body chafed beneath his self-imposed restraint. He ached to join her in blissful release, but James had to take his time. He pressed his thumb against her, soothing her aching core with the sweet honey she lavished on his fingers.

Elizabeth cried out against his lips, then shuddered deeply as her fragile control shattered, and she came apart in his arms, arching her hips wildly against his hand before collapsing on the chaise. She finally opened her eyes, and looked up at him with such an expression of sheer wonderment and joy that James's breath caught in his throat. He was humbled by the look in her eyes and rewarded tenfold for his remarkable restraint.

Elizabeth blushed. "What happened to me?"

"I hope you touched the stars," James said honestly.

"I not only touched them," she said, smiling at him, "but I saw them and felt them and kissed them and fell through them." Her eyes shimmered with emotion as she reached up and placed her palms on both sides of his face. "Thank you," she said simply as she pulled his face down to meet her lips.

"It was an honor," he whispered seconds before he captured her mouth with his own.

James kissed her again—this time with all the pent-up passion and frustration and longing he'd been holding in check so long. He kissed her until her breasts heaved with exertion, until her bones seemed to turn to jelly, until all she could do was cling to him while she fervently returned his kisses measure for measure. James's mind reeled from the flood of sensations she evoked as her tongue mated with his.

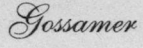

Shaking with need, James finally pulled his mouth away.

"What's wrong?" she asked in confusion.

"Nothing's wrong," he answered.

"Then why did you stop kissing me?"

"Because I want you." James leaned his forehead against hers and drew a shaky breath. "All of you."

"You have all of me," she told him.

James shook his head. "I'm not entirely certain you understand what I mean, Elizabeth. But I'm damned sure you weren't as compromised as your grandmother believed."

The smile Elizabeth gave him was beatific. "Then, why don't you show me how it should be done? Compromise me."

That was all the encouragement James needed. He scooped her into his arms, lifted her from the chaise, and headed toward his bedroom.

Elizabeth looped her arms around his neck and held on. They negotiated the distance from the chaise to the French doors leading to James's bedroom between kisses. "James," Elizabeth said as he entered his room and placed her on his bed, "not here."

James groaned aloud. "Why not?"

"The Treasures."

For the first time since he'd become a father, James remembered he was a man as well as a father and put his needs ahead of the needs of the Treasures. "What about them?"

"Cardinal rule number one: Never leave the Treasures alone."

James's blue eyes crinkled at the corners as he smiled down at her. "Then, we've got a real problem, my love, because I don't think what we're about to do is something they ought to witness just yet."

Elizabeth's breath caught in her throat at James's use of the casual endearment.

"That bad, huh?" she teased.

"That good," he pronounced.

"It gets better?" she asked in a voice so full of wonder that James couldn't help but laugh.

"I've always thought so," he said. "I've always thought that kissing the stars is a pasttime best experienced when two people do it together." He shrugged his shoulders. "But you may disagree."

"How can I disagree?" Elizabeth asked, her desire surging by leaps and bounds as James nipped her bottom lip with his teeth, then gently laved the tiny wound with his tongue. "When I've nothing with which to compare?"

James's leer was positively lustful as he placed a knee on the bed and leaned over her. "I was hoping you'd say that." He reached down and began unbuttoning her bodice. He kissed her hungrily as he fumbled with the tiny jet buttons that seemed determined to thwart his best efforts to slip them through their buttonholes. When she was finally unbuttoned, James searched the whalebone of her corset, feeling for more buttons or hooks, or laces anything he could undo. He had little experience with corsets. Mei Ling had quit wearing the torturous device shortly after they married, when she gave up Western dress and returned to her loose robes and silk and satin tunics and trousers.

"How do I open this thing?" he asked, his frustration rising along with his passion.

"Hooks," Elizabeth gasped as he took advantage of her open bodice and traced the tips of her breasts with his rough silk pads of his fingers. "The hooks are hidden beneath the front flap."

"Hidden?" James muttered. "Hidden from whom? You know where they are. And what man is going to look at hooks when he can feast his eyes on this magnificent bounty?" He felt beneath the front flap and groaned when he met with a hundred or so tiny hook and eye closures. "Bloody hell!"

Elizabeth should have cringed at his vivid curse, but she giggled instead. James's honest frustration with her feminine accouterments was proving to be a powerful aphrodisiac.

...ghed with relief as he finally unhooked the con-
...n and freed her. He lifted her to pull her corset and
...ght-fitting bodice of her dress from beneath her, then
...ged the hem of her chemise from the waistband of her
...irts and up and over her head, leaving her gloriously naked above the waist. Encouraged by his success with her
corset, James unhooked her skirts, untied the waistbands of
her petticoats and unbuttoned her lacy drawers. When
everything was unfastened, he peeled the garments down
her long, slender legs along with her silk stockings and
frilly garters.

Completely nude and suddenly shy, Elizabeth closed her
eyes and tried to roll to the side of the bed to extinguish
the lamp he'd left burning, but James wrapped his arm
around her waist and stopped her. "Leave it," he urged.
"I want to look at you."

"Please," she began, "I'm—"

"So damned beautiful you take my breath away," he
whispered, genuinely awestruck.

Elizabeth opened her eyes to see if the expression on his
face matched his tone of voice and was instantly gratified
to see that it did. She blushed. "What do I do?"

James raised an eyebrow at her and grinned. "Lie there
and enjoy while I see if you taste as good as you look."

Elizabeth met his heated gaze, trusting that James meant
to continue his intimate exploration with his fingers. She
was startled when he stretched out between her legs and
resting his head on her thigh, turned and pulled her toward
him. The feel of his hot breath came as a complete surprise.
Elizabeth clamped her legs together. James raised his head
and looked at her. "Trust me, Elizabeth. I'm not going to
hurt you," he coaxed. "I'm only going to love you. If
you'll let me."

When he looked at her like that, Elizabeth found she
couldn't deny him anything—didn't want to deny him anything. As long as he kept his promise to love her, her body
was his to do with as he pleased. "Please do," she begged
politely.

"My pleasure."

Elizabeth thought she'd kissed the stars while his ⸝ caressed her, but when James began to taste and teas⸝ places his fingers had explored, she captured the stars ⸝ held them inside her.

He drove her to the brink of rapture and beyond. James moved up her body and cradled her beside him, capturing her cries with his mouth as she shuddered back to the earth in his arms. He brushed her damp hair off her flushed face, wiped the tears from her eyes, and murmured love words of praise and encouragement in her ear.

She opened her eyes to find James staring down at her.

"Nice trip?" James remembered thinking, the first night they met, that a man could drown in those marvelous blue-green eyes of hers. Now he knew it was true.

"Hmm," she murmured, snuggling beside him and stretching languidly, like a cat.

"How were the stars?" he asked, kissing the tip of her nose.

Elizabeth gazed at him. "Lonely," she answered.

"Really?"

She nodded. "I've been told that the trip to the stars is much nicer when you have a companion on the journey."

"Just a companion?" He sounded disappointed.

"Well,"—she wet her lips with the tip of her tongue as she pretended to ponder his question—"a lover would be better."

James sucked in a breath as his body tightened and the bulge in his trousers threatened to pop his buttons. "Are you in the market for a lover, Miss Sadler?"

"I'd like to think I just found one, Mr. Craig," she said primly. "But you may disagree."

"I am not complaining," James assured her.

"I am," Elizabeth admitted. A wicked little smile played about the corners of her mouth and her eyes sparkled with merriment. She reached up and pulled him down to kiss her. "Because only one of us is naked."

...es kissed her quickly, then reached for the buttons ...s shirt.

...lizabeth brushed his hands away. "I've never undressed ...nan before," she told him shyly. "Allow me."

"Be my guest," he invited, giving himself up to the pleasure of having a woman's hands on him after so many years.

She untied the knot at his waist and slid his silk robe off his shoulders, down his arms, and over his hands, exposing the hard muscles of his chest and stomach. Elizabeth rubbed her hands over the mat of hair on his chest, then leaned over and indulged herself by allowing the tips of her breasts to rub against the soft hair.

James's blood rushed downward. The hard male part of him throbbed with each beat of his heart. He ached to sheathe himself in Elizabeth's warmth. He ached to end his exquisite torment. Wrapping his arms around her waist, James gently rolled her onto her back. Elizabeth followed the line of his spine, sliding her hands down his back and over his tight buttocks, then back to the waistband of his trousers. She followed the strip of fabric from his back to the front of his trousers. James groaned aloud as she brushed her fingers against him. She located the buttons of his trousers and carefully undid each one. James kicked free of his pants, moaning his immense satisfaction as the hard jutting length of him spilled into Elizabeth's waiting hands. She caressed him, marveling at the velvety soft feel encasing his iron-hard length. And she would have continued her exploration if James hadn't gently lifted her hands from around him, then guided her legs up over his hips, and pressed himself against her, delicately probing her entrance.

Lost in a frenzy of need, Elizabeth locked her legs around his waist and pulled him to her.

James thrust inside her. He closed his eyes, threw back his head, and gritted his teeth as he sheathed himself fully inside her warmth. His entire body shook with the effort as he fought to maintain his control.

Elizabeth cried out in pain as he entered her and tried to

pull away. James realized too late that he'd just ru~
pushed through her veil of innocence. He held on to .
keep her from squirming and causing herself more par
he soothed her with his words and kissed away the salt
her tears. "It's all right, love, the worst will be over in
moment. Lie still. Let me kiss you."

"It wasn't supposed to hurt," Elizabeth said. "It was
supposed to be beautiful."

"The first time always hurts, my sweet," he soothed,
"but the pain will go away soon, and I promise you, it will
be beautiful. We'll make it that way."

Her pain subsided just as he promised, and as it did,
Elizabeth began to move experimentally. James lost his battle to maintain control as her movement forced him deeper
inside her. He began to move his hips in a rhythm as old
as time. Elizabeth followed, matching his movements thrust
for thrust. She clung to him, reveling in the weight and feel
of him as he filled her again and again, gifting her with
himself in a way she'd never dreamed possible. She
squeezed her eyes shut. Tears of joy trickled from the corners, ran down her cheeks, and disappeared into the silk of
her hair. And as she felt the first tremors flow through her,
Elizabeth surrendered to the emotions swirling inside her,
gave voice to her passion with small incoherent cries that
escaped her lips as James rocked her to him and exploded
inside her.

He brushed his lips against her cheek as he buried his
face in her hair. He tasted the saltiness of her tears, then
lifted his head and looked down at her face. God, but she
was beautiful. James shuddered as a rush of emotions raced
through him. He should have spoken words of love instead
of words of passion. He should have cherished her and
treated her tenderly instead of using her to slake his raging
desire. Damn, but she'd been a virgin. She deserved more
than he was willing to offer. James sighed. He wouldn't
think about tomorrow yet. He wouldn't question his good
fortune or ask for more than he deserved. He'd simply love
her while it lasted.

were shimmering with emotion as James leaned

. touched his mouth to hers in a kiss so gentle, so

so precious, it brought fresh tears to her eyes.

captured the stars,'' he breathed at last. ''I brought

back with me.'' He stared down at her. ''And they're

ning in your eyes.''

Elizabeth touched his face with her palm of her hand. ''They're there to watch over you,'' she told him tenderly. ''So you never have to worry about ghosts in the dark.''

Twenty-eight

ELIZABETH FELT A movement beneath her face and awoke to find her head on James's shoulder, his arms wrapped tightly around her. She sighed, knowing at last that she was where she belonged. "What is it?" she whispered as James shifted her from his shoulder to the pillow.

"Diamond," he answered, kissing Elizabeth on her brow. "She's hungry."

"Already?" she grumbled. They had made love twice since they'd left the balcony, and James had carefully bathed her before he pulled her into his arms to sleep. But Elizabeth felt as if she'd just closed her eyes.

"Uh-huh," he murmured. "And I have to go feed her."

"Do you have to?" Elizabeth yawned widely, then cuddled up to him, pressing herself against his body like a demanding kitten.

James chuckled. "Well, we could wait for the governess to wake up and tend to her."

"Hmm, sounds like a plan," she agreed, closing her eyes and almost drifting back to sleep before she remembered. "*I'm* the governess."

"Uh-huh." he nodded. "And Diamond's crying. Do you want to go to her? Or shall I?"

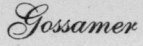

...eth eyed James and the distance to the door. She
...liciously exhausted and her body ached in places
... never be able to explain. James, on the other hand,
...ned well-rested, wide-awake, and relaxed. "You're
...oser."

James chuckled, then threw back his head and laughed.
He rolled out of bed and reached for his silk robe. Elizabeth
rolled to her side, propped herself on her elbow, and admired the line of his back and his nicely curved bottom
before he covered it with his robe. She sighed.

James glanced over his shoulder, read her expression,
and smiled. "Wanton."

"I'm twenty-five years old," she explained. "I have
years of catching up to do."

"Can we not do it all in one night?" he teased. "Not
that I haven't enjoyed every moment," he assured her,
leaning down to give her a proper good-morning kiss. "But
I'd like to live to see my children grow up, and at this rate,
I'm very much afraid I may not survive until breakfast."

"If I were as wanton and insatiable as you suggest,"
Elizabeth informed him, "you'd *be* breakfast."

James raised both eyebrows at her in comical fashion and
leered broadly. "Sounds like a plan." He leaned toward
her as Diamond's cries grew louder and more frustrated.
"After I go warm a bottle for the little one." James
couldn't keep his gaze off Elizabeth. "Would you care to
join me in greeting our little night owl?" He walked over
to the door and reached for the knob.

Elizabeth slid down on the bed, pulled his pillow into
her arms, and snuggled beneath the covers. "As soon as
the sun's up."

James chuckled. "And just last night, I was compli-
menting you on your remarkable maternal instincts."

She sat back up. "I have wonderful maternal instincts,"
she retorted. "And Ruby's living proof."

"How's that?" James stopped in his tracks and whirled
around to face her.

"Ruby escaped her bathing last night," Elizabeth joked.

"Because after the chaos she created yesterday, I
too tempted to drown her in the bathtub."

James went completely still. The color drained fror
face.

Elizabeth knew immediately that she'd said the wror
thing. "I was joking, James. I'm sorry." She stumbled ou.
of bed and ran to hug him around the waist. "James, I
didn't mean it. You know I would never do anything to
harm any of the Treasures. Or let anyone else harm them.
Nothing bad is going to happen to those children while I'm
around."

James met Elizabeth's gaze. "Look," he said, raking a
hand through his hair, torn between his deepening feelings
for Elizabeth and his unconditional love for his oldest child.
"I know Ruby's been a royal pain since you got here. I
saw what happened in the park yesterday. I'm not blind to
her faults. I know how she's behaving, or should I say,
misbehaving? And we both know she's responsible for Portia's disappearance."

"Portia's just a doll, James. Of no importance at all when
compared to living, breathing little girls. Forgive me for
making such a poor joke."

James managed a small smile. "There is nothing to forgive," he said, holding Elizabeth close as his heart resumed
its regular beat. "I'm fully aware that there are times when
Ruby can test the patience of a saint." He kissed Elizabeth
thoroughly, then turned her around in his arms, and play-
fully swatted her bare bottom as he sent her back to bed.
"Don't worry about it, sleepyhead. Go back to bed. You've
a long hard day ahead of you." He paused as he opened
the door.

Elizabeth winked saucily, then licked her lips provocatively. "Another long, hard workday. Is that all I have to
look forward to tomorrow?"

"You can always change your mind about joining me in
the nursery," he said. "And it's only fair to warn you that
I know several very *interesting* uses for that big rocking
chair."

...weighed her decision carefully. "Give me a
...grab my chemise."

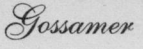

...CRAIG HOUSEHOLD ran as smoothly as it had ever
...n. Although he still didn't sleep through the night, James
slept better than he had in years. And Elizabeth no longer
missed dinner. Of course, James's often exhausted slumber
was the direct result of long hours spent in ardent lovemaking. And long days looking after the Treasures, too few
hours of sleep, and unusual amounts of night time physical
exertion increased Elizabeth's appetite.

After three weeks of living with James and the Treasures,
it seemed to Elizabeth and to all the other members of the
household that she had always been there. With one notable
exception. Portia had yet to make a reappearance, and Elizabeth and James had begun to despair that Ruby would
never return her or learn to accept Elizabeth as part of the
family. Ruby despised her, and every morning in the nursery was a battle for dominance between the governess and
the queen bee. Added to Elizabeth's woes was the fact that
Garnet awoke asking for Portia nearly every morning and
cried in disappointment when the doll failed to turn up.
Elizabeth had begun to heartily wish she'd left Portia sitting
on the shelf in her bedroom at her grandmother Sadler's
house.

"She'll turn up," James promised as he sat on the leather
wing chair he'd had brought up to the nursery from his
study. James hadn't seen Elizabeth since dinner. He had
spent the long hours after the evening meal working. The
clock in the downstairs hall had reminded him that it was
time for Diamond's early-morning feeding. James had put
aside his contracts and bids, grabbed a bottle of brandy and
a glass from the sideboard, and come up to the nursery for
his new favorite pastime of watching Elizabeth feed the
baby her bottle. Still dressed in his business suit, James
sat on his leather chair, kicked off his shoes, propped his
feet on the matching leather footstool, and crossed his legs

at the ankles. He leaned forward and lifted
brandy from its place and on the floor beside h.

"I know." Sitting in companionable silenc
rocked and fed Diamond her two o'clock bottle, E.
had spent the last few minutes staring up at the do.
the shelves, lost in thought. She looked over at James
smiled. "But can we endure it until she does?"

James shook his head. The rest of the household might
be running as smoothly as clockwork, but mornings in the
nursery were chaos. Ruby and Garnet were feuding over
the loss of Portia and there was very little he or Elizabeth
or anyone else could do to ease the tension. Ruby had di-
vided the nursery into two groups—the people she liked
and the people she didn't. Elizabeth and Garnet fell into
the latter category, everyone else fell into the former.

James was amazed to find that, far from lessening his
attraction for Elizabeth, the unrest in the nursery had
strengthened the feelings between them. He had spent every
two o'clock feeding for the past two and a half weeks with
Elizabeth in the nursery, taking turns feeding Diamond,
sharing the events of the day, and oftentimes, making inventive love in the rocking chair long after Diamond fell
asleep. He had missed this sharing even more than the lovemaking. He loved the closeness. He loved being able to
look at Elizabeth and know what she was thinking. And he
loved knowing that she could look at him and see past the
millionaire façade to the man deep inside. James had
planned to spend his life married to his wife, and when she
died, he'd decided to finish out his life by living on the
happy memories. He never expected to share this sort of
closeness with any woman other than Mei Ling. He hadn't
prepared for it. But somehow Elizabeth had quietly and
efficiently become a huge part of his life, willingly shoul-
dering so many of his daily burdens, that James had trouble
remembering how lonely and alone he'd been before she
arrived. And it was impossible for him to envision a future
without her.

He likened the past two and a half weeks to a honeymoon. The daily aggravations of life seemed easier to bear now that he had someone to share them with, now that the newness and the wonder of their lovemaking outweighed all other concerns. If only he could keep the outside world at bay a little longer.

But the demands of family, household, and business had a way of intruding. And James knew that the sleepless nights and the strain of enduring the endless battles for dominance in the nursery took their toll as well. "We have no choice," he said. "We'll have to endure."

"I wonder . . ." she mused aloud.

"What?" The determined expression on her face and the way she was concentrating on the dolls roused his curiosity.

"What was it about Portia that Garnet liked so much and Ruby didn't?"

James smiled at her. "That's easy. Portia looked like you. All tawny-blond hair and big blue-green eyes and an exquisite bow mouth."

"That's one of the things that drew me to her, too," Elizabeth explained. "I loved Portia, not just because my father gave her to me, but because she was the only doll I ever had who was a mirror image of me." She looked over at James, then up at the dolls on the shelf. "Maybe that's why Ruby and Garnet don't care anything about those." She nodded toward the red-haired, the brown-haired, and the blond-haired dolls. "Those dolls' faces don't look anything like the faces Ruby and Garnet see in the mirror."

"Hmm" James followed her train of thought, then without warning, he took his wallet out of his jacket, removed several bills, and walked over and tucked them in the pocket of Elizabeth's dressing gown.

"What's this for?" She couldn't quite disguise the nervous, wary note in her voice. Prostitutes were paid. Mistresses were paid. Lovers were not. But, then, James had never said anything about loving her.

"So you can stop by Kellerman's General Store tomorrow afternoon and order whatever dolls you think the

Treasures might like. Surely, they must have some dolls with Oriental features.''

"I doubt three dolls will cost that much,'' Elizabeth remarked dryly.

"I thought you might like to buy a few things for yourself, too.'' The tips of James's ears reddened in embarrassment.

"You don't have to buy me, James,'' she whispered. "I'm already in your employ and in your debt.''

James began to pace the nursery floor. "For God's sakes, Elizabeth, take the money!''

"I've been in Coryville for three weeks and so far, you haven't worried whether or not I had money to purchase a few things for myself. Why are you giving it to me now? As a salve to your conscience?'' The angry words were out before she could stop them. Elizabeth knew she was being prickly. She knew she might even be considered unreasonable, but she'd shared his bed for the past two and half weeks, and James hadn't breathed a word about his feelings for her.

"Yes,'' James answered. "As a salve to my conscience. Because I've kept your money on account and failed to provide you with any spending money, because I didn't trust you not to take the money and run away and leave me and the Treasures.''

The fight went out of her at his honest admission. She understood fear and doubts. She understood loss. And the fear of losing. "I lo . . .'' She almost said the words she instinctively knew he wasn't ready to hear. "You know I've no place else to go,'' Elizabeth improvised.

"Maybe so,'' James said. "But it's time I let you know I trust you. And I want you to take the money as a gift. Consider it your payday.''

"Payday,'' Elizabeth repeated, a stricken look on her face as she remembered the promise she'd made to Delia. "Oh, James, I forgot I promised Delia I'd talk to you about paying a nursery supplement to her mother and Rose for the extra laundry.''

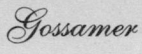

"What extra laundry?" he asked.

Elizabeth repeated the story Delia had told her about her mother and Rose and the seven brothers and sisters running around naked because it meant less wash to do. "I promised her you'd pay extra if she'd use clean facecloths and change the Treasures' clothes and diapers whenever they needed it."

James shuddered, thinking of all those children. "Of course I'll pay more. I'm ashamed the idea never occurred to me." He took out a few more bills. "I've already paid Delia and her mother for last week, but give Delia this tomorrow with my thanks."

"I will."

James waited while Elizabeth burped the baby, then leaned down and lifted Diamond from Elizabeth's arms and carried her into the bedroom. When he returned to the playroom, he paused for a moment, leaning against the doorjamb as he stood looking at Elizabeth as she closed her eyes and rested her head against the back of the rocking chair. James wanted to tell her what was in his heart, but Ruby kept him from it. Ruby was the stumbling block he couldn't go around or climb over.

How long before Ruby learned to accept Elizabeth? How long before she learned to trust her? To like her? Or to love her? He wanted to marry Elizabeth. He ached to marry her. But as long as Ruby disapproved of her, marriage to Elizabeth was out of the question. No matter how badly he wanted it. He'd made a promise three years ago when he heard her frantic cries and waded into the surf from a beach in Hong Kong to pluck Ruby out of the water. She hadn't been Ruby then, of course, just another baby girl whose family had abandoned her on the rocks for the ocean to swallow up. But James had fished her out of the surf and promised her that as long as he lived, she would never want for anything, never have to worry that he would place his needs above her own, never fear that her wishes would be dismissed or her welfare placed at risk simply because she was female. And James was duty bound to fulfill that promise. He'd named her for a gem of great value, and although she was only six or seven months old at the time, Ruby had forced him to earn her trust. He worked hard to earn it and to create a safe, secure world for her and for the sisters that came after her. He'd taken Garnet from the mouth of a stray dog outside a refuse bin in an alley in San Francisco's Chinatown, and he'd nearly run his carriage over Emerald while returning home from work one evening. His Treasures had all been gifts of fate. And James refused to risk their happiness and security for any reason— even if it meant sacrificing his happiness with Elizabeth.

Besides, Elizabeth had pride. She wouldn't ask him to choose between his oldest daughter and her. She wouldn't ask anything of him at all. But sooner or later Ruby's stubborn refusal to accept her would drive a wedge between them. She couldn't ignore Ruby. She couldn't dismiss one of the most important parts of his life. He loved his children and he believed that the best thing he could do for them was to marry Elizabeth and make her their mother. And James knew in his heart that Elizabeth wouldn't agree to marry him unless all the Treasures wanted her. For Elizabeth it was all or nothing. She wouldn't settle for less. He sighed. Although he wanted to declare his intentions, there was no hope for it. Not until Ruby capitulated. There was no reason to put Elizabeth through that agony of waiting. Of knowing her future hinged on the stubborn whim of a three-and-a-half-year-old child. So he kept his feelings to himself and endured the agony alone, very much afraid that now that he'd found Elizabeth, he was destined to lose her.

She opened her eyes as if she'd felt his presence and smiled a welcome. "Did she wake up?"

"No, all four of them are sound asleep."

"But we're wide awake," Elizabeth said softly. "What do we do now?"

James walked over to the rocking chair and stood towering over her. "Are you still angry with me?"

Elizabeth shook her head. "I wasn't angry with you. I was—surprised—confused—I don't know."

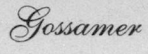

"Angry," James insisted. "And you had every right to be. Sometimes I have no tact."

That was a massive understatement, but Elizabeth refrained from pointing it out.

"I should have thought about your feelings, about how you'd feel when I handed you cash without warning, especially after . . ." He let his words drift off.

"I don't know what's expected of me." Elizabeth met his gaze without flinching. "I don't know who I am or what I am to you. A very convenient governess? Your mistress? Your who—"

James knelt down and placed his fingers over her lips to stop the words, then followed them with his mouth. "My woman," he breathed against her lips. "My own."

She closed her eyes and gave a trembling sigh as she heard James answer her most fervent prayer. Tears stung her eyes. She couldn't stop them. Since the night she had allowed James to carry her to his bed, Elizabeth had promised herself she wouldn't build castles in the air. She promised herself that she would take whatever James offered and not wish for more. She told herself that she could live for the moment, that she could survive in a state of limbo, but Elizabeth had known all along that those promises were impossible to keep. She simply wasn't a moment-by-moment person. She'd spent her whole life searching for a way to belong. People to belong to. But James Craig was the first person in her life who had ever taken her in his arms and made her feel as if she belonged there.

James rubbed the pad of his thumb over her bottom lip, gently caressing the plump flesh. "My own," he whispered again, in reverence, in awe. He scooted Elizabeth to the edge of the rocking chair and kissed her tenderly, before deepening his kiss and kissing her senseless.

When he released her, Elizabeth opened her eyes and found herself staring into James's dark blue ones. She met his gaze, her love for him shimmering in her eyes.

"If you're willing," he began, "I have an idea how we can pass the time until we get sleepy."

"Does your idea include a rocking chair?" she asked teasingly.

"No," James shook his head. "I was thinking more like a chaise longue and a blanket on the balcony beneath the stars."

"Stars," Elizabeth repeated.

"I can't offer you any more than that," he said softly. "I can't offer you the rest. Not until . . . Not yet." He studied her face, his intense gaze searching for a clue what she was thinking.

"I've always fancied myself as a stargazer," Elizabeth told him. And she certainly appreciated James's unique stargazing techniques.

"Elizabeth." Suddenly serious, James framed her face with his hands. "Please, understand that what we have now—at this moment—will have to be enough."

"It is," Elizabeth told him, silently promising herself that she'd make it enough.

~∞⟡∞~

A WEEK LATER James caught the flash of dark magenta skirts out of the corner of his eye as Elizabeth hurried past the open door of his study toward the kitchen with the large brown-paper wrapped package he'd picked up from Kellerman's and brought home to her. He glanced up from his stack of financial reports and assayer's assessments and called out to her. "Elizabeth?"

She paused in the doorway.

"Did the dolls come in?"

Elizabeth marched into his study and came to a stop beside his chair. She ripped the remainder of the paper from around the bundle, then reached inside and grabbed hold of one of the dolls and thrust it in his face. "If you call this *abomination* a doll!"

"*Christ!*" James uttered another more vicious oath and recoiled at the sight of it. Although it had a cloth body and two porcelain arms and two porcelain legs and a face and was dressed in a silk brocade robe, to call it a doll was a generous exaggeration. Elizabeth was right. The object she held before him was a grotesque abomination of what should have been a child's toy. The porcelain face was painted a sickening yellow, the eyes were mere black slits, the nose was broad and flat, and the mouth was a scarlet leer. The sly, malicious and faintly evil expression on the doll's face was a vicious caricature of a Chinese woman that bore even less resemblance to Ruby and Garnet and Emerald than the Caucasian dolls upstairs. Only the thick black hair resembled the Treasures' and it was elaborately braided and lacquered in the manner of a lady of the Emperor's court. James had seen plaster reliefs of stylized Chinese temple dogs that were prettier. "Who made these? From where were they shipped?"

"Mr. Kellerman ordered them from a toy supplier in New York City," Elizabeth told him, holding the doll by one tightly-bound foot, before turning it upside down so she could read the manufacturer's mark pressed into the porcelain at the base of the doll's skull. "But according to this, the faces were manufactured by Pearson's China Works of Chesterfield in England."

James pinched the bridge of his nose and rubbed his tired eyes before he looked up at Elizabeth. "Is that how the people in Chesterfield see my daughters? Is that the way the people here in Coryville see my daughters?"

Elizabeth saw the pain, the confusion, and the outrage on his face and answered honestly. "I don't know anyone in Chesterfield, but I suspect there are some people there who believe this is an accurate depiction of Chinese women because they've been taught to fear and ridicule foreigners who look and speak differently. As for the people here in Coryville, only the stubborn and ignorant and cold-hearted could fail to see beyond the color of the Treasures' skin and the shape of their eyes to the little girls they are."

James raked a hand through his hair in frustration. "You would think a *China* works would know better."

"Not if all they have heard are the horror stories. Not if

all they've ever seen are these grotesque dolls or equally grotesque drawings or paintings or descriptions they've read in travelogues. Not if they've never met any Chinese. You showed me that.''

James stared at her searchingly. ''Tell me, Elizabeth, am I wrong? Am I like Don Quixote tilting at windmills? Am I desperately trying to make silk purses out of sows' ears?''

He was and he wasn't. He couldn't change the whole world, or the attitudes of the people in it, in one lifetime. James knew that as well as she did. But he'd made a fine start. He'd changed *her* attitudes. And she would change Lois Marlin's and the others in town like her. And in time the Treasures would touch more lives and open more closed minds. In the end that was really all one man and one family could do. And if what he was doing was tilting at windmills, then the act of tilting was all that mattered. But Elizabeth didn't say those things to him. She said what she knew he wanted—and needed—to hear. ''That's absurd,'' she told him roundly. ''Everyone knows that to make a silk purse, you must start with the finest thread from China.''

In that moment James knew that if he didn't already love her, he'd fall desperately, hopelessly in love with her.

Elizabeth smiled at him. ''Could you do things differently? Could you feel any differently?''

''No,'' he admitted.

''Then how can following your heart be wrong?''

''Is that what I'm doing?'' he asked, even though he knew she was right.

''I hope so,'' Elizabeth said softly.

James sat silently for a moment, marveling at the woman who had followed her heart, then opened it and welcomed him and his children inside. ''I know silk when I see it,'' he said. And when he opened his arms, Elizabeth walked into them.

''What are you going to do with them?'' James asked, sometime later, as Elizabeth stuffed the Dragon-faced Lady, as he'd dubbed the doll, back into the bundle and started toward the door of the study.

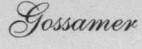

"I'm *not* giving them to Ruby and Garnet and Emerald. I'm taking them to the refuse bin in the kitchen where I intend to bury them."

"Why not return them to Kellerman's and get your money back?" James suggested.

Elizabeth raised both her eyebrows at that. "You don't seriously expect me to allow these dolls to be sold to anyone else, do you?"

James chuckled at the fire in her eyes and the indignation in her voice. "No. I don't guess I do."

"Good, because I'd hate to have to disappoint you."

"You, Elizabeth Sadler, could never disappoint me."

"That's what you say now," she replied smartly. "What will you say in forty or fif—" She broke off abruptly and hurried out the door before James could answer.

Twenty-nine

JAMES FOUND HER hours later, upstairs in the bathroom of the nursery. She had on what looked to be one of her oldest camisoles and pair of drawers and one of the Treasures' oilskin bedsheets wrapped around her waist. A large bottle of India ink, a sheet of very fine emery cloth, a pair of scissors, a stack of old towels, and a box of paints were spread out within easy reach. Two naked dolls with wet and shortened black hair and faces eerily covered in a thick layer of wax and bodies wrapped in oilcloth lay on a folded length of toweling amidst a tangle of red, blond, and brown human hair on the floor around her. As he watched, Elizabeth leaned over the bathtub and dipped the head of the third doll into a bowl of diluted ink, then carefully combed the ink through the strands with a toothbrush.

"What in the hell are you doing?"

Elizabeth didn't even pause in her work as she answered him. "I promised Ruby and Garnet and Emerald a doll of their own and I intend to see that they get them. And no bloody China factory in Chesterfield, England, is going to keep me from doing what I said I'd do when I said I'd do it!"

James's shoulders began to shake as he watched Elizabeth destroy the red-haired Parisian fashion plate he had bought for Ruby to transform her into a raven-haired Chinese beauty. A chuckle formed in his throat as Elizabeth continued her monologue. He coughed to disguise it.

"I thought about leaving their hair long," she said. "I know Chinese women have long hair, too, but I want to make these dolls look the way the Treasures look now. And contrary to what I was led to believe back at the jail before we arrived in Coryville"—Elizabeth cast James a pointed look over her shoulder—"none of the Treasures has hair long enough to braid yet."

James gave up all pretense of coughing. Instead, he threw back his head and roared with laughter.

"What's so funny?" she demanded, swiping a lock of hair off her cheek with the back of her hand.

"You," he said, laughing. "You cursing while you dip that poor wax-shrouded doll's head into a pot of India ink. You with ink splattered on your undergarments and hair and face and hands . . ."

Her hands. Elizabeth looked down to find that while she'd assembled everything she needed to protect the dolls while she recreated them, she had forgotten to protect her hands. Her lovely creamy-skinned hands. She reached for a towel.

"That won't do any good." James laughed even harder. "India ink is indelible."

"I know that!" Elizabeth snapped, carefully wringing out the doll's hair before she wrapped it in the towel. "Why do you think I poured wax over their porcelain faces?"

"I couldn't imagine," James gasped, laughing so hard his sides ached.

"Stop it!" she insisted, pointing a threatening ink-covered finger at him. But his laughter was contagious and by the time Elizabeth got to her feet and marched over to him, her shoulders were shaking, her mouth was trembling, and hot tears formed in her eyes. Elizabeth didn't know whether she was laughing or crying.

James held on to his side, pointed at her, and laughed even harder.

"This isn't funny!" she declared, laughing and crying right along with him.

"That depends on how you look at it." James caught her by the shoulders and turned her around to face the mirror.

A half-moon of India ink decorated her right cheekbone. Elizabeth was horrified. And he thought it was funny! The man she loved thought having a half-moon of India ink on her face less than a week away from her first scheduled tea for the women of Coryville was funny. "Bloody hell!" she squealed James's favorite oath.

"It will wear off," James told her. "Eventually."

"Not before my tea!"

James bit his lips to suppress another wave of laughter. He remembered Elizabeth asking permission to host a tea for the Coryville Ladies' League a week or so ago, but he'd forgotten all about it until now.

"It doesn't look so bad, sweetheart." He tried to placate her before she really burst into tears. "You're beautiful no matter what. And this"—he touched the crescent of ink— "will probably start a new fashion trend. All the ladies will want one."

"Oh, really?" Elizabeth whirled around in his arms and held up her stained hands. "And what do you suggest I do about these?"

"Wear gloves," he managed before he burst into another round of laughter.

"All right. Fine," Elizabeth announced, patting both sides of his face, "I'll wear gloves and start a new fashion trend. What are you going to do?"

James turned to look in the mirror as he realized what she had done. His mouth fell open at the sight of the two palm prints on either side of his face. It wouldn't take a genius to figure out that they were too big to be his daughters' and too small to belong to him.

A wave of desire took him by storm and nearly sent him

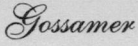

to his knees. James turned to look at Elizabeth, recognized the smug satisfaction on her face for what it was, and wanted her with an urgency he had never known was possible. His blue eyes darkened as his body tightened in reaction, and he grew hard against the buttons of his trousers. "Elizabeth," he murmured her name in a husky baritone layered with needs and emotion as he reached for her and lowered his mouth to hers.

Heat flared between them the moment their lips touched. His tongue plundered the depths of her mouth and Elizabeth's tongue returned the favor. He groaned her name and Elizabeth felt his need pressed up against her, nestled against the softness of her belly. She reached up and shoved the silk robe off his wide shoulders, pushing it down his arms, where it hung suspended until she slipped her hands between them to untie the silk cord at his waist. James sucked in a ragged breath as she brushed his stomach with the back of her hand. He tangled one hand in her hair and deepened the kiss. He worked his other hand between their bodies and cupped her, pressing the heel of his hand against her silken mound while he massaged her with his fingers through the slit in her linen drawers. Elizabeth's knees buckled at the contact, but James supported her weight. He leaned against the wall, wedging his knee between her legs while he continued to work magic with his fingers. His blood pounded in his ears, his heart raced, and his body trembled with the need to quench the fire flowing through him. James forgot about making love in his warm soft bed down the hall. Normally articulate, he forgot the soft words of love he had whispered to her before. He forgot to caress her. He forgot everything he'd ever learned about lovemaking except his one overwhelming, almost primal, need to bury himself in her warmth. Now. He withdrew his hand from her long enough to force open the buttons of his trousers. His hard shaft jutted through the opening. Elizabeth wiggled closer, trying to press his length where his fingers had been. No longer patient enough to fumble with ribbons and hooks, James reached for her camisole and ripped it from neck to hem down the front until it hung open on either side of her magnificent breasts. He tore his mouth away from hers, then bent his head and laved the nipples of her breasts before latching on to one and suckling like an eager baby. Elizabeth whimpered with a mix of excitement, anticipation, and an incredible hunger for him. James recognized her sounds of passion.

"Now," he said.

"Yes," she breathed.

And with that, James cupped his hands under her thighs and lifted her up to meet him. Elizabeth locked her long legs around his waist as James buried himself in her warmth. He threw back his head, bared his teeth, and hung on, as her woman's body tightened around him and he thrust higher, harder, spilling himself inside her.

"I CAN'T STAND it any longer," Will announced as he joined them for breakfast the following morning. He stared at the lavish buffet spread out in the dining room at Craig House and at the Treasures' bowls of porridge, then laid his knife and fork aside. Something strange was going on. Both sides of James's face was blotched with a dark stain and Elizabeth sported a black half moon on her right cheek and a pair of gloves—at breakfast. "What the devil is going on here this morning?"

James looked across the table at Will and said, with a perfectly serious expression on his face, "What makes you think there's something going on?"

"Well, cripes, Jamie," Will uttered, throwing his hands up in exasperation. "I'm not stupid or blind. I can see what's happening between the two of you." He turned to Elizabeth and smiled. "I don't mean to embarrass you, Beth," he said when she blushed. "I just want to let you know you have my best wishes. Both of you." He stared at his best friend. "What I don't understand is why we're enjoying steak and eggs today while the Treasures are eat-

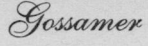

ing their usual mush or why Beth's a wee bit formal this morning.''

"Is she?" James asked. "I hadn't noticed."

Will leveled his gaze at James. "Oh, come now, Jamie, even your mother—a stickler for etiquette if I've ever seen one—removes her gloves for meals." He frowned as Elizabeth tried and failed to bite back a smile. "And what the devil is that on your faces?"

Elizabeth giggled.

"Is that all?" James asked, casting a brief conspiratory glance at Elizabeth. "I'm worried about you, Will," he continued. "You're usually much more observant."

"There's more?" Will appeared stunned.

"Look around you." James nodded at the little girls seated beside and across from Will.

Will followed his gaze to Ruby and Garnet, who sat calmly eating their oatmeal, each sharing their seat with a new doll. "Good heavens!" he exclaimed in mock horror. "The civil war has ended. It's actually quiet in here. And what are these?" He leaned closer to Garnet. "New dolls?"

Garnet looked up from her bowl of oatmeal and grinned. "Baby."

Will studied the dolls. Their glossy black hair was bobbed to just below the chin, and the doll Garnet held in her arms had a fringe of hair cut short and straight across her forehead, just like Garnet's. Their eyes were painted a warm shade of brown and lined to hint at their almond shape, and their mouths were bow-shaped and painted a delicate pink. Will was amazed by the resemblance to the Treasures. "Where did you find these dolls?" he asked. "They're exquisite."

"On the shelves in the nursery," James replied proudly.

Will wrinkled his brow. He'd been upstairs to the nursery many times, and he never remembered seeing them before. Two or three French fashion dolls, but not . . . He looked closer at the clothes they were wearing—the height of Parisian fashion.

"Elizabeth modified them a bit last night."

"You did this?" Will was impressed. "How?"

Elizabeth removed her gloves and held up her hands so he could see the black stains. "India ink."

Will began to laugh, then turned to look at James, and suddenly realized the marks on his face were palm prints. Obviously Elizabeth's palm prints.

"I helped," James added, grinning.

"I don't believe it!" Will laughed. "I wish I had been here. The sight of you two modifying those dolls must have been something."

James and Elizabeth shared another conspiratorial glance, and the temperature in the room seemed to rise a few degrees. Elizabeth blushed.

"Yes," James agreed in a low husky tone, "it was." And he had some very interesting ink marks on less visible parts of his anatomy to prove it.

◦◦◦◦◦

"JAMIE," WILL BEGAN when James returned from helping Elizabeth take the girls to the nursery. "We've got problems. In the camps."

James shrugged. "There are always problems in the camps."

"Not like this," Will said. "Jamie, the miners are feuding almost as badly as Ruby and Garnet were. I'm afraid it could get real ugly and real dangerous.

James looked at Will and read the seriousness of the situation in Will's eyes. "I don't suppose buying all the workers new dolls is going to bring peace and contentment to the settlements."

"Well, the buying part might work, but I don't know, Jamie. We already pay higher wages than any other company. And we've already implemented a five-day work week, instead of six. And we pay for overtime and holidays. I don't know what else we can do. But I don't like this situation, Jamie. I've never seen it so volatile. Anti-Chinese sentiment is running high. Tempers are flaring. And if we

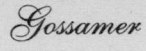

don't do something soon, somebody's going to get killed.''

"What do you suggest we do?"

Will shook his head. "I've talked to them until I'm blue in the face. They're not listening to me. You're the owner of Craig Capital, maybe you should go up there and try to negotiate.''

"What about offering blocks of common stock?''

Will thought about it. "It might work, but we're both going to have to go up there and make the offer in person.''

James shook his head as he paced the length of the dining room and back. "I can't go, Will. You'll have to go alone.''

"I've been up there alone, Jamie, and I'm telling you that it's no use. They don't want to deal with the second in command. They want you.''

"If I go," James began. "If we go, who's going to stay here and watch over Elizabeth and the girls? Would you want to leave them alone without knowing for sure whether or not Lo Peng's hatchet men were hanging around?''

"Cripes," Will cursed. "I forgot about that.''

"I haven't." James clenched his fists. If he stayed in Coryville, he put his company and all the men who worked for him at risk. And if he left town for the mining camps up in the high timber country, he could be leaving his family to face an even greater risk.

"Bring them with you," Will said suddenly.

"My children are Chinese, Will. I don't know if taking them into an area full of anti-Chinese sentiment will be good for them.''

"I don't see that we've any other choice, Jamie. And I don't think the anti-Chinese sentiment is personal. It's about labor, Jamie. And economics. I don't believe any of these men would make war on children. You know I wouldn't recommend this course of action if I thought the Treasures were in any danger from the workers. In fact, I think it might be good for the men to see your children— to see any children. Most of them are a long way away from their families. They need to be reminded of what they're working for. Besides," he added as an afterthought, "we'll both be there to protect them."

"It would be better than leaving them here," James agreed. "You may be right. At least, it's worth a shot."

"Agreed," Will said. "Bring Elizabeth and the Treasures and Delia and Mrs. G. and whoever else you need with you. You can have the cabin."

"What about you?" James asked.

"I'll bunk in the office," Will decided.

"All right," James said. "When do we leave?"

"As soon as you can," Will told him. "I'd like to get up there to head off any further trouble. Tomorrow, if possible."

"IT'S IMPOSSIBLE, JAMES," Elizabeth told him. "I can't have everyone packed and ready to leave by morning."

"Pack what you think you'll need," James told her. "And if we need anything else, we'll telegraph word to Mrs. G. and she can send it by express train to the camp."

"What about Diamond? How are we going to feed her?" she asked, looking at James. "Tell me you aren't planning to take the goat." Although the nursery was stocked with cans of evaporated milk, Elizabeth knew James and Mrs. G. preferred to use fresh milk from the nanny goat James kept in the stable.

James laughed. "No, we'll leave the goat here."

Elizabeth breathed a sigh of relief. "Thank goodness! Because I don't know how to milk a goat and I'm not eager to learn. And I don't even want to think about traveling with one."

"We'll stop at Kellerman's and pick up a case or two of canned milk. I hope we won't be gone too long, and Diamond should manage fine on that until we return home."

"What about Mrs. G.?" Elizabeth asked. "We're supposed to be planning the tea for the Coryville Ladies' League next Friday afternoon.''

''Mrs. G. can plan the tea without you. Besides,'' he added impishly, ''if you go with me, you won't have to wear gloves all the time for fear that someone will see your hands.''

Thirty

JAMES CRAIG'S FAMILY made quite a sight as they disembarked from the CCL express train at midafternoon the following day, after a three-hour journey. A dozen or so employees of Craig Capital paused to gape as the owner of Craig Capital, Ltd., exited the platform with his four children, their governess, the governess's assistant, assorted trunks of clothing, and other children's paraphernalia, including two baby carriages, and Will Keegan in tow. It was the first time any of the Craig Capital employees, other than Will, had ever seen James with his family.

The unease that had resided in the camp for weeks seemed to dissipate with the appearance of Elizabeth and Delia and the children. They seemed to represent James Craig's willingness to do whatever was needed to work out the problems in the camp. That he had brought his children along, rather than be separated from them for days at a time, seemed to show his willingness to negotiate. Everyone had heard how devoted James Craig was to his daughters; now they could witness that devotion for themselves. That the four Craig Treasures were foundlings was also known in the camp. Despite rumors to the contrary, the truth of the Treasures origins had gotten out. It was talked about in the Chinese section of the camp, where the word had spread from San Francisco through the Chinese grapevine, that Lo Peng allowed unwanted girl children to be taken to James Craig. And the Chinese workers were eager to get a look at the children to see how James Craig treated them. Speculation ran high among the Chinese as to why a man of James Cameron Craig's power and wealth would choose to build a fortune for worthless girl children rather than sons. Most of the Irishmen, Welshmen, and Cornishmen also knew the Treasures were James's adopted children. Word had spread among their groups of workers from the London and Edinburgh branch of Craig Capital that James Craig was an odd duck, choosing to adopt unwanted Chinese children, rather than remarry and have children of his own. Speculation ran high, in the London and Edinburgh branches of Craig Capital, as to whom James Craig intended to name as his heir, since he had no sons, only adopted daughters, to leave his fortune to.

The Treasures had napped during the journey and were now fairly crackling with excitement at the prospect of stretching their legs and exploring the camp. They'd been cooped up too long. They were accustomed to more freedom than they'd had on the train and were ready to play. Elizabeth watched the girls grow more and more excited and excitable as they followed Will into the cabin.

Although fairly roomy, the cabin was smaller than the area the girls were accustomed to in the nursery. Elizabeth looked around the main room with its Franklin stove with a reservoir, comfortable furniture, and at the two doors leading off it.

"There are two bedrooms," Will volunteered. "And a tub and a basin in the bathroom. I'm afraid the accommodations are a little rough. There's no running water, but there is a pump on the back porch and a privy a short distance away."

"I'm sure we'll be fine," Elizabeth said. She glanced down at the timepiece pinned to her bodice. "It's time for the Treasures' afternoon romp in the park," she said to

James. "Shall I keep to their regular schedule or would you rather I skip their exercise this afternoon while Delia and I get them settled into the cabin?"

James shook his head. "Unpack the things you need right now." He reached into the large leather bag Elizabeth had stuffed with diapers, talcum powder, fresh clothing, several cans of evaporated milk, and two of Diamond's feeding bottles and removed a bottle and a can of milk. James carried the can of milk over to a wooden table, pulled out his pocketknife, punched two holes in the lid, then removed the rubber nipple from Diamond's bottle and filled the bottle with evaporated milk. "Here." He jammed the nipple back on the bottle and stuck it the leather bag, then slipped the bag onto Elizabeth's shoulder. "In case Diamond gets hungry while you're gone," he offered by way of explanation.

"Where are we going?" Elizabeth asked.

"To take the Treasures for their afternoon romp. There's an open meadow bordering the forest down the path a quarter or a mile or so from here," James said as he walked into the nearest bedroom and returned with a folded quilt. He looked over at Will for confirmation, and Will nodded in agreement. "The girls will be safe playing there. As long as you and Delia keep them away from the mine entrances and out of the forest, they shouldn't be in anyone's way."

"Where will you be?" Elizabeth asked.

"I'll be in the main office near the entrance to the mine. The building across from the railroad platform," James told her. "I'll send someone over here to move the trunks into the bedrooms and set up the cots for the Treasures. Put Delia and Ruby and Garnet in one bedroom and you and Emerald and Diamond in the other."

"Where will you sleep?" Elizabeth asked, softly.

"In the office with Will," he answered gently.

Elizabeth frowned.

"It will be only be for a couple of days or so," James said in a voice so low only Elizabeth could hear it.

"But it will seem like an eternity," she whispered back.

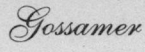

"Yes," he said. "It will." Then in a louder voice he added, "Load the girls into their buggies, and I'll walk you down to the meadow."

THE MEADOW, AN acre or so of cleared land at the edge of the forest, was just beginning to bloom with early spring phlox and trillium and new grasses. Elizabeth pushed Diamond's carriage while James wheeled Garnet and Emerald's buggy to a spot where a lone aspen stood at the edge of the forest shading a portion of the meadow and parked it. Elizabeth pushed Diamond's carriage beside her sisters'. James lifted Garnet and Emerald out of the buggy, then removed the quilt he'd brought along and spread it on top of the grass for Elizabeth, Emerald, and the baby to sit on. James took Emerald's and Garnet's dolls out of the buggy and a handful of wooden building blocks they'd been playing with during the journey and placed them in the center of the quilt. He set Emerald down among them to amuse herself. Delia let go of Ruby's hand, then followed her into the field of wildflowers as Ruby ran chasing after a butterfly. Garnet followed close behind.

James and Elizabeth stood watching as the girls careened through the meadow, running after the bright splashes of color that flitted from flower to flower, squealing at the top of their lungs.

"The Treasures should be able to run and jump to their hearts' content here," James said, pointing to the area close by. "Just don't let them wander too near the woods." He pointed toward a group of boulders a dozen or so yards deep inside the meadow. "Use that as your boundary. They're safe in the meadow, but some of the ventilation shafts from the abandoned mines extend into that stand of trees just beyond the clearing. And don't stay past four o'clock." He pulled out his pocket watch and looked at it. It was half past two. The Treasures normally played in the park for two hours from two until four every afternoon, but

James didn't want to take any chances. He gazed up at the sky, gauging the amount of afternoon sunlight left. "It gets dark early in the mountains."

Elizabeth nodded.

"If you have any trouble, yell. I won't be far away."

"We'll be fine," Elizabeth assured him. "And we'll meet you back at the cabin by four."

"I may not be able to get away by four," he told her, "but I'll be there in time to help bathe the girls and get them to bed. All right?" James wanted to kiss Elizabeth good-bye. He'd been wanting to kiss her all day, but Delia was there with the Treasures and James reached out and surreptitiously clasped Elizabeth's hand in his. "I want to steal a kiss or two from you tonight after Delia and the Treasures go to bed. Don't fall asleep on me before I get there," he teased in a low husky voice.

"I won't," Elizabeth promised. "Now, go before you're late for your meeting."

"Have fun," he said. "And take care of the girls for me."

"Trust me," Elizabeth said.

James looked down at her, a serious expression on his face. "If I didn't trust you," he said, "I wouldn't leave you alone with my Treasures." He glanced over to see if Delia or the girls were paying attention before he gently traced his finger over the half moon of India ink on Elizabeth's right cheek.

"I know you better than that, James Cameron Craig," she teased him. "Desperate times require desperate measures. You'd rather watch the Treasures yourself. And the only reason you're leaving them with me now is because I'm the only governess you've got."

"You're the only governess I want," he replied in the deep tone of voice that sent her pulses racing.

"Go," Elizabeth urged him. "The sooner you get started with the negotiations, the sooner you can get finished."

James smiled down at her. "And you're wrong, my sweet," he whispered as he brushed Elizabeth's ear with

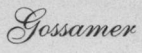

his lips, then bent to tickle Diamond on the chin, "I do trust you with my children. I trust you with their lives." He straightened and waved good-bye to the children, then started down the path, back toward the camp and the room full of disgruntled employees he knew were waiting for him.

Diamond awoke and began to fret. Elizabeth lifted her from her carriage, then settled down on the quilt to change Diamond's diaper and to feed her. Emerald crawled over to watch, shoving her building blocks in front of her as she made her way closer to Elizabeth. Emerald built three block towers on the fabric of Elizabeth's skirt while Elizabeth leaned back against the base of the aspen tree and fed the baby. Emerald amused herself by lifting the hem of the skirt and sending her blocks crashing onto the quilt.

Elizabeth hummed to Diamond as she fed her and watched with delight as Emerald built more towers on her skirt and sent them tumbling. She looked up from her pleasant task and followed the antics of Delia and Ruby and Garnet as they played ring-around-the-rosy in the meadow. Elizabeth found the meadow a peaceful, bucolic setting worthy of a Gainesborough painting. "Don't go too close to the woods," she called out to Delia as a reminder. "And don't let the girls out of your sight." Delia nodded in reply, before tumbling down to join Ruby and Garnet in the grass.

Elizabeth laughed at the calico skirts and white pinafores billowing like mushrooms on the ground. Delia was good with the children. She was diligent and hardworking and most of all she liked the Treasures and enjoyed frolicking with them. Although most fourteen-year-old girls would consider themselves far too old to be playing endless games of ring-around-the-rosy and tag with toddlers, Delia never seemed to mind.

Diamond finished her bottle and Elizabeth lifted the baby to her shoulder and patted her back until she burped, then rocked Diamond to sleep in her arms. Emerald continued to play quietly with her blocks as Ruby loudly and stri-

dently demanded that Delia be "it," before starting a noisy
game of hide-and-seek in the meadow.

Elizabeth settled Diamond into a cozy spot on the blanket
beside her and contented herself in a game of stacking
wooden building blocks with Emerald. She listened to the
squeals and the giggles of the girls playing hide-and-seek
in the meadow, looking up from her construction project
with Emerald every so often to keep an eye on the older
girls. At the moment Garnet was "it" and the other girls
were hiding from her. As Elizabeth watched, Garnet found
and tagged Delia, then continued merrily on her way in her
search for Ruby. Elizabeth waved at Delia and Garnet, then
turned her attention back to helping Emerald build and destroy another wooden tower of blocks.

Moments later Garnet's search for her sister took on a
serious tone. "Rwuby!" Garnet called to her sister.

Delia joined in. "Miss Ruby! You can come out now!
I'm it!"

Elizabeth shot to her feet and scanned the meadow. Delia
and Garnet were clearly visible, but Ruby was nowhere to
be found. "Delia? Have you found her?"

"Not yet, miss." Delia shook her head. "She's not in
any of her other hiding places. I've looked."

"Stay right there!" Elizabeth ordered. "Don't move!"
She bent and lifted the sleeping Diamond into her arms,
then carefully tucked the baby into the carriage before she
plucked Emerald from the center of the quilt and settled
her on her hip. "I'm coming!" With that, Elizabeth
grabbed hold of the handle on the baby carriage and pulled
it behind her, struggling through the high grass, as she carried Emerald across the field to where Delia and Garnet
stood waiting.

"I can't find her anywhere, Miss Elizabeth!" Delia's
voice took on a note of panic, and tears were already streak-
ing down her face. "I didn't mean to lose her."

"Do you think she wandered into the woods?" Elizabeth
asked.

"Oh, no, Miss," Delia answered. "I told them to stay

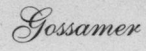

away from there. And I know Miss Ruby understood me. I don't think she went anywhere near the woods. We stayed out in the open." Delia stopped to catch her breath and began to cry harder. "We were just playing hide-and-seek like we always do."

"It's all right, Delia." Elizabeth offered comfort. "Don't worry. We'll find her." She handed Emerald over to Delia. "Stay here with the others. I'll look for Ruby."

Elizabeth searched the meadow, but it seemed as if Ruby had vanished. She retraced her steps across the field, carefully trying to cover each inch of ground that Delia and Ruby and Garnet had played on. "Ruby! This is Elizabeth. Come out now. It's time to go home." She called over and over again. "Please come out, Ruby!"

But Ruby didn't answer, and as Elizabeth listened in vain for sound, a reply of some kind, she began to worry. She glanced down at the watch pinned to the bodice of her dress. It was nearly four o'clock and the sun had already begun its descent toward the trees. She searched the meadow again—the entire meadow—but she found no sign of Ruby. Elizabeth began to shake. If Ruby wasn't in the meadow, she had to be in the forest, and the afternoon shadows were beginning to darken the forest. She couldn't wait any longer, she had to get help. She had to find James.

Elizabeth stood debating. She wanted to send Delia and the girls back to the camp for help, but she couldn't ask Delia to face James with the news that Ruby was missing. Delia felt bad enough about it as it was. Besides, *she* was the governess. She was the one to blame for Ruby's disappearance. She was the one to break the news to James. But unless she put Emerald and Garnet into their buggy and carried Diamond in her arms, Elizabeth couldn't manage the girls alone and she needed Delia to stay behind in case Ruby reappeared. And she needed to hurry and carrying a baby and pulling a buggy with two toddlers would slow her down.

Elizabeth turned to Delia and handed her the baby, then reached for Garnet and lifted her into the buggy beside her younger sister. "Stay here with Diamond in case Ruby comes out of hiding. I'll take Garnet and Emerald back to camp with me to get help."

"Miss Elizabeth, it's all my fault! I'm so sorry. . . ." Delia cried.

"Shh, shh." Elizabeth hugged her tightly. "It's nobody's fault. She'll be all right. You'll see. But it's beginning to get dark. We need help. Stay here. I'll be back with help as soon as I can. And keep calling her."

Elizabeth wheeled the buggy around, pushing it over the tall grass of the meadow as fast as she dared with Garnet and Emerald inside. But when she reached the hard-packed dirt of the path, Elizabeth gathered her skirts in her hand began to run, Emerald and Garnet laughing merrily as she pushed them down the path at a dizzying speed.

She didn't bother to park the carriage outside the door of the main office building once she reached the camp. She simply opened the door and wrestled the cumbersome wicker carriage inside.

"Miss." Someone rushed to stop her as Elizabeth pushed the carriage further into the room. "You can't interrupt right now. Mr. Craig is in a meeting."

"I know he's in a meeting," Elizabeth replied. "But I need to see him now." She fought to keep the edge of panic out of her voice as she stalked up to the closed door separating her from James, knocked once, then pushed it open.

---∽◎∾---

JAMES STARED AT the leaders of the different labor factions in the camp and bit back a sigh of frustration. It was no use. These men couldn't see the forest for the trees. They couldn't see the common good because they were searching so hard for the flaws. Every question they'd asked him had begun with "What's in it for us?" What was in it for the Welsh? The Irish? The Cornish? The Chinese? They couldn't seem to grasp that he wanted what was good for all of them, not just one group. He gritted his

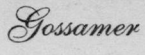

teeth, then took a deep breath. This meeting was a waste of time. These men weren't ready to negotiate because they weren't ready to listen to reason. But he'd finish what he started. The sooner he got through his proposal, the sooner he could pack up his family and go home. To hell with the lot of them. If they wanted to quit, fine. He'd hire other workers. Or he'd close the place down.

James halted his proposed sale of common stock in mid-sentence and frowned at the interruption as the door opened. What now? "I asked not to be disturbed—"

"I'm sorry, James," Elizabeth stood in the doorway. "But this is an emergency."

He looked over at her. Her eyes were wide, panic-stricken, and shimmering with unshed tears. Her face was white, and her voice quivered with emotion as she struggled to hang on to her composure. A knot of fear tightened in his belly. Perspiration dotted his brow. And he dreaded whatever it was she had to say. "What is it? What's happened?"

Elizabeth squeezed between the carriage and the doorway, forgetting the men in the room, forgetting everything except the need to throw herself in his arms and have him hold her as she broke the news. She ran toward him.

But James held her off. "What is it?" he demanded. "What's wrong?"

The tears that had shimmered in her eyes moments before rushed to the surface of her eyelids and brimmed over them, rolling down her cheeks in a steady stream. "It's Ruby," she breathed, reaching for him, wanting comfort, needing to comfort as she told him.

James stepped forward and grabbed her by the shoulders, placing distance between them so he could read the look in her eyes, the expression on her face. "What about Ruby?"

"She's gone!" Elizabeth tried again to hold him. "Oh, James, she's gone!"

"Oh, *Jesus*, no! Not again!" James let go of her shoulders and pushed away from her, instinctively recoiling from the bearer of bad news. Recoiling as if Elizabeth had stabbed at his heart with the sharpest of knives. His face turned an ashen shade of gray and his knees threatened to buckle as his world tilted beneath him and those words he'd hoped never to hear again came back to haunt him. Along with those words came the flood of memories and the rage—the overpowering sense of helpless rage. He stared at her as if he didn't see her, then took her by the shoulders and shook her. *"For the love of Christ, Mei Ling, what have you done with my child?"* he roared.

"I-I-I'm n-not M-Mei L-ling," she protested her teeth chattering in reaction, "I-I'm E-Elizabeth." She jerked away from him. "I'm Elizabeth," she said in a strong, angry voice. "And I didn't do anything with your child. She was playing hide-and-seek in the meadow with Delia and Garnet. I should have been watching more closely, but I . . . And I can't find her. She won't come out. She doesn't answer."

James stared down at her, then turned to Will. "Oh, God! Help me. We've got to find her. We've got to find her before . . . She's so little. She'll be so afraid." He turned to Elizabeth. "You were supposed to be watching her!" he accused. "You said you'd watch over them. I trusted you. Christ! I trusted you!" He shook his head. "I knew I shouldn't have left her with an inexperienced governess—" He broke off. "If anything happens to Ruby . . ."

Elizabeth sucked in a breath.

"I should have known you couldn't handle the responsibility. I should have known it was too much." He lashed out at her. "I should have known from your reaction the first time you saw her. Christ! What was I thinking of? What was I thinking with? You didn't even know how to change a diaper, and I hired you to be their governess. Delia does a better job of looking after them."

"James, I . . ." Elizabeth stood before him. "It's my fault. It's all my fault. I'm so sorry. I—"

"You're sorry? You think that makes everything all right? I'm going to go find her, and I just pray—"

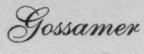

"So do I, James," she told him. "I pray she's all right. And I'm coming with you to see that she is."

"No," he ordered. "You stay here. I don't need any more problems. I don't need any more distractions. If anything happens to my child, I'll never forgive myself." He looked Elizabeth right in the eyes. "And I'll never be able to forgive you."

Then he took hold of the handle of Emerald and Garnet's baby carriage, wheeled it past Elizabeth, and was out the door, shouting for men, shouting for volunteers as the search for Ruby began.

Thirty-one

"HE DOESN'T MEAN it, Beth," Will said, stepping from the shadows, reaching out to enfold Elizabeth in his arms as she stood hugging herself with tears running silently down her cheeks, alone in the center of the meeting room. "He's just terrified and railing at the fates that have put him in this position once again."

Elizabeth looked up at the underside of Will's chin. "You should be out helping James look for Ruby."

"And leave you to blame yourself for something that isn't your fault? Not a chance." Will shook his head. "I made that mistake with Jamie years ago. I should have helped him to understand what happened then, instead of allowing him to blame himself and shoulder responsibility for a tragedy he couldn't have prevented. Or waited nearly four years to correct my mistake."

Elizabeth pushed against Will's chest and leaned back so she could look at him. "He called me Mei Ling."

Will nodded. "His wife."

Elizabeth shivered. "Who starved to herself to death because James couldn't forgive her."

"Jamie told you that?" Will was surprised.

Elizabeth nodded.

"Did he tell you why?" Will asked. "Did Jamie tell you why he couldn't forgive her? Did he tell you what Mei Ling did that made his forgiveness impossible?"

"No," Elizabeth whispered. "He didn't."

"She killed his child," Will replied baldly. "She waited until Jamie had to go to Macao on business for a couple of days, then she took their six-week-old daughter and gave her to the old woman next door to bathe."

Elizabeth shook her head in shock. "I don't understand."

" 'Bathing the infant' is a polite Chinese euphemism for drowning the infant. It's what families do with unwanted children, especially daughters."

"I can't believe that any child of James's was unwanted," she protested in horror.

"Exactly," Will agreed. "And that's why Mei Ling waited until Jamie went to Macao on business. Mei Ling knew Jamie loved his daughter. She knew he wanted the baby and that he would never allow his daughter to be killed to make way for that all-important son and heir. The old lady next door had been Mei Ling's midwife, and Jamie had forbidden the old woman to enter his house after the baby was born because he'd had to prevent her from strangling it when she realized Cory was a girl."

"Cory," Elizabeth breathed the word.

"Yes, Cory," Will said. "She was baptized Julia Coral, but Jamie called her Cory. Mei Ling gave her to the woman next door. She took Cory down to a pond not far from where Jamie and Mei Ling lived and drowned her. Jamie came home from his trip to Macao, went in to see the baby, and found the crib empty. He knew what had happened when Mei Ling refused to offer any explanation except that Cory was gone. Jamie searched the area until he found Cory's body. It took him several days to find her remains because she'd been dragged from the pond by wild animals. There wasn't much left. There was no way Jamie could really be sure if the bits of baby he found was Cory, but . . ." Will stopped and swallowed hard twice. "That's why Jamie doesn't sleep much. He still has nightmares about it. The Lord knows I'll never forget how he looked at Mei Ling when he returned with Cory's body.''

"Coryville.'' Tears burned Elizabeth's eyes and nose and throat as she looked up at Will for confirmation. "He built the town and named it after his daughter.''

"That's right. He envisioned a perfect town, a haven for children to grow up in, and he built it as a monument to Cory. Because she'd died. Because he hadn't been there to save her.''

"And Mei Ling?'' Elizabeth knew the answer, but she had to ask. "What happened to her?''

"She begged Jamie's forgiveness. And he tried. He honestly tried. But some things are unforgivable. Mei Ling was too ashamed to face him unless he forgave her. She withdrew to her room with her maid and slowly wasted away. By the time Jamie came out of his grief over Cory long enough to realize what was happening to Mei Ling, it was too late.''

"And Ruby?'' Elizabeth asked. "What about Ruby's mother?''

"We don't know anything about Ruby's mother,'' Will told her. "Jamie found her after Mei Ling died. She'd been abandoned on the rocks along the shoreline to await the incoming tide. Jamie waded out and rescued her.'' He smiled at the memory. "Then he showed up at the office with a wet, naked, and squalling girl baby, soaked himself, and grinning from ear to ear. Ruby's been with him ever since. He left Hong Kong with her and brought her to Coryville. And the others—Garnet, Emerald, and Diamond— are all foundlings, too. Girls who would have died if Jamie hadn't taken them in. He loves them all. But Ruby . . .'' Will walked away from Elizabeth and began to pace the width of the room. He ran his fingers through his hair, then shook his head as if to clear it. "I don't know if he saved Ruby or she saved him. All I know is that Ruby is Jamie's favorite. The apple of his eye. I don't know what he'll do if something happens to that child. . . .''

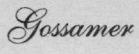

"I do," Elizabeth said, meeting Will's gaze and struggling not to flinch as she said what they were both thinking. "He'll blame himself for hiring me to take care of her. And he'll never forgive either one of us."

IT WAS THE longest afternoon of his life, and there was every reason to believe that the night would be no different. James watched as the darkness closed over the meadow, watched as his employees lit torches and canvassed the area for the hundredth time. He watched as they paused at the edge of the forest and began shouting Ruby's name. It was too dark to search the forest, even with torches and lanterns, too dark to see the treacherous network of ventilation shafts reaching out from the abandoned mines. And although his employees were willing to risk it, James couldn't let them. It was best to wait until morning. To resume the search at first light when it was safer. He couldn't risk having them trample any signs—any trail Ruby might have left. They had searched the meadow, and Ruby wasn't there. The only place left to search was the forest. And James couldn't risk having his employees miss something at night, something they should have seen, some clue they might have noticed if they'd waited for light. He took a deep breath and slowly let it out. Although his every instinct as a father railed against it, it was time to postpone the search until morning.

He walked to the center of the path where the men had made a ring of protective stones and built a fire on the hard-packed earth inside it. "Thank you all," James said in a voice hoarse from hours spent calling Ruby's name and from choking back the tears that threatened to strangle him. "Thank you all very much for your hard work and cooperation." He managed a crooked, halfhearted smile as he stared at the oriental and occidental faces of the men standing shoulder to shoulder before him. "I knew you could find a way to work together as a team; I just wish my daughter's disappearance hadn't provided the means." He

stopped to regain control of his emotions as his voice broke.
"But it's too dark to see anything and it's late and you've
all worked a full day. Go home to your beds and get some
sleep. I'll be here at first light if any of you would like to
help with the search. If not, take the day off. Stay in bed.
Rest. Whatever. Go see your wives. Go see your children."
James lifted a hand to his brow and covered his eyes. "I
wish to God I could see all of mine." He waved the men
away, then walked over and sank down on the quilt beneath
the aspen tree.

"Mr. Craig?"

James opened his eyes to find Delia standing before him,
holding Diamond in her arms. The carriage with Garnet and
Emerald was parked nearby.

"Mr. Craig, the Treasures—I mean, Miss Garnet and
Miss Emerald—are asleep and Miss Diamond needs a
change of diapers and another bottle." She rocked the baby
in her arms to keep her from crying. "I thought I'd walk
back to the cabin with the men if you don't mind. I know
you want the girls with you, sir. But they're real tired and
hungry and all, and it's way past their bedtime."

James buried his face in his hands. He did want the
Treasures with him. But keeping them out all night wasn't
the answer. Just because he intended to keep vigil, just
because he didn't intend to leave the meadow without
Ruby, didn't mean that Delia and the other children had to
keep vigil with him. "Take them back to the cabin, Delia.
And get some rest. You've done a good job managing tonight. I'm proud of you."

"Thank you, sir," Delia answered. "I'll go check on
Miss Elizabeth, too. I know you said she was too distraught
to come back out here and search, but I'd like to check on
her if that's okay with you. I know she's worried sick about
Miss Ruby. She nearly tore the meadow apart looking for
her when I told her I'd lost her."

James lifted his head. "*You* lost her?"

Delia shuddered beneath the look he gave her, but she
stood her ground bravely. "Yes, sir. I was playing hide-

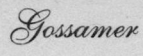

and-seek with Miss Ruby and Miss Garnet in the meadow and I lost sight of her. She hid real good and I couldn't find her.''

''Where was Miss Elizabeth when this was happening?''

''She was sitting here on this quilt tending to the baby and to Miss Emerald.''

''Why weren't you taking care of Emerald and the baby? Why wasn't Miss Elizabeth watching the older girls?'' James asked, though he was fairly sure he knew the reason.

''Because Miss Ruby won't play if Miss Elizabeth watches her. She gets mad and pitches a fit and won't do anything except sit on her bottom. So Miss Elizabeth always watches us from a safe distance so Miss Ruby doesn't notice and lets me play with the older girls 'cause it's important that they get their exercise.''

James squeezed his eyes shut and pinched the bridge of his nose in anguish, remembering the scene in the park that he'd witnessed from his office window; remembering how Ruby refused to allow Elizabeth to participate and refused to do most of the things Elizabeth asked of her. *''Miss Elizabeth always watches us from a safe distance so Miss Ruby doesn't notice.''* He remembered the ugly things he'd said to her at the office in front of all those witnesses. *''Delia does a better job of looking after them.''* And that was just part of the ugly accusations he'd flung at her. *Christ!* He'd been blaming Elizabeth for the crime Mei Ling had committed, confusing the two, believing that accidentally allowing a toddler to slip past her guard was the same as deliberately allowing a baby to be murdered. He turned his attention back to Delia. ''Thank you for explaining everything to me,'' he said at last. ''I'd appreciate it very much if you'd take the Treasures back to the cabin and check on Miss Elizabeth for me before you go to bed. And, Delia, tell Miss Elizabeth . . .'' James stopped, then shook his head. He wanted to say, ''Tell Miss Elizabeth I love her,'' but he knew those words should come from him. After everything that had happened between them, Elizabeth deserved to hear those words spoken through his lips, not Delia's.

"Sir?"

James looked up and realized Delia stood waiting expectantly for him to continue. "Never mind," he answered softly. "I'll tell her myself."

⸻❦⸻

ELIZABETH FOUND HIM hours later where she knew she would—outside sitting on the quilt and leaning against the aspen tree. The fire had burned down to glowing embers that flared into flames occasionally and flickered out again, casting little light. She thought he must have fallen into an exhausted sleep and carefully lowered the wick on her lantern to keep from waking him as she set it on the ground. But it was too late. He'd heard her approach.

"You should be in bed, asleep," he said.

"You think I can sleep after what happened? You think I can sleep knowing Ruby's lost and that it's my fault?" she asked. "My, how your opinion of me has fallen, James."

"I didn't mean what I said this afternoon," he told her. "I confused what happened today with something that happened a long time ago."

"You confused me with your wife, Mei Ling," Elizabeth answered. "And you accused me of negligence. Maybe I am negligent," she admitted. "But I didn't deliberately allow Ruby to become lost. I didn't deliberately rid myself of Ruby the way Mei Ling rid herself of Cory."

James whirled around and faced her.

Elizabeth could see the look of surprise on his face, the shimmer of unshed tears in his eyes and the stains his previous tears had left behind.

"Will told me."

James nodded. "Then you know everything."

"Yes."

"So, tell me, have I botched it, Elizabeth?" he asked. "Have I ruined what we have together?"

"I don't know," she answered honestly, coming to stand at the edge of the quilt, close enough to touch, but not touching. "It's cold out," she shivered, running her hands up and down her arms to dispel the chill. "You should be keeping warm in that quilt instead of sitting on it."

"I can't," he said simply. "Ruby's out there somewhere without a quilt. How can I wrap myself in a quilt knowing she doesn't have one?"

"You can't," Elizabeth said. "Neither can I."

James looked past her face and saw that she was wearing the same lightweight dress she'd had on that afternoon. James stared at the lantern. "I found my oldest daughter," he said, at last. "Or rather, I found what was left of her."

"I know." Elizabeth knelt down and placed her hand on his shoulder. "That's why I'm here. I knew you'd refuse to leave until Ruby's found. And after Will told me what happened with Cory, I knew you'd be sitting here remembering and wondering if the fates could be so cruel to you a second time."

James turned to her, wrapped his arms around her waist, and pulled her to him. "Sometimes I can't sleep at night for remembering. Oh, God, Elizabeth, I can't go through this another time. I can't stand to think about what I may find." He buried his face against her bodice, and Elizabeth held him while he wept.

And when he'd cried all his tears, she held him in a different way and showed him how much—how very much—she cared.

"I love you, James Cameron Craig," she said as he lay spent in her arms. "I love you."

He kissed her hungrily, then followed it with a kiss so tender it took her breath away. "I-I—" He faltered. "I want to say it, Elizabeth. I want to say the words. But I'm afraid. If we don't find Ruby alive . . . If we don't find Ruby . . ." He searched her face, begging for another dram of understanding. "I don't know if I'll be able to . . ."

"Forgive me?" she asked, already knowing the answer.

"I couldn't forgive Mei Ling," he said. "Not even when she begged me with her dying breath."

Elizabeth smiled at him and her eyes filled with tears. "Then I have my answer."

"Elizabeth," he reached for her again, but she rolled away and began to straighten her clothes. "I-I . . ."

She placed her fingers against his lips. "Don't. Not now. Not until we have Ruby back in our arms safe and sound," she told him.

"Stay," he said when she got to her feet and started to leave. "Stay with me. Keep the ghosts at bay."

"I can't," she said. "Diamond will be wanting her bottle soon."

"Delia's there. She can feed her," James said.

Delia does a better job of looking after them. James's words echoed in her head. "No." Elizabeth shook her head. "I need to feed her. I want to feed her. I may not—" she broke off abruptly, held her breath to keep from sobbing, then turned and hurried down the path before she had a chance to change her mind, before she allowed the look on James's face to change her mind.

She was sobbing by the time she reached the cabin. "Go to him," she begged when Will opened the door to let her in. "Go to him. Don't let him stay out there alone."

Thirty-two

THE SOUNDS OF men cheering awoke her from a fitful doze the following morning. Will burst into the cabin, made a beeline for Elizabeth, and lifted her out of the chair where she'd spent the night. He swung her around in his arms. "They've found her!" he said. "Praise God, they've found her!"

"Is she . . . ?" Elizabeth asked when he set her on her feet.

"She's alive. Cold, scared, and hungry, but she doesn't seem to be hurt," Will said.

"Where is she? When can I see her?" Elizabeth asked, pulling on her shawl and racing for the door.

"Well"—he cleared his throat—"that's a problem. You see, they haven't gotten her out yet."

Elizabeth stopped in her tracks. "Out? Out of where?"

"A ventilation shaft of one of the old abandoned mines."

"Ruby fell down a ventilation shaft? In the forest?"

Will shook his head. "In the meadow. There's a group of boulders in the meadow covering the opening of one of the ventilation shafts."

Elizabeth put a hand to her throat. "But James said the meadow was safe."

"He thought it was," Will told her. "Jamie didn't realize that one of the old shafts reached that far out of woods and into the meadow. None of us did."

"But I searched the meadow," Elizabeth protested. "I searched near the boulders."

"You couldn't have seen her," Will said. "Apparently she crawled between two of the large boulders covering the opening and tumbled down the shaft when the ground gave way."

"How did they find her?"

"Jamie heard her crying before dawn, and he crawled over the meadow, following the sound until he got to the boulders. Even then he couldn't see where she was until the sun came up and he could see the hole between the rocks that he missed yesterday afternoon."

"Where is he now?"

"He's in the meadow. He sent me to get you."

"What about Delia and the girls?" Elizabeth asked, knowing James would want the other girls with him when Ruby was rescued.

"I'll come back for them. He needs you now. You're the only one who can help. I'll explain on the way." He grabbed hold of Elizabeth's hand. "Hurry!"

❦

"NO! NO! DADDY! Daddy!" Ruby's screams of terror and her plaintive cries for her father echoed up from the depths of the ventilation shaft as James lay flat on his belly on the ground in front of the opening, bracing himself and steadying the rope that held one of the few men small enough to go down the shaft and try to get her. But Ruby was fighting him, hampering his struggle to reach her. James cursed beneath his breath in frustration. "It's all right, Button. The nice man is trying to help you," he called down to her, trying to soothe her. But Ruby's

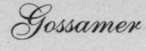

screams grew more frantic and James could hear the chunks of dirt and debris raining down on top of them as Ruby's struggles intensified.

James was too big. The shaft had filled with dirt and debris over the years and the opening had narrowed. He didn't fit. He couldn't get down the shaft and Ruby was frightened of the Chinese laborer who'd volunteered. James could hear him, now, speaking to her, attempting to soothe her in Cantonese, but Ruby didn't understand Cantonese and the laborer didn't speak English and James was very much afraid that Ruby's fear stemmed from the fact that the last time she'd been so close to a Chinese man or heard Chinese spoken, she'd been abandoned on a pile of rocks in the ocean. He listened as the man tried again to soothe Ruby. And heard the scuffle and the screams. "No! No! Daddy!"

James couldn't stand it any longer, nor could he risk having the walls of the shaft cave in around her. He called down to the laborer in Cantonese, then motioned for the men and the team of oxen to slowly pull him up.

"I've brought her, Jamie, she's here." Carefully avoiding the ground above the shaft, Will led Elizabeth forward, then knelt on the ground and touched James on the shoulder to get his attention as the laborer surfaced from the depths of the shaft.

It was worse than he expected, James learned as he untied the man from the swing chair he'd fashioned. Ruby was wedged on a ledge of rock, too frightened to do anything but lash out at the man who hadn't been able to make her understand that he was there to help her—to take her to her daddy.

James glanced around and saw Will with Elizabeth. "Thank God," he breathed. "I'm too big to get down the shaft. So are most of the men here, and I don't want to try to tunnel her out unless we fail to get her out this way. The shaft is narrow and dry and crumbly and I'm afraid digging will trigger a collapse." He paused, then raked Elizabeth with his urgent gaze. "I need you to talk to her while we send the man back down,'' he said. "See if you can calm her down. She won't listen to me," he said. "She just keeps screaming my name, begging me to come down and get her."

Elizabeth took a breath. "What if I make it worse? She doesn't like me, James. You know that."

"I know," he said, "but I've got to try something."

He nodded to the next Chinese volunteer who climbed into the swing chair, then at Elizabeth. "Talk to her. Tell her that it's you and that a nice man is coming down to get her."

Elizabeth did. She lay on her stomach in the dirt beside James and talked to Ruby as the men lowered the second volunteer and then a third one, into the shaft, but Ruby didn't listen. She cried. She screamed for James, and she fought the young men sent down to rescue her like a termagant.

Finally Elizabeth could stand it no longer and turned to James. "Pull him up," she ordered, getting to her feet. "Pull him up. He's terrifying her. She doesn't understand."

"I know," James snapped.

"That's why I'm going down to get her."

"I can't let you," James said. "I can't risk your life, too."

"Try stopping me," she challenged. Then ignoring the crowd of men gathered to offer help or to watch, Elizabeth unbuttoned her skirt and pushed it over her hips, untied her petticoats and bustle, and pulled her chemise over her head, stripping off clothing until she stood before James and the rest of the assembly in her camisole and drawers. When she'd shed all the cumbersome garments she could shed, Elizabeth climbed into the chair the last volunteer had vacated. "Strap me in," she ordered James. "Strap me in before I have time to think about what I'm doing."

She took a deep breath as James tied the ropes around her waist that secured her to the chair.

Alone in the shaft, Ruby began to cry.

"It's all right, Ruby," Elizabeth soothed as James carefully lowered her into the dark, dirty tunnel. "Stay right where you are and don't cry, sweetie. I'll be there in a minute. I'm coming down to get you."

"Daddy!" Ruby cried.

Dirt and debris rained down on Elizabeth, filling the air with dust as she inched her way down the shaft. Her eyes stung and her nose and throat burned from the dust she breathed. Roots and bits of rock and wood scratched her arms and legs as she scraped the narrow walls. She bit back a frightened cry as a clump of dirt broke loose and bounced off her shoulder.

"Be a brave little girl," Elizabeth said to Ruby as her feet touched the ledge. She looked down to find Ruby crouched behind a broken beam. "I can reach her," she called up to James to tell him to tighten the slack in the rope. "Come on, sweetheart, come to me and let me hold you."

"Want Daddy," Ruby said.

"Then come with me," Elizabeth coaxed. "He's waiting for you at the top of this nasty old hole."

Ruby debated a moment longer, then lunged off the ledge and into Elizabeth's arms. The swing rocked violently, bounced off the walls, and sent a cascade of dirt and pebbles tumbling down the shaft, but Elizabeth grabbed hold of her precious cargo and refused to let go. She hugged Ruby to her, burying her face in Ruby's hair as a flood of tears poured unchecked down her face and left jagged tracks in the dirt on her face.

"I've got her," she called out to James. "Bring us up."

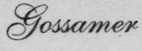

THE CELEBRATION BEGAN as soon as Elizabeth and Ruby appeared at the surface and lasted late into the morning. James declared a holiday and ordered the cooks in the canteen to break out the barrels of beer, but for Elizabeth, the celebration ended the moment Ruby pushed out of her embrace and ran for James. Elizabeth would never forget the expression of gratitude on James's face as he fell to his knees, wrapped his arms around Ruby, and covered her little face with kisses, nor would she forget the pang in her heart as he reached out to include her in their embrace and Ruby pushed her away.

James started to speak, but there was nothing he could say, nothing he could do to change the fact that while Ruby had allowed Elizabeth to rescue her, she wouldn't allow Elizabeth to share in his love. He covered his frustration and his embarrassment by yelling for the company doctor as he lifted Ruby into his arms.

Elizabeth stood off to the side, her heart nearly bursting with love for James and for Ruby, as she watched them together. Ruby was safe and secure in her father's arms. Safe and secure in the warmth and knowledge of James's love. And James was secure in the knowledge that he had dodged a horrible fate and been given another chance to take care of the child who had saved him by securing the place in his heart Cory's death had left empty. James and Ruby were together. A family again—as they were meant to be. Elizabeth had done her duty and made up for her terrible mistake; now it was time to go on. She bent and picked up her discarded skirts and petticoats and slowly walked away.

"Wait, Elizabeth!" James called to her. "Where are you going?"

Elizabeth held up her discarded clothing.

"You should have the doctor look at you," he said.

"I'm fine," she told him. "I don't need a doctor."

Ruby wiggled in his arms and James turned his attention back to his daughter. "Are you sure?" he asked again, his voice laced with concern for Elizabeth.

Elizabeth managed a teary smile. "I'm sure," she said. There was nothing the doctor could do for a broken heart.

By the time James returned to the cabin to put Ruby to bed, Elizabeth was gone.

"Where is she?" James demanded of Will when he turned around in Elizabeth's empty bedroom and found

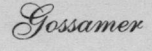

Will standing in the doorway looking at him.

"She's gone," Will said. "She left on the express train while you were with Ruby. I loaned her some traveling money and sent Delia and Garnet and Emerald and Diamond with her to keep her company. Delia and the girls are getting off at Coryville. But I don't think Elizabeth is planning to get off with them."

"How do you know?"

"She asked me to send her belongings."

Stunned, James sank down onto the edge of the bed. "She didn't say good-bye. She didn't tell me good-bye."

"I thought she said a rather eloquent good-bye last night," Will told him.

"You knew she was leaving last night?"

"I suspected it," Will said, "when she came in crying after making love with you."

James raised an eyebrow at that.

Will snorted. "Unlike some men in this room, I'm not a fool. All you had to do was tell her you love her and ask her to stay."

"I couldn't," James said. "Ruby . . ."

"Ruby is a child. A jealous, spoiled little girl who wants her daddy all to herself," Will answered brutally.

"Ruby went through a terrible ordeal," James said. "She's a little girl. It's understandable that she wants me to herself for a while. Is there anything wrong with that?" he demanded.

"No, Jamie," Will said. "Except that Ruby won't always be a little girl. She's going to grow up and meet someone and fall in love and leave you. So will Garnet and Emerald and Diamond and any others you adopt. And where will you be?" Will didn't wait for him to answer. "Alone, Jamie, and just as lonely as you are now. And all because you let Ruby decide the course of your life, instead of following your heart."

"I made a promise to Ruby when I found her in the ocean. I promised her that as long as I was alive, she wouldn't have to worry about the people around her not loving her.''

"You've kept your promise, Jamie!" Will thundered. "Do you really believe Ruby has suffered under Elizabeth's care? Do you really believe that the woman who stayed up all night modifying a doll for your daughter doesn't love her? For God's sake, Jamie, open your eyes! Elizabeth risked her life for Ruby after she'd offered her heart to you on a platter and had it tossed aside. She did it willingly because she loves you and those children. How long are you going to punish yourself for something you didn't do? How long are you going to deny yourself someone to love—and someone to love you back? *Christ*, Jamie, how can you let Mei Ling ruin the rest of your life? How can you let Elizabeth walk away?'' Will waved his hand in disgust. "If I thought I could make her love me, I'd go after her myself.''

"Where?" James asked.

"I don't know," Will answered. "But she asked that I send her belongings to a Samuel Wright in Cincinnati.''

James didn't wait to hear any more. "Have the extra engine and a passenger car readied,'' James ordered as he exited the bedroom and headed across the hall to get Ruby.

"Where are you going?'' Will demanded, a small smile turning up the corner of his mouth.

"To tell Elizabeth I love her and to keep her from trying to Samuel Wright a wrong!''

⤜⤚⫯

HE MISSED HER in Coryville. Mrs. G. was furious with him, and the household was in an uproar. "What did you do to that girl up in that mining camp?" she kept wanting to know. "She left here crying as if her heart would break.''

"I'm going after her," James said grimly. "The train's at the water tank now. I've only got a minute to drop off

Ruby and say good-bye to the other Treasures.'' He handed
Ruby over to the housekeeper.

The little girl squirmed and pushed until Mrs. G. set her
on the floor. She ran through the foyer, darted into James's
study, then ran up the stairs, clutching something in her
arms, and screaming at the top of her lungs before she
disappeared into James's bedroom.

''You'd better go after her,'' Mrs. G. said.

''I am.''

''I meant Ruby,'' she clarified.

''I meant Elizabeth,'' he said. ''You'll have to manage
Ruby alone for a while.''

''What do you intend to do when you find her?'' Mrs.
G. shouted after him as James took the stairs two at a time.

''Marry her,'' he shouted back. ''And help her hire a
new governess.''

''Thank the Lord,'' Mrs. G. breathed.

The train whistle sounded once in warning as James
kissed each of the Treasures good-bye and started out the
nursery door. Ruby ran to him and held on, clinging to him
and crying. ''No, Ruby,'' he said firmly, ''Daddy's got to
go find Elizabeth.''

Ruby stared at him. ''Libeth,'' she said clearly, then
reached out and grabbed hold of James's hand and began
pulling him toward his bedroom.

''What about Elizabeth?'' he asked.

''Libeth.'' Ruby pointed to the pillows on James's bed.
Portia rested against them, her hair slightly mussed, and her
clothes rumpled, looking for all the world as if, like Elizabeth, she belonged there.

He scooped Ruby up in his arms. ''All right, little imp,''
he said. ''Let's go find Libeth and make her your
mommy.''

Thirty-three

ELIZABETH STOOD LOOKING down at the new marble headstone marking the middle grave in the row of three. *Owen Sadler*, it read, *beloved brother of Elizabeth. Born 03 August 1852. Died February 1873. Our hearts grieve from the loss.* Tears stung her eyes. She had gone to Dorminey's Stone Works to make the final installment on the headstone and to arrange to have it delivered and discovered the arrangements had already been made. Days ago.

"I knew you'd come here eventually," James said, coming up to stand behind her. "I've been waiting and watching this place for days."

"Have you?" she asked coolly.

"San Francisco is a big city. I tried the Russ House and Bender's and every place I knew to try to find you before I came here."

"You must have skipped the jail," she said.

"Is that where you've been?"

"It seemed as good a place as any to get away from the pain of losing you. I've come full circle," she said. "I went to the jail to serve my three days in lieu of paying my fine, and Sergeant Darnell took me home to stay with his wife and family. But I've imposed on them long enough. It's time I moved on, so I've come to say good-bye to Owen and to San Francisco.''

"What about me?" James asked.

"I said good-bye to you four nights ago."

"I'm not ready to say good-bye," he said. "Not then. Not now. Not ever."

"Oh, James," Elizabeth pleaded. "Don't make this any more painful than it has to be. Please let me go."

"No," he said, turning her in his arms and kissing her. "I can't let you go. Have you forgotten that you invited the entire Coryville Ladies' League to the house for tea? Are you going to make me face that alone?"

"You said yourself that Mrs. G. can handle a simple tea. And I'm sure you can manage to endure it for one afternoon."

"What about the rest of my life, Elizabeth? How am I supposed to endure being without you for the rest of my life? What about you? What about the rest of your life? How are you going to endure being alone? Or worse, being married to Samuel Wright?"

"I don't know, James," she said. "I don't know how I'll manage." That was a lie. She knew exactly how she'd manage to endure the rest of her life. She'd manage the same way she'd managed the last four days of it—only half alive and with a great big empty hole where her heart used to be. "But I will. And so will you."

"I don't want to be alone," James told her. "I don't want to endure and exist. I want to be with you."

"I'm sorry." Elizabeth answered softly.

"Can you honestly say you don't want me? That you don't want to stay with me and the Treasures?"

"Ruby doesn't want *me*."

"Are you sure?" he asked. "Maybe the problem is that you don't want her. Or the other Treasures. Or me."

"Don't be ridiculous!" Elizabeth snapped at him. "I love Ruby. I love Garnet and Emerald and Diamond."

"And me?" he asked hopefully.

"I love you most of all.''

"Good," he announced, scooping her up in his arms before she had time to protest and carrying her out of the cemetery and over to one of the two closed carriages parked on the street in front of Saint Mary's Church. "Because we've got a little surprise for you." He set Elizabeth on her feet and opened the carriage door. Delia and the Treasures filed out. All four Treasures were dressed in their finest clothes and the three oldest girls were clutching the dolls Elizabeth had made for them. Mrs. G. and Annie climbed out of the other carriage and joined them. They, too, were dressed in their Sunday best. "Will's waiting with Father Paul inside," he said. "He's the best man. And Mrs. G. offered to be the matron of honor."

"For what?" Elizabeth asked.

James dropped to his knees on the sidewalk. "I love you, Elizabeth. I want to marry you. I want you to be my wife and the mother of these children. Don't you want to marry me?"

"Of course I do," she said. "But what about Ruby?"

James smiled. "I think she approves," he said. "She brought you a wedding present." He reached inside the carriage and presented Portia. "I found her in my bed the day you left. Ruby seems to think she belongs there." He leaned down and kissed Elizabeth with all the love and passion he'd been holding in check since she left. "I think you do."

"Ruby?" Elizabeth asked in wonder. "Are you sure?"

"Ask her yourself."

Elizabeth knelt on the sidewalk. "Ruby?" she asked, hesitantly, with all the love and hope and heartbreak in her voice.

Ruby walked over to Elizabeth and stood facing her.

James prompted her. "Isn't there something you wanted to say to Libeth?"

Ruby leaned forward and wrapped her arms around Elizabeth's neck. "When you coming home, Libeth?" she demanded.

"Do you want me to come home?" Elizabeth asked.

Ruby nodded. "I love you, Libeth. When you gonna be my mommy?"

Tears filled Elizabeth's eyes, brimmed over, and ran unchecked down her face as she clutched Ruby to her breast. "Soon, sweetheart. Just as soon as your daddy and I can say, 'I do,' " Elizabeth answered, half laughing and half crying, able to breathe once again now that she knew that James and Ruby wanted her and that everything was going to be all right.

Ruby turned to her father. "Say I do, Daddy," she ordered. "Now!"

"I do," James told Elizabeth tenderly. "Now and always."

The End

AUTHOR'S NOTE

James Cameron Craig is a fictional hero. During the writing of this book I liked to think that there were real men like him, men who refused to allow little girls to be abandoned or murdered by their parents or family simply because they were born female in a male culture. Imagine how delighted I was to discover during the course of my research that at least one such man did exist. His name was Yu Chih, and he started an Infant Protection Society in his home village in Wu-hsi County, Kiangsu Province, China, in 1843. For the next ten years, until 1853, the Infant Protection Society supported between sixty and one hundred infants every year, most of them girls. In his efforts to gain support for the society and to educate his fellow countrymen, Yu Chih explained the custom of drowning infants and described the heartbreaking results as newborns struggled to survive.

I attempted to recreate the outrage Yu Chih felt as he recorded the history of his Infant Protection Society when I created James Cameron Craig.

For Yu Chih's and other firsthand accounts of Chinese history and culture, I am indebted to Patricia Buckley Ebrey, Assistant Professor, University of Illinois at Urbana-Champaign for her book, *Chinese Civilization and Society*: *A Sourcebook* and to Fox Butterfield for his book, *China: Alive in the Bitter Sea.*

And because hundreds of thousands of baby girls still wait for families in orphanages throughout China, I am including the phone number for the National Adoption Information Clearinghouse: 1-888-251-0075, which puts potential parents in touch with agencies who specialize in Chinese adoptions, in the hope that some of you may find Treasures of your own.

—*Rebecca Hagan Lee*

REBECCA HAGAN LEE

Rebecca Hagan Lee set out to make her mark in the world of television journalism but somewhere along the way, decided she was a small-town girl at heart and settled in a town where the media consists of a weekly newspaper and an AM radio station. Seeking a creative outlet, she turned to writing romance stories far different from the world of television news, but not that far removed from the hundreds of episodes of *Bonanza*, *Big Valley*, *Gunsmoke*, and *The Virginian* she had watched growing up. She decided to create stories where good guys win, bad guys lose, prostitutes have hearts of gold, and the heroes and heroines who fall in love and perservere are richly rewarded with incredibly bright futures and happy endings. In her world, heroines don't die or get killed off to make way for the next episode's new love interest; they get their men and help them become ideal husbands, lovers, friends, and fathers.

Rebecca Hagan Lee is the author of five bestselling romances, and has won numerous awards including a Waldenbooks Award for Bestselling Original Long Historical Romance by a New Author. She lives in south Georgia with her hero husband, three miniature schnauzers, a rat terrier, a cat, and a a host of imaginary heroes and heroines waiting to be introduced.